THE DEVIL'S OWN

A Romance of the Black Hawk War

RANDALL PARRISH

1st WORLD
LIBRARY
Literary Society

The Devil's Own

Randall Parrish

© 1st World Library, 2007
PO Box 2211
Fairfield, IA 52556
www.1stworldlibrary.com
First Edition

LCCN: 2007927860

Softcover ISBN: 978-1-4218-4570-8
Hardcover ISBN: 978-1-4218-4486-2
eBook ISBN: 978-1-4218-4654-5

Purchase *"The Devil's Own"*
as a traditional bound book at:
www.1stWorldLibrary.com/purchase.asp?ISBN=978-1-4218-4570-8

1st World Library is a literary, educational organization
dedicated to:

- Creating a free internet library of downloadable ebooks

- Hosting writing competitions and offering book publishing
scholarships.

Interested in more 1st World Library books? contact:
literacy@1stworldlibrary.com
Check us out at: www.1stworldlibrary.com

1st World Library Literary Society

Giving Back to the World

"If you want to work on the core problem, it's early school literacy."

- James Barksdale, former CEO of Netscape

"No skill is more crucial to the future of a child, or to a democratic and prosperous society, than literacy."

- Los Angeles Times

"Literacy... means far more than learning how to read and write... The aim is to transmit... knowledge and promote social participation."

- UNESCO

"Literacy is not a luxury, it is a right and a responsibility. If our world is to meet the challenges of the twenty-first century we must harness the energy and creativity of all our citizens."

- President Bill Clinton

"Parents should be encouraged to read to their children, and teachers should be equipped with all available techniques for teaching literacy, so the varying needs and capacities of individual kids can be taken into account."

- Hugh Mackay

CONTENTS

CHAPTER I

AT OLD FORT ARMSTRONG

It was the early springtime, and my history tells me the year was 1832, although now that seems so far away I almost hesitate to write the date. It appears surprising that through the haze of all those intervening years—intensely active years with me—I should now be able to recall so clearly the scene of that far-off morning of my youth, and depict in memory each minor detail. Yet, as you read on, and realize yourself the stirring events resulting from that idle moment, you may be able to comprehend the deep impression left upon my mind, which no cycle of time could ever erase.

I was barely twenty then, a strong, almost headstrong boy, and the far wilderness was still very new to me, although for two years past I had held army commission and been assigned to duty in frontier forts. Yet never previously had I been stationed at quite so isolated an outpost of civilization as was this combination of rock and log defense erected at the southern extremity of Rock Island, fairly marooned amid the sweep of the great river, with Indian-haunted land stretching for leagues on every side. A mere handful of troops was quartered there, technically two companies of infantry, yet numbering barely enough for one; and this in spite of rumors daily drifting to us that the Sacs and Foxes, with their main village just below, were already becoming restless and warlike, inflamed by the slow approach of white settlers into the valley of the Rock. Indeed, so short was the garrison of officers, that the harassed commander had ventured to retain me for field service, in spite of the fact that I was detailed to staff duty, had borne dispatches up the Mississippi from General Gaines, and expected to return again by the first boat.

The morning was one of deep-blue sky and bright sunshine, the soft spring air vocal with the song of birds. As soon as early drill ended I had left the fort-enclosure, and sought a lonely perch on the great rock above the mouth of the cave. It was a spot I loved. Below, extended a magnificent vista of the river, fully a mile wide from shore to shore, spreading out in a sheet of glittering silver, unbroken in its vast sweep toward the sea except for a few small, willow-studded islands a mile or two away, with here and there the black dot of an Indian canoe gliding across the surface. I had been told of a fight amid those islands in 1814, a desperate savage battle off the mouth of the Rock, and the memory of this was in my mind as my eyes searched those distant shores, silent now in their drapery of fresh green foliage, yet appearing strangely desolate and forlorn, as they merged into the gray tint of distance. Well I realized that they only served to screen savage activity beyond, a covert amid which lurked danger and death; for over there, in the near shadow of the Rock Valley, was where Black Hawk, dissatisfied, revengeful, dwelt with his British band, gathering swiftly about him the younger, fighting warriors of every tribe his influence could reach. He had been at the fort but two days before, a tall, straight, taciturn Indian; no chief by birth, yet a born leader of men, defiant in speech, and insolent of demeanor in spite of the presence also at the council of his people's true representative, the silent, cautious Keokuk.

Even with my small knowledge of such things it was plain enough to be seen there existed deadly hatred between these two, and that Keokuk's desire for peace with the whites alone postponed an outbreak. I knew then but little of the cause. The Indian tongue was strange to me, and the interpreter failed to make clear the under-lying motive, yet I managed to gather that, in spite of treaty, Black Hawk refused to leave his oldtime hunting grounds to the east of the river, and openly threatened war. The commandant trusted Keokuk, with faith that his peaceful counsels would prevail; but when Black Hawk angrily left the chamber and my eyes followed him to his waiting canoe, my mind was convinced that this was not destined to be the end—that only force of arms would ever tame his savage spirit.

This all came back to me in memory as I sat there, searching out that distant shore line, and picturing in imagination the restless Indian camp concealed from view beyond those tree-crowned bluffs. Already tales reached us of encroaching settlers advancing along the valley, and of savage, retaliating raids which could only terminate in armed encounters. Already crops had been destroyed, and isolated cabins fired, the work as yet of prowling, irresponsible bands, yet always traced in their origin to Black Hawk's village. That Keokuk could continue to control his people no longer seemed probable to me, for the Hawk was evidently the stronger character of the two, possessed the larger following, and made no attempt to conceal the depth of his hatred for all things American.

Now to my view all appeared peaceful enough—the silent, deserted shores, the desolate sweep of the broad river, the green-crowned bluffs, the quiet log fort behind me, its stockaded gates wide open, with not even a sentry visible, a flag flapping idly at the summit of a high pole, and down below where I sat a little river steamboat tied to the wharf, a dingy stern-wheeler, with the word "Warrior" painted across the pilot house. My eyes and thoughts turned that way wonderingly. The boat had tied up the previous evening, having just descended from Prairie du Chien, and, it was rumored at that time, intended to depart down river for St. Louis at daybreak. Yet even now I could perceive no sign of departure. There was but the thinnest suggestion of smoke from the single stack, no loading, or unloading, and the few members of the crew visible were idling on the wharf, or grouped upon the forward deck, a nondescript bunch of river boatmen, with an occasional black face among them, their voices reaching me, every sentence punctuated by oaths. Above, either seated on deck stools, or moving restlessly about, peering over the low rail at the shore, were a few passengers, all men roughly dressed—miners from Fevre River likely, with here and there perchance an adventurer from farther above—impatient of delay. I was attracted to but two of any interest. These were standing alone together near the stern, a heavily-built man with white hair and beard, and a younger, rather slender fellow, with clipped, black moustache. Both were unusually well dressed, the latter exceedingly natty and fashionable in attire, rather overly so I thought, while the former wore a long coat, and high white stock. Involuntarily I had placed them in my mind as river gamblers, but was still observing their movements with some curiosity, when Captain Thockmorton crossed the gangplank and began ascending the steep bluff. The path to be followed led directly past where I was sitting, and, recognizing me, he stopped to exchange greetings.

"What! have you finished your day's work already, Lieutenant?" he exclaimed pleasantly. "Mine has only just begun."

"So I observe. It was garrison talk last night that the *Warrior* was to depart at daylight."

"That was the plan. However, the *Wanderer* went north during the night," he explained, "and brought mail from below, so we are being held for the return letters. I am going up to the office now."

My eyes returned to the scene below.

"You have some passengers aboard."

"A few; picked up several at the lead mines, besides those aboard from Prairie du Chien. No soldiers this trip, though. They haven't men enough at Fort Crawford to patrol the walls."

"So I'm told; and only the merest handful here. Frankly, Captain, I do not know what they can be thinking about down below, with this Indian uprising threatened. The situation is more serious than they imagine. In my judgment Black Hawk means to fight."

"I fully agree with you," he replied soberly. "But Governor Clark is the only one who senses the situation. However, I learned last night from the commander of the *Wanderer* that troops were being gathered at Jefferson Barracks. I'll probably get a load of them coming back. What is your regiment, Knox?"

"The Fifth Infantry."

"The Fifth! Then you do not belong here?"

"No; I came up with dispatches, but have not been permitted to return. What troops are at Jefferson—did you learn?"

"Mostly from the First, with two companies of the Sixth, Watson told me; only about four hundred altogether. How many warriors has Black Hawk?"

"No one knows. They say his emissaries are circulating among the Wyandottes and Potawatamies, and that he has received encouragement from the Prophet which makes him bold."

"The Prophet! Oh, you mean Wabokieshiek? I know that old devil, a Winnebago; and if Black Hawk is in his hands he will not listen very long even to White Beaver. General Atkinson passed through here lately; what does he think?"

I shook my head doubtfully.

"No one can tell, Captain; at least none of the officers here seem in his confidence. I have never met him, but I learn this: he trusts the promises of Keokuk, and continues to hold parley. Under his orders a council was held here three days since, which ended in a quarrel between the two chiefs. However, there is a rumor that dispatches have already been sent to Governors Clark and Reynolds suggesting a call for volunteers, yet I cannot vouch for the truth of the tale."

"White Beaver generally keeps his own counsel, yet he knows Indians, and might trust me with his decision, for we are old friends. If you can furnish me with a light, I'll start this pipe of mine going."

I watched the weather-beaten face of the old riverman, as he puffed away in evident satisfaction. I had chanced to meet him only twice before, yet he was a well-known character between St. Louis and Prairie du Chien; rough enough to be sure, from the very nature of his calling, but generous and straightforward.

"Evidently all of your passengers are not miners, Captain," I ventured, for want of something better to say. "Those two standing there at the stern, for instance."

He turned and looked, shading his eyes, the smoking pipe in one hand.

"No," he said, "that big man is Judge Beaucaire, from Missouri. He has a plantation just above St. Louis, an old French grant. He went up with me about a month ago—my first trip this season—to look after some investment on the Fevre, which I judge hasn't turned out very well, and has been waiting to go back with me. Of course you know the younger one."

"Never saw him before."

"Then you have never traveled much on the lower river. That's Joe Kirby."

"Joe Kirby?"

"Certainly; you must have heard of him. First time I ever knew of his drifting so far north, as there are not many pickings up here. Have rather suspected he might be laying for Beaucaire, but the two haven't touched a card coming down."

"He is a gambler, then?"

"A thoroughbred; works between St. Louis and New Orleans. I can't just figure out yet what he is doing up here. I asked him flat out, but he only laughed, and he isn't the sort of man you get very friendly with, some say he has Indian blood in him, so I dropped it. He and the Judge seem pretty thick, and they may be playing in their rooms."

"Have you ever told the planter who the other man is?"

"What, me, told him? Well, hardly; I've got troubles enough of my own. Beaucaire is of age, I reckon, and they tell me he is some poker player himself. The chances are he knows Kirby better than I do; besides I've run this river too long to interfere with my passengers. See you again before we leave; am going up now to have a talk with the Major."

My eyes followed as he disappeared within the open gates, a squatty, strongly-built figure, the blue smoke from his pipe circling in a cloud above his head. Then I turned idly to gaze once again down the river, and observe the groups loitering below. I felt but slight interest in the conversation just exchanged, nor did the memory of it abide for long in my mind. I had not been close enough to observe Beaucaire, or glimpse his character, while the presence of a gambler on the boat was no such novelty in those days as to chain my attention. Indeed, these individuals were everywhere, a recognized institution, and, as Thockmorton had intimated, the planter himself was fully conversant with the game, and quite able to protect himself. Assuredly it was none of my affair, and yet a certain curiosity caused me to observe the movements of the two so long as they remained on deck. However, it was but a short while before both retired to the cabin, and then my gaze returned once more to the sullen sweep of water, while my thoughts drifted far away.

A soldier was within a few feet of me, and had spoken, before I was even aware of his approach.

"Lieutenant Knox."

I looked about quickly, recognizing the major's orderly.

"Yes, Sanders, what is it?"

"Major Bliss requests, sir, that you report at his office at once."

"Very well. Is he with Captain Thockmorton?"

"Not at present, sir; the captain has gone to the post-sutler's."

Wondering what might be desired of me, yet with no conception of the reality, I followed after the orderly through the stockade gate, and across the small parade ground toward the more pretentious structure occupied by the officers of the garrison.

CHAPTER II

ON FURLOUGH

A number of soldiers off duty were loitering in front of the barracks, while a small group of officers occupied chairs on the log porch of their quarters, enjoying the warmth of the sun. I greeted these as I passed, conscious that their eyes followed me curiously as I approached the closed door of the commandant's office. The sentry without brought his rifle to a salute, but permitted my passage without challenge. A voice within answered my knock, and I entered, closing the door behind me. The room was familiar—plain, almost shabbily furnished, the walls decorated only by the skins of wild beasts, and holding merely a few rudely constructed chairs and a long pine table. Major Bliss glanced up at my entrance, with deep-set eyes hidden beneath bushy-gray eyebrows, his smooth-shaven face appearing almost youthful in contrast to a wealth of gray hair. A veteran of the old war, and a strict disciplinarian, inclined to be austere, his smile of welcome gave me instantly a distinct feeling of relief.

"How long have you been here at Armstrong, Lieutenant?" he questioned, toying with an official-looking paper in his hands.

"Only about three weeks, sir. I came north on the *Enterprise*, with dispatches from General Gaines."

"I remember; you belong to the Fifth, and, without orders, I promptly dragooned you into garrison service." His eyes laughed. "Only sorry I cannot hold you any longer."

"I do not understand, sir."

"Yet I presume you have learned that the *Wanderer* stopped here for an hour last night on its way north to Prairie du Chien?"

"Captain Thockmorton just informed me."

"But you received no mail?"

"No, sir; or, rather, I have not been at the office to inquire. Was there mail for me?"

"That I do not know; only I have received a communication relating to you. It seems you have an application pending for a furlough."

"Yes, sir."

"It is my pleasure to inform you that it has been granted— sixty days, with permission to proceed east. There has been considerable delay evidently in locating you."

A sudden vision arose before me of my mother's face and of the old home among the hills as I took the paper from his extended hands and glanced at the printed and written lines.

"The date is a month ago."

"That need not trouble you, Knox. The furlough begins with

this delivery. However, as I shall require your services as far as St. Louis, I shall date its acceptance from the time of your arrival there."

"Which is very kind, sir."

"Not at all. You have proven of considerable assistance here, and I shall part from you with regret. I have letters for Governor Clark of Missouri, and Governor Reynolds of Illinois; also one to General Atkinson at Jefferson Barracks, detailing my views on the present Indian situation. These are confidential, and I hesitate to entrust them to the regular mail service. I had intended sending them down river in charge of a non-commissioned officer, but shall now utilize your services instead—that is, if you are willing to assume their care?"

"Very gladly, of course."

"I thought as much. Each of these is to be delivered in person. Captain Thockmorton informs me that he will be prepared to depart within an hour. You can be ready in that time?"

I smiled.

"In much less. I have little with me but a field kit, sir. It will not require long to pack that."

"Then return here at the first whistle, and the letters will be ready for you. That will be all now."

I turned toward the door, but paused irresolutely. The major was already bent over his task, and writing rapidly.

"I beg your pardon, sir, but as I am still to remain on duty, I

Randall Parrish

presume I must travel in uniform?"

He glanced up, his eyes quizzical, the pen still grasped in his fingers.

"I could never quite understand the eagerness of young officers to get into civilian clothing," he confessed reflectively. "Why, I haven't even had a suit for ten years. However, I can see no necessity for your proclaiming your identity on the trip down. Indeed, it may prove the safer course, and technically I presume you may be considered as on furlough. Travel as you please, Lieutenant, but I suggest it will be well to wear the uniform of your rank when you deliver the letters. Is that all?"

"I think of nothing more."

Fifteen minutes sufficed to gather together all my belongings, and change from blue into gray, and, as I emerged from quarters, the officers of the garrison flocked about me with words of congratulation and innumerable questions. Universal envy of my good fortune was evident, but this assumed no unpleasant form, although much was said to express their belief in my early return.

"Anyway, you are bound to wish you were back," exclaimed Hartley, the senior captain, earnestly. "For we are going to be in the thick of it here in less than a month, unless all signs fail. I was at that last council, and I tell you that Sac devil means to fight."

"You may be certain I shall be back if he does," I answered. "But the Major seems to believe that peace is still possible."

"No one really knows what he believes," insisted Hartley soberly. "Those letters you carry south may contain the truth, but if I was in command here we would never take the chances we do now. Look at those stockade gates standing wide open, and only one sentry posted. Ye gods! who would ever suppose we were just a handful of men in hostile Indian territory." His voice increased in earnestness, his eyes sweeping the group of faces. "I've been on this frontier for fourteen years, and visited in Black Hawk's camp a dozen times. He's a British Indian, and hates everything American. Ask Forsyth."

"The Indian agent?"

"Yes, he knows. He's already written Governor Reynolds, and I saw the letter. His word is that Keokuk is powerless to hold back an explosion; he and the Hawk are open enemies, and with the first advance of settlers along the Rock River Valley this whole border is going to be bathed in blood. And look what we've got to fight it with."

"Thockmorton told me," I explained, "that Atkinson is preparing to send in more troops; he expects to bring a load north with him on his next trip."

"From Jefferson?"

"Yes; they are concentrating there."

"How many regulars are there?"

"About four hundred from the First and Sixth regiments."

He laughed scornfully.

"I thought so. That means that Atkinson may send two or three hundred men, half of them recruits, to be scattered between Madison, Armstrong and Crawford. Say we are lucky enough to get a hundred or a hundred and fifty of them stationed here. Why, man, there are five hundred warriors in Black Hawk's camp at this minute, and that is only fifteen miles away. Within ten days he could rally to him Kickapoos, Potawatamies and Winnebagoes in sufficient force to crush us like an eggshell. Why, Gaines ought to be here himself, with a thousand regulars behind him."

"Surely we can defend Armstrong," broke in a confident voice. "The savages would have to attack in canoes."

Hartley turned, and confronted the speaker.

"In canoes!" he exclaimed. "Why, may I ask? With three hundred men here in garrison, how many could we spare to patrol the island? Not a corporal's guard, if we retained enough to prevent an open assault on the fort. On any dark night they could land every warrior unknown to us. The Hawk knows that."

His voice had scarcely ceased when the boat whistle sounded hoarse from the landing below. Grasping my kit I shook hands all around, and left them, hastening across the parade to the office. Ten minutes later I crossed the gangplank, and put foot for the first time on the deck of the *Warrior*. Evidently the crew had been awaiting my arrival to push off, for instantly the whistle shrieked again, and immediately after the boat began to churn its way out into the river current, with bow pointing down stream. Little groups of officers and enlisted men gathered high up on the rocky headland to watch us getting under way, and I lingered beside the rail, waving to them, as the struggling boat swept down, constantly increasing its speed. Even when the last of those black spots had vanished in the far distance, the flag on the high staff remained clearly outlined against the sky, a symbol of civilization in the midst of that vast savage wilderness. Thockmorton leaned out from the open window of the pilot house and hailed me.

"Put your dunnage in the third cabin, Knox—here, you, Sam, lay hold and help."

It was nothing to boast of, that third cabin, being a mere hole, measuring possibly about four feet by seven, but sufficient for sleeping quarters, and was reasonably clean. It failed, however, in attractiveness sufficient to keep me below, and as soon as I had deposited my bag and indulged in a somewhat captious scrutiny of the bedding, I very willingly returned to the outside and clambered up a steep ladder to the upper deck.

The view from this point was a most attractive one. The little steamer struggled forward through the swift, swirling water, keeping nearly in the center of the broad stream, the white spray flung high by her churning wheel and sparkling like diamonds in the sunshine. Lightly loaded, a mere chip on the mighty current, she seemed to fly like a bird, impelled not only by the force of her engines, but swept irresistibly on by the grasp of the waters. We were already skirting the willow-clad islands, green and dense with foliage to the river's edge; and beyond these could gain tantalizing glimpses of the mouth of the Rock, its waters gleaming like silver between grassy banks. The opposite shore appeared dark and gloomy in comparison, with great rock-crowned bluffs outlined against the sky, occasionally assuming grotesque forms, which the boatmen pointed out as familiar landmarks.

Once we narrowly escaped collision with a speeding Indian canoe, containing two frightened occupants, so intent upon saving themselves they never even glanced up until we had swept by. Thockmorton laughed heartily at their desperate struggle in the swell, and several of the crew ran to the stern to watch the little cockle-shell toss about in the waves. It was when I turned also, the better to assure myself of their safety, that I discovered Judge Beaucaire standing close beside me at the low rail. Our eyes met inquiringly, and he bowed with all the ceremony of the old school.

"A new passenger on board, I think, sir," and his deep, resonant voice left a pleasant impression. "You must have joined our company at Fort Armstrong?"

"Your supposition is correct," I answered, some peculiar constraint preventing me from referring to my military rank. "My name is Knox, and I have been about the island for a few weeks. I believe you are Judge Beaucaire of Missouri?"

He was a splendidly proportioned man, with deep chest, great breadth of shoulders, and strong individual face, yet bearing unmistakable signs of dissipation, together with numerous marks of both care and age.

"I feel the honor of your recognition, sir," he said with dignity. "Knox, I believe you said? Of the Knox family at Cape Girardeau, may I inquire?"

"No connection to my knowledge; my home was at Wheeling."

"Ah! I have never been so far east; indeed the extent of my travels along the beautiful Ohio has only been to the Falls. The Beaucaires were originally from Louisiana."

"You must have been among the earlier settlers of Missouri?"

"Before the Americans came, sir," proudly. "My grandfather arrived at Beaucaire Landing during the old French regime;

but doubtless you know all this?"

"No, Judge," I answered, recognizing the egotism of the man, but believing frankness to be the best policy. "This happens to be my first trip on the upper river, and I merely chanced to know your name because you had been pointed out to me by Captain Thockmorton. I understood from him that you represented one of the oldest families in that section."

"There were but very few here before us," he answered, with undisguised pride. "Mostly wilderness outcasts, *voyageurs, coureurs de bois*; but my grandfather's grant of land was from the King. Alphonse de Beaucaire, sir, was the trusted lieutenant of D'Iberville—a soldier, and a gentleman."

I bowed in acknowledgment the family arrogance of the man interesting me deeply. So evident was this pride of ancestry that a sudden suspicion flared into my mind that this might be all the man had left—this memory of the past.

"The history of those early days is not altogether familiar to me," I admitted regretfully. "But surely D'Iberville must have ruled in Louisiana more than one hundred years ago?"

The Judge smiled.

"Quite true. This grant of ours was practically his last official act. Alphonse de Beaucaire took possession in 1712, one hundred and twenty years ago, sir. I was myself born at Beaucaire, sixty-eight years ago."

"I should have guessed you as ten years younger. And the estate still remains in its original grant?"

The smile of condescension deserted his eyes, and his thin

Randall Parrish

lips pressed tightly together.

"I—I regret not; many of the later years have proven disastrous in the extreme," he admitted, hesitatingly. "You will pardon me, sir, if I decline to discuss misfortune. Ah, Monsieur Kirby! I have been awaiting you. Have you met with this young man who came aboard at Fort Armstrong? I—I am unable to recall the name."

"Steven Knox."

I felt the firm, strong grip of the other's hand, and looked straight into his dark eyes. They were like a mask. While, indeed, they seemed to smile in friendly greeting, they yet remained expressionless, and I was glad when the gripping fingers released mine. The face into which I looked was long, firm-jawed, slightly swarthy, a tightly-clipped black moustache shadowing the upper lip. It was a reckless face, yet appeared carved from marble.

"Exceedingly pleased to meet you," he said carelessly. "Rather a dull lot on board—miners, and such cattle. Bound for St. Louis?"

"Yes—and beyond."

"Shall see more of you then. Well, Judge, how do you feel? Carver and McAfee are waiting for us down below."

The two disappeared together down the ladder, and I was again left alone in my occupancy of the upper deck.

CHAPTER III

HISTORY OF THE BEAUCAIRES

The first two days and nights of the journey southward were devoid of any special interest or adventure. The lonely river, wrapped in the silence of the wilderness, brought to me many a picture of loveliness, yet finally the monotony of it all left the mind drowsy with repetition. Around each tree-crowned bend we swept, skirting shores so similar as to scarcely enable us to realize our progress. In spite of the fact that the staunch little *Warrior* was proceeding down stream, progress was slow because of the unmarked channel, and the ever-present danger of encountering snags. The intense darkness and fog of the first night compelled tying up for several hours. The banks were low, densely covered with shrubbery, and nothing broke the sameness of the river scene, except the occasional sight of an Indian canoe skimming across its surface. Towns there were none, and seldom even a sign of a settlement greeted the eye on either shore. The only landings were made at Yellow Banks, where there was a squalid group of log huts, and Fort Madison, where I spent a pleasant hour with the officers of the garrison. Occasionally the boat warped in against the bank to replenish its exhausted supply of wood, the crew attacking the surrounding trees with axes, while the wearied passengers exercised their cramped limbs ashore. Once, with some hours at our disposal, we organized a hunt, returning with a variety of wild game. But most of the time I idled the hours away alone.

No one aboard really attracted my companionship. The lead miners were a rough set, boasting and quarrelsome, spending the greater part of their time at the bar. They had several fights, in one of which a man was seriously stabbed, so that he had to be left in care of the post-surgeon at Madison. After the first day Kirby withdrew all attention from me, and ceased in his endeavor to cultivate my acquaintance, convinced of my disinclination to indulge in cards. This I did not regret, although Beaucaire rather interested me, but, as the gambler seldom permitted the Judge out of his sight, our intimacy grew very slowly. Thockmorton, being his own pilot, seldom left the wheelhouse, and consequently I passed many hours on the bench beside him, gazing out on the wide expanse of river, and listening to his reminiscences of early steam-boating days. He was an intelligent man, with a fund of anecdote, acquainted with every landmark, every whispered tale of the great stream from New Orleans to Prairie du Chien. At one time or another he had met the famous characters along the river banks, and through continual questioning I thus finally became possessed of the story of the house of Beaucaire.

In the main it contained no unusual features. Through the personal influence of D'Iberville at Louis' court, Alphonse de Beaucaire had originally received a royal grant of ten thousand acres of land bordering the west bank of the Mississippi a few miles above St. Louis. When his master returned to France leaving him unemployed, Beaucaire, possessing ample means of his own, had preferred to remain in America. In flatboats, propelled by *voyageurs*, and accompanied by a considerable retinue of slaves, he, with his family, had ascended the river, and finally settled on his princely estate. Here he erected what, for those early days, was a stately mansion, and devoted himself to cultivating the land. Twenty years later, when his death occurred, he possessed the finest property along the upper river, was shipping heavily to the New Orleans market, and was probably the most influential man in all that section. His home was considered a palace, always open to frontier hospitality, the number of his slaves had increased, a large proportion of his land was utilized, and his name was a familiar one the length of the river.

His only son, Felipe, succeeded him, but was not so successful in administration, seriously lacking in business judgment, and being decidedly indolent by nature. Felipe married into one of the oldest and most respectable families of St. Louis, and, as a result of that union, had one son, Lucius, who grew up reckless of restraint, and preferred to spend his time in New Orleans, rather than upon the plantation. Lucius was a young man of twenty-six, unsettled in habits when the father died, and, against his inclination, was compelled to return to Missouri and assume control of the property. He found matters in rather bad condition, and his was not at all the type of mind to remedy them. Much of the land had been already irretrievably lost through speculation, and, when his father's obligations had been met, and his own gambling debts paid, the estate, once so princely and magnificent, was reduced to barely five hundred acres, together with a comparatively small amount of cash. This condition sufficed to sober Lucius for a few years, and he married a Menard, of Cape Girardeau, of excellent family but not great wealth, and earnestly endeavored to rebuild his fortunes. Unfortunately his reform did not last. The evil influences of the past soon proved too strong for one of his temperament. A small town, redolent of all the vices of the river, grew up about the Landing, while friends of other days sought his hospitality. The plantation house became in time a rendezvous for all the wild spirits of that neighborhood, and stories of fierce drinking bouts and mad gambling were current in St. Louis.

Common as such tales as these were in those early days of the West, I still remained boy enough in heart to feel a fascination in Thockmorton's narrative. Besides, there was at the time so little else to occupy my mind that it inevitably drifted back to the same topic.

"Have you ever been at Beaucaire, Captain?" I asked, eager for more intimate details.

"We always stop at the Landing, but I have only once been up the bluff to where the house stands. It must have been a beautiful place in its day; it is imposing even now, but showing signs of neglect and abuse. The Judge was away from home—in St. Louis, I believe—the day of my visit. He had sold me some timber, and I went out with the family lawyer, a man named Haines living at the Landing, to look it over."

"The house was closed?"

"No; it is never closed. The housekeeper was there, and also the two daughters."

"Daughters?"

"Certainly; hadn't I told you about them? Both girls are accepted as his daughters; but, if all I have heard is true, one must be a granddaughter." He paused reminiscently, his eyes on the river. "To all appearances they are about of the same age, but differing rather widely in looks and character. Both are attractive girls I judge, although I only had a glimpse of them, and at the time knew nothing of the difference in relationship. I naturally supposed them to be sisters, until

Haines and I got to talking about the matter on the way back. Pshaw, Knox, you've got me gossiping like an old woman."

I glanced aside at his face.

"This, then, is not common river talk? the truth is not generally known?"

"No; I have never heard it mentioned elsewhere, nor have I previously repeated the story. However, now that the suggestion has slipped out, perhaps I had better go ahead and explain." He puffed at his pipe, and I waited, seemingly intent on the scene without. The captain was a minute or two in deciding how far he would venture. "Haines told me a number of strange things about that family I had never heard before," he admitted at last. "You see he has known them for years, and attended to most of Beaucaire's legal business. I don't know why he chanced to take me into his confidence, only he had been drinking some, and, I reckon, was a bit lonely for companionship; then those two girls interested me, and I asked quite a few questions about them. At first Haines was close as a clam, but finally loosened up, and this is about how the story runs, as he told it. It wasn't generally known, but it seems that Lucius Beaucaire has been married twice— the first time to a Creole girl in New Orleans when he was scarcely more than a boy. Nobody now living probably knows what ever became of her, but likely she died early; anyway she never came north, or has since been heard from. The important part is that she gave birth to a son, who remained in New Orleans, probably in her care, until he was fourteen or fifteen years old. Then some occurrence, possibly his mother's death, caused the Judge to send for the lad, whose name was Adelbert, and had him brought to Missouri. All this happened before Haines settled at the Landing, and previous to Beaucaire's second marriage to Mademoiselle Menard. Bert, as the boy was called, grew up wild, and father and son quarreled so continuously that finally, and before he was twenty, the latter ran away, and has never been heard of since. All they ever learned was that he drifted down the river on a flatboat."

"And he never came back?"

"Not even a letter. He simply disappeared, and no one knows to this day whether he is alive or dead. At least if Judge Beaucaire ever received any word from him he never confessed as much to Haines. However, the boy left behind tangible evidence of his existence."

"You mean—"

"In the form of a child, born to a quadroon slave girl named Delia. The mother, it seems, was able in some way to convince the Judge of the child's parentage. All this happened shortly before Beaucaire's second marriage, and previous to the time when Haines came to the Landing. Exactly what occurred is not clear, or what explanation was made to the bride. The affair must have cut Beaucaire's pride deeply, but he had to face the conditions. It ended in his making the girl Delia his housekeeper, while her child—the offspring of Adelbert Beaucaire—was brought up as a daughter. A year or so later, the second wife gave birth to a female child, and those two girls have grown up together exactly as though they were sisters. Haines insists that neither of them knows to this day otherwise."

"But that would be simply impossible," I insisted. "The mother would never permit."

"The mother! which mother? The slave mother could gain nothing by confession; and the Judge's wife died when her baby was less than two years old. Delia practically mothered the both of them, and is still in complete charge of the house."

"You met her?"

"She was pointed out to me—a gray-haired, dignified woman, so nearly white as scarcely to be suspected of negro blood."

"Yet still a slave?"

"I cannot answer that. Haines himself did not know. If manumission papers had ever been executed it was done early, before he took charge of Beaucaire's legal affairs. The matter never came to his attention."

"But surely he must at some time have discussed this with the Judge?"

"No; at least not directly. Beaucaire is not a man to approach easily. He is excessively proud, and possesses a fiery temper. Once, Haines told me, he ventured a hint, but was rebuffed so fiercely as never to make a second attempt. It was his opinion the Judge actually hated the sight of his son's child, and only harbored her in the house because he was compelled to do so. All Haines really knew about these conditions had been told him secretly by an old negro slave, probably the only one left on the estate knowing the facts."

"But, Captain," I exclaimed, "do you realize what this might mean? If Judge Beaucaire has not issued papers of freedom, this woman Delia is still a slave."

"Certainly."

"And under the law her child was born into slavery?"

Randall Parrish

"No doubt of that."

"But the unspeakable horror of it—this young woman brought up as free, educated and refined, suddenly to discover herself to be a negro under the law, and a slave. Why, suppose Beaucaire should die, or lose his property suddenly, she could be sold to the cotton fields, into bondage to anyone who would pay the price for her."

Thockmorton knocked the ashes out of his pipe.

"Of course," he admitted slowly. "There is no question as to the law, but I have little doubt but what Beaucaire has attended to this matter long ago. If he dies, the papers will be found hidden away somewhere. It is beyond conception that he could ever leave the girl to such a fate."

I shook my head, obsessed with a shadow of doubt.

"A mistake men often make—the putting off to the last moment doing the disagreeable task. How many, expecting to live, delay the making of a will until too late. In this case I am unable to conceive why, if Beaucaire has ever signed papers of freedom, for these two, the fact remains unknown even to his lawyer. One fact is certain, nothing bearing upon the case has been recorded, or Haines would know of it."

"There is nothing on record, Haines assured himself as to that some years ago. The fact is, Knox, that while I hope this provision has been made, there remains a doubt in my mind. Beaucaire has traveled on my boat several times, but he's an unsociable fellow; I don't like him; he's not my kind. If he still harbors hatred toward that run-away son—and to my notion he is exactly that sort—he will never feel any too kindly toward Delia, or her child. If he has not freed them, that will be the reason—no neglect, but a contemptible revenue."

"What are the two girls named?"

"Rene, and Eloise."

"Which one is the daughter?"

"Really, Lieutenant, I do not know. You see I was never introduced, but merely gained a glimpse of them in the garden. I doubt if I would recognize the one from the other now. You see all this story was told me later."

I sat there a long while, after he had gone below, the taciturn mate at the wheel. The low, wooded shores swept past in changing panorama, yet I could not divorce my mind from this perplexing problem. Totally unknown to me as these two mysterious girls were, their strange story fascinated my imagination. What possible tragedy lay before them in the years? what horrible revelation to wrench them asunder? to change in a single instant the quiet current of their lives? About them, unseen as yet, lurked a grim specter, waiting only the opportunity to grip them both in the fingers of disgrace, and make instant mock of all their plans. In spite of every effort, every lurking hope, some way I could not rid myself of the thought that Beaucaire—either through sheer neglect, or some instinct of bitter hatred—had failed to meet the requirements of his duty. Even as I sat there, struggling vainly against this suspicion, the Judge himself came forth upon the lower deck, and began pacing back and forth restlessly beside the rail. It was a struggle for me not to join him; the impetuosity of youth urging me even to brave his anger in my eagerness to ascertain the whole truth. Yet I possessed sense enough, or discretion, to refrain, realizing dimly that, not even in the remotest degree, had I any excuse for such action. This was no affair of mine. Nor, indeed, would I have found much opportunity for private conversation, for, only a moment or two later, Kirby joined him, and the two remained together, talking earnestly, until the gong called us all to supper.

Across the long table, bare of cloth, the coarse food served in pewter dishes, I was struck by the drawn, ghastly look in Beaucaire's face. He had aged perceptibly in the last few hours, and during the meal scarcely exchanged a word with anyone, eating silently, his eyes downcast. Kirby, however, was the life of the company, and the miners roared at his humorous stories, and anecdotes of adventure—while outside it grew dark, and the little *Warrior* struggled cautiously through the waters, seeking the channel in the gloom.

CHAPTER IV

THE END OF THE GAME

Unconscious that the stage had thus been set for a great life drama, a drama in which, through strange circumstances, I was destined to play my part, amid stirring scenes of Indian war, and in surroundings that would test my courage and manhood to the utter-most; yet, although I heard it not, the hour had already struck, and I stood on the brink of a tragedy beyond my power to avert.

I left the others still seated about the table, and returned alone to the outer deck. I had no plans for the evening, and retain now only slight recollection as to the happenings of the next few hours, which I passed quietly smoking in the darkened pilot house, conversing occasionally with Thockmorton, who clung to the wheel, carefully guiding his struggling boat through the night-draped waters. The skill with which he found passage through the enshrouding gloom, guided by signs invisible to my eyes, aided only by a fellow busily casting a lead line in the bows, and chanting the depth of water, was amazing. Seemingly every flitting shadow brought its message, every faint glimmer of starlight pointed the way to safety.

It must have been nearly midnight before I finally wearied of this, and decided to seek a few hours' rest below, descending the short ladder, and walking forward along the open deck for one last glance ahead. Some time the next day we were to be in St. Louis, and this expectation served to brighten my thoughts. It was a dark night, but with a clear sky, the myriad of stars overhead reflecting their lights along the river surface, and bringing into bold relief the dense shadows of the shores on either side. The boat, using barely enough power to afford steering way, swept majestically down stream, borne by the force of the current, which veered from bank to bank. We were moving scarcely swifter than from eight to ten miles an hour, and the monotonous voice of the man casting the lead line arose continuous through the brooding silence. The only other perceptible sounds were the exhaust of the steam pipes and the splash of running water. Thockmorton had told me we were already approaching the mouth of the Illinois, and I lingered against the rail, straining my eyes through the gloom hoping to gain a distant glimpse of that beautiful stream. We were skirting the eastern shore, the wooded bank rising almost as high as our smokestack, and completely shutting off all view of the horizon.

As I stood there, gripping the rail, half fearful lest we strike, the furnace doors below were suddenly flung open for a fresh feeding of the fire, and the red glare of the fire lit up the scene. Close in against the shore nestled a flatboat, evidently tied up for the night, and I had a swift glimpse as we shot by of a startled man waving his arms, and behind him a wildly barking dog. An instant more and the vision had vanished as quickly as it had appeared; even the dog's sharp bark dying away in the distance. The furnace doors banged shut, and all was again darkness and silence.

I turned back along the deserted deck, only pausing a moment to glance carelessly in through the front windows of the main cabin. The forward portion was wrapped in darkness, and unoccupied, but beyond, toward the rear of the long salon, a considerable group of men were gathered closely about a small table, above which a swinging lamp burned brightly, the rays of light illuminating the various faces. I recognized several, and they were apparently a deeply interested group, for, even at that distance, I could plainly note the excitement stamped upon their countenances, and the nervousness with which they moved about seeking clearer view. There were so many closely wedged together as to obstruct my vision of what was occurring, yet I felt no doubt but that they watched a game of cards; a desperate struggle of chance, involving no small sum to account for such intense feeling on the part of mere onlookers. Gambling was no novelty on the great river in those days, gambling for high stakes, and surely no ordinary game, involving a small sum, would ever arouse the depth of interest displayed by these men. Some instinct told me that the chief players would be Kirby and Beaucaire, and, with quickening pulse, I opened the cabin door and entered.

No one noted my approach, or so much as glanced up, the attention of the crowd riveted upon the players. There were four holding cards—the Judge, Kirby, Carver, and McAfee; but I judged at a glance that the latter two were merely in the game as a pretense, the betting having already gone far beyond the limit of their resources. Without a thought as to the cards they held, my eyes sought the faces of the two chief players, and then visioned the stakes displayed on the table before them. McAfee and Carter were clearly enough out of it, their cards still gripped in their fingers, as they leaned breathlessly forward to observe more closely the play. The Judge sat upright, his attitude strained, staring down at his hand, his face white, and eyes burning feverishly. That he had been drinking heavily was evident, but Kirby fronted him in apparent cold indifference, his feelings completely masked, with the cards he held bunched in his hands, and entirely concealed from view. No twitch of an eyelash, no quiver of a muscle revealed his knowledge; his expressionless face might have been carved out of stone. Between the two rested a stack of gold coin, a roll of crushed bills, and a legal paper of some kind, the exact nature of which I could not determine. I leaned forward, but could only perceive that it bore the official stamp of some recording office—a deed, perhaps, to some of the remaining acres of Beaucaire. It was evident that a fortune already rested on that table, awaiting the flip of a card. The silence, the breathless attention, convinced me that the crisis had been reached—it was the Judge's move; he must cover the last bet, or throw down his hand a loser.

Perspiration beaded his forehead, and he crunched the cards savagely in his hands. His glance swept past the crowd, as though he saw nothing of their faces.

"Another drink, Sam," he called, the voice trembling. He tossed down the glass of liquor as though it were so much water, but made no other effort to speak. You could hear the strained breathing of the men.

"Well," said Kirby sneeringly, his cold gaze surveying his motionless opponent. "You seem to be taking your time. Do you cover my bet?"

Someone laughed nervously, and a voice sang out over my shoulder, "You might as well go the whole hog, Judge. The niggers won't be no good without the land ter work 'em on. Fling 'em into the pot—they're as good as money."

Beaucaire looked up, red-eyed, into the impassive countenance opposite. His lips twitched, yet managed to make words issue between them.

"How about that, Kirby?" he asked hoarsely. "Will you accept a bill of sale?"

Kirby grinned, shuffling his hand carelessly.

"Why not? 'twon't be the first time I've played for niggers. They are worth so much gold down the river. What have you got?"

"I can't tell that offhand," sullenly. "About twenty field hands."

"And house servants?"

"Three or four."

The gambler's lips set more tightly, a dull gleam creeping into his eyes.

"See here, Beaucaire," he hissed sharply. "This is my game and I play square and never squeal. I know about what you've got, for I've looked them over; thought we might get down to this sometime. I can make a pretty fair guess as to what your niggers are worth. That's why I just raised you ten thousand, and put up the money. Now, if you think this is a bluff, call me."

"What do you mean?"

"That I will accept your niggers as covering my bet."

"The field hands?"

Kirby smiled broadly.

"The whole bunch—field hands and house servants. Most of

them are old; I doubt if all together they will bring that amount, but I'll take the risk. Throw in a blanket bill of sale, and we'll turn up our cards. If you won't do that, the pile is mine as it stands."

Beaucaire again wet his lips, staring at the uncovered cards in his hands. He could not lose; with what he held no combination was possible which could beat him. Yet, in spite of this knowledge, the cold, sneering confidence of Kirby, brought with it a strange fear. The man was a professional gambler. What gave him such recklessness? Why should he be so eager to risk such a sum on an inferior hand? McAfee, sitting next him, leaned over, managed to gain swift glimpse at what he held, and eagerly whispered to him a word of encouragement. The Judge straightened up in his chair, grasped a filled glass some one had placed at his elbow, and gulped down the contents. The whispered words, coupled with the fiery liquor, gave him fresh courage.

"By God, Kirby! I'll do it!" he blurted out. "You can't bluff me on the hand I've got. Give me a sheet of paper, some-body—yes, that will do."

He scrawled a half-dozen lines, fairly digging the pen into the sheet in his fierce eagerness, and then signed the document, flinging the paper across toward Kirby.

"There, you blood-sucker," he cried insolently. "Is that all right? Will that do?"

The imperturbable gambler read it over slowly, carefully deciphering each word, his thin lips tightly compressed.

"You might add the words, 'This includes every chattel slave legally belonging to me,'" he said grimly.

"That is practically what I did say."

"Then you can certainly have no objection to putting it in the exact words I choose," calmly. "I intend to have what is coming to me if I win, and I know the law."

Beaucaire angrily wrote in the required extra line.

"Now what?" he asked.

"Let McAfee there sign it as a witness, and then toss it over into the pile." He smiled, showing a line of white teeth beneath his moustache. "Nice little pot, gentlemen—the Judge must hold some cards to take a chance like that," the words uttered with a sneer. "Fours, at least, or maybe he has had the luck to pick a straight flush."

Beaucaire's face reddened, and his eyes grew hard.

"That's my business," he said tersely. "Sign it, McAfee, and I'll call this crowing cockerel. You young fool, I played poker before you were born. There now, Kirby, I've covered your bet."

"Perhaps you would prefer to raise it?"

"You hell-hound—no! That is my limit, and you know it. Don't crawl now, or do any more bluffing. Show your hand—I've called you."

Kirby sat absolutely motionless, his cards lying face down upon the table, the white fingers of one hand resting lightly upon them, the other arm concealed. He never once removed his gaze from Beaucaire's face, and his expression did not change, except for the almost insulting sneer on his lips. The silence was profound, the deeply interested men leaning forward, even holding their breath in intense eagerness. Each realized that a fortune lay on the table; knew that the old Judge had madly staked his all on the value of those five unseen cards gripped in his fingers. Again, as though to bolster up his shaken courage, he stared at the face of each, then lifted his blood-shot eyes to the impassive face opposite.

"Beaucaire drew two kayards," whispered an excited voice near me.

"Hell! so did Kirby." replied another. "They're both of 'em old hands."

The sharp exhaust of a distant steam pipe below punctuated the silence, and several glanced about apprehensively. As this noise ceased Beaucaire lost all control over his nerves.

"Come on, play your hand," he demanded, "or I'll throw my cards in your face."

The insinuating sneer on Kirby's lips changed into the semblance of a smile. Slowly, deliberately, never once glancing down at the face of his cards, he turned them up one by one with his white fingers, his challenging eyes on the Judge; but the others saw what was revealed—a ten spot, a knave, a queen, a king, and an ace.

"Good God! a straight flush!" someone yelled excitedly. "Damned if I ever saw one before!"

For an instant Beaucaire never moved, never uttered a sound. He seemed to doubt the evidence of his own eyes, and to have lost the power of speech. Then from nerveless hands his own cards fell face downward, still unrevealed, upon the table. The next moment he was on his feet, the chair in which he had been seated flung crashing behind him on the deck.

"You thief!" he roared, "You dirty, low-down thief; I held four aces—where did you get the fifth one?"

Kirby did not so much as move, nor betray even by change of expression his sense of the situation. Perhaps he anticipated just such an explosion, and was fully prepared to meet it. One hand still rested easily on the table, the other remaining hidden.

"So you claim to have held four aces," he said coldly. "Where are they?"

McAfee swept the discarded hand face upward, and the crowd bending forward to look saw four aces, and a king.

"That was the Judge's hand," he declared soberly. "I saw it myself before he called you, and told him to stay."

Kirby laughed, an ugly laugh showing his white teeth.

"The hell, you did? Thought you knew a good poker hand, I reckon. Well, you see I knew a better one, and it strikes me I am the one to ask questions," he sneered. "Look here, you men; I held one ace from the shuffle. Now what I want to know is, where Beaucaire ever got his four? Pleasant little trick of you two—only this time it failed to work."

Beaucaire uttered one mad oath, and I endeavored to grasp him, but missed my clutch. The force of his lurching body as he sprang forward upturned the table, the stakes jingling to the deck, but Kirby reached his feet in time to avoid the shock. His hand which had been hidden shot out suddenly, the fingers grasping a revolver, but he did not fire. Before the

Judge had gone half the distance, he stopped, reeled suddenly, clutching at his throat, and plunged sideways. His body struck the upturned table, and McAfee and I grasped him, lowering the stricken man gently to the floor.

CHAPTER V

KIRBY SHOWS HIS HAND

That scene, with all its surroundings, remains indelibly impressed upon my memory. It will never fade while I live. The long, narrow, dingy cabin of the little *Warrior*, its forward end unlighted and in shadow, the single swinging lamp, suspended to a blackened beam above where the table had stood, barely revealing through its smoky chimney the after portion showing a row of stateroom doors on either side, some standing ajar, and that crowd of excited men surging about the fallen body of Judge Beaucaire, unable as yet to fully realize the exact nature of what had occurred, but conscious of impending tragedy. The air was thick and stifling with tobacco smoke, redolent of the sickening fumes of alcohol, and noisy with questioning voices, while above every other sound might be distinguished the sharp pulsations of the laboring engine just beneath our feet, the deck planks trembling to the continuous throbbing. The overturned table and chairs, the motionless body of the fallen man, with Kirby standing erect just beyond, his face as clear-cut under the glare of light as a cameo, the revolver yet glistening in his extended hand, all composed a picture not easily forgotten.

Still, this impression was only that of a brief instant. With the next I was upon my knees, lifting the fallen head, and seeking eagerly to discern some lingering evidence of life in the inert, body. There was none, not so much as the faint flutter of a pulse, or suggestion of a heart throb. The man was already dead before he fell, dead before he struck the overturned table. Nothing any human effort might do would help him now. My eyes lifting from the white, ghastly face encountered those of McAfee, and, without the utterance of a word, I read the miner's verdict, and arose again to my feet.

"Judge Beaucaire is dead," I announced gravely. "Nothing more can be done for him now."

The pressing circle of men hemming us in fell back silently, reverently, the sound of their voices sinking into a subdued murmur. It had all occurred so suddenly, so unexpectedly, that even these witnesses could scarcely grasp the truth. They were dazed, leaderless, struggling to restrain themselves. As I stood there, almost unconscious of their presence, still staring down at that upturned face, now appearing manly and patrician in the strange dignity of its death mask, a mad burst of anger swept me, a fierce yearning for revenge—a feeling that this was no less a murder because Nature had struck the blow. With hot words of reproach upon my lips I gazed across toward where Kirby had been standing a moment before. The gambler was no longer there—his place was vacant.

"Where is Kirby?" I asked, incredulous of his sudden disappearance.

For a moment no one answered; then a voice in the crowd croaked hoarsely:

"He just slipped out through that after door to the deck—him and Bill Carver."

"And the stakes?"

Another answered in a thin, piping treble.

"I reckon them two cusses took along the most ov it. Enyhow 'tain't yere, 'cept maybe a few coins that rolled tinder the table. It wasn't Joe Kirby who picked up the swag, fer I was a watchin' him, an' he never onct let go ov his gun. Thet damn sneak Carver must a did it, an' then the two ov 'em just sorter nat'rally faded away through that door thar."

McAfee swore through his black beard, the full truth swiftly dawning upon him.

"Hell!" he exploded. "So that's the way of it. Then them two wus in cahoots frum the beginnin'. That's what I told the Jedge last night, but he said he didn't give a whoop; thet he knew more poker than both ov 'em put tergether. I tell yer them fellers stole that money, an' they killed Beaucaire—"

"Hold on a minute," I broke in, my mind cleared of its first passion, and realizing the necessity of control. "Let's keep cool, and go slow. While I believe McAfee is right, we are not going to bring the Judge back to life by turning into a mob. There is no proof of cheating, and Kirby has the law behind him. Let me talk to the captain about what had best be done."

"Who, Thockmorton?"

"Yes; he'll know the better action for us to take. He's level-headed, and an old friend of Beaucaire's."

"I'm fer swingin' that damn gambler up, without askin' nobody," shouted a fellow fiercely. "He's bin raisin' hell frum one end o' this river ter the other fer ten years. A rope is whut he needs."

"What good would that do in this case?" I questioned before anyone else could chime in, "either to the dead man, or his family? That's what I am thinking about, men. Suppose you strung him up, that money, the plantation, and those slaves would still belong to him, or his heirs. I'm for getting all these back, if there is any way of accomplishing it. See here, men," I pleaded earnestly, "this affair doesn't necessarily end here on board the *Warrior*, and if you were to kill Kirby it wouldn't benefit matters any."

"It would get rid ov a skunk."

"Yes, but he is only one of a hundred between here and New Orleans. Look at the other side a minute. Beaucaire bet everything he possessed—everything, land, niggers, and money. Kirby sneered him on to it, and saw that he had the kind of a hand that would do the business right. When the Judge died he didn't own enough to pay his funeral expenses. Now see here; I happen to know that he left two young daughters. Just stop, and think of them. We saw this game played, and there isn't a man here who believes it was played on the square—that two such hands were ever dealt, or drawn, in poker. We can't prove that Kirby manipulated things to that end; not one of us saw how he worked the trick. There is no chance to get him that way. Then what is it we ought to do? Why I say, make the thief disgorge—and hanging won't do the business."

"Well then, what will?"

"I confess I do not yet know. I want to talk with Thockmorton first. He may know something."

There was a moment's silence, then a suspicious voice, "Who

the hell are you? How do we know you ain't in on this yerself?"

"Listen, men," and I fronted them, looking straight into their eyes. "You have a right to ask that question, and I'll tell you who I am. I am not here in uniform, but I am an officer of the United States Army. Captain Thockmorton will vouch for that. I pledge you my word that this affair does not end here. I never met any of these men until I came on board the boat at Fort Armstrong, but I have letters with me for Governor Clark of Missouri, and Governor Reynolds of Illinois. Either man will accept my statement regarding this matter, and I promise you that either Kirby and Carver will return the papers and money before we reach St. Louis, or I'll swear out a warrant for their arrest. If you boys will stay with me we'll scare it out of them for the sake of those girls. What do you say?"

No one spoke immediately, although there was a muttering of voices, sounding antagonistic, and sprinkled with oaths. It was, indeed, a poor time and place in which to appeal to the law, nor were these men accustomed to the pleadings of mercy. I glanced across Beaucaire's extended body, and caught the eyes of McAfee. The man lifted his hand.

"The leftenant has got this thing sized up about proper," he said gruffly. "He's an army officer all right, fer I saw him back thar on the island, when we wus tied up at the dock. Now look yere, boys, I'm fer hangin' both ov them cusses just as much as eny ov the rest ov yer—a bit more, I reckon, fer they stripped me ov my pile; along with Beaucaire, only I was easier ter strip—but, as the leftenant says, that ain't the p'int now. What we want ter do is get back them bills o' sale, so them two young women won't be left with nuthin' ter live on. Let's make the fellers cough up furst, an' then, if we think best, we kin hang 'em afterwards. It's my vote we let the leftenant tackle the job—what do yer say?"

The rise and fall of voices, although punctuated by oaths, and indistinct in expression, seemed generally to signify assent. The faces of the men, as they pushed and crowded about us, remained angry and resentful. Clearly enough prompt action alone would carry the day.

"Very well then, boys," I broke in sharply. "You agree to leave this settlement with me. Then I'll go at it. Two or three of you pick up the body, and carry it to Beaucaire's state-room—forward there. The rest of you better straighten up the cabin, while I go up and talk with Thockmorton a moment. After that I may want a few of you to go along when I hunt up Kirby. If he proves ugly we'll know how to handle him. McAfee!"

"I'm over here."

"I was just going to say that you better stay here, and keep the fellows all quiet in the cabin. We don't want our plan to leak out, and it will be best to let Kirby and Carver think that everything is all right; that nothing is going to be done."

I waited while several of them gently picked up the body, and bore it forward into the shadows. Others busied themselves in straightening the overturned furniture, and gathered into a small pile those few scattered coins which had fallen to the deck, and been overlooked by the two gamblers in their eagerness to escape. No one attempted to appropriate any of these. McAfee apparently knew most of the fellows intimately, calling them by name, and seemed to be recognized as a leader among them. This fact was encouraging, as to all appearance they were a rough set, unaccustomed to law of any kind, and to be controlled only by physical strength, and some one of their own sort. In spite of my position and rank, I was far too young in appearance to exercise much weight of authority over such border men, but fortunately I possessed sufficient good sense to rely now in this emergency upon the black-bearded McAfee, who served well. His voice, strongly resembling a foghorn, arose in threat and expostulation unceasingly, and the miners, who evidently knew him well, and perhaps had previously tested the weight of his fist, were lamb-like and obedient to his control.

"They'll be quiet enough fer a while, leftenant," he managed to whisper hoarsely to me. "But they is jest boys growed up, an' if eny one o' them should really take a notion ter raise hell, all the cussin' I might do wouldn't make no diffrance. Whatever yer aim at, better be done right off, while I kin sorter keep 'em busy down yere; onct they git loose on the deck the devil himself couldn't stop 'em frum startin' a row."

This advice was so good that I slipped instantly away, silently gained the door, and, unobserved, emerged on to the deserted deck without. The sudden change in environment sobered me, and caused me to pause and seriously consider the importance of my mission. Through the thin walls of the cabin the murmuring voices of those within became indistinct, except as an occasional loudly spoken oath, or call, might be distinguished. The struggling *Warrior* was close within the looming shadows of the western shore, and seemed to be moving downward more swiftly with the current, as though the controlling mind in the darkened wheelhouse felt confident of clear water ahead. The decks throbbed to the increased pulsation of the engine, and I could plainly hear the continuous splash of the great stern wheel as it flung spray high into the air.

I paused a moment, hand gripping the rail, and eyes seeking vainly to peer across the wide expanse of river, really fronting the situation for the first time, and endeavoring to think out calmly some definite course of action. Thus far, spurred only by necessity, and a sense of obligation, I had merely been blindly grasping at the first suggestion which had occurred to mind. The emergency had demanded action, rather than reflection. But now, on cooler consideration, and alone, the result I sought did not appear so apparent, nor so easily attained. Hitherto, in the midst of the excitement occasioned by Beaucaire's tragic death, my mind had grasped but one idea clearly—if I permitted Kirby to be mobbed and killed by those enraged men, his death would benefit no one; would remedy no wrong. That mad mob spirit must be fought down, conquered. Yet now, when I had actually accomplished this, what must be my next step? Nothing less potent than either fear, or force, would ever make Kirby disgorge. Quite evidently the gambler had deliberately set out to ruin the planter, to rob him of every dollar. Even at the last moment he had coldly insisted on receiving a bill of sale so worded as to leave no possible loophole. He demanded all. The death of the Judge, of course, had not been contemplated, but this in no way changed the result. That was an accident, yet, I imagined, might not be altogether unwelcome, and I could not rid my memory of that shining weapon in Kirby's hand, or the thought that he would have used it had the need arose. Would he not then fight just as fiercely to keep, as he had, to gain? Indeed, I had but one fact upon which I might hope to base action—every watcher believed those cards had been stacked, and that Beaucaire was robbed by means of a trick. Yet, could this be proven? Would any one of those men actually swear that he had seen a suspicious move? If not, then what was there left me except a mere bluff? Absolutely nothing.

Gambling was a recognized institution, with which even the law did not interfere. Of course there were statutes in both Missouri and Illinois, but no enforcement. Indeed the gambling fraternity was so firmly intrenched, through wealth and influence, that no steamer captain even, autocratic as he often was, would dare encroach on their prerogatives. Interested as Thockmorton would be in serving Beaucaire's dependents, and as much as he cordially disliked Kirby, all I could rely upon from him in this emergency would be a certain moral support, and possibly some valuable advice. He would never dare ally himself openly, for the cost of such action would be too high. On the other hand, from my knowledge of Kirby's desperate character, and previous exploits, I seriously doubted the efficacy of threatening him with lynch law. He would be far more liable to defy a mob than yield to its demands. Yet memory of those two helpless girls—more particularly that one over whose unconsciousness there hung the possibility of slavery—urged me strongly to attempt even the apparently impossible. I had it in my mind to fight the man personally if, in no other way, I could attain my end; at least I would face him with every power and authority I could bring to bear.

With no other object in mind, and unarmed, never once dreaming of attack, I advanced alone along the dark, narrow strip of deck, leading toward the ladder which mounted to the wheelhouse. There were no lights, and I was practically compelled to feel my way by keeping one hand upon the rail. The steamer was sweeping around a great bend, and a leadsman forward was calling the depth of water, his monotonous voice chanting out strange river terms of guidance. I had reached the foot of the ladder, my fingers blindly seeking the iron rungs in the gloom, when a figure, vague, indistinct, suddenly emerged from some denser shadow and confronted me. Indeed the earliest realization I had of any other presence was a sharp pressure against my breast, and a low voice breathing a menacing threat in my ear.

"I advise you not to move, you young fool. This is a cocked

pistol tickling your ribs. Where were you going?"

The black night veiled his face, but language and voice, an spite of its low grumble, told me the speaker was Kirby. The very coldness of his tone served to send a chill through me.

"To have a word with Thockmorton," I answered, angered at my own fear, and rendered reckless by that burst of passion. "What do you mean by your threat? Haven't you robbed enough men already with cards without resorting to a gun?"

"This is no robbery," and I knew by the sharpness of his reply my words had stung, "and it might be well for you to keep a civil tongue in your head. I overheard what you said to those men in the cabin. So you are going to take care of me, are you?" There was a touch of steel in the low voice. "Now listen, you brainless meddler. Joe Kirby knows exactly what he is doing when he plays any game. I had nothing to do with Beaucaire's death, but those stakes are mine. I hold them, and I will kill any man who dares to interfere with me."

"You mean you refuse to return any of this property?"

"Every cent, every nigger, every acre—that's my business. Beaucaire was no child; he knew what he was betting, and he lost."

"But," I insisted almost hopelessly, "perhaps you do not wholly understand this matter—the entire situation. Judge Beaucaire risked every penny he possessed in the world."

"I suppose he did, but he expected to gain it all back again, with as much more of mine."

"That may be true, Kirby. I am not defending his action, but surely this is no reason, now that he is dead, why you should not show some degree of mercy to others totally innocent of any wrong. The man left two daughters, both young girls, who will now be homeless and penniless."

He laughed, and the sound of that laugh was more cruel than the accompanying words.

"Two daughters!" he sneered. "According to my information that strains the relationship a trifle, friend Knox—at least the late Judge never took the trouble to acknowledge the fact. Permit me to correct your statement. I happen to know more about Beaucaire's private affairs than you do. He leaves one daughter only. I have never met the young lady, but I understand from excellent authority that she possesses independent means through the death some years ago of her mother. I shall therefore not worry about her loss—and, indeed, she need meet with none, for if she only prove equal to all I have heard I may yet be induced to make her a proposition."

"A proposition?"

"To remain on the plantation as its mistress—plainly an offer of marriage, if you please. Not such a bad idea, is it?"

I stood speechless, held motionless only by the pressing muzzle of his pistol, the cold-blooded villainy of the man striking me dumb. This then had probably been his real purpose from the start. He had followed Beaucaire deliberately with this final end in view—of ruining him, and thus compelling the daughter to yield herself. He had egged the man on, playing on the weakness of his nature, baiting him to finally risk all on a game of chance, the real stake not the money on the table, but the future of this young girl.

"You—you have never seen her?"

"No, but I have met those who have. She is reported to be beautiful, and, better still, worth fifty thousand dollars."

"And you actually mean that you propose now to force Judge Beaucaire's daughter to marry you?"

"Well hardly that, although I shall use whatever means I possess. I intend to win her if I can, fair means, or foul."

I drew a deep breath, comprehending now the full iniquity of his plot, and bracing myself to fight it.

"And what about the other girl, Kirby? for there is another girl."

"Yes," rather indifferently, "there is another."

"Of course you know who she is?"

"Certainly—a nigger, a white nigger; the supposed illegitimate daughter of Adelbert Beaucaire, and a slave woman. There is no reason why I should fret about her, is there? She is my property already by law." He laughed again, the same ugly sneering laugh of triumph, "That was why I was so particular about the wording of that bill of sale—I would rather have her than the whole bunch of field hands."

"You believe then the girl has never been freed—either she, or her mother?"

"Believe? I know. I tell you I never play any game with my eyes shut."

"And you actually intend to—to hold her as a slave?"

"Well, I'll look her over first before I decide—she would be worth a pot full of money down the river."

Randall Parrish

CHAPTER VI

INTO THE BLACK WATER

The contemptuous, utterly indifferent manner in which he voiced his villainous purpose, would have crazed any man. Perhaps he intended that it should, although it was my belief that he merely expressed himself naturally, and with no thought of consequences. The man was so steeped in crime as to be ignorant of all sense of honor, all conception of true manhood. But to me this utterance was the last straw, breaking down every restraint, and leaving me hot, and furious with anger. I forgot the muzzle of the pistol pressed against my side, and the menacing threat in Kirby's low voice. The face of the man was indistinct, a mere outline, but the swift impulse to strike at it was irresistible, and I let him have the blow—a straight-arm jab to the jaw. My clinched knuckles crunched against the flesh, and he reeled back, kept from falling only by the support of the deckhouse. There was no report of a weapon, no outcry, yet, before I could strike again, I was suddenly gripped from behind by a pair of arms, which closed about my throat like a vise, throttling me instantly into silent helplessness. I struggled madly to break free, straining with all the art of a wrestler, exerting every ounce of strength, but the grasp which held me was unyielding, robbing me of breath, and defeating every effort to call for help; Kirby, dazed yet by my sudden blow, and eager to take a hand in the affray, struck me a cowardly blow in the face, and swung his undischarged pistol to a level with my eyes.

"Damn you!" he ejaculated, and for the first time his voice really exhibited temper. "I'd kill you with this, but for the noise. No, by God! there is a safer way than that to settle with you. Have you got the skunk, Carver?"

"You can bet I have, Joe. I kin choke the life out o' him—shall I?"

"No; let up a bit—just enough so he can answer me first, I want to find out what all this means. Now look here, Knox, you're an army officer, are you?"

"Yes," I managed to gasp, sobbing in an effort to catch breath, as the iron fingers at my throat relaxed slightly.

"Well then, what is all this to you? Why are you butting in on my game? Was Beaucaire a friend of yours?"

"I can hardly claim that," I admitted. "We never met until I came aboard this steamer. All I am interested in is justice to others."

"To others? Oh, I suppose you mean those girls—you know them then?"

"I have never even seen them," I said, now speaking more easily. "Thockmorton chanced to tell me about them yesterday, and their condition appealed to me, just as it naturally would to any true man. I thought probably you did not understand the situation, and hoped that if I told you the truth you might respond."

"Oh, you did, did you? You must have figured me as being pretty soft. Well, what do you think now?"

His tone so completely ended my hope of compromise that I replied hotly, "That you are a dirty, piratical cur. I may have doubted your purpose at first, for I am not used to your kind, but this is so no longer. You deliberately ruined and robbed Beaucaire, in order to gain possession of these two girls. You have admitted as much."

He laughed, in no way angered by my plain speech; indeed it almost seemed as though he felt complimented.

"Hardly admit, my friend, for that is not my style. I let others do the guessing. What do you think of that, Carver? It seems we rank rather high in the estimation of the young man." His eyes again centered on me. "And you are really not acquainted with either of the ladies?"

"No."

"I see; a self-appointed squire of dames; actuated merely by a romantic desire to serve beauty in distress. Extremely interesting, my dear boy. But, see here, Knox," and his tone changed to seriousness. "Let the romance go, and talk sense a minute. You are not going to get very far fighting me alone. You haven't even got the law with you. Even if I cheated Beaucaire, which I do not for a moment admit, there is no proof. The money is mine, and so is the land, and the niggers. You can be ugly, of course, but you cannot overturn the facts. Now I don't care a whoop in hell for that bunch of miners back there in the cabin. If left alone they will forget all about this affair in an hour. It's nothing to them, and they are no angels if it was. But, in a way, it is different with you. I understand that, and also that you are in a position where you might make me some trouble. People would listen to what you had to say—and some of them might believe you. Now you acknowledge that what has occurred is personally nothing to you; Beaucaire was no special friend, and you don't even know the two girls—all right then, drop the whole matter. I hold no grudge on account of your striking me, and am even willing to share up with you to avoid trouble."

"And if I refuse?"

"Then, of course, we shall be compelled to shut your mouth for you. Self preservation is the first law."

"Which simply means that you intend to go on, and yield nothing?"

"That is about right. We'll hold tight to what we've got—hey, Carver?"

"That's allers bin my way o' doin' business," chimed in the other brutally. "An' we've sure got you, mister soldier man, where we kin handle yer, I reckon."

I looked about at them both, scarcely able to distinguish clearly even their outlines in the dense gloom. The seriousness of my situation, coupled with my helplessness, and inability to achieve the object proposed, was very evident. These men were reckless, and determined, unable to even grasp my point of view. It might, under these circumstances, have been the part of wisdom to me to have sought some means of compromise, but I was young and hot, fiery blood swept through my veins. The words of Kirby stung me with their breath of insult—his sneering, insolent offer to pay me to remain still.

"You must rank me as one of your own kind," I burst forth. "Now you listen to a plain word from me. If that was intended as an offer, I refuse it. When I first left the cabin, and came here on deck, I honestly believed I could talk with you, Kirby, appeal to your better nature, and gain some consideration for those two girls. Now I know better. From the start this has been the working out of a deliberately planned plot. You, and your confederate, have coolly robbed Beaucaire, and propose to get away with the spoils. Perhaps you will, but that end will not be accomplished through any assistance of mine. At first I only felt a slight interest in the affair, but from now on I am going to fight you fellows with every weapon I possess."

Kirby chuckled, apparently greatly amused.

"Quite glad, I am sure, for the declaration of war. Fighting has always agreed with me. Might I ask the nature of those weapons?"

"That remains for you to discover," I ejaculated sharply, exasperated by his evident contempt. "Carver, take your dirty hands off of me."

In spite of the fact of their threat, the ready pistol pressing against my ribs, the grip of Carver's fingers at my throat, I did not anticipate any actual assault. That either would really dare injure me seemed preposterous. Indeed my impression was, that Kirby felt such indifference toward my attempt to block his plan, that he would permit me to pass without opposition—certainly without the slightest resort to violence. The action of the two was so swift, so concerted, as though to some secret signal, that, almost before I realized their purpose, they held me helplessly struggling, and had forced me back against the low rail. Here I endeavored to break away, to shout an alarm, but was already too late. Carver's hands closed remorselessly on my throat, and, when I managed to strike out madly with one free fist, the butt of

Kirby's pistol descended on my head, so lacerating my scalp the dripping blood blinded my eyes. The blow partially stunned me, and I half fell, clutching at the rail, yet dimly conscious that the two straining men were uplifting my useless body. Carver swearing viciously as he helped to thrust me outward over the wooden bar. The next instant I fell, the sneering cackle of Kirby's laugh of triumph echoing in my ears until drowned in the splash as I struck the black water below.

I came back to the surface dazed and weakened, yet sufficiently conscious to make an intelligent struggle for life. The over-hang of the rapidly passing boat still concealed me from the observation of those above on the deck, and the advantage of permitting them to believe that the blow on my head had resulted in drowning, together with the knowledge that I must swiftly get beyond the stroke of that deadly wheel, flashed instantly through my brain. It was like a tonic, reviving every energy. Waiting only to inhale one deep breath of air, I plunged back once more into the depths, and swam strongly under water. The effort proved successful, for when I again ventured to emerge, gasping and exhausted, the little *Warrior* had swept past, and become merely a shapeless outline, barely visible above the surface at the river. Even if the two men had rushed to the stern, seeking thus to ascertain what had happened to their victim, they could not have detected my presence in that darkness, or determined whether or not I had met death in the depths, or been crushed lifeless by those revolving paddles.

Slowly treading water, my lips held barely above the surface, I drew in deep draughts of cool night air, my mind becoming more active as hope returned. The blow I had received was a savage one, and pained dully, but the cold water in which I had been immersed had caused the bleeding to cease, and likewise revived all my faculties. The water was so icy, still fed by the winter snow of the north, as to make me conscious of chill, and awaken within me a fear of cramps. The steamer melted swiftly away into nothingness, and the last indication of its presence in the distance was the faint gleam of a stern light piercing the night shadows. The very fact that no effort was made to stop was sufficient proof that Thockmorton in the wheelhouse remained unconscious of what had occurred on the deck below. My fate might never be discovered, or suspected. I was alone, submerged in the great river, the stars overhead alone piercing the night shadows. They seemed cold, and far away, their dull glow barely sufficient to reveal the dim outline of the western shore; and even this would have remained invisible except for the trees lining the higher bank beyond, and silhouetted against the slightly lighter background of sky. In the other direction all was apparently water, a turbulent waste, and one glance deciding my action, I quickly struck out, partially breasting the downward sweep of the current, in a desperate struggle to attain land.

I discovered this to be no easy task, as the swirl of the river bore strongly toward the opposite shore, yet I had always been a powerful swimmer, and although now seriously hampered by boots, and heavy, sodden clothing, succeeded in making steady progress. A log swept by me, white bursts of spray illuminating its sides, and I grappled it gratefully, my fingers finding grip on the sodden bark. Using this for partial support, and ceasing to battle so desperately against the down-sweep of the current, I managed finally to work my way into an eddy, struggling onward until my feet at last touched bottom at the end of a low, out-cropping point of sand. This proved to be a mere spit, but I waded ashore, water streaming from my clothing, conscious now of such complete exhaustion that I sank instantly outstretched upon the sand, gasping painfully for breath, every muscle and nerve throbbing.

The night was intensely still, black, impenetrable. It seemed as though no human being could inhabit that desolate region. I lifted my head to listen for the slightest sound of life, and strained my eyes to detect the distant glimmer of a light in any direction. Nothing rewarded the effort. Yet surely along here on this long-settled west bank of the Mississippi I could not be far removed from those of my race, for I knew that all along this river shore were cultivated plantations and little frontier towns irregularly served by passing steamboats. We had not been far to the northward of St. Louis at midnight, and Thockmorton confidently expected to tie up the *Warrior* at the wharf before that city early the next morning. So, surely, somewhere near at hand, concealed amid the gloom, would be discovered the habitations of men—either the pretentious mansion of some prosperous planter, or the humble huts of his black slaves. Could I attain to either one I would be certain of welcome, for hospitality without questioning was the code of the frontier.

The night air increased in chilliness as the hours approached dawn, and I shivered in my wet clothes, although this only served to arouse me into immediate action. Realizing more than ever as I again attempted to move my weakness and exhaustion from struggle, I succeeded in gaining my feet, and stumbled forward along the narrow spit of sand, until I attained a bank of firm earth, up which I crept painfully, emerging at last upon a fairly level spot, softly carpeted with grass, and surrounded by a grove of forest trees. The shadows here were dense, but my feet encountered a depression in the soil, which I soon identified as a rather well-defined path leading inland. Assured that this must point the way to some door, as it was evidently no wild animal trail, I felt my way forward cautiously, eager to attain shelter, and the comfort of a fire.

The grove was of limited extent, and, as I emerged from

beneath its shadow, I came suddenly to a patch of cultivated land, bisected by a small stream, the path I was following leading along its bank. Holding to this for guidance, within less than a hundred yards I came to the house I was seeking, a small, log structure, overshadowed by a gigantic oak, and standing isolated and alone. It appeared dark and silent, although evidently inhabited, as an axe stood leaning against the jamb of the door, while a variety of utensils were scattered about. Believing the place to be occupied by a slave, or possibly some white squatter, I advanced directly to the door, and called loudly to whoever might be within.

There was no response, and, believing the occupant asleep, I used the axe handle, rapping sharply. Still no voice answered, although I felt convinced of some movement inside, leading me to believe that the sleeper had slipped from his bed and was approaching the door. Again I rapped, this time with greater impatience over the delay, but not the slightest sound rewarded the effort Shivering there in my wet clothes, the stubborn obduracy of the fellow awakened my anger.

"Open up, there," I called commandingly, "or else I'll take this axe and break down your door."

In the darkness I had been unobservant of a narrow slide in the upper panel, but had scarcely uttered these words of threat when the flare of a discharge almost in my very face fairly blinded me, and I fell backward, aware of a burning sensation in one shoulder. The next instant I lay outstretched on the ground, and it seemed to me that life was fast ebbing from my body. Twice I endeavored vainly to rise, but at the second attempt my brain reeled dizzily and I sank back unconscious.

CHAPTER VII

PICKING UP THE THREADS

I turned my head slightly on the hard shuck pillow and gazed curiously about. When my eyes had first opened all I could perceive was the section of log wall against which I rested, but now, after painfully turning over, the entire interior of the single-room cabin was revealed. It was humble enough in all its appointments, the walls quite bare, the few chairs fashioned from half-barrels, a packing box for a table, and the narrow bed on which I lay constructed from saplings lashed together, covered with a coarse ticking, packed with straw. The floor was of hard, dry clay; a few live coals remained, smoking in the open fireplace, while a number of garments, among them to be recognized my own clothing, dangled from wooden pegs driven into the chinks of the farther wall. I surveyed the entire circuit of the room wonderingly, a vague memory of what had lately occurred returning slowly to mind. To all appearances I was there alone, although close beside me stood a low stool, supporting a tin basin partially filled with water. As I moved I became conscious of a dull pain in my left shoulder, which I also discovered to be tightly bandaged. It was late in the day, for the rays of the sun streamed in through the single window, and lay a pool of gold along the center of the floor.

Randall Parrish

I presume it was not long, yet my thoughts were so busy it seemed as if I must have been lying there undisturbed for some time, before the door opened quietly, and I became aware of another occupant of the room. Paying no attention to me he crossed to the fireplace, stirred the few smouldering embers into flame, placing upon these some bits of dried wood, and then idly watched as they caught fire. The newcomer was a negro, gray-haired but still vigorous, evidently a powerful fellow judging from his breadth of shoulder, and possessing a face denoting considerable intelligence. Finally he straightened up and faced me, his eyes widening with interest as he caught mine fastened upon him, his thick lips instantly parting in a good-natured grin.

"De good Lord be praised!" he ejaculated, in undisguised delight. "Is yer really awake agin, honey? De docthar say he done thought ye'd cum round by terday sure, sah. Enyhow I's almighty glad fer ter see yer wid dem eyes open onct mor'— yas, sah, I sure am."

"The doctor?" I questioned in surprise, my voice sounding strange and far away. "Have I been here long?"

"Goin' on 'bout ten days, sah. Yer was powerful bad hurt an' out o' yer head, I reckon."

"What was it that happened? Did some one shoot me?"

The negro scratched his head, shuffling his bare feet uneasily on the dirt floor.

"Yas, sah, Mister Knox," he admitted with reluctance. "I's sure powerful sorry, sah, but I was de boy whut plugged yer. Yer see, sah, it done happened dis-a-way," and his black face registered genuine distress. "Thar's a mean gang o' white folks 'round yere thet's took it inter their heads ter lick every free nigger, an' when yer done come up ter my door in de middle ob de night, a cussin', an' a-threatenin' fer ter break in, I just nat'larly didn't wanter be licked, an'—an' so I blazed away. I's powerful sorry 'bout it now, sah."

"No doubt it was more my fault than yours. You are a free negro, then?"

"Yas, sah. I done belong onct ter Colonul Silas Carlton, sah, but afore he died, just because I done saved his boy frum drownin' in de ribber, de ol' Colonul he set me free, an' give me a patch o' lan' ter raise corn on."

"What is your name?"

"Pete, sah. Free Pete is whut mostly de white folks call me." He laughed, white teeth showing and the whites of his eyes. "Yer see, thar am a powerful lot o' Petes round 'bout yere, sah."

I drew a deep breath, conscious of weakness as I endeavored to change position.

"All right, Pete; now I want to understand things clearly. You shot me, supposing I was making an assault on you. Your bullet lodged in my shoulder. What happened then?"

"Well, after a while, sah, thar wan't no mor' noise, an' I reckoned I'd either done hit yer er else ye'd run away. An' thar ye wus, sah, a lyin' on yer back like ye wus ded. Just so soon as I saw ye, I know'd as how ye never wus no nigger-hunter, but a stranger in des yere parts. So I dragged ye inside de cabin, an' washed up yer hurts. But ye never got no bettah, so I got skeered, an' went hoofin' it down fer de docthar at Beaucaire Landin', sah, an' when he cum back along wid me he dug the bullet outer yer shoulder, an' left som truck fer me ter giv' yer. He's done been yere three times, sah."

"From Beaucaire Landing—is that a town?"

"A sorter a town, sah; 'bout four miles down ribber."

The mentioning of this familiar word brought back instantly to my darkened understanding all those main events leading up to my presence in this neighborhood. Complete memory returned, every separate incident sweeping through my brain—Kirby, Carver, the fateful game of cards in the cabin of the *Warrior*, the sudden death of the Judge, the mob anger I sought to curb, the struggle on deck, my being thrown overboard, and the danger threatening the two innocent daughters of Beaucaire. And I had actually been lying in this negro hut, burning up with fever, helplessly delirious, for ten days. What had already occurred in that space of time? What villainy had been concocted and carried out? What more did the negro know?—something surely, for now I remembered he had addressed me by name.

"Now see here, Pete," I began earnestly. "How did you learn what my name was?"

"De docthar he foun' dat out, sah. I reckon' he thought maybe he ought ter know; fearin' as how ye might die. He done looked through yer pockets, sah, an' he took two papers whut he foun' dar away wid him. He done tol' me as how yer wus an offercer in de army—a leftenant, er sumthin'—an' thet dem papers ought fer ter be sint ter de Gov'ner et onct. De las' time he wus yere he tol' me thet he wint down ter Saint Louee hisself, an' done gif bof dem papers ter Gov'ner Clark. So yer don't need worry none 'bout dem no mor'."

I sank back onto the hard pillow, greatly relieved by this

information. The burden of official duty had been taken from me. I was now on furlough, and free to act as I pleased. I suddenly became conscious that I was hungry. I expressed this desire for food, and the negro instantly busied himself over the fire. I watched his movements with interest, although my thoughts quickly drifted to other matters.

"Have you picked up any news lately from the Beaucaire plantation?" I asked, at last.

He twisted his head about at sound of my voice.

"I heerd said dey done brought de body ob de ol' Jedge home, sah—he died mighty sudden sumwhar up de ribber. Thet's 'bout all I know."

"When was this?"

"'Bout a week maybe mor'n dat ago. De *Warrior* brought de body down, sah."

"The *Warrior*? Did anyone go ashore with it?"

"Pears like thar wus two men stopped off at de Landin'. I disremember de names, but one ob 'em wus an ol' friend ob de Jedge's."

I turned my head away silently, but only for a moment. The two men were in all probability Kirby and his satellite, Carver. Evidently they intended to lose no time. The accident, the period of my unconsciousness, had left the villains ample opportunity in which to carry out the details of their devilish plot. The silence had convinced them of my death, leaving them nothing to fear, no opposition to guard against. Doubtless the Beaucaire property was already legally in Kirby's possession, and any possible chance I might have once had to foil him in his nefarious purpose had now completely vanished.

To be sure I had reasoned out no definite means whereby I could circumvent his theft, except to take legal advice, confer with Governor Clark, and warn those threatened girls of their danger. But now it was too late even to do this. And yet it might not be. If Kirby and his confederate believed that I was dead, were convinced that I had perished beneath the waters of the river, they might feel safe in taking time to strengthen their position; might delay final action, hoping thus to make their case seem more plausible. If Kirby was really serious in his intention of marrying Beaucaire's daughter he would naturally hesitate immediately to acknowledge winning the property at cards, and thus indirectly being the cause of her father's death. He would be quite likely to keep this hidden from the girl for a while, until he tried his luck at love. If love failed, then the disclosure might be made to drive the young woman to him; a threat to render her complacent. The negro evidently knew very little as to what had occurred, merely the floating gossip of the slave quarters, and some few things the doctor had mentioned. But there was a man living at the Landing who would be informed as to all the facts.

"I believe the Judge left two daughters, did he not?"

"Yas, sah—mighty pretty gals dey am too."

"And they still remain in possession of the house?"

"I reckon dey do, sah. Pears like the dochtar sed sumthin' 'bout treating one ob 'em—Miss Eloise—one time he wus ober yere. Sure, deys dere all right."

"Do you know a lawyer named Haines?"

"Livin' down at de Landin'? Yas, sah."

I lifted myself up in the bed, too deeply interested to lie still any longer.

"Now listen, Pete," I explained earnestly. "I've got sufficient money to pay you well for all you do, and, just as soon as you get me something to eat, I want you to go down to the Landing and bring Lawyer Haines back here with you. Just tell him a sick white man wants to see him at once, and not a word to anyone else. You might tell Haines this is a private matter—you understand?"

"Yas, sah," the whites of his eyes rolling. "He done know ol' Pete, an' I'll sure bring him back yere."

It was dark when they came, the fire alone lighting up the interior of the dingy cabin with a fitful glow of red flame. I had managed to get out of bed and partially dress myself feeling stronger, and in less pain as I exercised my muscles. They found me seated before the fireplace, indulging in a pot of fresh coffee. Haines was a small, sandy-complexioned man, with a straggling beard and light blue eyes. He appeared competent enough, a bundle of nervous energy, and yet there was something about the fellow which instantly impressed me unfavorably—probably his short, jerky manner of speech, and his inability to look straight at you.

"Pete has been telling me who you are, Lieutenant," he said, as we shook hands, "and putting some other things together I can guess the rest. You came south on the *Warrior*."

"From Fort Armstrong—yes; who told you this?"

"Captain Thockmorton. I saw him in St. Louis, and he seemed deeply grieved by your sudden disappearance. No one on board was able to explain what had occurred."

"Yet there were two men on the boat who could have explained, if they had cared to do so," I answered drily. "I mean Kirby and Carver; they were the ones who threw me overboard."

He dropped into a chair, his keen, ferret eyes on my face.

"Kirby and Carver? They went ashore with the Judge's body at the Landing. So there is a story back of all this," he exclaimed jerkily. "Damn it, I thought as much. Was Beaucaire killed?"

"No—not at least by any violence. No doubt the shock of his loss hastened his death. Surely you must know that he risked all he possessed on a game of cards and lost?"

"Thockmorton knew something about it, and there were other rumors floating about the Landing, but I have heard no details."

"You did not see the two men, then?"

"No, I was not at home, and they went on down the river the next day on a keel-boat. You saw the play?"

"I saw the last part of the game and was convinced, as all the others present were, that the Judge was deliberately ruined for a purpose. I believe it was all planned beforehand, but of this we have no tangible proof."

"His opponent was Joe Kirby?"

"And a fellow named Carver, a mere hanger-on."

Haines wet his lips, his eyes narrowing to mere slits, his professional nature coming to the front.

"First, let me ask you why you believe Beaucaire was cheated?" he piped. "I know Joe Kirby, and consider him quite capable of such a trick, but we shall need more than suspicion to circumvent his scheme."

"I have every reason, Haines, to feel convinced that both Kirby and Carver trailed Beaucaire up the river with the intention of plucking him. Kirby practically confessed this to me, boastingly, afterwards. All the way down he was bantering the Judge to play. That last night he so manipulated the cards—or rather Carver did, for it was his deal—as to deceive Beaucaire into firmly believing that he held an absolutely unbeatable hand—he was dealt four aces and a king."

The lawyer leaned forward, breathing heavily.

"Four aces! Only one hand is better than that, and it would be impossible to get such a hand out of one pack."

"That is exactly true, Haines. I am no card player, but I do know that much about the game. Yet Kirby took the pot with a straight flush. Now, either he, or Carver, slipped an extra ace into the pack, or else Beaucaire did. In my opinion the Judge had no chance to work such a trick. And that's the case, as it stands."

Haines jumped to his feet and began pacing the dirt floor excitedly, his hands clasped behind his back.

"By God, man!" he cried, pausing suddenly. "Even if he did have a chance, the Judge never did it—never. He was a good sport, and always played a straight game. You say he bet everything he had?"

"To the last dollar—Kirby egged him on. Besides the money, a deed to his land, and a bill of sale for his negroes were on the table."

"The field hands, you mean?"

"Yes, and the house servants. Kirby insisted that he write these words, 'This includes every chattel slave legally belonging to me,' and made Beaucaire sign it in that form."

Haines' face was white, his eyes staring at me incredulously.

"God help us, man! Do you know what that means?" he gasped.

"I am almost afraid I do," I answered, yet startled by his manner. "That was why I sent for you. Would that include his son's daughter?"

He buried his face in his hands.

"Yes," he confessed brokenly. "To the best of my knowledge Rene Beaucaire is a slave."

CHAPTER VIII

I DECIDE MY DUTY

The silence following this blunt statement was sickening. Up to that moment, in spite of every fact brought to my knowledge, I had secretly believed this condition of affairs impossible. Surely somewhere, through some legal form, Judge Beaucaire had guarded the future safety of this young woman, whom he had admitted into his household. Any other conception seemed impossible, too monstrous, too preposterous for consideration. But now the solemn words of the lawyer, his own legal counselor, brought conviction, and for the moment all power of speech deserted me. It was actually true then—the girl was a slave, a thing belonging to Kirby. Nothing broke the stillness within the cabin, except the sharp crackling of flames in the open fireplace, and the heavy breathing of the negro. He was seated on the edge of the bed, his black face showing a greenish tint, and revealing puzzled amazement, with wide-opened eyes staring blankly at Haines, who stood motionless before the fire.

"Whut wus dat yer sed, Mister Haines?" he asked thickly. "You say as how Missus Rene Beaucaire is a slave, sah? Pears like I don't just rightfully understan'."

"Still that is true, Pete," and the lawyer lifted his head and surveyed us both. "She is the illegitimate daughter of Delia, Judge Beaucaire's housekeeper; her father was Adelbert Beaucaire, the Judge's only son. No one knows where he is, dead or alive."

"De good Lord! An' de ol' Jedge never set her free?"

The lawyer shook his head, words evidently failing him.

"But are you absolutely certain of this?" I broke in impatiently. "Have you searched the records?"

"Not only searched them, Knox, but, before he left for the north on this last trip, Beaucaire was in my office, and I practically forced him to acknowledge the negligence. He even authorized me to draw up the necessary papers for him to sign on his return—for both Delia and the girl. They are in my desk now, unexecuted. There is no mistake—Rene is legally a slave, together with her mother."

"My God!" I exclaimed. "What an indictment of slavery. Could anyone conceive a more horrible position! Here is a young girl, educated, refined, of more than ordinary attractiveness Thockmorton tells me, brought up amid every comfort, and led to believe herself the honored daughter of the house, awakening in an instant to the fact that she is a slave, with negro blood in her veins—a mere chattel, owned body and soul by a gambler, won in a card game, and to be sold to the highest bidder. Haines, I tell you Kirby knew all this."

"Kirby knew? Why do you say that?"

"He boasted of it. I thought little about what he said at the time, but I believe now one of his main objects was to gain possession of this girl. That would account for his insistence upon that peculiar clause in the bill of sale—he either suspected, or had discovered through some source, that Rene Beaucaire had never been set free. For some reason he desired possession of both Beaucaire girls; they meant more to him than either the money or the property. This card game gave him one; the other—"

"Eloise, you mean? Did the fellow threaten her?"

"Here is what he said sneeringly, you can judge yourself what he meant, 'She's worth fifty thousand dollars by her mother's will, and I intend to win her if I can, fair means or foul.'"

Haines did not speak for some moments, his eyes on my face. Then he paced back and forth across the floor, finally stopping before the fire.

"This is as near hell as anything I ever knew," he said, "and so far as I can see there is no legal way out of it. We are utterly helpless to assist."

"We are not," I answered hotly, "if we are men. There may be no legal way in which we can beat this villain, but there is an illegal one, unless we are already too late, and I propose to use it, whether you join me or not."

"You have a plan? What is it?"

"The only one feasible. I thought of its possibility before on the boat, when a suspicion of this situation first came to me. You are sure the girls are still at the plantation house? that they know nothing of this condition?"

"I have reason to believe so. Delia was buying provisions at the Landing yesterday; I talked with her a moment."

"And you said that Kirby and Carver were only in town for one night, leaving the next morning on a keel-boat for St. Louis. Probably they did not visit the plantation at all, unless it was to scout around. My idea is they were not quite ready to take possession; that they have gone to St. Louis to file the papers, and will come back with officers prepared to execute them. This means that we must work fast to get out of their way."

"What do you propose doing?"

"Let me ask a question first. Is it true that Eloise Beaucaire is heiress to fifty thousand dollars through her mother's estate?"

"Yes, I invested most of it."

"In what?"

"New Orleans property principally."

"Then it is safe enough whatever happens. The only thing we can do is this: Tell those girls and the mother the whole truth—tell them at once, before Kirby can return, and then help them to get out of this country. It is not necessary for Eloise to go, unless she desires to, but there is no other safe course for Delia and Rene. They must reach a northern state before Kirby can lay hands on them. Could Delia pass for a white woman?"

"Not in the South; still she could travel as Rene's maid. But I do not believe it is possible for the two to escape in that way, Knox. Understand I'd be willing to risk it if there were any show. How can it be done? On the average at this time of year there isn't a steamboat along here once a month. If we did get them onto a boat they would have to travel straight south as far as the Ohio. Kirby wouldn't be more than a day or two behind them, with friends on every boat on the river. Illinois is no free state for fugitive slaves—they might just as well be caught in Missouri as over there. There is not one chance in a thousand that they make it."

"And less than that, if they remain here for Kirby to get his hands on," I retorted bitterly. "Now look here, Haines. I am going to carry out this plan alone, if you will not back me in it. I am not talking about steamboats; they could travel by night, and hide along shore during the day. All they would need would be two negro oarsmen, sufficient food, and a boat big enough to carry them safely. You have small boats, surely?"

"I got one, Massa Knox," burst out Pete eagerly. "She's down by de mouth ob de creek, sah, an' she sure am a mighty good boat. We could load her up right here, an' I'd be one ob de niggers fer ter take dem ladies down ribber. I'se a free boy, an' nobody care whar I done go."

These unexpected words heartened me, strengthened my own resolve, and I obeyed the first impulse, instantly crossing the room and frankly extending my hand to the surprised negro.

"That sounds like a man, Pete," I exclaimed warmly. "Yes, of course I mean it—shake hands. You are white enough for me, boy, and I do not propose letting you do any more than I am willing to do. I'll go along with you on this trip. I have sixty days furlough."

I turned and faced the lawyer, my mind firmly settled on the scheme, and determined upon carrying it out instantly.

"And now, what about you, Haines?" I demanded. "Are you ready to help? Come, man, surely this is not something we have any time to debate. Kirby is liable to show up at any moment with full authority, and the sheriff to back him. It is still early in the evening and we must work tonight, if at all."

"You haven't the strength for such a venture," he protested.

"Haven't I?" and I laughed. "Oh, yes I have. I am young and this wound is nothing. I may be a bit stiff in the shoulder for a few days, but I can pull an oar with one hand. That never will stop me. Are you with us?"

He was slow in replying, and, as I eagerly watched his face, I could almost comprehend the working of the lawyer mind. He saw and argued every doubt, considered every danger.

"In spirit, yes," he answered at last, "but not physically. I believe under the circumstances you are justified, Knox. Perhaps I'd do the same thing if I was in your place and had your youth behind me. But I am a lawyer, fifty years old, and this is my home. If the story ever got out that I took part in nigger stealing, that would be the end of me in Missouri. As you say, you are a young man, and I reckon you were not brought up in the South either. That makes a difference. You can take the risk, but about all I can do will be to keep a quiet tongue in my head. Nobody will ever learn what has happened through me—I'll promise you that. But that is all I can promise."

"Yet you acknowledge this is the only way? No legal course is open to us?"

"Absolutely none. If there was I should never consent to be a party to this plan, or shield you in any way. Kirby has undoubtedly got the law with him. We cannot establish fraud; the property actually belongs to him—both mother and daughter are his slaves."

"And how about the other girl—Eloise?"

"He has no legal hold on her; she is a free white woman. He could only hope to overcome her resistance by threats. The plantation is irrevocably lost to the Beaucaires, but she possesses the power to defy him because of her mother's property. If Kirby marries her, it will only be through her consent."

He picked up his hat from the table, and a stout stick he had brought along with him, taking a step toward the door.

"I might as well tell you I consider this a mad scheme," he paused to add gravely, "and that it will probably fail. There is a possible chance of success, I admit, and for that reason I permit you to go ahead with it, and pledge myself to keep the secret. I was rather intimately associated with Beaucaire for a number of years, and to see his granddaughter sold into slavery, even if she does have a drop of nigger blood in her veins, is more than I can stand, without giving her a chance to get away. That is why I consent to abet a crime, and keep still about it. But beyond that I'll not go. I am a southerner, Knox; my father owned slaves. I believe in the system, and have always upheld it. Nobody in Missouri hates a Black Abolitionist worse than I do; if anyone had ever said I would help a nigger run away, I'd call him a liar in a minute. Do you understand the position this damned affair puts me into?"

"Yes, I do, Haines," and I held out my hand to him, with fresh cordiality. "It is uncommonly white of you to even go that far. On the other hand I was brought up to despise slavery. I'll pledge you this—for Pete here, as well as myself—that if we are caught, your name shall never be mentioned. Have you any advice to give?"

He paused uncertainly, his hand on the latch, the firelight flashing up into his face.

"Only this," he said slowly. "If I were you I'd never attempt to go south. Below St. Louis boats are numerous, and you would be almost certain to be discovered. If Kirby chases you—and I know him well enough to be sure he will—he will naturally take it for granted that you have headed for the Ohio. The very fact that the fugitives are women would convince him of this. To my mind the one chance of your getting away, lies to the north—up the Illinois."

"That thought was in my mind also," I admitted, thoroughly satisfied now that he was really friendly, and to be trusted. "I have been told that the settlers north of that stream came mostly from New England—is that true?"

"To a large extent. We have reason to believe there is an underground road in operation from the river to Canada, and many a runaway nigger makes the trip every year. That ought to be your best course, but there is no time now to put the women in the care of those men. Of course I don't know who they are—perhaps Pete does?"

"No, sah," protested the black quickly. "'Pears like I never heerd tell 'bout dem. I'se a free nigger, sah."

The lawyer's shrewd eyes twinkled.

"And that is exactly why, you black rascal, I believe you really do know. I reckon, Knox, he'll tell you what he wouldn't tell me. Anyhow, good luck to you both, and good night."

The door closed behind him, and the negro and I were alone. All at once I realized the desperate nature of this adventure I had undertaken, and its possible consequences. Haines' words had driven it home to my mind, causing me to comprehend the viewpoint of this neighborhood, the hatred men felt for a nigger-stealer, and what my fate would be if once caught in the act. Yet the die was already cast; I had pledged myself to action; was fully committed to the attempted rescue of Rene Beaucaire, and no thought of any retreat once occurred to me. I opened the door cautiously, glancing out into the night, to thus assure myself we were alone, closed it again, and came back. The negro still remained seated on the edge of the bed, digging his toes into the hard earth of the floor.

"Pete," I began earnestly. "You trust me, don't you? You do not suspect me of being any slave-hunter?"

"No, sah, Massa Knox, I ain't 'feared o' yer—yers one o' dem down-easterners."

"Well, not exactly that. I came from a slave state, but my family is of New England blood and breeding. I am just as much your friend as though you were white. Now you and I have got a hard job before us."

"Yas, sah, we sure has."

"And the first thing we have got to do, is to trust each other. Now I am going to ask you a question—is that the best way for us to go, up the Illinois?"

He was slow to answer, evidently turning the whole matter over in his mind. I waited impatiently, feeling the delay to be a serious loss of time.

"Well then, let me put this differently. Have you ever assisted any slaves to run away from Missouri?"

"Well, Massa Knox, I reckon thet maybe I knew'd 'bout som' gittin' a-way—'pears like I did, sah."

"And these escaped by way of the Illinois?"

His dumb, almost pathetic eyes met mine pleadingly, but some expression of my face served to yield him courage.

"I—I reckon I—I don't know much 'bout all dis, Massa Knox," he stammered doubtfully, his hands locking and unlocking nervously. "I—I sure don'; an' fer de mattah o' dat, ther ain't nobody whut does, sah. All I does know, fer sure, is dat if a nigger onct gets as fer as a certain white man up de ribber, 'bout whar de mouth ob de Illinois is, he's got a mighty good chance fer ter reach Canada. De next place whar he's most likely ter stop is Beardstown, long wid som' sorter preacher whut lives thar. An' thet's as fer as dey ever done tol' me, sah."

"About this first white man—the one near the mouth of the Illinois—do you know his name?"

Pete rose to his feet, and crossed the room to where I stood, bending down until his lips were close to my ear. His answer was spoken in a thick whisper.

"Massa Knox, I never did 'spect to say dis ter no white man, but it seems I just nat'larly got fer ter tell yer. I done heerd thet man say onct just whut yer did, thet a nigger wus just as much his frien' as though he wus white—thet it wan't de skin nohow what counted, but de heart. No, sah, I ain't feered fer ter tell yer, Massa Knox. He's got a cabin hid way back in de bluffs, whar nobody don't go, 'cept dem who know whar it is. I reckon he don't do nuthin' but hunt an' fish nohow— leastways he don't raise no corn, nor truck fer ter sell. He's a tall, lanky man, sah, sorter thin, with a long beard, an' his name wus Amos Shrunk. I reckon maybe he's a Black Abolitionist, sah."

"Quite likely, I should say. And you could take a boat from here to his place?"

"Sure, the darkest night yer ever see. Inter the mouth ob a crick, 'bout a hundred rods up de Illinois. Den thar's a path, a sorter path, whut goes ter de cabin; but most genir'ly he's down thar waitin' et night. Yer see dey never sure knows when som' nigger is goin' fer ter git away—only mostly it's at night."

This knowledge greatly simplified matters. If there was already in operation an organized scheme by means of which fugitives from this side of the great river were taken through to Canada, protected and assisted along the way by the friends of freedom, then all we would be required to do in this case would be to safely convey the unfortunate Rene and her mother in Pete's boat up the river, and there turn them over to the care of this Amos Shrunk. Undoubtedly he could be trusted to see to it that they were promptly forwarded to others, fanatics like himself, who would swiftly pass them along at night across the Illinois prairies, until beyond all danger of pursuit. Hundreds, no doubt, had traveled this route, and, once these two were in Shrunk's care our responsibility would be over with. It was to me a vast relief to realize this. The distance to the mouth of the Illinois could not be far, surely not to exceed fifty miles as the river ran. It ought not to prove difficult to baffle Kirby for that short distance, and then we would be free to return, and no one could prove any charge against us. Indeed it was my purpose to immediately proceed down the river on my furlough, and probably it would never so much as be suspected that the negro had been away. Ever since my boyhood I had listened to stories concerning the operation of Underground Railroads

Randall Parrish

by means of which slaves were assisted to freedom, and now felt no hesitancy in confiding these two women to the care of their operators. The only important fact fronting us was that we must act quickly, before Kirby and his aides, armed with legal authority, could return—this very night.

"Pete," I said shortly, my tone unconsciously one of authority, "we must be out of here before daylight, and safely hidden somewhere up the river. The first thing to be done, and the hardest, is to explain to those women the situation, and persuade them to accompany us. They may not believe my story; that was why I was so anxious to have Haines go to the house. They would have confidence in him. Do they know you?"

"Lord love yer—ob course dey do. I'se knowed all ob 'em for a long while, sah. Why when I furst don' see dem Beaucaire gals dey wus just infants. Dey'll sure believe ol' Pete."

"Well, we can only try our best. Have you any conveyance here?"

"Any whut, sah?"

"Any wheeled vehicle in which we can ride to Beaucaire, and by means of which we can bring the women back? The distance is too far to walk."

"I'se got a sorter khart, an' an ol' muel, sah. Dey's out yonder in de bush."

"Hitch them up at once, while I put a few things we may need in the boat. Show me how to find it."

He pointed out the path, with the directions necessary, and disappeared, while I returned to the cabin, dragged a blanket from off the bed, and filled it with whatever miscellaneous articles of food I was able to discover about the place. My wound, now that I was busily engaged, troubled me very little, and, gathering the four corners of the blanket together, I easily transported this stock of provisions to the river bank, and safely stowed them away in the boat found there. I returned to discover the mule and cart ready, and a few moments later we were creaking slowly along a gloomy wood road, jolting over the stumps, with Pete walking beside the animal's head, whispering encouragement into the flapping ear. The great adventure had begun.

CHAPTER IX

THE HOME OF JUDGE BEAUCAIRE

The road we followed appeared to be endless, and so rough that I soon climbed down from my seat, an unplaned board, uncomfortable enough under any conditions, in the swaying, bumping cart, and stumbled blindly along behind, tripping over stumps in the darkness, and wrenching my ankles painfully in deep ruts. Progress was slow, not only because of the difficulties of the passage, but equally on account of the obstinacy of the mule. Indeed, it required no small diplomacy on the part of the negro to induce the animal to proceed at all, and finally, despairing of the efficiency of words, he drew a club, evidently reserved for such emergencies, from the interior of the cart, and gave utterance to an ultimatum. Following this display of force our advance became a trifle more rapid.

I endeavored to think, to plan more definitely my course upon arriving at the Beaucaire plantation, but discovered it quite impossible to concentrate my mind upon anything. My entire attention had to be riveted on the intricacies of the road, which wound in and out among the bluffs, down one gully and up another, until I finally lost all sense of direction, and merely stumbled on after the dark outlines of the cart, through a black cave formed by the branches of over-arching trees.

It was considerably after ten o'clock when we emerged upon an open plateau, and a glimmer of stars overhead revealed to me afar off the silver thread of the great river. Even in that dim light I could trace its winding course along the valley, and the view by daylight from this point must have been a delight to the eye. Pete stopped the straining mule, a feat not at all difficult of accomplishment, the animal's sides rising and falling as he wheezed for breath, and came back to where I stood, staring about at the dimly perceived objects in the foreground.

"Out dar am de Beaucaire place," he announced, as soon as he could distinguish my presence, waving his arm to indicate the direction. "An' I reckon we bettah not ride no further, fer if Alick shud smell corn, he'd nat'larly raise dis whol' neighborhood—he's got a powerful voice, sah."

"Equal to his appetite no doubt."

"Yas, sah; that's mostly whut Alick am."

"How far away is the house?"

"Likely 'bout a hundred yards. Yer see dat light out yonder; well dat's it, an' I reckon de ladies mus' be up yet, keepin' de lamp burnin'. Here's de slave cabins 'long de edge ob de woods, but dey's all dark. What's yer a goin' fer ter do now, Massa Knox?"

I was conscious that my heart was beating rapidly, and that my mind was anything but clear. The problem fronting me did not appear so easily solved, now that I was fairly up against it, and yet there seemed only one natural method of procedure. I must go at my unpleasant task boldly, and in

Randall Parrish

this case only the truth would serve. I was an officer in the United States Army, and had in my pocket papers to prove my identity. These would vouch for me as a gentleman, and yield me a measure of authority. And this fact, once established, ought to give me sufficient standing in the eyes of those girls to compel from them a respectful hearing. I would tell the story exactly as I knew it, concealing nothing, and adding no unnecessary word, outline my plan of action, and then leave them to decide what they thought best to do. This was the simple, sensible way, and I had implicit faith that they would accept my statement, and believe my offer of assistance an honest one. I could not perceive how they could do otherwise. Strange, unbelievable as the situation was, proof was not lacking. Delia could be compelled to acknowledge that Rene was her child—she would scarcely dare deny this truth in face of my positive knowledge—and she, at least, must know that Judge Beaucaire had never during his lifetime given her her freedom. This fact could be established beyond question, and then they must surely all comprehend the necessity of immediate flight—that there remained no other possible means of escape from hopeless slavery. Desperate as the chance appeared, it was the only one.

It was a disagreeable, heart-rending task which I had taken upon myself, but it could be no longer avoided. It dawned upon me now with more intense force than ever before the position in which I stood, and I shrank from the ordeal. A perfect stranger, not even a chance acquaintance of those directly involved in this tragedy, I would have to drag out from the closet, where it had been hidden away for years, this old Beaucaire skeleton, and rattle the dried bones of dishonor before the horrified understanding of these two innocent, unsuspecting girls. I knew nothing of their characters, or of how they would meet such a revelation, and yet they must be made to see, and thoroughly comprehend the situation; must be compelled to face the horror and disgrace of their position, and aroused to action. I had little thought then for the slave mother; doubtless she had been expecting some such exposure for years, and was, at least, partially steeled to meet it. But for the two girls, brought up as sisters, close companions since infancy, having no previous suspicion of the dreadful truth, this sudden revelation would be worse than death. Yet now concealment would be no kindness; indeed, the tenderest mercy I could show was to tell them in all frankness the whole miserable story of crime and neglect; and then point out to them the only remaining means of escape from the consequence of others' sins.

These thoughts, definite and compelling, flashed through my mind as I stood there in the darkness, vainly seeking to distinguish the distant outlines of the great house, from one window alone of which the glow of light streamed. In that moment of decision the conviction came to me that I had best do this alone; that the presence of the negro would hinder, rather than help the solution of the problem. I must appeal directly to the intelligence, the courage, of those so deeply involved, and trust my own personality to win their confidence. In this the negro would be useless.

"Pete," I said, measuring my words, my plan of action shaping itself even as I spoke. "What lies in there between us and the house?"

"A truck patch mostly, wid a fence 'round it. Den thar comes som' flower beds."

"No path?"

"Well, I done reckon as how thar might be a sorter path, sah, but you'd hardly find it in de dark. De bes' way'd be ter sorter feel 'long de fence, 'til yer git sight o' de front porch."

"All right, then. I am going to leave you here while I scout around. Keep your eyes open, and have the mule ready to leave at any minute."

"'Bout how lon' yer be gone, sah?"

"I cannot tell you that. As short a time as possible. It may require considerable explanation and urging to get those three women to trust me. However, all you have to do is wait, and be sure that no one sees you. If you should be needed for anything at the house, I'll get word to you some way; and if I should send Delia and Rene out here alone, without being able to come with them myself, load them into the cart at once, and drive to the boat. I'll manage to join you somewhere, and the important thing is to get them safely away. You understand all this?"

"Yas, sah; leastways I reckon I does. I'se ter take keer ob dem all, an' let yer take keer o' yerself."

"Exactly, because, you see, I haven't the slightest idea what I am going to run up against. There may be others in the house, and I might not dare to leave Miss Eloise behind alone without some protection. In a way she is in almost as much danger as the others if she falls into Kirby's hands. I shall endeavor to induce her to go to Haines at once."

Following some impulse I shook hands with him, and then plunged into the darkness, my only guidance at first that single ray of light streaming through the unshaded window. The ground underfoot was roughly irregular, cleared forest land evidently, as I occasionally stumbled over an unremoved stump, although there was nothing to seriously obstruct my passage until I reached the fence surrounding the garden. By this time the outlines of the house were plainly visible against the skyline beyond, and I realized that it was indeed quite a mansion for that country, a great square frame structure, two full stories in height, appearing black and deserted, except for that single window through which the light continued to stream. While this window was upon the lower floor, directly opposite where I stood, and no great distance away, it was still sufficiently elevated above the ground, and obscured by a small outside balcony, so as to afford me no glimpse within. All I could distinguish clearly was the ceiling of what appeared to be a rather large apartment.

As I advanced cautiously along the fence, a low structure built of rough rails, and thus approached more closely to the front of the main building, other lights began to reveal themselves, enabling me to perceive that the inner hallway was likewise illuminated, although not brilliantly. These dim lights proved sufficient, however, to unable me to trace the general form of the broad veranda in front, with its high roof upheld by pillars of wood—doubtless giant forest trees—and also the wide wooden steps leading down to a circling carriage drive. In spite of previous descriptions I had scarcely anticipated encountering so fine a home in this land which to me was wilderness. The contrast of what life had undoubtedly been to its inmates, and what it would now become through the medium of this unwelcome message I bore, struck me with new force. My mission became instantly a hateful thing, yet I only set my lips tighter, determined to end it as quickly as possible.

By groping about with my feet I succeeded in discovering the path of which Pete had spoken, and managed with difficulty to follow it slowly. Winding in and out amid shrubbery, and what may have been reserved for flower beds, this ended at a side door, which was locked.

Randall Parrish

Discovering this fact, and that it resisted all efforts at opening, I turned once more toward the front, and advanced in that direction, securely hidden by the dense shadow of the house. All about me was silence, not even the sound of a voice or the flap of a wing breaking the intense stillness of the night. I almost imagined I heard the murmur of the distant river, but this was probably the night breeze sighing through the tree branches. I came below the veranda, still in the deep shadow, utterly unconscious of any other presence, when suddenly, from just above me, and certainly not six feet distant, a man spoke gruffly, the unexpected sound of his strange voice interrupted by the sharp grate of a chair's leg on the porch floor, and a half-smothered yawn.

"Say, Sheriff, how long are we all goin' ter set yere, do yer know? This don't look much like Saint Louee afore daylight ter me."

I stopped still, crouching low, my heart leaping into my throat, and every nerve tingling.

"No, it sure don't, Tim," replied another, and the fellow apparently got down from off his perch on the porch rail. "Yer see Kirby is bound he'll get hold o' them two missin' females furst, afore he'll let me round up the niggers."

"But yer told him yer wouldn't round the niggers up, an' stow 'em away in the boat."

"Not till I get service on the young lady. It wouldn't do no good."

"Whut's the idee?"

"Damned if I know exactly. All I know is whut I kin do accordin' ter law, an' whut I can't. The papers is all straight

'nough, but they've got ter be served afore we kin lay hands
on a damned thing. The Jedge tol' me fer ter do everything
just as Kirby sed, an' I aim ter do it, but just the same I got
ter keep inside the law. I reckon thar's a hitch sumwhar', but
thet's none o' my business. Kirby is liberal 'nough with his
money, an' I dunno as it makes much difference when we
strike the ol' town."

"'Tain't so much that, Sheriff. I kin stan' it fer ter be up all
night, but Bill wus tellin' me we might hav' som' trouble
down ter the Landin' unless we finished up our job yere afore
mornin'."

"Oh, I reckon not; whut was it Bill said?"

"Quite a rigmarole frum furst ter last. Giv' me a light fer the
pipe, will yer?"

There was a flare above me, and then darkness once more,
and then the slow drawl of the man's voice as he resumed.
"Some feller by the name ov McAdoo, down ter Saint Louee,
who's just com' down frum the lead mines, tol' him thet Joe
Kirby got all this yere property in a game o' kyards on the
boat, an' thet it wan't no square game either. I didn't git it all
straight, I reckon, but accordin' ter the deal handed me thar
wus two dead men mixed up in the affair—Beaucaire, an' a
young army offercer. Seems ter me his name wus Knox."

"I didn't hear that."

"Well, enyhow, that's the way Bill told it. Beaucaire he
naturally fell dead—heart, er som'thin'—an' the other feller,
this yere army man, he went out on deck fer ter see Kirby,
an' he never cum' back. McAdoo sorter reckoned as how
likely he wus slugged, an' throwed overboard. An' then, on
top' all that, we're sent up yere in the night like a passel o'

thieves ter take these niggers down ter Saint Louee. What do yer make ov it, Jake?"

"Wal," said the other slowly, his mouth evidently loaded with tobacco, "I ain't never asked no questions since I wus made sheriff. I'm doin' whut the court says. Hell! thar's trouble 'nough in this job without my buttin' in on other people's business. But this is how it stacks up ter me. Kirby's got the law on his side—no doubt 'bout that—but I reckon as how he knows it wus a damn mean trick, and so he's sorter skeered as ter how them fellers livin' down ter the Landin' might act. Thar's a lawyer thar named Haines, as sharp as a steel trap, who tended ter all the ol' Jedge's business, an' Joe he don't wanter run foul o' him. Thet's why we tied up ter the shore below town, in the mouth o' thet crick, an' then hed ter hoof it up yere in the dark. Of course we got the law with us, but we wanter pull this job off an' not stir up no fight—see?"

"Sure," disgustedly. "I reckon I know all that; I heerd the Jedge tell yer how we wus ter do the job. But why's Kirby in such a sweat ter git all these niggers down ter Saint Louee?"

"Ter sell 'em, an' git the cash. Onct they're outer the way there won't be no row. He'll let the land yere lie idle fer a year or two, an' by that time nobody'll care a whoop how he got it. But he's got ter git rid o' them niggers right away."

"Well, who the hell's goin' ter prevent? They're his'n, ain't they? Thar ain't no Black Abolitionists 'round yere, I reckon. I never know'd yer had ter run off your own niggers in the night, so's ter sell 'em down South. My Gawd, is this yere Mussury!"

"Seems sorter queer ter me," admitted the sheriff, "but I did get a little outer that feller Carver comin' up. He's a close-mouthed cuss, an' didn't say much, but puttin' it with what yer just told me, I reckon I kin sorter figger it out. Carver is som' sorter partner with Kirby—a capper I reckon—an' enyhow he had a hand in that kayrd game. 'Tain't the niggers thet are makin' the trouble—leastways not the black 'uns. Nobody's likely ter row over them. It seems that Beaucaire kept a quadroon housekeeper, a slave, o' course, an' a while back she giv' birth ter a child, the father o' the infant bein' Judge Beaucaire's son. Then the son skipped out, an' ain't ever bin heard frum since—dead most likely, fer all this wus twenty years ago. 'Course the child, which wus a girl, is as white as I am—maybe more so. I ain't never set eyes on her, but Carver he says she's damn good lookin'. Enyhow the Jedge he brought her up like his own daughter, sent her ter school in Saint Louee, an' nobody 'round yere even suspected she wus a nigger. I reckon she didn't know it herself."

"The hell you say."

"Yes, but that ain't all o' it. I don't know how it happened— maybe he forgot, er put it off too long, er aimed ter git revenge—but, it seems, he never executed no paper freein' either her or her mother."

"Yer mean the girl's still a slave?"

"Yer bet! That's the law, ain't it?"

"And Kirby knew about this?"

"I reckon he did. I sorter judge, Tim, frum whut Carver sed, that he wus more anxious fer ter git thet girl than all the rest o' the stuff; an' it's her he wants ter git away frum yere on the dead quiet, afore Haines er any o' them others down at the Landin' kin catch on."

"They couldn't do nuthin'; if thar ain't no papers, then she's his, accordin' ter law. I've seen that tried afore now."

"Of course; but what's the use o' runnin' eny risk? A smart lawyer like Haines could make a hell ov a lot o' trouble just the same, if he took a notion. That's Kirby's idee—ter cum' up yere in a boat, unbeknownst to enybody, tie up down thar at Saunders', an' run the whole bunch o' niggers off in the night. Then it's done an' over with afore the Landin' even wakes up. I reckon the Jedge told him that wus the best way."

There was a moment of silence, the first man evidently turning the situation over in his mind. The sheriff bent across the rail, and spat into the darkness below.

"The joke of it all is," he continued, with a short laugh, as he straightened up, "this didn't exactly work out 'cordin' ter schedule. When we dropped in yere we rounded up the niggers all right, an' we got the girl whar there's no chance fer her ter git away—"

"Is that the one back in the house?"

"I reckon so; leastways she tol' Kirby her name was Rene Beaucaire, an' that's how it reads in the papers. But thar ain't no trace ov her mother, ner ov the Jedge's daughter. They ain't in the house, ner the nigger cabins. Whar the hell they've gone, I don't know, an' the girl won't tell. Leaves me in a deuce ov a fix, fer I can't serve no papers less we find the daughter. Her name's Eloise; she's the heir et law, an' I ain't got no legal right fer ter take them niggers away till I do. Looks ter me like they'd skipped out."

"Maybe som'body blowed the whole thing."

"I dunno who it wud be. Then whut did they leave thet girl

behind fer? She'd most likely be the furst ter run—thar's Kirby an' Carver, a comin' now, an' they're alone; ain't got no trace ov 'em, I reckon."

Where I crouched in the shadows I could gain no glimpse of the approaching figures, but I heard the crunch of their boots on the gravel of the driveway, and a moment later the sound of their feet as they mounted the wooden steps. Kirby must have perceived the forms of the other men as soon as he attained the porch level, and his naturally disagreeable voice had a snarly ring.

"That you, Donaldson? Have either of those women come back?"

"No," and I thought the sheriff's answer was barely cordial. "We ain't seen nobody. What did you learn down at the Landin'?"

"Nothing," savagely. "Haven't found a damn trace, except that Haines hasn't been home since before dark; some nigger came for him then. Is that girl safe inside?"

"Sure; just as you left her, but she won't talk. Tim tried her again, but it's no use; she wudn't even answer him."

"Well, by God! I'll find a way to make her open her mouth. She knows where those two are hiding. They haven't had no time to get far away, and I'll bring her to her senses before I am through. Come on, Carver; I'll show the wench who's master here, if I have to lick her like a common nigger."

The front door opened, and closed, leaving the two without standing in silence, the stillness between them finally broken by a muttered curse.

CHAPTER X

A GIRL AT BAY

I drew back hastily, but in silence, eager to get away before the sheriff and his deputy should return to their seats by the porch rail. My original plan of warning the women of the house of their peril was blocked, completely overturned by the presence of these men. The situation had thus been rendered more complicated, more difficult to solve, and I could only act on impulse, or as guided by these new conditions. Beyond all question, those I had hoped to serve were already aware of their position—someone had reached them before me—and two, at least, were already in hiding. Why the third, the one most deeply involved, had failed to accompany the others, could not be comprehended. The mystery only made my present task more difficult. Could the others have fled and deliberately left her to her fate? Had some mistake been made? or had some accident led to their absence, and her falling into the inhuman clutches of Kirby? Why should Delia, the slave, disappear in company with Eloise, the free, and leave her own daughter Rene behind to face a situation more terrible than death? I could not answer these questions; but, whatever the cause, the result had been the complete overthrow of the gambler's carefully prepared plans. Not that I believed he would hesitate for long, law or no law; but Donaldson, the sheriff, refused to be a party to any openly illegal act, and this would for the present tie the fellow's hands. Not until Miss Eloise was found and duly served with the eviction papers would Donaldson consent to take possession of a single slave. This might still give me time for action.

Kirby, angry and baffled, could rave and threaten; but to no end. Whether this condition of affairs had been attained as a result of legal advice, or through a mere accident, made no difference; the present inability to reach the daughter of the Judge—the legal heiress to his estate—completely blocked the conspiracy. Yet Kirby was not the kind to surrender without a fight, and a desperate one; all that was savagely brutal in the man had been aroused by this check. The very sound of his voice indicated his intention—he proposed to drive, with a whip if necessary, the helpless girl in his power to a full confession. She was his slave, his chattel, and, under the influence of ungoverned passion, he was capable of any degree of cruelty to attain his end. I knew—seemed to realize—all this in an instant, and as swiftly decided to risk life if need be in her defense. There was at that moment no thought in my mind of her stain of negro blood; she was not a slave to me, but merely a woman helpless and alone, fronting dishonor and degradation.

I slipped along in the shadow of the house, without definite plan of action, but with a firm purpose to act. The side door I knew to be securely locked, yet, first of all, it was essential that I attain to the interior. But one means to this end occurred to me—the unshaded window through which the glow of light continued to stream. I found I could reach the edge of the balcony with extended fingers, and drew myself slowly up, until I clung to the railing, with feet finding precarious support on the outer rim. This was accomplished noiselessly, and, from the vantage point thus obtained, I was enabled to survey a large portion of the room. The illumination came from a chandelier pendent from the center of the high ceiling, but only one lamp had been lighted, and the apartment was so large that both ends and sides remained in partial shadow. It might have been originally intended as either a sitting room or library, for there were bookcases against the walls, and a large writing table, holding books and writing material, stood directly beneath the chandelier, while on the sofa in one corner reposed a bit of women's sewing, where it had apparently been hastily dropped. A fireplace, black and gloomy, evidently unused for some time, yawned in a side wall, and above it hung a rifle and powder horn.

I clambered over the rail, assured by this first glance that the room was empty, and succeeded in lifting the heavy sash a few inches without any disturbing noise. Then it stuck, and, even as I ventured to exert my strength to greater extent to force it upward, the single door directly opposite, evidently leading into the hall, was flung violently open, and I sank back out of view, yet instantly aware that the first party to enter was Joe Kirby.

Without venturing to lift my eyes to the level of the opening, I could nevertheless imagine his movements, while the sound of his voice when he spoke was as distinct as though I stood beside him. He strode forward to the table, striking the wooden top angrily with his fist and knocking something crashing to the floor.

"You know where she is, don't you?" he asked, in the same threatening tone he had used without.

"Of course I do; didn't I help put her there?" It was Carver who replied, standing in the open doorway.

"Then bring the hussy in here. By God! I'll make the wench

talk, if I have to choke it out of her; she'll learn what it means to be a nigger."

The door closed, and Kirby strode across to the fireplace, muttering to himself, and stood there, an arm on the mantel, nervously stirring up the dead ashes with one foot. Plainly enough the events of the night had overcome all his boasted self-control, his gambler's coolness, and the real underlying brutality of his nature demanded expression. He yearned to crush, and hurt something—something that would cringe before him. I ventured to raise my head cautiously, so as to gain a glimpse of the man, and was surprised to note the change in his face. It was as though he had removed a mask. Heretofore, always holding the winning hand, and able to sneer at opposition, he had always in my presence assumed an air of cold bravado, insolent and sarcastic; but now, baffled in his plans, checkmated by a girl, and believing himself unobserved, the gambler had given way to his true nature, both expression and manner exhibiting a temper beyond control.

I had but a moment in which to observe this new exhibit of the man's personality, for almost immediately Carver flung the door of the room open, and Kirby swung impatiently about to face the entrance. Except for a possibility of thus attracting the attention of the newcomer, I was in no special danger of being detected by those within. Nevertheless I sank lower, with eyes barely above the edge of the sill, eager to witness this meeting, and especially interested in gaining a first view of their prisoner. Carver thrust her forward, but remained himself blocking the doorway. I use the word thrust, for I noted the grip of his hand on her arm, yet in truth she instantly stepped forward herself, her bearing in no way devoid of pride and dignity, her head held erect, her eyes fearlessly seeking the face of Kirby. Their glances met, and she advanced to the table, the light of the swinging lamp full upon her. The impression she made is with me yet. Hers was a refined, patrician face, crowned by a wealth of dark hair. Indignant eyes of hazel brown, shadowed by long lashes, brightened a face whitened by intense emotion, and brought into agreeable contrast flushed cheeks, and red, scornful lips. A dimpled chin, a round, full throat, and the figure of young womanhood, slender and yet softly curved, altogether formed a picture so entrancing as to never again desert my imagination. With one bound my heart went out to her in sympathy, in admiration, in full and complete surrender. Yet, even in that instant, the knowledge of the truth, in all its unspeakable horror, assailed me—this girl, this proud, beautiful girl, was a slave; within her veins a cursed drop of negro blood stained her with dishonor, made of her a chattel; and the sneering brute she faced was by law her master. My hands clinched in the agony of the thought, the knowledge of my own impotence. Yet all this was but the flash of an instant. Before I could change posture, almost before I could draw fresh breath, her voice, trembling slightly with an emotion she was unable wholly to suppress, yet sounding clear as a bell, addressed the man confronting her.

"May I ask, sir, what this outrage means? I presume you are responsible for the insolence of this fellow who brought me here?"

Kirby laughed, but not altogether at ease.

"Well, not altogether," he answered, "as his methods are entirely his own. I merely told him to go after you."

"For what purpose?"

"So pretty a girl should not ask that. Carver, close the door, and wait outside."

I could mark the quick rise and fall of her bosom, And the look of fear she was unable to disguise. Yet not a limb moved as the door closed, nor did the glance of those brown eyes waver.

"You are not the same man I met here before," she began doubtfully. "He said he was connected with the sheriff's office. Who are you?"

"My name is Kirby; the sheriff is here under my orders."

"Kirby!—the—the gambler?"

"Well I play cards occasionally, and you have probably heard of me before. Even if you never had until tonight, it is pretty safe to bet that you do now. Donaldson, or his man, told you, so there is no use of my mincing matters any, nor of your pretence at ignorance."

"I know," she admitted, "that you won this property at cards, and have now come to take possession. Is that what you mean?"

"That, at least, is part of it," and he took a step toward her, his thin lips twisted into a smile. "But not all. Perhaps Donaldson failed to tell you the rest, and left me to break the news. Well, it won't hurt me any. Not only this plantation is mine, but every nigger on it as well. You are Rene Beaucaire?"

"Yes," she replied, slowly, almost under her breath, and hesitating ever so slightly, "I am Rene Beaucaire."

"And you don't know what that means, I suppose?" he insisted, savagely, angered by her coolness. "Perhaps the sheriff did not explain this. Yet, by God! I believe you do know. Someone spread the word before we ever got up here—that damn lawyer Haines likely enough. That is why the others have disappeared; why they have hidden themselves away. Who was it?"

"I cannot answer."

"Oh, I reckon you can. Why did they run off and leave you here?"

"I cannot answer."

"Damn you, stop that! Don't try any of your fine airs on me. Do you know who and what you are?"

She rested one hand on the table in support, and I could note the nervous trembling of the fingers, yet her low voice remained strangely firm.

"I know," she said distinctly, "I am no longer a free white woman; I am a negro, and a slave."

"Oh, so you know that, do you? Then you must also be aware that you are my property. Perhaps it will be well for you to remember this in answering my questions. Now tell me who informed you of all this?"

"I cannot answer."

"Cannot! You mean you will not. Well, young woman, I'll find means to make you, for I have handled your kind before. Drop this dignity business, and remember you are a slave, talking to your master. It will be better for you, if you do. Where is Eloise Beaucaire?"

"Why do you seek to find her? There is no slave blood in

her veins."

"To serve the necessary papers, of course."

He spoke incautiously, urged on by his temper, and I marked how quickly her face brightened at this intelligence.

"To serve papers! They must be served then before—before you can take possession? That is what I understood the sheriff to say."

"Why, of course—the law requires that form."

"Then I am not really your slave—yet?" her voice deepening with earnestness and understanding. "Oh, so that is how it is—even if I am a negro, I do not belong to you until those papers have been served. If you touch me now you break the law. I may not be free, but I am free from you. Good God! but I am glad to know that!"

"And damn little good it is going to do you," he growled. "I was a fool to let you know that; but just the same you are here in my power, and I care mighty little what the law says. Sheriff, or no sheriff, my beauty, you are going to St. Louis with me tonight; so I advise you to keep a grip on that tongue of yours. Do you think I am going to be foiled altogether by a technical point of law? Then, by God! you don't know Joe Kirby. Possession is the main thing, and I have you where you can't get away. You hear me?"

She had not moved, although her form had straightened, and her hand no longer rested on the table. Kirby had stepped close in front of her, his eyes glowing with anger, his evident intention being to thus frighten the girl into compliance with his wishes, but her eyes, defiant and unafraid, looked him squarely in the face.

Randall Parrish

"I certainly hear," she replied calmly. "Your voice is sufficiently distinct. I am a slave, I suppose, and in your power; but I despise you, hate you—and you are not going to take me to St. Louis tonight."

"What can stop me?"

"That I am not obliged to tell you, sir."

"But what will prevent? The sheriff? Puh! a few dollars will take care of him. The Judge is a friend of mine."

"It is not the sheriff—nor the Judge; I place reliance on no friend of yours."

He grasped at her arm, but she stepped back quickly enough to avoid contact, and the red lips were pressed together in a thin line of determination. Kirby could not have seen what I did, or if he did see, failed to attach the same significance to the action. Her hand had suddenly disappeared within the folds of her skirt; but the angry man, apparently blinded by the violence of his passion, his eagerness to crush her spirit, thought only that she counted on outside aid for deliverance.

"You silly little fool," he snapped, his moustache bristling. "Why, what could you do to stop me? I could break your neck with one hand. So you imagine someone is going to save you. Well, who will it be? Those yokels down at the Landing? Haines, the lawyer? You have a surprise up your sleeve for me, I suppose! Hell! it makes me laugh; but you might as well have your lesson now, as any other time. Come here, you wench!"

He caught her arm this time, brutally jerking her toward him, but as instantly staggered backward, grasping at the table, the flash of anger in his eyes changing to a look of startled surprise. A pistol was leveled full in his face, the polished black barrel shining ominously in the light of the overhead lamp.

"Now perhaps you know what I mean," she said. "If you dare to touch me I will kill you like a dog. That is no threat; it is true as God's gospel," and the very tone of her voice carried conviction. "You say I am a slave—your slave! That may be so, but you will never possess me—never! Life means nothing to me any more, and I never expect to go out of this house alive; I do not even care to. So I am not afraid of you. Do you know why? Probably not, for men of your kind would be unable to understand. It is because I would rather die than have your dirty hand touch me—a thousand times rather. Do not drop your arms, you low-lived cur, for you have never been nearer death in all your miserable life than you are now. God knows I want to kill you; it is the one desire of my heart at this moment to rid the earth of such a beast. But I'll give you one chance—just one. Don't you dare call out, or answer me. Do what I say. Now step back—back along the table; that's it, a step at a time. Oh, I knew you were a cowardly bully. Go on—yes, clear to that window; don't lower those hands an inch until I say you may. I am a slave—yes, but I am also a Beaucaire. Now reach behind you, and pull up the sash—pull it up higher than that."

Her eyes dilated with sudden astonishment and terror. She had caught sight of me, emerging from the black shadow just behind her victim. Kirby also perceived the quick change in the face fronting him, read its expression of fright, and sought to twist his head so as to learn the truth. Yet before he could accomplish this, or his lips could give utterance to a sound, my hands closed on his throat, crushing him down to the sill, and throttling him into silence between the vise of my fingers.

CHAPTER XI

TO SAVE A "NIGGER"

It proved to be a short, sharp struggle, from the first the advantage altogether with me. Kirby, jerked from off his feet from behind, his head forced down against the wooden sill, with throat gripped remorselessly in my clutch, could give utterance to no outcry, nor effectively exert his strength to break free. I throttled the very breath out of him, knowing that I must conquer then and there, silently, and with no thought of mercy. I was battling for her life, and my own. This was no time for compassion, nor had I the slightest wish to spare the man. With all the oldtime dislike in my heart, all the hatred aroused by what I had overheard, I closed down on his throat, rejoicing to see the purple of his flesh turn into a sickening black, as he fought desperately for breath, and as he lost consciousness, and ceased from struggle. I was conscious of a pang in my wounded shoulder, yet it seemed to rob me of no strength, but only added to my ferocity. The fellow rested limp in my hands. I believed I had killed him, and the belief was a joy, as I tossed the helpless body aside on the floor, and stepped through the open window into the room. Dead! he was better off dead.

I stood above him, staring down into the upturned face. It was breathless, mottled, hideously ugly, to all appearances the face of a dead man, but it brought to me no sense of remorse. The cur—"the unspeakable cur." In my heart I hoped he was dead, and in a sudden feeling of utter contempt, I struck the inert body with my foot. Then, as my eyes lifted, they encountered those of the girl. She had drawn back to the table, startled out of all reserve by this sudden apparition, unable to comprehend. Doubt, questioning, fright found expression in her face. The pistol yet remained clasped in her hand, while she stared at me as though a ghost confronted her.

"Who—who are you?" she managed to gasp, in a voice which barely reached my ears. "My God! who—who sent you here?"

"It must have been God," I answered, realizing instantly that I needed to make all clear in a word. "I came only to help you, and was just in time—no doubt God sent me."

"To help me? You came here to help me? But how could that be? I—I never saw you before—who are you?"

I stood straight before her, my eyes meeting her own frankly. I had forgotten the dead body at my feet, the incidents of struggle, the pain of my own wound, comprehending only the supreme importance of compelling her to grasp the truth.

"There is no time now to explain all this, Miss Rene. You must accept the bare facts—will you?"

"Yes—I—I suppose I must."

"Then listen, for you must know that every moment we waste here in talk only makes escape more difficult. I tell you the simple truth. I am Steven Knox, an officer in the army. It chanced I was a passenger on the boat when Judge

Beaucaire lost his life. I witnessed the game of cards this man won, and afterwards, when I protested, was attacked, and flung overboard into the river by Kirby here, and that fellow who is outside guarding the door. They believe me to be dead; but I managed to reach shore, and was taken care of by a negro—'Free Pete' he calls himself; do you know him?"

"Yes—oh, yes; he was one of the Carlton slaves." Her face brightened slightly in its bewilderment.

"Well, I knew enough of what was bound to occur to feel an interest, and tonight he brought me here for the purpose of warning you—you, your mother, and Eloise Beaucaire. He has his cart and mule out yonder; we intended to transport you across the river, and thus start you safely on the way to Canada."

"Then," she said slowly, seeming to catch at her breath, her voice trembling, "then it must be really true what these men say—Delia is my mother? I—I am a slave?"

"You did not really know. You were not warned by anyone before their arrival?"

"No, there was no warning. Did anyone in this neighborhood understand?"

"Haines the lawyer did. He furnished me with much of the information I possess. But I am the one puzzled now. If the truth was not known to any of you, how does it happen the others are gone?"

"So far as I am aware that is merely an accident. They walked over to the old Carlton place early this evening; there is sickness in the family, and they hoped to be of help. That is everything I know. They were to return two hours ago, for

I was here all alone, except for the negroes in their quarters. I cannot conceive what has occurred—unless they have learned in some way of the trouble here."

"That must be the explanation; they have hidden themselves. And these men told you why they came?"

"The only one I saw at first did. He came in all alone and claimed to be a deputy sheriff. I was terribly frightened at first, and did not at all understand; but I questioned him and the man liked to talk. So he told me all he knew. Perhaps I should have thought he was crazy, only—only some things had occurred of late which led me to half suspect the truth before. I—I wouldn't believe it then, but—but I made him repeat everything he had heard. Horrible as it was, I—I wanted to know all."

"And you acknowledged to him that you were Rene Beaucaire?"

Her dark eyes flashed up into my face questioningly.

"Why—why, of course. I—I could not deny that, could I?"

"Perhaps not; yet if none of them knew you, and you had claimed to be Eloise, they would never have dared to hold you prisoner."

"I never once thought of that; the only thing which occurred to me was how I could best protect the others. My plan was to send them warning in some way. Still, now I am very glad I said I was Rene."

"Glad! why?"

"Because it seems it is Eloise they must find to serve their papers on. They dare not take away the slaves until this is done. As for me, I am nothing—nothing but a slave myself; is that not true?"

To look into her eyes, her face, and answer was a hard task, yet one I saw no way to evade.

"Yes; I am afraid it is true."

"And—and then Delia, the housekeeper, is actually my mother?"

"That is the story, as it has reached me."

She held tightly to the table for support, all the fresh color deserting her face, but the lips were firmly set and her head remained as proudly poised as ever above the round throat. Whatever might be the stain of alien blood in her veins, she was still a Beaucaire. Her eyes, filled with pain as they were, met mine unflinchingly.

"And—and knowing all this, convinced of its truth—that—that I am colored," she faltered, doubtfully. "You came here to help me?"

"I did; that can make no difference now."

"No difference! Why do you say that? Are you from the North, an Abolitionist?"

"No; at least I have never been called one or so thought of myself. I have never believed in slavery, yet I was born in a southern state. In this case I merely look upon you as a woman—as one of my own class. It—it does not seem as though I could ever consider you in any other way. You must believe this."

"Believe it! Why you and I are caught in the same net. I am a slave to be sold to the highest bidder; and you—you have killed a man to save me. Even if I was willing to remain and face my fate, I could not now, for that would mean you must suffer. And—and you have done this for me."

My eyes dropped to the upturned face of Kirby on which the rays of light rested. The flesh was no longer black and horrid, yet remained ghastly enough to increase my belief that the man was actually dead—had perished under my hand. He was not a pleasant sight to contemplate, flung as he had been in a shapeless heap, and the sight brought home to me anew the necessity of escape before those others of his party could learn what had occurred.

"From whatever reason the deed was done," I said, steadying my voice, "we must now face the consequences. As you say, it is true we both alike have reason to fear the law if caught. Flight is our only recourse. Will you go with me? Will you trust me?"

"Go—go with you? Where?"

"First across the river into Illinois; there is no possible safety here. Once over yonder we shall, at least, have time in which to think out the proper course, to plan what shall be best to do. In a way your danger is even more serious than mine. I have not been seen—even Kirby had no glimpse of my face—and might never be identified with the death of this man. But you will become a fugitive slave and could be hunted down anywhere this side of Canada."

"Then being with me would add to your danger."

"Whether it will or not counts nothing; I shall never let you go alone."

She pressed the palms of both her hands against her forehead as though in a motion of utter bewilderment.

"Oh, I cannot seem to realize," she exclaimed. "Everything is like a dream to me—impossible in its horror. This situation, is so terrible; it has come upon me so suddenly, I cannot decide, I cannot even comprehend what my duty is. You urge me to go away with you—alone?"

"I do; there is no other way left. You cannot remain here in the hands of these men; the result of such a step is too terrible to even contemplate. There are no means of determining where the others are—Delia and Miss Eloise. Perhaps they have had warning and fled already," I urged, desperately.

Her eyes were staring down at Kirby's body.

"Look, he—he is not dead," she sobbed, excitedly. "Did you see then, one of his limbs moved, and—and why he is beginning to gasp for breath."

"All the more reason why we should decide at once. If the fellow regains consciousness and lives, our danger will be all the greater."

"Yes, he would be merciless," her lips parted, her eyes eloquent of disgust and horror as she suddenly lifted them to my face. "I—I must not forget that I—I belong to him; I am his slave; he—he, that hideous thing there, can do anything he wishes with me—the law says he can." The indignant color mounted into her face. "He can sell me, or use me, or rent me; I am his chattel. Good God! think of it! Why, I am as white as he is, better educated, accustomed to every care, brought up to believe myself rich and happy—and now I belong to him; he owns me, body and soul." She paused suddenly, assailed by a new thought, a fresh consideration.

"Do you know the law?"

"I am no expert; what is it you would ask?"

"The truth of what they have told me. Is it so, is it the law that these men can take possession of nothing here until after Eloise has been found and their papers served upon her?"

"Yes, I believe it is," I said. "She is the legal heiress of Judge Beaucaire; the estate is hers by inheritance, as, I am told, there was no will. All this property, including the slaves, would legally remain in her possession until proper steps had been taken by others. Serving of the papers would be necessary. There is no doubt as to that—although, probably, after a certain length of time, the court might presume her dead and take other action to settle the estate."

"But not for several years?"

"No; I think I have heard how many, but have forgotten."

She drew a deep breath and stepped toward me, gazing straight into my face.

"I believe in you," she said firmly. "And I trust you. You look like a real man. You tell me you serve in the army—an officer?"

"A lieutenant of infantry."

She held out her hand and my own closed over it, the firm, warm clasp of her fingers sending a strange thrill through my whole body. An instant she looked directly into my eyes, down into the very soul of me, and what I read in the depths of her brown orbs could never find expression in words. I have thought of it often since—that great, dimly-lighted room, with the guard at the outer door; the inert, almost lifeless body huddled on the floor beside us, and Rene Beaucaire, her hand clasped in mine.

"Lieutenant Knox," she said softly, yet with a note of confidence in the low voice, "no woman was ever called upon to make a more important choice than this. Although I am a slave, now I am free to choose. I am going to trust you absolutely; there are reasons why I so decide which I cannot explain at this time. I have not known you long enough to venture that far. You must accept me just as I am—a runaway slave and a negress, but also a woman. Can you pledge such as I your word of honor—the word of a soldier and a gentleman?"

"I pledge it to you, Rene Beaucaire," I answered soberly.

"And I accept the pledge in all faith. From now on, whatever you say I will do."

I had but one immediate purpose in my mind—to escape from the house as quickly as possible, to attain Pete's cart at the edge of the woods and be several miles up the river, hidden away in some covert before daylight, leaving no trail behind. The first part of this hasty program would have to be carried out instantly, for any moment a suspicion might cause Carver to throw open the door leading into the hallway and expose our position. Kirby was already showing unmistakable symptoms of recovery, while those other men idling on the front porch might begin to wonder what was going on so long inside and proceed to investigate. By this time they must be nervously anxious to get away. Besides, it would prove decidedly to our advantage if I was not seen or recognized. The very mystery, the bewilderment as to who had so viciously attacked the gambler and then spirited away the girl, would serve to facilitate our escape. Theories as to how it had been accomplished would be endless and the pursuit delayed.

I stooped and removed a pistol from Kirby's pocket, dropping it, together with such ammunition as I could find, into one of my own. The man by this time was breathing heavily, although his eyes remained closed, and he still lay exactly as he had fallen.

"Keep your own weapon," I commanded her. "Hide it away in your dress. Now come with me."

She obeyed, uttering no word of objection, and stepping after me through the open window onto the narrow balcony without. I reached up and drew down the shade, leaving us in comparative darkness. The night was soundless and our eyes, straining to pierce the black void, were unable to detect any movement.

"You see nothing?" I whispered, touching her hand in encouragement. "No evidence of a guard anywhere?"

"No—the others must still be out in front waiting."

"There were only the four of them then?"

"So I understood. I was told they came up the river in a small keel-boat, operated by an engine, and that they anticipated no resistance. The engineer was left to watch the boat and be ready to depart down stream at any moment."

"Good; that leaves us a clear passage. Now I am going to drop to the ground; it is not far below. Can you make it alone?"

"I have done so many a time."

We attained the solid earth almost together and in silence.

"Now let me guide you," she suggested, as I hesitated. "I know every inch of the way about here. Where is the negro waiting?"

"At the edge of the wood where the wagon road ends, beyond the slave quarters."

"Yes, I know; it will be safer for us to go around the garden."

She flitted forward, sure-footed, confident, and I followed as rapidly as possible through the darkness, barely keeping her dim figure in sight. We skirted the rear fence, and then the blacker shadow of the wood loomed up somber before us. Our feet stumbled over the ruts of a road and I seemed to vaguely recognize the spot as familiar. Yes, away off yonder was the distant gleam of the river reflecting the stars. This must be the very place where Pete and I had parted, but— where had the fellow gone? I caught at her sleeve, but as she paused and turned about, could scarcely discern the outlines of her face in the gloom.

"Here is where he was directed to wait," I explained, hurriedly. "Before I left he had turned his mule around under this very tree. I am sure I am not mistaken in the spot."

"Yet he is not here, and there is no sign of him. You left no other instructions except for him to remain until your return?"

"I think not—oh; yes, I did tell him if you women came without me, he was to drive you at once to the boat and leave me to follow the best way I could. Do you suppose it possible the others reached here and he has gone away with them?"

I felt a consciousness that her eyes were upon me, that she was endeavoring to gain a glimpse of my face.

"No, I can hardly imagine that. I—I do not know what to think. When I see you I believe all you say, but here in the darkness it is not the same. You—you are not deceiving me?"

"No; you must trust my word. This is unfortunate, but neither of us could venture back now. There is a pledge between us."

She stood silent and I strove by peering about to discover some marks of guidance, only to learn the uselessness of the effort. Even a slight advance brought no result, and it was with some difficulty I even succeeded in locating her again in the darkness—indeed, only the sound of her voice made me aware of her immediate presence.

"The negro's boat is some distance away, is it not?"

"Four miles, over the worst road I ever traveled." A sudden remembrance swept into my mind, bringing with it inspiration.

"Have you ever visited the mouth of Saunder's Creek? You have! How far away is that from here?"

"Not more than half a mile, it enters the river just below the Landing."

"And, if I understood you rightly," I urged, eagerly, "you said that these fellows left their keel-boat there; that it had been rigged up to run by steam, and had no guard aboard except the engineer; you are sure of this?"

"That was what the man who talked to me first said—the deputy sheriff. He boasted that they had the only keel-boat on the river equipped with an engine and had come up from St. Louis in two hours. The Sheriff had it fitted up to carry him back and forth between river towns. You—you think we could use that?"

"It seems to be all that is left us. I intend to make the effort, anyway. You had better show me the road."

CHAPTER XII

WE CAPTURE A KEEL-BOAT

I followed her closely, a mere shadow, as she silently led the way along the edge of the wood and back of the negro quarters. The path was narrow and apparently little used, extremely rough at first until we finally came out upon what was seemingly a well-built road descending to a lower level in the general direction of the river. The girl, however, was sufficiently familiar with her surroundings to advance rapidly even in the dark, and I managed to stumble blindly along after her at a pace which kept her in sight, comprehending the urgent need of haste. We crossed the front of the house, but at a distance enabling us to gain no glimpse of the two men who guarded the porch, or to even hear their voices. The only evidence of their presence there still was the dim glow of a pipe. Here we were cautious enough, slinking past in complete silence, watchful of where we placed our feet; but once beyond this point of danger I joined her more closely, and we continued down the sharp decline together side by side, exchanging a few words in whispers as she attempted to describe to me briefly the lay of the land about the mouth of the creek and where the boat probably rested, awaiting the return of its owners.

She made this sufficiently clear, answering my few questions promptly, so that I easily visioned the scene and felt confident of being able to safely approach the unsuspecting engineer and overcome any resistance before he should realize the possibility of attack. I was obliged to rely upon a guess at the time of night, yet surely it could not be long after twelve and there must yet remain hours of darkness amply sufficient for our purpose. With the boat once securely in our possession, the engineer compelled to serve, for I had no skill in that line, we could strike out directly for the opposite shore and creep along in its shadows past the sleeping town at the Landing until we attained the deserted waters above. By then we should practically be beyond immediate pursuit. Even if Carver or the sheriff discovered Kirby, any immediate chase by river would be impossible. Nothing was available for their use except a few rowboats at the Landing; they would know nothing as to whether we had gone up or down stream, while the coming of the early daylight would surely permit us to discover some place of concealment along the desolate Illinois shore. Desperate as the attempt undoubtedly was, the situation, as I considered it in all its details, brought me faith in our success and fresh encouragement to make the effort.

The distance was covered far more quickly than I had anticipated. The road we followed was by now fairly visible beneath the faint star-gleam, and once we were below the bluff the broad expanse of river appeared at our left, a dim, flowing mystery, the opposite shore invisible. To our strained eyes it seemed an endless flood of surging water. Immediately about us, all remained dark and silent, the few trees lining the summit of the overhanging bluff assuming grotesque shapes, and occasionally startling us by their strange resemblance to human beings. Not even the moaning of wind through the branches broke the intense midnight stillness. I could feel her hand, grasping my sleeve, tremble from nervous tension.

"Saunder's Creek is just beyond that ridge—see," she whispered, causing me to pause. "I mean the darker line in front. This road we are on goes straight ahead, but we must turn off here in order to reach the mouth where the boat lies."

I stooped low, close to the earth, so as to better perceive any outline against the sky, and, with one hand shadowing my eyes, stared earnestly in the direction indicated.

"It will be over there, then. Kneel down here beside me a moment. There is a whisp of smoke yonder, curling up over the bank. I suppose it will be safe enough for us to venture that far?"

"Yes, unless the engineer has come ashore."

"Is there any path?"

"Not that I remember, but there are plenty of dead rushes along the side of the bank. It will be safe enough to go where we can look over."

We moved forward slowly, but this time I took the lead myself, bending low, and feeling carefully for footing in the wiry grass. The bank was not high, and once safely at its edge, we could peer out through the thick growth of rushes with little fear of being observed from below. The darkness, however, so shrouded everything, blending objects into shapeless shadows, that it required several moments before I could clearly determine the exact details. The mouth of the creek, a good-sized stream, was only a few yards away, and the boat, rather a larger craft than I had anticipated seeing, lay just off shore, with stern to the bank, as though prepared for instant departure. It was securely held in position by a rope, probably looped about a convenient stump, and my eyes were finally able to trace the outlines of the wheel by which it was propelled. Except for straggling rushes extending to the edge of the water, the space between was vacant, yet sufficiently mantled in darkness to enable one to creep forward unseen.

At first glance I could distinguish no sign of the boatman left in charge, but, even as I lay there, breathless and uncertain, he suddenly revealed his presence by lighting a lantern in the stern. The illumination was feeble enough, yet sufficient to expose to view the small, unprotected engine aft, and also the fact that all forward of the little cockpit in which it stood, the entire craft was decked over. The fellow was busily engaged in overhauling the machinery, leaning far forward, his body indistinct, the lantern swinging in one hand, with entire attention devoted to his task. Occasionally, as he lifted his head for some purpose, the dim radiance fell upon his face, revealing the unmistakable countenance of a mulatto, a fellow of medium size, broad of cheek with unusually full lips, and a fringe of whisker turning gray. Somehow this revelation that he was a negro, and not a white man, brought with it to me an additional confidence in success. I inclined my head and whispered in the girl's ear:

"You are not to move from here until I call. This is to be my part of the work, handling that lad. I am going now."

"He is colored, is he not, a slave?"

"We can only guess as to that. But he does not look to me like a hard proposition. If I can only reach the boat without being seen, the rest will be easy. Now is the proper time, while he is busy tinkering with the engine. You will stay here?"

"Yes, of course; I—I could be of no help."

She suddenly held out her hand, as though impelled to the action of some swift impulse, and the warm pressure of her fingers meant more than words. I could not see the expression on her face, yet knew the slender body was trembling nervously.

"Surely you are not afraid?"

"Oh, no; it is not that—I—I am all unstrung. You must not think of me, at all."

This was far easier said than done, however, for she was more in my mind as I crept forward than the indistinct figure below in the boat. It was becoming a constant struggle already—indeed, had been from the first—to hold her for what I actually knew her to be—negress, a slave, desperately seeking to escape from her master. The soft, refined voice, the choice use of language, the purity of her thought and expression, the girlish face as I had seen it under the light, all combined to continually blind me to the real truth. I could not even force myself to act toward her from any standpoint other than that of equality, or regard her as in any way removed from my most courteous consideration. I think it was equally hard for her to adapt her conduct to these new conditions. Accustomed all her life to respect, to admiration, to the courtesy of men, she could not stoop to the spirit of servitude. It was this effort to humble herself, to compel remembrance, which caused her to speak of herself so often as a slave.

These thoughts assailed, pursued me, as I crept cautiously down the steep bank, concealed by the shadows of the rushes. Yet in reality I remained intent enough upon my purpose. Although unable to wholly banish all memory of the young girl just left behind, I still realized the gravity of my task, and my eyes were watchful of the shrouded figure I was silently approaching. I drew nearer inch by inch, advancing so slowly, and snake-like, that not even the slightest sound of movement aroused suspicion. Apparently the fellow was engaged in oiling the machinery, for he had placed the lantern on deck, and held a long-spouted can in his fingers. His back remained toward me as I drew near the stern, and, consequently, I no longer had a glimpse of his face. The wooden wheel of the boat, a clumsy appearing apparatus, rested almost directly against the bank, where the water was evidently deep enough to float the vessel, and the single rope holding it in position was drawn taut from the pressure of the current. Waiting until the man was compelled to bend lower over his work, utterly unconscious of my presence, I straightened up, and, pistol in hand, stepped upon the wooden beam supporting the wheel. He must have heard this movement, for he lifted his head quickly, yet was even then too late; already I had gained the after-deck, and my weapon was on a level with his eyes.

"Don't move, or cry out!" I commanded, sternly. "Obey orders and you will not be hurt."

He shrank away, sinking upon the bench, his face upturned so that the light fell full upon it, for the instant too greatly surprised and frightened to give utterance to a sound. His mouth hung open, and his eyes stared at me.

"Who—who wus yer? Whatcha want yere?"

"I am asking questions, and you are answering them. Are you armed? All right, then; hand it over. Now put out that light."

He did exactly as I told him, moving as though paralyzed by fear, yet unable to resist.

"You are a negro—a slave?"

"Yas, sah; Ah's Massa Donaldson's boy frum Saint Louee."

"He is the sheriff?"

"Yas, sah—yas, sah. Whar is Massa Donaldson? Yer ain't done bin sent yere by him, I reckon. 'Pears like I never see yer afore."

"No, but he is quite safe. What is your name?"

"Sam, sah—just plain Sam."

"Well, Sam, I understand you are an engineer. Now it happens that I want to use this boat, and you are going to run it for me. Do you understand I am going to sit down here on the edge of this cockpit, and hold this loaded pistol just back of your ear. It might go off at any minute, and surely will if you make a false move or attempt to foul the engine. Any trick, and there is going to be a dead nigger overboard. I know enough about engines to tell if you play fair—so don't take any chances, boy."

"Ah—Ah—reckon as how I was goin' fer ter run her all right, sah; she's sum consid'ble contrary et times, sah, but Ah'll surely run her, if thar's eny run in her, sah. Ah ain't carryin' 'bout bein' no corpse."

"I thought not; you'd rather be a free nigger, perhaps? Well, Sam, if you will do this job all right for me tonight, I'll put you where the sheriff will never see hide nor hair of you again—no, not yet; wait a moment, there is another passenger."

She came instantly in answer to my low call, and, through

the gloom, the startled negro watched her descend the bank, a mere moving shadow, yet with the outlines of a woman. I half believe he thought her a ghost, for I could hear him muttering inarticulately to himself. I dared not remove my eyes from the fellow, afraid that his very excess of fear might impel him to some reckless act, but I extended one hand across the side of the boat to her assistance.

"Take my hand, Rene," I said pleasantly to reassure her, "and come aboard. Yes, everything is all right. I've just promised Sam here a ticket for Canada."

I helped her across into the cockpit and seated her on the bench, but never venturing to remove my eyes from the negro. His actions, and whatever I was able to observe of the expression of his face, only served to convince me of his trustworthiness, yet I could take no chances.

"She's just a real, live woman, sah?" he managed to ejaculate, half in doubt. "She sure ain't no ghost, sah?"

"By no means, Sam; she is just as real as either you or I. Now listen, boy—you know what will happen to you after this, if Donaldson ever gets hold of you?"

"I 'spects Ah does, sah. He'd just nat'larly skin dis nigger alive, Ah reckon."

"Very well, then; it is up to you to get away, and I take it that you understand this river. Where is the main current along here?"

"From de p'int yonder, over ter de east shore."

"And the depth of water across from us? We are going to head up stream."

"Yas, sah; yer plannin' fer ter go nor'. Wal, sah, dars planty o' watah fer dis yere boat right now, wid de spring floods. Nothin' fer ter be a'feered of 'bout dat."

"That is good news. Now, Sam, I am going to cut this line, and I want you to steer straight across into the shadows of the Illinois shore. I believe you are going to play square, but, for the present, I'm going to take no chances with you. I am holding this pistol within a foot of your head, and your life means nothing to me if you try any trick. What is the speed of this boat up stream?"

"'Bout ten mile an hour, sah."

"Well, don't push her too hard at first, and run that engine as noiselessly as possible. Are you ready? Yes—then I'll cut loose."

I severed the line and we began to recede from the shore, cutting diagonally across the decidedly swift current. Once beyond the protection of the point the star-gleam revealed the sturdy rush of the waters, occasionally flecked with bubbles of foam. Sam handled the unwieldy craft with the skill of a practiced boatman and the laboring engine made far less racket than I had anticipated. Ahead, nothing was visible but the turbulent expanse of desolate water, the Illinois shore being still too far away for the eye to perceive through the darkness. Behind us the Missouri bluffs rose black, and fairly distinct against the sky, but dimming constantly as the expanse of water widened to our progress. Pistol in hand, and vigilant to every motion of the negro, my eyes swept along that vague shore line, catching nowhere a spark of light, nor any evidence that the steady chug of our engine had created alarm. The churning wheel flung white spray into the air, which glittered in the silver of the star-rays, and occasionally showered me with moisture. At last the western shore imperceptibly merged into the night shadows, and we were alone upon the mysterious bosom of the vast stream, tossed about in the full sweep of the current, yet moving steadily forward, and already safely beyond both sight and sound.

CHAPTER XIII

SEEKING THE UNDERGROUND

Every moment of progress tended to increase my confidence in Sam's loyalty. His every attention seemed riveted upon his work, and not once did I observe his eyes turned backward for a glimpse of the Missouri shore. The fellow plainly enough realized the situation—that safety for himself depended on keeping beyond the reach of his master. To this end he devoted every instant diligently to coaxing his engine and a skillful guidance of the boat, never once permitting his head to turn far enough to glance at me, although I could occasionally detect his eyes wandering in the direction of the girl.

She had not uttered a word, nor changed her posture since first entering the boat, but remained just as I had seated her, one hand grasping the edge of the cockpit, her gaze on the rushing waters ahead. I could realize something of what must be passing through her mind—the mingling of doubt and fear which assailed her in this strange environment. Up until now she had been accorded no opportunity to think, to consider the nature of her position; she had been compelled to act wholly upon impulse and driven blindly to accept my suggestions. And now, in this silence, the reaction had come, and she was already questioning if she had done right.

It was in my heart to speak to her, in effort to strengthen her faith, but I hesitated, scarcely knowing what to say, deeply touched by the pathetic droop of her figure, and, in truth, uncertain in my own mind as to whether or not we had chosen the wiser course. All I dared do was to silently reach out one hand, and rest it gently on those fingers clasping the rail. She did not remove her hand from beneath mine, nor, indeed, give the slightest evidence that she was even aware of my action. By this time the eastern shore became dimly defined through the black mist, and the downward sweep of the current no longer struck in force against our bow.

"Wus Ah ter turn nor', sah?" asked the negro, suddenly.

"Yes, up-stream, but keep in as close to the shore as you think safe. There is no settlement along this bank, is there?"

"No, sah; dar's jus' one cabin, 'bout a mile up-stream, but dar ain't nobody livin' thar now. Whar yer all aim fer ter go?"

I hesitated an instant before I answered, yet, almost as quickly, decided that the whole truth would probably serve us best. The man already had one reason to use his best endeavors; now I would bring before him a second.

"Just as far up the river before daylight as possible, Sam. Then I hope to uncover some hiding place where we can lie concealed until it is dark again. Do you know any such place?"

He scratched his head, muttering something to himself; then turned half about, exhibiting a line of ivories.

"On de Illinois shore, sah? Le's see; thar's Rassuer Creek, 'bout twenty mile up. 'Tain't so awful big et the mouth, but I reckon we mought pole up fer 'nough ter git outer sight. Ah spects you all knows whut yer a headin' fer?"

"To a certain extent—yes; but we had to decide on this action very quickly, with no chance to plan it out. I am aiming at the mouth of the Illinois."

He glanced about at me again, vainly endeavoring to decipher my expression in the gloom.

"De Illinois ribber, boss; what yer hope fer ter find thar?"

"A certain man I've heard about. Did you ever happen to hear a white man mentioned who lives near there? His name is Amos Shrunk?"

I could scarcely distinguish his eyes, but I could feel them. I thought for a moment he would not answer.

"Yer'l surely excuse me, sah," he said at last, humbly, his voice with a note of pleading in it. "Ah's feelin' friendly 'nough, an' all dat, sah, but still yer mus' 'member dat Ah's talkin' ter a perfict stranger. If yer wud sure tell me furst just whut yer was aimin' at, then maybe Ah'd know a heap mor'n Ah do now."

"I guess you are right, Sam. I'll tell you the whole of it. I am endeavoring to help this young woman to escape from those men back yonder. You must know why they were there; no doubt you overhead them talk coming up?"

"Yas, sah; Massa Donaldson he was goin' up fer ter serve sum papers fer Massa Kirby, so he cud run off de Beaucaire niggers. But dis yere gal, she ain't no nigger—she's just a white pusson."

"She is a slave under the law," I said, gravely, as she made no effort to move, "and the man, Kirby, claims her."

I could see his mouth fly open, but the surprise of this statement halted his efforts at speech.

"That explains the whole situation," I went on. "Now will you answer me?"

"'Bout dis yere Massa Shrunk?"

"Yes—you have heard of him before?"

"Ah reckon as how maybe Ah has, sah. Mos' all de niggers down dis way has bin tol' 'bout him—som'how dey has, sah."

"So I thought. Well, do you know where he can be found?"

"Not perzackly, sah. Ah ain't never onct bin thar, but Ah sorter seems fer ter recollec' sum'thin' 'bout whar he mought be. Ah reckon maybe Ah cud go thar, if Ah just hed to. Ah reckon if yer all held dat pistol plum 'gainst mah hed, Ah'd mos' likely find dis Amos Shrunk. Good Lord, sah!" and his voice sank to a whisper, "Ah just can't git hol' o' all dis—Ah sure can't, sah—'bout her bein' a nigger."

Rene turned about, lifting her face into the starlight.

"Whether I am white or colored, Sam," she said, quietly, "can make little difference to you now. I am a woman, and am asking your help. I can trust you, can I not?"

The negro on his knees stared at her, the whites of his eyes conspicuous. Then suddenly he jerked off his old hat.

"Ah 'spects yer kin, Missus," he pledged himself in a tone of conviction which made my heart leap. "Ah's bin a slave-nigger fer forty-five years, but just de same, Ah ain't never bin mean ter no woman. Yas, sah, yer don't neither one ob yer eber need ter ask Sam no mor'—he's a goin' thro' wid yer all ter de end—he sure am, Ma'm."

Silence descended upon us, and I slipped the pistol back into my pocket. Rene rested her cheek on her hand and gazed straight ahead into the night. Her head seemed to droop, and I realized that her eyes saw nothing except those scenes pictured by her thoughts. Sam busied himself about his work, muttering occasionally under his breath, and shaking his head as though struggling with some problem, but the few words I caught were disconnected, yielding me no knowledge of what he was trying to solve. The bow of the boat had been deflected to the north, and was silently cleaving the sluggish downward trend of the water, for we had passed out of the swifter current and were close in to the eastern shore. The bank appeared low and unwooded, a mere black line barely above the water level and I guessed that behind it stretched uninhabitable marshes overflowed by the spring floods.

As we fought our way up stream the boat gradually drew away, the low shore fading from view as the negro sought deeper water, until finally the craft was nearly in the center of the broad stream where the eye could see only turbulent water sweeping past on every side. Occasionally a log scraped along our side, dancing about amid foam, or some grotesque branch, reaching out gaunt arms, swept by. The stars overhead reflected their dim light from off the surface, rendering everything more weird and desolate. The intense loneliness of the scene seemed to clutch my soul. Far off to the left a few winking lights appeared, barely perceptible, and I touched the negro, pointing them out to him and whispering my question so as not to disturb the motionless girl.

"Is that the Landing over there?"

"Ah certainly 'spects it must be, sah; dar ain't no other town directly 'round dese parts."

"Then those lights higher up must be on the bluff at Beaucaire?"

"Yas, sah; looks like de whol' house was lit up. I reckon things am right lively up thar 'bout now." He chuckled to himself, smothering a laugh. "It's sure goin' fer ter bother Massa Donaldson ter lose dis nigger, sah, fer Ah's de only one he's got."

The lights slowly faded away in the far distance, finally disappearing altogether as we rounded a sharp bend in the river bank. The engine increased its stroke, giving vent to louder chugging, and I could feel the strain of the planks beneath us as we battled the current. This new noise may have aroused her, for Rene lifted her head as though suddenly startled and glanced about in my direction.

"We have passed the village?" she asked, rather listlessly.

"Yes; it is already out of sight. From the number of lights burning I imagine our escape has been discovered."

"And what will they do?" an echo of dismay in her voice.

All fear of any treachery on the part of the negro had completely deserted me, and I slipped down from my perch on the edge of the cockpit to a place on the bench at her side. She made no motion to draw away, but her eyes were upon my face, as though seeking to read the meaning of my sudden action.

"We can talk better here," I explained. "The engine makes so much noise."

"Yes; and—and somehow I—I feel more like trusting you when I am able to see your face," she admitted frankly. "I am actually afraid to be alone."

"I have felt that this was true from the first. Indeed, I seriously wonder at the trust you have reposed in me—a total stranger."

"But—but how could I help it? Have I been unwomanly? I think I scarcely know what I have done. I could very easily have told what was right in the old days; but—but surely you understand—this was not to be decided by those rules. I was no longer free. Do you mean that you blame me for what has been done?"

"Far from it. You have acted in the only way possible. To me you are a wonderfully brave woman. I doubt if one in a thousand could have faced the situation as well."

"Oh I can hardly feel I have been that. It seems to me I have shown myself strangely weak—permitting you to do exactly as you pleased with me. Yet you do not understand; it has not been wholly my own peril which caused me to surrender so easily."

"But I think I do understand—it was partly a sacrifice for others."

"In a way, yes, it was; but I cannot explain more fully, even to you, now. Yet suppose I make this sacrifice, and it fails; suppose after all they should fall into the hands of these men?"

"I will not believe that," I protested, stoutly. "I feel convinced they had warning—there is no other way in which to account for their disappearance, their failure to return to the house. They must have encountered Pete and gone away with him."

"If I only knew that."

"Perhaps we can assure ourselves; we can go ashore at his place up the river, and if his boat is gone, there will be no longer any doubt. In any case, it is clearly your duty to save yourself."

"Do you really think so? It has seemed to me cowardly to run away."

"But, Rene," I urged. "They were the ones who deserted first. If they had warning of danger, they fled without a word to you—leaving you alone in the hands of those men."

"They—they, perhaps they failed to realize my peril. Oh you cannot see this as I do," she faltered, endeavoring to conjure up some excuse. "They may have thought they could serve me best in that way."

I laughed, but not in any spirit of humor.

"Hardly that, I imagine. Far more likely they fled suddenly in a panic of fear, without pausing to think at all. Why, you were the very one whose danger was the greatest; you were the one plunged into slavery."

"Yes—yes; I had forgotten that. Never for a moment does it seem real to me. I have to keep saying over and over again to myself, 'I am a negro and a slave.'"

"And so do I," I confessed, unthinkingly. "And even then, when I remember you as I first saw you in that lighted room back yonder, it is unbelievable."

Her eyes fell from my face, her head drooping, as she stared over the rail at the sullen rush of black water alongside. She remained silent and motionless for so long that I felt impelled to speak again, yet before I could decide what to say, her voice addressed me, although with face still averted.

"Yes, it is indeed most difficult—for both of us," she acknowledged, slowly. "We are in an extremely embarrassing position. You must not think I fail to realize this. It would be comparatively easy for me to choose my course but for that. I do not know why you serve me thus—risking your very life and your professional future—but neither of us must forget, not for a moment, that I am only a runaway slave. I can only consent to go with you, Lieutenant Knox, if you promise me this."

I hesitated to make the pledge, to put it into binding words, my lips pressed tightly together, my hands clinched. Feeling the rebuke of my silence, she turned her head once more, and her questioning eyes again sought my face in the star-gleam.

"You must promise me," she insisted, firmly, although her sensitive lips trembled as she gave utterance to the shameful words. "I am nothing else. I am no white woman of your own race and class appealing for protection. I cannot ask of you the courtesy a gentleman naturally gives; I can only beg your mercy. I am a negress—you must not forget, and you must not let me forget. If you will give me your word I shall trust you, fully, completely. But it must be given. There is no other way by which I can accept your protection; there can be no equality between us—only an impassable barrier of race."

"But I do not see this from the same viewpoint as you of the South."

"Oh yes, you do. The viewpoint is not so dissimilar; not in the same degree, perhaps, but no less truly. You believe in my right of freedom; you will even fight for that right, but at the same time you realize as I do, that the one drop of black blood in my veins is a bar sinister, now and forever. It cannot be overcome; it must not be forgotten. You will pledge me this?"

"Yes—I pledge you."

"And, in spite of that drop of black blood, as long as we are together, you will hold me a woman, worthy of respect and honor? Not a creature, a chattel, a plaything?"

"Will you accept my hand?"

"Yes."

"Then I will answer you, Rene Beaucaire," I said, soberly, "with all frankness, black or white I am your friend, and never, through any word or act of mine, shall you ever regret that friendship."

Her wide-open eyes gazed straight at me. It seemed as if she would never speak. Then I felt the tightening pressure of her hand, and her head bent slowly forward as though in the instinct of prayer.

"Thank God!" she whispered softly. "Now I can go with you."

I waited breathless, conscious of the trembling of her body against mine. Once again the bowed head was lifted, and this time a sparkle of unshed tears were visible in the shadowed eyes.

"You have not yet explained to me what we were to do? Your plans for tomorrow?"

"Because I scarcely have any," I replied, comprehending that now she claimed partnership in this adventure. "This has all occurred so suddenly, I have only acted upon impulse. No doubt those back at the Landing will endeavor to pursue us; they may have discovered already our means of escape and procured boats. My principal hope is that they may take it for granted that we have chosen the easier way and gone down stream. If so we shall gain so much more time to get beyond their reach. Anyway we can easily out-distance any rowboat, and Sam tells me there is nothing else to be had at the Landing."

"But why have you chosen the northern route? Surely you had a reason?"

"Certainly; it was to deceive them and get out of slave territory as quickly as possible. There are friends in this direction and none in the other. If we should endeavor to flee by way of the Ohio, we would be compelled to run a thousand-mile gauntlet. There are slaves in Illinois—it has never been declared a free state—but these are held almost exclusively in the more southern counties. North of the river the settlers are largely from New England, and the majority of them hate slavery and are ready to assist any runaway to freedom."

"But you have spoken of a man—Amos Shrunk—who is he?"

"You have certainly heard rumors, at least, that there are

regular routes of escape from here to Canada?"

"Yes; it has been discussed at the house. I have never clearly understood, but I do know that slaves disappear and are never caught. I was told white men helped them."

"It is accomplished through organized effort by these men— Black Abolitionists, as they are called—haters of slavery. They are banded together in a secret society for this one purpose and have what they call stations scattered all along at a certain distance apart—a night's travel—from the Mississippi to the Canadian line, where the fugitives are hidden and fed. The runaways are passed from one station to the next under cover of darkness, and are seldom recaptured. A station keeper, I am told, is only permitted to know a few miles of the route, those he must cover—the system is perfect, and many are engaged in it who are never even suspected."

"And this man, is he one?"

"Yes, a leader; he operates the most dangerous station of all. The escaping slaves come to him first."

"And he passes them on to the next man—do you know who?"

"Only what little Pete told me; the second agent is supposed to be a preacher in Beardstown."

She asked no further questions, and after a moment turned away, resting back against the edge of the cockpit with chin cupped in the hollow of her hand. The profile of her face was clearly defined by the starlight reflected by the river, and I found it hard to withdraw my eyes. A movement by the negro attracted my attention.

"There is a small creek about four miles above the Landing, Sam," I said shortly. "Do you think you can find it?"

"On de Missouri side, sah? Ah reckon Ah cud."

CHAPTER XIV

THE DAWN OF DEEPER INTEREST

It tested his skill as a boatman to locate the exact spot sought amid that gloom, yet he finally attained to it closely enough so I was able to get ashore, wading nearly thigh deep in water and mud, but only to learn that the boat, which I had provisioned earlier in the evening, had disappeared from its moorings. No trace of it could be found in the darkness, although I devoted several minutes to the search. To my mind this was positive evidence that Pete had returned, accompanied by the two frightened women, and that, finally despairing of my arrival, had departed with them up the river. In all probability we would overhaul the party before morning, certainly before they could attain the mouth of the Illinois. Their heavy rowboat would be compelled to creep along close in shore to escape the grasp of the current, while our engine gave us every advantage. I made my way back to the keel-boat with this information, and the laboring engine began to chug even while I was briefly explaining the situation to Rene. She listened almost wearily, asking but few questions, and both of us soon lapsed into silence. A little later she had pillowed her head on her arms and apparently had fallen asleep.

I must have dozed, myself, as the hours passed, although

hardly aware of doing so. The soft, continuous chugging of the engine, the swash of water alongside, the ceaseless sweep of the current, and the dark gloom of the shadows through which we struggled, all combined to produce drowsiness. I know my eyes were closed several times, and at last they opened to a realization that gray, sickly dawn rested upon the river surface. It was faint and dim, a promise more than a realization of approaching day, yet already sufficient to afford me view of the shore at our right, and to reveal the outlines of a sharp point of land ahead jutting into the stream. The mist rising from off the water in vaporous clouds obscured all else, rendering the scene weird and unfamiliar. It was, indeed, a desolate view, the near-by land low, and without verdure, in many places overflowed, and the river itself sullen and angry. Only that distant point appeared clearly defined and real, with the slowly brightening sky beyond. I endeavored to arouse myself from stupor, rubbing the sleep from my eyes. Rene had changed her posture, but still slumbered, with face completely concealed in her arms; but Sam was wide awake, and turned toward me grinning at my first movement. He had a broad, good-humored face, and a row of prominent teeth, slightly shadowed by a very thin moustache. Instinctively, I liked the fellow on sight—he appeared both intelligent and trustworthy.

"Daylight, is it?" I said, speaking low so as not to awaken the girl. "I must have been asleep."

"Yas, sah; yer's bin a noddin' fer de las' hour. Ah wus 'bout ter stir yer up, sah, fer Ah reckon as how we's mos' dar."

"Most where?" staring about incredulously. "Oh, yes, Rassuer Creek. Have we made that distance already?"

Sam's teeth glittered in another expanding of his mouth.

"Wal', we's bin a goin' et a mighty good gait, sah. She ain't done fooled none on me all dis night," his hand laid lovingly on the engine. "Nebber kicked up no row o' no kind—just chug, chug, chug right 'long. 'Pears like she sorter know'd dis nigger hed ter git away. Enyhow, we bin movin' lon' now right smart fer 'bout four hours, an' Rassuer Creek am just 'round dat p'int yonder—Ah's mighty sure ob dat, sah."

He was right, but it was broad daylight when we reached there, the eastern sky a glorious crimson, and the girl sitting up, staring at the brilliant coloring as though it pictured to her the opening of a new world. I was too busily engaged helping Sam at the wheel, for the swirl of the current about the headland required all our strength to combat it, and eagerly scanning the irregular shore line, to observe her closely in the revealing light; yet I knew that she had studied us both attentively from beneath her long lashes, before turning her head away.

Rounding the headland brought us immediately into a new country, the river bank high and firm, a bank of rather vivid yellow clay, with trees thickly covering the rising ground beyond. The passage of a few hundred yards revealed the mouth of Rassuer Creek, a narrow but sluggish stream, so crooked and encroached upon by the woods as to be practically invisible from the center of the river. The water was not deep, yet fortunately proved sufficiently so for our purpose, although we were obliged to both pole and paddle the boat upward against the slow current, and it required an hour of hard labor to place the craft safely beyond the first bend where it might lie thoroughly concealed by the intervening fringe of trees. Here we made fast to the bank.

I assisted Rene ashore, and aided her to climb to a higher level, carpeted with grass. The broad river was invisible, but we could look directly down upon the boat, where Sam was already busily rummaging through the lockers, in search of something to eat. He came ashore presently bearing some corn pone, and a goodly portion of jerked beef. Deciding it would be better not to attempt a fire, we divided this, and made the best meal possible, meanwhile discussing the situation anew, and planning what to do next. The negro, seated at one side alone upon the grass, said little, beyond replying to my questions, yet scarcely once removed his eyes from the girl's face. He seemed unable to grasp the thought that she was actually of his race, a runaway slave, or permit his tongue to utter any words of equality. Indeed, I could not prevent my own glance from being constantly attracted in her direction, also. Whatever had been her mental strain and anguish, the long hours of the night had in no marked degree diminished her beauty. To me she appeared even younger, and more attractive than in the dim glare of the lamplight the evening before; and this in spite of a weariness in her eyes, and the lassitude of her manner. She spoke but little, compelling herself to eat, and assuming a cheerfulness I was sure she was far from feeling. It was clearly evident her thoughts were elsewhere, and finally the conviction came to me, that, more than all else, she desired to be alone. My eyes sought the outlines of the boat lying in the stream below.

"What is there forward of the cockpit, Sam?" I questioned. "Beneath the deck, I mean; there seem to be several portholes."

"A cabin, sah; 'tain't so awful big, but Massa Donaldson he uster sleep dar off an' on."

"The young lady could rest there then?"

"Sure she cud. 'Twas all fixed up fine afore we lef Saint Louee. Ah'll show yer de way, Missus."

She rose to her feet rather eagerly, and stood with one hand resting against the trunk of a small tree. Her eyes met mine, and endeavored a smile.

"I thank you for thinking of that," she said gratefully. "I—I really am tired, and—and it will be rest just to be alone. You—you do not mind if I go?"

"Certainly not. There is nothing for any of us to do, but just take things easy until night."

"And then we are to go on, up the river?"

"Yes, unless, of course, something should occur during the day to change our plan. Meanwhile Sam and I will take turns on guard, while you can remain undisturbed."

She gave me her hand simply, without so much as a thought of any social difference between us, and I bowed low as I accepted it, equally oblivious. Yet the realization came to her even as our fingers met, a sudden dash of red flaming into her cheeks, and her eyes falling before mine.

"Oh, I forgot!" she exclaimed, drawing away. "It is so hard to remember."

"I beg you not to try. I have but one aim—to serve you to the best of my ability. Let me do it in my own way."

"Your own way?"

"Yes, the way of a gentleman, the way of a friend. You can look into my face now by daylight. Please look; am I unworthy to be trusted?"

She did not answer at once, or even seem to hear my

question, yet slowly her downcast eyes lifted, until she gazed frankly into my own. Beneath the shading lashes they were wistful, pleading, yet steadfastly brave.

"I am at your mercy, Lieutenant Knox," she said quietly. "I must trust you—and I do. Yes, you may serve me in your own way. We—we cannot seem to play a part very well, either of us, so, perhaps, it will be easier just to be natural."

I watched the two as they went down the steep bank together, and Sam helped her over the rail into the cockpit. The narrow entrance leading into the cabin forward was to the right of the engine, and she disappeared through the sliding door without so much as glancing upward toward where I remained standing. The negro left the door open, and returned slowly, clambering up the bank.

"'Cuse me, sah," he said clumsily, as he paused before me, rubbing his head, his eyes wandering below. "Did Ah hear right whut yer sed las' night, 'bout how dat young woman was a nigger, a runaway frum Massa Kirby? 'Pears like Ah don't just seem fer ter git dat right in my head, sah."

"That is the truth, Sam, although it appears quite as impossible to me as to you. She is a natural lady, and worthy of all respect—a beautiful girl, with no outward sign that she is not wholly white—yet she has the blood of your race in her veins, and is legally a slave."

"Lordy, an she nebber know'd it till just now?"

"No; I can only wonder at her meeting the truth as she does. Perhaps I had better tell you the story—it is very brief. She is the illegitimate daughter of a son of the late Judge Beaucaire, and a slave mother known as Delia, a quadroon woman. The boy disappeared years ago, before she was born, and is probably dead, and she has been brought up, and educated exactly as if she was the Judge's own child. She has never known otherwise, until those men came to the house the other night."

"An'—an' de ol' Jedge, he nebber done set her free?"

"No; nor the mother. I do not know why, only that it is a fact."

"An' now she done b'long ter dis yere Massa Kirby?"

"Yes, he won all the Beaucaire property, including the slaves, in a poker game on the river, the night Beaucaire died."

"Ah done heered all 'bout dat, sah. An' yer nebber know'd dis yere girl afore et all?"

"No, I never even saw her. I chanced to hear the story, and went to the house to warn them, as no one else would. I was too late, and no other course was left but to help her escape. That is the whole of it."

He asked several other questions, but at last appeared satisfied, and after that we discussed the guard duty of the day, both agreeing it would not be safe for us to permit any possible pursuit to pass by us up the river unseen. Sam professed himself as unwearied by the night's work, and willing to stand the first watch; and my eyes followed his movements as he scrambled across the intervening ravine, and disappeared within a fringe of woods bordering the shore of the river. Shortly after I lay down in the tree shade, and must have fallen asleep almost immediately. I do not know what aroused me, but I immediately sat upright, startled and instantly awake, the first object confronting me being Sam on the crest of the opposite ridge, eagerly beckoning me to join him. The moment he was assured of my coming, and without so much as uttering a word of explanation, he vanished again into the shadow of the woods.

I crossed the ravine with reckless haste, clambering up the opposite bank, and sixty feet beyond suddenly came into full view of the broad expanse of water. Scarcely had I glimpsed this rolling flood, sparkling under the sun's rays, when my gaze turned up stream, directed by an excited gesture of the negro. Less than a mile away, its rapidly revolving wheel churning the water into foam in ceaseless battle against the current, was a steamboat. It was not a large craft, and so dingy looking that, even at that distance, it appeared dull gray in color. A number of moving figures were perceptible on the upper deck; two smokestacks belched forth a vast quantity of black smoke, sweeping in clouds along the water surface, and a large flag flapped conspicuously against the sky. I stared at the apparition, scarcely comprehending the reality of what I beheld.

"Yer bettah stoop down more, sah," Sam urged. "Fer sum o' dem fellars might see yer yit. Ah nebber heerd nuthin', ner saw no smoke till she cum a puffin' 'round de end 'o dat p'int. Ah cudn't dare go fer yer then, sah, fer fear dey'd see me, so Ah jus' nat'larly lay down yere, an' watched her go by."

"Is it a government boat?"

"Ah reckon maybe; leastwise thar's a heap o' sojers aboard her—reg'lars Ah reckon, fer dey's all in uniform. But everybody aboard wan't sojers."

"You know the steamer?"

"Yas, sah. Ah's seed her afore dis down et Saint Louee. She

uster run down de ribber—she's de *John B. Glover*. She ain't no great shakes ob a boat, sah."

His eyes, which had been eagerly following the movements of the craft, turned and glanced at me.

"Now dey's goin' fer ter cross over, sah, so's ter keep de channel. Ah don't reckon es how none o' dem men kin see back yere no more. Massa Kirby he wus aboard dat steamer, sah."

"Kirby! Are you sure about that, Sam?"

"'Course Ah's sure. Didn't Ah see him just as plain as Ah see you right now? He wus for-rad by de rail, near de pilot house, a watchin' dis whole shore like a hawk. Dat sure wus Massa Kirby all right, but dar wan't nobody else 'long wid him."

"But what could he be doing there on a troop boat?"

The negro scratched his head, momentarily puzzled by my question.

"Ah sure don't know, sah," he admitted. "Only dat's perzackly who it was. Ah reckon dar ain't no boat whut won't take a passenger, an' Kirby, he knows ebery captain 'long dis ribber. Ah figur' it out 'bout dis way, sah; dat nobody kin tell yit which way we went—up de ribber, er down de ribber. Long cum de *John B. Glover*, an' Massa Kirby he just take a chance, an' goes aboard. De sheriff he goes der odder way, down stream in a rowboat; an' dat's how dey aims ter sure head us off."

I sat down at the edge of the bluff, convinced that the conclusions of the negro were probably correct. That was undoubtedly about how it had happened. To attempt pursuit up stream with only oars as propelling power, would be senseless, but the passage upward of this troop boat afforded Kirby an opportunity he would not be slow to accept. Getting aboard would present no great difficulty, and his probable acquaintance with the captain would make the rest easy.

The steamer by this time was moving diagonally across the river, head toward the other shore, and was already so far away the men on deck were invisible. It was scarcely probable that Kirby would go far northward, but just what course the man would take when once more ashore was problematical. Where he might choose to seek for us could not be guessed. Yet the mere fact that he was already above us on the river was in itself a matter for grave consideration. Still, thus far we remained unlocated, and there was less danger in that direction than down stream. Donaldson, angered by the loss of his boat, and the flight of Sam, would surely see to it that no craft slipped past St. Louis unchallenged. In this respect he was more to be feared than Kirby, with a hundred miles of river to patrol; while, once we attained the Illinois, and made arrangements with Shrunk, the immediate danger would be over. Then I need go no farther—the end of the adventure might be left to others. I looked up—the steamer was a mere smudge on the distant bosom of the river.

Randall Parrish

CHAPTER XV

THE CABIN OF AMOS SHRUNK

Beyond this passing of the *John B. Glover*, the day proved uneventful, although all further desire for sleep deserted me. It was late afternoon before Rene finally emerged from the cabin to learn the news, and I spent most of the time on watch, seated at the edge of the bluff, my eyes searching the surface of the river. While Kirby's presence up stream, unquestionably increased our peril of capture, this did not cause me as much anxious thought as did the strange disappearance of Free Pete, and the two women. What had become of them during the night? Surely they could never have out-stripped us, with only a pair of oars by which to combat the current, and yet we had obtained no glimpse of them anywhere along that stretch of river.

The knowledge that the steamer which had passed us was heavily laden with troops was most encouraging. In itself alone this was abundant proof of the safe delivery of my dispatches, and I was thus relieved to realize that this duty had been performed. My later disappearance was excusable, now that I was convinced the papers intrusted to me had reached the right hands. There might be wonder, and, later, the necessity of explanation, yet no one would suffer from my absence, and I was within the limits of my furlough—the reinforcements for Forts Armstrong and Crawford were already on their way. So, altogether, I faced the task of eluding Kirby with a lighter heart, and renewed confidence. Alone, as I believed him to be, and in that new country on the very verge of civilization, he was hardly an antagonist I needed greatly to fear. Indeed, as man to man, I rather welcomed an encounter.

There is little to record, either of the day or the night. The latter shut down dark, but rainless, although the sky was heavily overcast by clouds. Satisfied that the river was clear as far as eye could reach in every direction, we managed to pole the heavy boat out of its berth in the creek while the twilight yet lingered, the western sky still remaining purple from the lingering sunset as we emerged into the broader stream. The following hours passed largely in silence, each of us, no doubt, busied with our own thoughts. Sam made no endeavor to speed his engine, keeping most of the way close to the deeper shadow of the shore, and the machinery ran smoothly, its noise indistinguishable at any distance. Twice we touched bottom, but to no damage other than a slight delay and the labor of poling off into deeper water, while occasionally overhanging limbs of trees, unnoticed in the gloom, struck our faces. By what uncanny skill the negro was able to navigate, how he found his way in safety along that ragged bank, remains a mystery. To my eyes all about us was black, impenetrable, not even the water reflecting a gleam of light; indeed, so dense was the surrounding gloom that in the deeper shadows I could not even distinguish the figure of the girl seated beside me in the cockpit. Yet there was scarcely a break in the steady chug of the engine, or the gentle swish of water alongside.

The clouds broke slightly after midnight, occasionally yielding a glimpse of a star, but the uninhabited shore remained desolate and silent. Day had not broken when we came to the mouth of the Illinois, and turned our bow cautiously up that stream, becoming immediately aware that we had entered new waters. The negro, ignorant of what was before us, soon beached the boat onto a sand bar, and we decided it would be better for us to remain there until dawn. This was not long in coming, the graying sky of the east slowly lighting up the scene, and bringing into view, little by little, our immediate surroundings. These were lonely and dismal enough, yet revealed nothing to create alarm. A desolate flat of sand extended from either shore back to a high ridge of clay, which was thickly wooded. Slightly higher up the river this ridge approached more closely the bank of the stream, with trees actually overhanging the water, and a rather thick growth of underbrush hiding the ground. The river was muddy, flowing with a swift current, and we could distinguish its course only so far as the first bend, a comparatively short distance away. Nowhere appeared the slightest evidence of life, either on water or land; all was forlorn and dead, a vista of utter desolation. Sam was standing up, his whole attention concentrated on the view up stream.

"Do steamers ever go up this river?" I asked, surprised at the volume of water.

He glanced around at me, as though startled at my voice.

"Yas, sah; putty near eny sorter boat kin. Ah nebber tried it, fer Massa Donaldson hed no bus'ness ober in dis kintry, but Ah's heerd 'em talk down ter Saint Louee. Trouble is, sah, we's got started in de wrong place—dar's plenty watah t'other side dis yere bar."

"Who told you the best way to find Shrunk?"

His eyes widened and searched my face, evidently still

somewhat suspicious of any white man.

"A nigger down Saint Louee way, sah. Dey done cotched him, an' brought him back afore he even got ter Beardstown."

"And you believe you can guide us there?"

"Ah sure can, if whut dat nigger sed wus correct, sah. Ah done questioned him mighty par'ticlar, an' Ah 'members ebery sign whut he giv' me." He grinned broadly. "Ah sorter suspicion'd Ah mought need dat informa'ion."

"All right, then; it is certainly light enough now—let's push off."

We had taken the sand lightly, and were able to pole the boat into deep water with no great difficulty. I remained crouched at the bow, ready for any emergency, while the engine resumed its chugging, and Sam guided us out toward the swifter current of the stream. The broader river behind us remained veiled in mist, but the gray light was sufficient for our purpose, enabling us to proceed slowly until our craft had rounded the protruding headland, out of sight from below. Here the main channel cut across to the left bank, and we forced into the deeper shadows of the overhanging woods.

"'Tain't so awful fur from yere, sah," Sam called to me.

"What, the place where we are to land?"

"Yas, sah. It's de mouth ob a little crick, whut yer nebber see till yer right plum at it. Bettah keep yer eyes open 'long dat shore, sah."

The girl, alertly bent forward, was first among us to detect the concealed opening, which was almost completely screened by the over-arching trees, her voice ringing excitedly, as she pointed it out. Sam was quick to respond, and, almost before I had definitely established the spot, the bow of the boat swerved and we shot in through the leafy screen, the low-hung branches sweeping against our faces and scraping along the sides. It was an eery spot, into which the faint daylight scarcely penetrated, but, nevertheless, revealed itself a secure and convenient harbor. While the stream was not more than twelve feet in width and the water almost motionless, the banks were high and precipitous and the depth amply sufficient. The dim light, only occasionally finding entrance through the trees, barely enabled us to see for a short distance ahead. It looked a veritable cave, and, indeed, all I remember noting in my first hasty glance through the shadows, was the outline of a small boat, moored to a fallen tree. Sam must have perceived this at the same instant, for he ran our craft alongside the half-submerged log and stopped his engine. I scrambled over, found precarious footing on the wet bank, and made fast.

"So this is the place?" I questioned incredulously, staring about at the dark, silent forest; which still remained in the deep night shade. "Why, there's nothing here."

"No, sah; dar certenly don't 'pear fer ter be much," and the negro crept out of the cockpit and joined me, "'ceptin' dat boat. Dar ain't no boat 'round yere, les' folks hes bin a ridin' in it, Ah reckon. Dis sure am de spot, all right—an' dar's got ter be a trail 'round yere sumwhar."

Rene remained motionless, her eyes searching the shadows, as though half frightened at finding herself in such dismal surroundings. The girl's face appeared white and drawn in that twilight. Sam advanced cautiously from off the log to the shore, and began to anxiously scan the ground, beating back and forth through the underbrush. After watching him a moment my gaze settled on the strange boat, and I crept along the log curious to examine it more closely. It had the appearance of being newly built, the paint unscratched, and exhibiting few marks of usage. A single pair of oars lay crossed in the bottom and beside these was an old coat and some ordinary fishing tackle—but nothing to arouse any interest. Without doubt it belonged to Amos Shrunk, and had been left here after the return from some excursion either up or down the river. I was still staring at these things, and speculating about them, when the negro called out from a distance that he had found the path. Rene answered his hail, standing up in the boat, and I hastened back to help her ashore.

We had scarcely exchanged words during the entire night, but now she accepted my proffered hand gladly, and with a smile, springing lightly from the deck to the insecure footing of the log.

"I do not intend that you shall leave me behind," she said, glancing about with a shudder. "This is such a horrid place."

"The way before us looks scarcely better," I answered, vainly endeavoring to locate Sam. "Friend Shrunk evidently is not eager for callers. Where is that fellow?"

"Somewhere over in that thicket, I think. At least his voice sounded from there. You discovered nothing in the boat?"

"Only a rag and some fishing tackle. Come; we'll have to plunge in somewhere."

She followed closely as I pushed a passage through the obstructing underbrush, finally locating Sam at the edge of a small opening, where the light was sufficiently strong to enable us to distinguish marks of a little-used trail leading along the bottom of a shallow gully bisecting the sidehill. The way was obstructed by roots and rotten tree trunks, and so densely shaded as to be in places almost imperceptible, but Sam managed to find its windings, while we held close enough behind to keep him safely in sight. Once we came into view of the river, but the larger part of the way lay along a hollow, heavily overshadowed by trees, where we could see only a few feet in any direction.

At the crossing of a small stream we noticed the imprint of several feet in the soft mud of the shore. One plainly enough was small and narrow, beyond all question that of a woman, but the others were all men's, one being clad in moccasins. Beyond this point the path trended downward, winding along the face of the hill and much more easily followed. Sam, still ahead, started to clamber across the trunk of a fallen tree, but came to a sudden halt, staring downward at something concealed from our view on, the other side.

"Good Lord o' mercy!" he exclaimed, excitedly.

"What's dat?"

I was close beside him by this time and saw the thing also—the body of a man lying on the ground. The light was so dim only the bare outlines of the recumbent figure were visible, and, following the first shock of discovery, my earliest thought was to spare the girl.

"Wait where you are, Rene!" I exclaimed, waving her back. "There is a man lying here beyond the log. Come, Sam; we will see what he looks like."

He was slow in following, hanging back as I approached

closer to the motionless form, and I could hear the muttering of his lips. Unquestionably the man was dead; of this I was assured before I even knelt beside him. He lay prone on his face in a litter of dead leaves, and almost the first thing I noticed was the death wound back of his ear, where a large caliber bullet had pierced the brain. His exposed hands proved him a negro, and it was with a feeling of unusual repugnance that I touched his body, turning it over sufficiently to see the face. The countenance of a negro in death seldom appears natural, and under that faint light, no revealed feature struck me, at first, as familiar. Then, all at once, I knew him, unable to wholly repress a cry of startled surprise, as I stared down into the upturned face—the dead man, evidently murdered, shot treacherously from behind, was Free Pete. I sprang to my feet, gazing about blindly into the dim woods, my mind for the instant dazed by the importance of this discovery. What could it mean? How could it have happened? By what means had he reached this spot in advance of us, and at whose hand had he fallen? He could have been there only for one purpose, surely—in an attempt to guide Eloise Beaucaire and the quadroon Delia. Then what had become of the women? Where were they now?

I stumbled backward to the support of the log, unable to answer any one of these questions, remembering only in that moment that I must tell Rene the truth. Her eyes already were upon me, exhibiting her fright and perplexity, her knowledge that I had viewed something of horror. She could keep silent no longer.

"Tell me—please," she begged. "Is the man dead? Who is he, do you know?"

"Yes," I replied desperately. "He is dead, and I recognize his face. He is the negro Pete, and has been killed, shot from behind. I cannot understand how it has happened."

"Pete," she echoed, grasping at the log to keep erect, her eyes on that dimly revealed figure in the leaves. "Free Pete, Carlton's Pete? How—how could he have got here? Then—then the others must have been with him. What has become of them?"

"It is all mystery; the only way to solve it is for us to go on. It can do no one any good to stand here, staring at this dead body. When we reach the cabin we may learn what has occurred. Go on ahead, Sam, and we will follow—don't be afraid, boy; it is not the dead who hurt us."

She clung tightly to me, shrinking past the motionless figure. She was not sobbing; her eyes were dry, yet every movement, each glance, exhibited her depth of horror. I drew her closer, thoughtless of what she was, my heart yearning to speak words of comfort, yet realizing there was nothing left me to say. I could almost feel the full intensity of her struggle for self-control, the effort she was making to conquer a desire to give way. She must have known this, for once she spoke.

"Do not mind me," she said, pausing before the utterance of each word to steady her voice. "I—I am not going to break down. It—it is the suddenness—the shock. I—I shall be strong again, in a minute."

"You must be," I whispered, "for their lives may depend on us."

It was a short path before us and became more clearly defined as we advanced. A sharp turn brought us into full view of the cabin, which stood in a small opening, built against the sidehill, and so overhung with trees as to be invisible, except from the direction of our approach. We could see only the side wall, which contained one open window, and was a one-room affair, low and flat-roofed, built of logs. Its outward appearance was peaceful enough, and the swift beat of my pulse quieted as I took rapid survey of the surroundings.

"Sam," I commanded, "you are to remain here with Rene, while I learn the truth yonder. Yes," to her quick protest, "that will be the better way—there is no danger and I shall not be gone but for a moment."

I seated her on a low stump and left them there together, Sam's eyes rolling about in a frightened effort to perceive every covert in the woods, but the girl satisfied to watch me intently as I moved cautiously forward. A dozen steps brought me within view of the front of the cabin. The door had been smashed in and hung dangling from one hinge. Another step, now with a pistol gripped in my hand, enabled me to obtain a glimpse within. Across the puncheon threshold, his feet even protruding without, lay a man's body; beyond him, half concealed by the shadows of the interior, appeared the outlines of another, with face upturned to the roof, plainly distinguishable because of a snow-white beard.

CHAPTER XVI

THE TRAIL OF THE RAIDERS

Shocked and unmanned as I was at this discovery, to pause there staring at those gruesome figures would have only brought fresh alarm to the two watching my every movement from the edge of the clearing. Gripping my nerves I advanced over the first body, watchful for any sign of the presence of life within the cabin. There was none—the work of the murder had been completed, and the perpetrators had fled. I saw the entire interior at a glance, the few articles of rude, hand-made furniture, several overturned, the fire yet smouldering on the hearth, some broken crockery, and pewter dishes on the floor, and on every side the evidences of a fierce, brutal struggle. The dead man, with ghastly countenance upturned to the roof rafters, and the snowy beard, was undoubtedly the negro helper, Amos Shrunk. Pete's description of the appearance of the man left this identification beyond all dispute. He had been stricken down by a savage blow, which had literally crushed in one side of his head, but his dead hands yet gripped a rifle, as though he had fallen fighting to the last.

The other man, the one lying across the threshold, had been shot, although I did not ascertain this fact until after I turned the body over sufficiently to reveal the face. This was disfigured by the wound and covered with blood, so that the features could scarcely be seen, yet I instantly recognized the fellow—Carver. Surprised out of all control by this unexpected discovery, I steadied myself against the log wall, fully aroused to the sinister meaning of his presence. To a degree the complete significance of this tragedy instantly gripped my mind. It this fellow Carver had been one of the assailants, then it was absolutely certain that Kirby must have also been present—the leader of the attack. This inevitably meant that both men had been aboard the steamer, and later were put ashore at the mouth of the Illinois. And now that I thought about it, why not? It was no accident, and I wondered that the possibility had never occurred to me before. The gambler naturally knew all the gossip of the river, and, beyond question, he would be aware of the reported existence of this underground station for runaway slaves. It was common talk as far down as St. Louis, and his mind would instantly revert to the possibility that the fleeing Rene might seek escape through the assistance of Shrunk. The mysterious vanishing of the boat would serve to increase that suspicion. Even if this had not occurred to him at first, the steamer would have brought news that no keel-boat had been seen on the lower river, while the captain of the *John B. Glover*, or someone else on board, would have been sure to have mentioned the negro-helper and suggest that he might have had a hand in the affair. To follow that trail was, indeed, the most natural thing for Kirby to do.

And he had promptly accepted the chance; blindly, no doubt, and yet guided by good fortune. He had not overtaken Rene, because she was not yet there, but he had unexpectedly come upon the other fugitives, and, even though the encounter had cost the life of his henchman, Carver, it also resulted in the death of two men who had come between him and his prey— the negro, and the abolitionist. The scene cleared in my brain and became vivid and real. I could almost picture in detail each act of the grim tragedy. The two revengeful trackers—if there were only two engaged, for others might have been recruited on the steamer—must have crept up to the hut in the night, or early morning. Possibly Kirby had learned of some other means of approach from the direction of the big river. Anyway, the fact that Shrunk had been trapped within the cabin would indicate the final attack was a surprise. The negro might have been asleep outside, and met his death in an attempt at escape, but the old white man, finding flight impossible, had fought desperately to the last and had killed one antagonist before receiving his death blow. This was all plain enough, but what had become of Kirby, of the two women—Eloise, and the quadroon mother?

I searched the cabin without uncovering the slightest trace of their presence, or finding a single article which could be associated with them. Kirby himself must have fled the scene of the tragedy immediately—without even pausing long enough to turn his companion over to ascertain the nature of his wound. Had something occurred to frighten him? Had the fellow fled alone back to a waiting boat at the shore, perchance seriously injured himself in the melee, or had he secured the two women, and, reckless as to all else, driven them along with him to some place of concealment until they could be transported down the river? Nothing could answer these questions; no discovery enabled me to lift the veil. Uncertain what to do, or how to act, I could only return to the waiting girl and the negro to tell them what I had found.

They listened as though scarcely comprehending, Sam uttering little moans of horror, and appearing helpless from fright, but Rene quiet, merely exhibiting her emotion in the whiteness of her face and quickened breathing. Her eyes, wide-open, questioning, seemed to sense my uncertainty. As I ended the tale and concluded with my theory as to what had occurred following the deed of blood, her quick mind asserted itself.

"But this must have happened very lately; the men were not long dead?"

"I cannot judge how long; their bodies were cold."

"Yet the fire still smouldered, you said. When do you think that steamer could have landed here?"

"Why, perhaps early last evening."

"And it has not occurred to you that the boat might have waited here while the man Kirby went ashore?"

"No; that could scarcely be true, if the steamer was transporting troops; what was it you were thinking about?"

She buried her face in her hands; then lifted it once more to mine, with a new conviction in her eyes.

"It is all dark, of course," she said slowly, "we can only guess at what happened. But to me it seems impossible that the man Kirby could have accomplished all this alone—without assistance. The boat we saw at the landing was not his; it must have been Pete's, and there is no evidence of any other trail leading here from the river. If, as you imagine, he knew the captain of that steamer, and some of the other men aboard were Missourians and defenders of slavery, he would have no trouble in enlisting their help to recover his runaway slaves. They would be only too glad to break up an abolitionist's nest. That is what I believe has happened; they came ashore in a party, and the steamer waited for them. Even if it was a troop boat, the captain could easily make excuses for an hour's delay."

"And you think the prisoners were taken along? Yet Kirby would not want to transport them up the river."

"As to that," she insisted, "he could not help himself. He needed to get away quickly, and there were no other means available. He could only hope to connect later with some craft south-bound on which to return. There are keel-boats and barges always floating down stream from the mines. He dare not remain here; that was why they were in such haste; why, they did not even wait to bury the bodies."

"You may be right," I admitted, impressed, yet not wholly convinced. "But what can we do?"

She looked at me reproachfully.

"You should not ask that of a girl."

The words stung me.

"No; this is my task. I was thoughtlessly cruel. Neither can we remain here, only long enough to bury those bodies. It would be inhuman not to do that. Sam, there is an old spade leaning against the cabin wall—go over and get it."

"Ah ain't goin' fer ter tetch no daid man, sah."

"I'll attend to that; all you need do is dig. Over there at the edge of the wood will answer, and we shall have to place all three in one grave—we can do no more."

He started on his mission reluctantly enough, glancing constantly backward over his shoulder to insure himself of our presence, and carefully avoiding any approach to the open door.

"Am I to simply remain here?" the girl asked, as I took the first step to follow him. "Can I not be of some help?"

"I think not; I can get along very nicely. It is not a pleasant sight inside. Here is the best place for you, as it might not be safe for you to go any further away. We do not know positively where those men have gone. They might be hiding somewhere in the woods. You can turn away and face the forest, so as to see nothing. We shall not be long."

"And—and," she faltered, "what will be done after that?"

"I will endeavor to think out some plan. I confess I do not yet know what will be best. To remain here is, of course, impossible, while to return down the river means certain capture. Perhaps you may be able to suggest something."

Unpleasant as our task was, it proved to be less difficult of accomplishment than I had anticipated. There were blankets in the cabin bunks, and in these I wrapped the bodies. They were too heavy, however, for me to transport alone, and it required some threatening to induce Sam to give me the assistance necessary to deposit them in the shallow grave. Only the fear that I would not have him with us longer compelled his joining me. He was more frightened at the thought of being left alone than of contact with the dead. In bearing Pete's body from where it lay in the woods, we were compelled to pass by near where Rene sat, but she kept her eyes averted, and I experienced no desire to address her with empty words. Sam filled in the loose earth, rounding it into form, and the two of us stood above the fresh mound, our bent heads bared to the sunlight, while I endeavored to repeat brokenly a few words of prayer. As I finally turned gladly away, it was to note that the girl had risen to her feet and stood motionless, with face toward us. Her attitude and expression is still in memory the one dear remembrance of the scene. My inclination was to join her at once, but I knew that the negro would never enter the cabin alone, and now our first necessity was food. Of this I found a fair supply, and, compelling him to assist me, we hastily prepared a warm meal over the open fire. It was eaten without, no one of us desiring to remain in the midst of that scene of death; and the very knowledge that the dreaded burial was completed and that we were now free to depart, brought to all of us a renewed courage.

The sun was high in the heavens by this time, the golden light brightening the little clearing and dissipating the gloom of the surrounding forest. All suspicion that the murderer, or murderers, might still remain in the immediate neighborhood of their crime had entirely deserted my mind. Where, and by what means, they had fled could not be determined, but I felt assured they were no longer near by, I had sought in vain for any other path than the one we had followed from the mouth of the creek, while the suggestion which Rene had advanced, that the steamer had tied up to the shore, permitting the raiding party to land, grew more and more plausible to my mind. It scarcely seemed probable that one man alone, or even two men, had committed this crime, and the sole survivor disappear so completely with the prisoners. I had turned each detail over and over in my thought, while I worked, yet to but little purpose. The only present solution of the problem seemed to be our return to that hidden basin where our boat lay, and the remaining there in concealment until the darkness of another night rendered it safe to once more venture upon. the river. Perhaps during those inter-vening hours, we might, by conferring together, decide our future course; some new thought might guide us in the right direction, or some occurrence drive us into definite action.

I spoke of this to her, as I finally approached where she rested on the stump, eager and glad to escape from all memories of that somber cabin I had just left. She stood before me, listening quietly, her eyes lifting to my face, as though she sought to read there the exact meaning of my words.

"You—you are no longer so confident," she said, "your plan has failed?"

"I am afraid it has," I admitted, "for it was based altogether on the assistance of Amos Shrunk. He is no longer alive, and I do not know where to turn for guidance. There would seem to be danger in every direction; the only question is—in which way lies the least?"

"You begin to regret your attempt to aid me?"

"No," impulsively. "So far as that goes, I would do it all over again. Your safety means more to me now than ever before—you must believe that."

"Why should I? All I have brought you is trouble. I can read in your face how discouraged you are. You must not think I do not understand. I do understand—perfectly. I can see how all this has happened. You cannot really care. What you have done has been only a response to impulse; merely undertaken through a spirit of adventure. Then—then why not let it end here, and—Sam and I can go on to—to whatever is before us? It is nothing to you."

"You actually believe I would consent to that?" I asked, in startled surprise at the vehemence of her words. "That I could prove such a cur?"

"But why not? It would not be a cowardly act at all. I could not blame you, for I have no claim on your service—never have had. You have done a thousand times too much already;

you have risked honor, reputation, and neglected duty to aid my escape; and—and I am nothing to you—can be nothing."

"Nothing to me!"

"Certainly not. Why speak like that? Have you forgotten again that I am a slave—a negress? Think, Lieutenant Knox, what it would mean to you to be caught in my company; to be overtaken while attempting to assist me in escaping from my master. Now no one dreams of such a thing, and no one ever need dream. You have had your adventure; let it end here. I shall be grateful to you always, but—but I cannot bear to drag you deeper into this mire."

"You order me to leave you?"

"I cannot order; I am a slave. My only privilege is to request, urge, implore. I can merely insist that it will be best—best for us both—for you to go. Surely you also must realize that this is true?"

"I do not know exactly what I realize," I said doubtfully. "Nothing seems altogether clear in my mind. If I could leave you in safety, in the care of friends, perhaps I should not hesitate—but now—"

"Am I any worse off than the others?" she interrupted. "I, at least, have yet the chance of escape, while they remain helplessly in Kirby's clutches. When—when I think of them, I no longer care about myself; I—I feel almost responsible for their fate, and—and it would kill me to know that I had dragged you down also. You have no right to sacrifice yourself for such as I."

"You have been brooding over all this," I said gently, "sitting here alone, and thinking while we worked. I am not going to answer you now. There is no need. Nothing can be done until night, whatever we decide upon. You will go back with us to the boat?"

"Yes; I simply cannot stay here," her eyes wandering toward the cabin.

I took the lead on the return, finding the path easy enough to follow in the full light of day. The sincere honesty of her plea—the knowledge that she actually meant it—only served to draw me closer, to strengthen my determination not to desert. Her face was ever before me as I advanced—a bravely pathetic face, wonderfully womanly in its girlish contour—appealing to every impulse of my manhood. I admitted the truth of what she said—it had been largely love of adventure, the rash recklessness of youth, which had brought me here. But this was my inspiration no longer. I had begun to realize that something deeper, more worthy, now held me to the task. What this was I made no attempt to analyze—possibly I did not dare—but, nevertheless, the mere conception of deserting her in the midst of this wilderness was too utterly repugnant for expression. No, not that; whatever happened, it would never be that.

The last few rods of our journey lay through thick underbrush, and beneath the spreading branches of inter-lacing trees. It was a gloomy, primitive spot, where no evidence of man was apparent. Suddenly I emerged upon the bank of the creek, with the rude log wharf directly before me. I could hear in that silence the sound of those following, as they continued to crunch a passage through the thicket, but I stopped transfixed, staring at the water—nothing else greeted my eyes; both the boats were gone.

CHAPTER XVII

WE FACE DISASTER

This unexpected discovery came to me like a blow; the very breath seemed to desert my lungs, as I stared down at the vacant stream. We had been out-generaled, tricked, and all our theories as to what had occurred were wrong. The duty we had performed to the dead had cost us our own chance to escape. Instead of being alone, as we had supposed, we were in the midst of enemies; we had been seen, watched, and while we loitered ashore, the murderers had stolen our boat and vanished, leaving us there helplessly marooned. All this was plain enough now, when it was already too late to remedy the evil. The struggling girl emerged through the tangle of shrubs, and paused suddenly at my side, her lips giving utterance to a cry of surprise.

"The—the boat! It is not here?"

"No; there is not a sign of it. Those fellows must be still in the neighborhood; must have seen us when we first came."

"But, what are we to do?"

I had no ready answer, yet the echo of utter despair in her voice stirred me to my own duty as swiftly as though she had thrust a knife into my side. Do? We must do something! We could not sit down idly there in the swamp. And to decide what was to be attempted was my part. If Kirby, and whoever was with him, had stolen the missing boat, as undoubtedly they had, they could have possessed but one purpose—escape. They were inspired to the act by a desire to get away, to flee from the scene of their crime. They must believe that we were left helpless, unable to pursue them, or create alarm. Yet if it was Kirby, why had he fled so swiftly, making no effort to take Rene captive also? It was she he was seeking; for the purpose of gaining possession of her these murders had been committed. Why, then, should he run away when he must have known the girl was already in his grasp? The same thought apparently occurred to her.

"You—you believe that Kirby did this?"

"What other conclusion is possible? We know that he passed us on the steamer—Sam saw him plainly. It was his man, Carver, whom we found dead in the hut. It could have been no one else."

"But," she questioned, unsatisfied, "he would have only one reason for being here—hunting me, his slave. That was his one purpose, was it not? If he saw us, then he must have known of my presence, that I was here with you. Why should he make no attempt to take me with him? Why should he steal our boat and run away?"

I shook my head, my glance shifting toward the negro, who stood just behind us, his mouth wide open, evidently smitten speechless.

"One theory is as good as another," I said, "and mine so far have all been wrong. What do you make of it, Sam?"

"Who, sah? Me, sah?"

"Yes, take a guess at this."

"'Pears like," he said, deliberately, rubbing his ear with one hand, "as how it mought hav' happen'd dis yere way, sah. Ah ain't a' sayin' it wus, it mought be. Maybe Massa Kirby nebber got no sight ob us 'tall, an' wus afeerd fer ter stay. He just know'd a party wus yere—likely 'nough sum Black Abolitionists, who'd be huntin' him if he didn't cl'ar out, just so soon as dey foun' dat Amos Shrunk wus ded. Her' wus his chance, an' he done took it."

"Yet he would surely recognize the boat?"

"Yas, sah; Ah reckon he wud, sah. Dat's de truth, whut stumps me. Dat white man am certenly full o' tricks. Ah sure wish Ah know'd just whar he wus now. Ah'd certenly feel a heap easier if Ah did." He bent suddenly forward, his glance at the edge of the log. "Dey ain't took but just de one boat, sah, fer de odder am shoved under dar out'r sight."

As I stooped further over I saw that this was true, the small rowboat, with the oars undisturbed in its bottom, had been pressed in beneath the concealment of the log wharf, almost completely hidden from above, yet to all appearances uninjured. The very fact that it should have been thus left only added to the mystery of the affair. If it had been Kirby's deliberate purpose to leave us there stranded ashore, why had he failed to crush in the boat's planking with a rock? Could the leaving of the craft in fit condition for our use be part of some carefully conceived plan; a bait to draw us into some set trap? Or did it occur merely as an incident of their hurried night? These were unanswerable questions, yet the mere knowledge that the boat was actually there and in navigable condition, promised us an opportunity to escape. While hope remained, however vague, it was not my nature to despair. Whether accident or design had been the cause, made no odds—I was willing to match my wits against Kirby and endeavor to win. And I must deal with facts, just as they were.

"It is my guess," I said, "that their only thought was to get away before the crime was discovered. The leaving of this boat means nothing, because the steam-operated keel-boat they escaped in, could never be overtaken, once they had a fair start. If Kirby was alone in this affair, and had those two women in his charge, getting away would be about all he could attend to. He'd hardly dare leave them long enough to sink this craft. But what does he know about running an engine?"

"Ah reckon as how he cud, sah, if he just had to," interposed the negro. "He wus a' foolin' mor' or les' wid dat one a' comin' up frum Saint Louee; an' he sure ask'd me a big lot o' questions. He done seemed right handy; he sure did."

"Then that probably is the explanation. Rene, would you be afraid to remain here alone for a little while?"

She glanced about into the gloom of the surrounding woods, her hesitancy answering me.

"It is not a pleasant prospect I admit, but there is no possible danger. Kirby has gone, beyond all question, but I wish to learn, if I can, the direction he has taken. All this must have happened only a short time ago—while we were at the cabin. The keel-boat can scarcely be entirely out of sight yet on either river, if we could only find a place to offer us a wide view."

"But could I not go with you?"

"Hardly with me, for I intend to swim the creek and try to reach the point at the mouth of the Illinois, from where I can see up and down the Mississippi. I am going to send Sam back through the woods there and have him climb that ridge. From the top he ought to have a good view up the valley of the Illinois. I suppose you might go with him."

"Ah sure wish yer wud, Missus," broke in the negro pleadingly. "Ah ain't perzackly feered fer ter go 'lone, but Ah's an' ol' man, an' Ah reckon as how a y'ung gal wus likely fer ter see mor'n Ah wud. 'Pears like Ah's done los' my glasses."

A faint smile lighted up her face—a mere glimmer of a smile.

"Yes, Sam, I'll go," she said, glancing up into my eyes and holding out her hand. "You wish me to, do you not?"

"I think it will be fully as well. I have some doubts as to Sam, but can absolutely trust you. Besides there is nothing to be done here. I shall not use the boat, then if anyone does chance this way, they will find nothing disturbed. You still retain the pistol?"

She nodded her response and without delaying my departure longer, I lowered myself into the water and swam toward the opposite shore, creeping forth amid a tangle of roots, and immediately disappearing in the underbrush. Sam had already vanished, as I paused an instant to glance back, but she lingered at the edge of the wood to wave her hand. I found a rough passage for the first few rods, being obliged to almost tear a way through the close growth and unable to see a yard in advance. But this ended suddenly at the edge of the sand flat, with the converging waters of the two rivers visible just beyond. My view from here was narrowed, however, by high ridges on both sides, and, with a desire not to expose myself to any chance eye, I followed the line of forest until able to climb the slope, and thus attain the crest of the bluff.

From this vantage point the view was extensive, both up and down the big river, as well as across to the opposite bank. For miles nothing could escape my eyes, the mighty stream sweeping majestically past where I lay, liquid silver in the sunshine. Its tremendous volume had never so impressed me as in that moment of silent observation, nor had I ever realized before its sublime desolation. Along that entire surface but three objects met my gaze—a small island, green with trees, seemingly anchored just beyond the mouth of the Illinois; a lumbering barge almost opposite me, clearly outlined against the distant shore, and barely moving with the current; and far away below a thin smudge of smoke, arising from behind a headland, as though curling upward from the stack of some steamer. I watched this closely, until convinced the craft was bound down stream and moving swiftly. The smudge became a mere whisp and finally vanished entirely. I waited some time for the vessel to appear at the lower end of the bend, but it was then only a speck, scarcely distinguishable. I felt no doubt but what this was the stolen keel-boat, speeding toward St. Louis.

Armed, as I believed, with this knowledge that Kirby had actually fled, beyond any possibility of doing us any further injury, I did not hurry my return, but remained for some time on the bluff, watching those rushing waters, and endeavoring to outline some feasible plan for the coming night. With this final disappearance of the gambler we were left free to proceed, and it seemed to me with no great danger of arousing suspicion, so long as we exercised reasonable precautions. The girl to all appearances was white; no one would ever question that, particularly as she possessed sufficient intelligence and refinement to thus impress anyone she might meet, If necessary we might travel as man and wife, with Sam as our servant. Our means of travel would attract no particular attention in that country—the edge of the wilderness; it was common enough. This struck me as the most reasonable course to pursue—to work our way quietly up the Illinois by night, keeping close in shore to avoid any passing steamer, until we arrived close to Beardstown. There, if necessary, we might begin our masquerade, but it need not be a long one. Undoubtedly there were blacks in the town, both slaves and free negroes, with whom Sam could easily establish an acquaintance. By this means we would soon be able to identify that particular preacher into whose care I hoped to confide Rene. Of course, the girl might refuse to enter into the game, might decline to assume the role assigned her, however innocent I intended it to be—indeed, I felt convinced she would meet the suggestion with indignation. But why worry about that now? Let this be kept as a last resort. There was no necessity for me to even mention this part of my plan until after our approach to Beardstown; then the necessity of our going forward with it might be so apparent, she could not refuse to carry out her part. With this point thus settled in my own mind I felt ready to rejoin the others.

I must have been absent in the neighborhood of two hours, and they had returned to the bank of the creek some time in advance of me. As I appeared at the edge of the wood, Sam hailed, offering to row the boat across.

"All right," I replied, confident we were alone. "It will save me another wetting. You saw nothing?"

"No, sah; leastways, not much," busily fitting the oars into the row-locks. "We cud see up de Illinois mor'n ten mile. Ah reckon, but dar wan't no boat nowhar, 'cepting an o' scow tied up ter de bank."

"I thought so. The keel-boat has gone down the Mississippi."

"Yer done saw her, sah?"

"I saw her smoke; she was hidden by a big bend just below. Don't sit there staring at me—come across."

Rene greeted me with a smile, as I scrambled up on the slippery log, and asked a number of questions. I answered these as best I could and then explained, so far as I deemed it desirable, the general nature of the plans I had made. Both she and the listening negro in the boat below agreed that the safer course for us to choose led up the Illinois, because every mile traversed in that direction brought us nearer the goal sought, and among those who were the enemies of slavery. To proceed northward along the Mississippi would only serve to plunge us into an unbroken wilderness, already threatened by Indian war, while to venture down that stream meant almost certain capture. The Illinois route offered the only hope, and we decided to venture it, although Rene pleaded earnestly that she and the negro be permitted to go on alone. To this suggestion, however, I would not consent, and the girl finally yielded her reluctant permission for me to accompany them until she could be safely left in the care of white friends.

She took anxious part in our discussion, bravely endeavoring to hide the anguish she felt, yet I knew her real thought was elsewhere—with those two in Kirby's hands, already well on their way to St. Louis. Try as she would she was unable to banish from her mind the conception that she was largely to blame for their misfortune, or submerge the idea that it was cowardly in her to seek escape, while leaving them in such peril. I lingered, talking with her for some time after Sam had fallen asleep, yet the only result was the bringing of tears to her eyes and a reluctantly given pledge that she would do whatever I believed to be best and right. The girl was not wholly convinced by my argument, but no other course of action seemed open to her. She appeared so tired and worn that I left her at last in the little glade where we had found refuge, hoping she might fall asleep. I doubt if she did, although I dozed irregularly, my back against a tree, and it was already growing dusk when she came forth again from her retreat, and joined us in a hastily prepared meal.

Sam and I stowed away in the boat whatever provender remained, and I assisted her to a seat at the stern, wrapping a blanket carefully about her body, for the night air in those dank shadows already began to chill. I took possession of the oars myself, believing the negro would serve best as a lookout in the bow, and thus settled we headed the boat out through the tangle of trees toward the invisible river. The silent gloom of night shut about us in an impenetrable veil, and we simply had to feel our slow way to the mouth of the creek, Sam calling back directions, and pressing aside the branches that impeded progress. I sat facing the motionless girl, but could barely distinguish her shapeless form, wrapped in the blanket; and not once did her voice break the stillness. The night hung heavy; not even the gentle ripple of water disturbed the solemn silence of our slow progress.

Suddenly we shot out through the screen of concealing boughs into the broader stream beyond, and I struggled hastily to swerve the boat's bow upward against the current. The downward sweep of the water at this point was not particularly strong, the main channel being some distance further out, and we were soon making perceptible progress. The light here in the open was better, although dim enough still, and revealing little of our surroundings. All was wrapped in gloom along shore, and beyond the radius of a few yards no objects could be discerned. The river itself swept past us, a hidden mystery. Sam knelt on his knees, peering eagerly forward into the blackness, an occasional growl of his voice the only evidence of his presence. I doubt if I had taken a dozen strokes, my whole attention centered on my task, when the sudden rocking of the boat told me he had scrambled to his feet. Almost at the same instant my ears distinguished the sharp chugging of an engine straight ahead; then came his shout of alarm, "God, A'mighty! Dar's de keelboat, sah. Dey's goin' fer ter ram us!"

I twisted about in my seat, caught a vague glimpse of the advancing shadow, and leaped to my feet, an oar gripped in my hands. Scarcely was I poised to strike, when the speeding prow ripped into us, and I was catapulted into the black water.

CHAPTER XVIII

THE LOSS OF RENE

There was the echo of an oath, a harsh, cruel laugh, the crash of planking, a strange, half-human cry of fright from the negro—that was all. The sudden violence of the blow must have hurled me high into the air, for I struck the water clear of both boats, and so far out in the stream, that when I came again struggling to the surface, I was in the full sweep of the current, against which I had to struggle desperately. In the brief second that intervened between Sam's shout of warning, and the crash of the two boats, I had seen almost nothing—only that black, menacing hulk, looming up between us and the shore, more like a shadow than a reality. Yet now, fighting to keep my head above water, and not to be swept away, I was able to realize instantly what had occurred. I had been mistaken; Kirby had not fled down the river; instead he had craftily waited this chance to attack us at a disadvantage. Convinced that we would decide to make use of the rowboat, which he had left uninjured for that very purpose, and that we would venture forth just so soon as the night became dark enough, he had hidden the stolen craft in some covert along shore, to await our coming. Then he sprang on us, as the tiger leaps on his prey. He had calculated well, for the blunt prow of the speeding keel-boat had struck us squarely, crushing in the sides of our frail craft, and flinging me headlong.

What had become the fate of the others I could not for the moment determine. I could see little, with eyes scarcely above the surface, and struggling hard to breast the sweep of the current. The darkness shadowed everything, the bulk of the keel-boat alone appearing in the distance, and that, shapelessly outlined. The craft bore no light, and had it not been for a voice speaking, I doubt if I could have located even that. The rowboat could not be distinguished—it must have sunken, or else drifted away, a helpless wreck. The first sound my ears caught, echoing across the water, was an oath, and a question, "By God! a good job; do you see that fellow anywhere?"

"Naw," the response a mere growl. "He's a goner, I reckon; never knowed whut hit him, jedgin' frum the way he upended it."

"Well, then he isn't likely to bother us any more. Suppose he was the white man?"

"Sure he wus; it wus the nigger who was up ahead. We hit him, an' he dropped in 'tween ther boats, an' went down like a stone. He never yeeped but just onct, when I furst gripped ther girl. I don't reckon as she wus hurt et all; leastwise I never aimed fer ter hurt her none."

"Has she said anything?"

"Not a damned twitter; maybe she's fainted. I dunno, but that's ther way females do. What shall I do with the bird, Kirby?"

"Oh, hold on to her there awhile, long as she's quiet. I'm going to try the steam again, and get outside into the big river. Hell, man, but this hasn't been such a bad night's work. Now if we only make it to St. Louis, we'll have the laugh on Donaldson."

"I reckon he won't laugh much," with a chuckle. "It's cost him a valuable nigger."

"You mean Sam? Yes, that's so. But I'd like to know who that other fellow was—the white one."

"Him! oh, sum abolitionist likely; maybe one o' ol' Shrunk's gang. It's a damn good thing fer this kintry we got him, an' I ain't worryin' none 'bount any nigger-stealer. The boat must 'er gone down, I reckon; enyhow ther whol' side wus caved in. What's ther matter with yer engine?"

"It's all right now—keep your eyes peeled ahead."

The steam began to sizz, settling swiftly into a rhythmatic chugging, as the revolving wheel began to churn up the water astern. Confident of being safely hidden by the darkness, I permitted the current to bear me downward, my muscles aching painfully from the struggle, and with no other thought in my mind except to keep well out of sight of the occupants of the boat. To be perceived by them, and overtaken in the water, meant certain death, while, if they continued to believe that I had actually sunk beneath the surface, some future carelessness on their part might yield me an unexpected opportunity to serve Rene. The few words overheard had made sufficiently plain the situation. Poor Sam had already found freedom in death, crushed between the two colliding boats, but the girl had been grasped in time, and hauled uninjured aboard the heavier craft. This had been the object of the attack—to gain possession of her. Very evidently I had not been seen, at least not closely enough to be recognized by Kirby. In a measure this afforded me a decided advantage, provided we ever encountered each other again—and I meant that we should. The account between us was not closed by this incident; far from it. There in that black water, struggling to keep afloat, while being swept resistlessly out into the river, with no immediate object before me except to remain concealed by the veil of darkness, I resolved solemnly to myself that this affair should never end, until it was ended right. In that moment of decision I cared not at all for Rene Beaucaire's drop of negro blood, nor for the fact that she was a slave in her master's hands. Her appeal to me ignored all this. To my mind she was but a woman, a sweet, lovable, girlish woman, in the unrestrained power of a brute, and dependent alone on me for rescue. That was enough; I cared for nothing more.

The intense blackness hid me completely, as I held my head barely above the surface, no longer making any effort to stem the downward sweep of the stream. Conscious of being thus borne rapidly to the mouth of the river, my only endeavor was to keep afloat, and conserve my strength. The ceaseless noise of the engine told me accurately the position of the keel-boat, although, by this time, there was a stretch of rushing water between us which prevented me even seeing the hulking shadow of the craft. Judging from the sound, however, it was easy to determine that the heavy boat was traveling much faster than I, and was steadily passing me, close in against the dense shadow of the southern shore. With silent strokes I waited patiently, until the steady chugging of the engine grew faint in the distance, and then finally ceased entirely.

I was alone in the grasp of the waters, wrapped in the night silence, both shores veiled beneath the dense shadows; every dim outline had vanished, and I realized that the swift current had already swept me into the broad Mississippi. Uncertain in that moment which way to turn, and conscious of a strange lassitude, I made no struggle to reach land, but permitted myself to be borne downward in the grip of the water. Suddenly something drifted against my body, a black, ill-defined object, tossing about on the swell of the waves, and instinctively I grasped at it, recognizing instantly the shell of our wrecked boat. It was all awash, a great hole stove in its side well forward, and so filled with water the added weight of my body would have sunk it instantly. Yet the thing remained buoyant enough to float, and I clung to its stern, thankful even for this slight help.

There was no occasion for fear, although I became aware that the sweep of the current was steadily bearing us further out toward the center of the broad stream, and soon felt convinced that escape from my predicament would be impossible until after daylight. I could perceive absolutely nothing by which to shape a course, the sky above, and the water beneath being equally black. Not a star glimmered overhead, and no revealing spark of light appeared along either shore, or sparkled across the river surface. The only sound to reach my ears was the soft lapping of water against the side of the boat to which I clung. The loneliness was complete; the intense blackness strained my eyes, and I constantly felt as though some mysterious weight was dragging me down into the depths. Yet the struggle to keep afloat was no longer necessary, and my head sank in relief on the hands gripping at the boat's stern, while we floated silently on through the black mystery.

I know not how long this lasted—it might have been for hours, as I took no account of time. My mind seemed dazed, incapable of consecutive thought although a thousand illogical conceptions flashed through the brain, each in turn fading away into another, before I was fully aware of its meaning. Occasionally some far-off noise aroused me from lethargy, yet none of these could be identified, except once the mournful cry of a wild animal far away to the right; while twice we were tossed about in whirlpools, my grip nearly dislodged before the mad water swept us again into the sturdy current. I think we must have drifted close in toward the western shore, for once I imagined I could vaguely distinguish the tops of trees outlined against the slightly lighter sky. Yet this vision was so fleeting, I dare not loosen my hold upon the boat to swim in that direction; and, even as I gazed in uncertainty, the dim outline vanished as though it had been a dream, and we were again being forced outward into the swirling waters.

Suddenly the wrecked boat's bow grated against something immovable; then became fixed, the stern swinging slowly about, until it also caught, and I could feel the full volume of down-pouring water pressing against my body. It struck with such force I was barely able to work my way forward along the side of the half-submerged craft in an effort to ascertain what it was blocking our progress. Yet a moment later, even in that darkness, and obliged to rely entirely upon the sense of touch, the truth of my situation became clear. The blindly floating boat had drifted upon a snag, seemingly the major portion of a tree, now held by some spit of sand. I struggled vainly in an attempt to release the grip which, held us, but the force of the current had securely wedged the boat's bow beneath a limb, a bare, leafless tentacle, making all my efforts useless. The ceaseless water rippled about me, the only sound in the silent night, and despairing of any escape, I found a submerged branch on which to stand, gripped the boat desperately to prevent being swept away, and waited for the dawn.

It seemed a long while coming, and never did man gaze on a more dismal, ghastly scene than was revealed to me by those first gray gleams dimly showing in the far east. All about stretched utter desolation; wherever my eyes turned, the vista

Randall Parrish

was the same—a wide stretch of restless, brown water surging and leaping past, bounded by low-lying shores, forlorn and deserted. There was no smoke, no evidence of life anywhere visible, no sign of habitation; all was wilderness. The snag on which I rested was nearly in the center of the great river, an ugly mass of dead wood, sodden with water, forking out of the stream, with grotesque limbs thrust up into the air. The force of the current had driven the nose of the boat so firmly beneath one branch as to sink it below the surface, making it impossible to be freed. In the dull light I struggled hopelessly to extricate the craft, my feet slipping on the water-soaked log. Twice I fell into the stream, barely able to clamber back again, but my best efforts were without results. The increase in light gave me by this time a wider view of my surroundings, but brought with it no increase of hope. I was utterly alone, and only by swimming could I attain either bank.

How far I had aimlessly drifted down stream during the night was a mere matter of conjecture. I possessed no knowledge of where I was. No familiar object along shore afforded any clue as to my position, and I could not even determine which bank offered me the greater chance of assistance. Each appeared about equally bare and desolate, entirely devoid of promise. However, I chose the west shore for my experiment, as the current seemed less strong in that direction, and was about to plunge in, determined to fight a way across, when my eyes suddenly detected a faint wreath of smoke curling up into the pale sky above a headland far to the southward. As I stared at this it became black and distinct, tossed about in the wind. I watched intently, clinging to my support, scarcely trusting my eyesight, while that first wisp deepened into a cloud, advancing slowly toward me. There was no longer doubt of what it was—unquestionably some steamer was pushing its course up stream. Even before my ears could detect the far-off chug of the engine, the boat itself rounded the sharp point of the headland, and came forth into full view, heading out toward the middle of the river in a search for deeper water.

It was an unusually large steamboat for those days, a lower river packet I guessed, with two funnels painted yellow, and a high pilot house, surmounted by a huge brazen eagle. At first, approaching me, bow on, I could perceive but little of its dimensions, nor gain clear view of the decks, but when it veered slightly these were revealed, and I had a glimpse of a few figures grouped forward, the great wheel astern splashing the water, and between a long row of windows reflecting the glare of the early sun. Even as I gazed at this vision a flag crept up the slender staff at the bow, and reaching the top rippled out in the crisp breeze. A moment later I deciphered the lettering across the white front of the pilot house, *Adventurer, of Memphis.*

Indifferent at that moment as to where the approaching boat might be bound, or my reception on board; desirous only of immediate escape from my unfortunate predicament, I managed to remove my sodden coat, and furiously wave it in the air as a signal. At first there was no response, no evidence that I had even been seen; then slowly, deliberately, the steamer changed its course, and came straight up the river, struggling against the full strength of the current. I could see a man step from out the pilot house onto the upper forward deck, lean out over the rail, and speak to the others below, pointing toward me across the water. A half-dozen grouped themselves at the bow, ready for action, their figures growing more sharply defined as the struggling craft approached. The man above stood shading his eyes with one hand, and gesticulating with the other. Finally the sound of his voice reached me.

"Hey! you out there! If you can swim, jump for it. I'm not

going to run into that snag."

I measured the distance between us with my eye, and leaped as far out as possible, striking out with lusty strokes. The swift current swung me about like a chip, and swept me downward in spite of every struggle. I was squarely abreast of the boat, already caught in her suction, and being drawn straight in toward her wheel, when the looped end of a flying noose struck my shoulder.

"Keep your head, lad!" roared out a hoarse voice. "Hang on now, an' we'll get yer."

It was such a rush, such a breathless, desperate struggle, I can scarcely recall the details. All I really remember is that I gripped the rope, and clung; was dragged under again and again; was flung against the steamer's side, seemingly losing all consciousness, yet dimly realizing that outstretched hands grasped me, and lifted me up by main strength to the narrow footway, dropping me there in the pool of water oozing from my clothes. Someone spoke, lifting my head on his arm, in answer to a hail from above.

"Yes, he's all right, sir; just a bit groggy. What'll we do with him?"

"Bring him along up to Haines' cabin, and get him the old suit in my room. You might warm him up with a drink first. You tend to it, Mapes."

The liquor I drank out of a bottle burnt like fire, but brought me new strength, so that, with Mapes' help, I got to my feet, and stared about at the group of faces surrounding us. They were those of typical river men, two negroes and three whites, ragged, dirty, and disreputable. Mapes was so bushily bearded, that about all I could perceive of his face was the eyes, yet these were intelligent, and I instantly picked him out as being the mate.

"How long yer all bin roostin' on thet snag?" he questioned, evidently somewhat amused. "Dem me, stranger, if I ever see thet sorter thing done afore."

"I was caught there last night," I answered, unwilling to say more, "Boat got snagged in the dark, and went down."

"Live round yere, I reckon?"

"No; just floating. Came down the Illinois. Where is this steamer bound?"

"Hell alone knows," dryly. "Yeller Banks furst, enyhow; we're loaded with supplies."

"Supplies! For Yellow Banks?" in surprise. "Why; what's going on there? My friend, there aren't ten families within a hundred miles of that place."

Mapes laughed, his mouth opening like a red gash, exhibiting a row of yellow fangs.

"No, I reckon not; but thar's a hell ov a lot o' fellers thar whut ain't families, but kin eat. Didn't yer know, pardner, thar's a right smart war on? thet the Illinoy militia is called out, an' is a marchin' now fer Yeller Banks? They're liable fer ter be thar too afore ever this damn scow makes it, if we hav' ter stop an' pick eny mor' blame fools outer the river. Come on, let's go up."

"Wait a minute. This is an Indian war? Black Hawk has broken loose?"

"Sure; raised perticular hell. We heerd down et Saint Louee he'd killed 'bout a hundred whites, an' burned sum ov 'em—ther ol' devil."

"And where is he now?"

"Dunno; never wus up in yer afore. We bin runnin' 'tween Saint Louee an' New Orleans, 'till the Gov'ment took us. Maybe the captain kin tell yer—sumwhar up Rock River, I reckon, wharever that is."

We climbed the steep steps to the upper deck, and were met at the head of the ladder by the captain, evidently desirous of looking me over. He was a solidly-built individual, wearing white side-whiskers, and a bulbous nose, and confronted me not altogether pleasantly.

"All right, are you? Water pretty cold yet, I reckon. Been sticking on that snag for long?"

"Several hours; but my boat was wrecked before we lodged there."

The captain laughed, and winked aside at the mate.

"Seems to be a mighty populous river up this way, hey, Mapes?" he remarked genially. "Castaways round every bend."

"What do you mean? Have you picked up others?"

"Certainly have. Hit a keel-boat twenty miles below."

"A keel-boat, operated by steam?"

"Couldn't say as to that. Was it, Mapes? The craft had gone

down when I got on deck. Had four aboard, but we got 'em all off, an' stowed 'em back there in the texas. You better get along now, and shuck those wet clothes."

CHAPTER XIX

ON BOARD THE *ADVENTURER*

The captain turned rather sharply away, and I was thrust through an open cabin door by the grasp of the mate before I could really sense the true meaning of this unexpected news. Mapes paused long enough to gruffly indicate a coarse suit of clothes draped over a stool, and was about to retire without further words, when I recovered sufficiently from the shock to halt him with a question.

"I suppose you saw those people picked up from the keel-boat?"

"Sure; helped pull 'em aboard. A damned queer combination, if you ask me; two nigger wenches, Joe Kirby, an' a deputy sheriff from down Saint Louee way."

"Two women, you say? both negresses?"

"Well, thet whut Joe sed they wus, an' I reckon he knew; an' neither ov 'em put up a holler whin he sed it. However one ov 'em looked ez white as enybody I ever saw. The deputy he tol' ther same story—sed they wus both slaves thet Kirby got frum an ol' plantation down below; som' French name, it wus. Seems like the two wenches hed run away, an' the deputy hed caught 'em, an' wus a takin' 'em back. Kirby cum 'long ter help, bein' as how they belonged ter him."

"You knew Kirby then?"

"Hell, ov course. Thar ain't many river men who don't, I reckon. What is it to you?"

"Nothing; it sounds like a strange story, that's all. I want to get this wet stuff off, and will be out on deck presently."

I was shivering with the cold, and lost no time shifting into the warm, dry clothing provided, spreading out my own soaked garments over the edge of the lower bunk, but careful first to remove my packet of private papers, which, wrapped securely in oiled silk, were not even damp. It was a typical steamer bunkhouse in which I found myself, evidently the abiding place of some one of the boat's petty officers, exceedingly cramped as to space, containing two narrow berths, a stool and a washstand, but with ample air and light. The slats across the window permitted me a view of the river, and the low-lying shore beyond, past which we were slowly moving. The sun was just rising above the eastern horizon, and the water reflected a purple tinge. With no desire to return immediately to the deck, I seated myself on the stool to consider the situation.

Fate had played a strange trick, and I knew not how best to turn it to advantage. One thing only was clear; whatever was to be accomplished, I would have to do it alone—nowhere could I turn for help. In the first place Kirby undoubtedly had the law with him, and besides was among friends—those who would naturally believe him, and were loyal to the institution of slavery. The very fact that this was a Memphis boat we were on precluded any possibility that the crew would sympathize with a nigger-stealer. Nor could I anticipate any assistance from without. Steamboats were few and far between on these northern waters, and at this time, if the report of war was true, everything afloat would be headed up stream, laden with troops and provisions. That the report was true I had no doubt. The probability of an outbreak was known before I left Fort Armstrong; the crisis had come earlier than expected, that was all.

This, then, was the situation—through an odd intervention of Providence here we were all together on this steamer, which was steadily churning its way northward, every turn of the wheel bearing us deeper into the wilderness. The chances were that we should thus be aboard for several days; certainly until we encountered some other boat bound down stream, which would accept us as passengers. Meanwhile what should I do? How escape observation? How reach Rene, without encountering Kirby? The answer was not an easy one. The deputy would not know me, for I had never been seen by him. Kirby believed me dead, yet might recognize me in spite of that conviction if we met face to face. Still, would he? The daring hope that he might not came to me in a flash. Might it not be possible to so disguise myself as to become unnoticeable? I sprang up to stare at my features in the small mirror hanging over the washstand. The face which confronted me in surprise was almost a strange one even to my eyes. Instead of the smart young soldier, smoothly shaven, with closely-trimmed hair, and rather carefully attired, as I had appeared on board the *Warrior*, the glass reflected a bearded face, the skin visibly roughened and reddened by exposure, the hair ragged and uncombed. Even to my view there remained scarcely a familiar feature—the lack of razor and shears, the exposure to sun and water, the days of sickness and neglect, had all helped to transform me into a totally different-appearing person from what I had formerly been; the officer and gentleman had, by the mystery of environment, been changed into the outward semblance of a river roustabout. Nor was this all. The new character was emphasized by the clothes I wore—far too large to fit, also the texture and color, not to mention the dirt and grease, speaking loudly of a rough life, and the vicissitudes of poverty. The metamorphosis was complete; so complete that I laughed aloud, assured by that one glance that the gambler, confident that I was dead, would never by any possibility recognize me in this guise, or while habilitated in such nondescript garments. Unless some happening should expose me, some occurrence arouse suspicion, I felt convinced of my ability to even slouch past him on deck unobserved, and unrecognized.

But the girl—Rene? And so this was how I had appeared to her. No wonder she questioned me; doubted my first explanation. The thought that my personal appearance was so disreputable had never occurred to me before, and even then, staring into that glass, I could scarcely bring myself to acknowledge the truth. I had first approached her confident that my appearance as a gentleman would awaken her trust; I had felt myself to be a most presentable young man in whom she must instantly repose faith. Yet, this had not been true at all—instead I came to her with the outward bearing of a worthless vagabond, a stubble-bearded outcast. And yet she had trusted me; would trust me again. More; she could never be deceived, or fail to recognize my presence aboard if she had the freedom of the deck. Kirby might be deceived, but not Rene. Still she was a woman of quick wit; once recovered from her first surprise at thus encountering me, neither by word or look would she ever betray her knowledge. If I could only plan to meet with her first alone, the peril of her recognition would not be extreme.

But I must also figure upon the other woman. Who could she be? Not Eloise Beaucaire surely, for the mate had only mentioned one of the two as being sufficiently white to be noticeable. That one would surely be Rene, and it was scarcely probable that Eloise, with no drop of negro blood in her veins, could appear colored. Perhaps this second woman was Delia, the quadroon mother. But if so, how did she chance to fall alone into Kirby's clutches? Was she aboard the keel-boat, locked below in the cabin, when it rammed into us? If she had been captured at Shrunk's camp during their murderous raid, what had become of her companion? Where was Eloise Beaucaire? The harder I sought to straighten out this mystery the more involved it became. I knew so little of the facts, there was nothing I could argue from. All that remained was for me to go forward blindly, trusting implicitly to the god of luck.

With every additional glance at the face reflected by the mirror, my confidence strengthened in the ability to encounter Kirby, and pass unrecognized. Convinced as he undoubtedly was of my death beneath the black waters of the river he could not possibly imagine my presence aboard the *Adventurer*, while my personal appearance was so utterly changed as to suggest to his mind no thought of familiarity. The conditions were all in my favor. I was smiling grimly at this conceit, well pleased at the chance thus afforded me, when the stateroom door was suddenly flung open, and the hairy face of the mate thrust within.

"I reckon yer better tote them wet duds down ter the boiler room," he said, gruffly, "an' then git sum grub. Likely 'nough yer wound't mind eatin' a bit. Be yer a river man?"

"I've never worked on a steamboat, if that is what you mean."

"No; well I reckoned not, but the captain he thought maybe yer had. I tol' him yer didn't talk like no steamer hand. Howsumever we're almightly short o' help aboard, an' maybe yer'd like a job ter help pay yer way?"

My fingers involuntarily closed on some loose gold pieces in my pocket, but a sudden thought halted me. Why not? In what better way could I escape discovery? As an employe of the boat I could go about the decks unsuspected, and unnoticed. Kirby would never give me a second thought, or glance, while the opportunity thus afforded of speaking to Rene, and being of service to her, would be immeasurably increased. I withdrew my hand, swiftly deciding my course of action.

"I suppose I might as well earn a bit," I admitted, hesitatingly. "Only I had about decided I'd enlist, if the war was still going on when we got up there."

"That'll be all right. We'll keep yer busy til' then, enyhow. Go on down below now, an' eat, an' when yer git through, climb up the ladder, an' report ter me. What'll I call yer?"

"Steve."

"Steve—hey; sorter handy man, ain't yer?"

"Well, I've done a little of everything in my time. I'm not afraid to work."

During most of the remaining hours of the morning the mate kept me employed below, in company with a number of others of the crew, in sorting over the miscellaneous cargo, which had evidently been very hastily loaded. I began to think that I had made a wrong choice, and that, in the guise of a passenger, with the freedom of the upper decks, my chances for observation would have been decidedly better. The work was hard, and dirty, and, after a few hours of it, I must have looked my assumed part to perfection. However,

Randall Parrish

it was now too late to assert myself, and I could only trust blindly to Fate to furnish me with the information I needed. Mapes merely glanced in upon us occasionally, leaving the overseeing of the gang to a squatty, red-faced white man, whose profanity never ceased. There were ten of us in the gang, several being negroes, and I was unable to extract any information of value from those I attempted to converse with. One had assisted in rescuing the party from the wrecked keel-boat, and had seen the two women, as they came aboard under the glare of a torch, but his description of their appearance was far from clear, and as to what had become of them since, he knew nothing.

As we worked in the heat and dirt below, the steamer steadily plowed its way up stream, meeting with no vessel bound down, or even a drifting barge; nor did I perceive the slightest sign of any settlement along the banks. Our course ran zig-zag from shore to shore in an endeavor to follow the main channel, and progress was slow, the wheelsman evidently not being well acquainted with the stream. The cry of a leadsman forward was almost constant. Once we tied up against the western bank for nearly an hour to remove a bit of driftwood from the wheel, and I heard voices speaking above on the upper deck as though passengers were grouped along the rail. I obtained no glimpse of these, however, although one of the negroes informed me that there were several army officers on board. The possibility that some of these might recognize me was not a pleasant thought. I saw nothing of the captain, but heard him shouting orders to the men engaged tinkering at the paddle-wheel. The overseer gave me a hat which added little to my personal appearance, and by the time we were called to knock off for the noon meal, I was thoroughly tired, and disgusted, feeling as much a roustabout as I certainly looked.

The meal was served on an unplaned plank, the ends resting

on kegs in front of the boilers. The unwashed gang simply helped themselves, and then retired to any convenient spot where they chose to eat. I discovered a fairly comfortable seat on a cracker box, and was still busily munching away on the coarse, poorly-cooked food, when Mapes, prowling about, chanced to spy me among the shadows.

"Hullo; is that you, Steve?" he asked, gruffly. "Well, when yer git done eatin' I got another job fer yer on deck. Yer hear me?"

I signified that I did, and indeed was even then quite ready to go, my heart throbbing at this opportunity to survey other sections of the boat. I followed him eagerly up the ladder, and ten minutes later was busily employed with scrubbing brush, and a bucket of water, in an endeavor to improve the outward appearance of the paint of the upper deck. Nothing occurred about me for some time, the passengers being at dinner in the main cabin. I could hear the rattle of dishes, together with a murmur of conversation, and even found a partially opened skylight through which I could look down, and distinguish a small section of the table. Kirby was not within range of my vision, but there were several officers in fatigue uniforms, none of their faces familiar, together with one or two men in civilian dress, I judged there were no women present, as I saw none, or heard any sound of a feminine voice. The principal topic of conversation appeared to be in connection with the war, and was largely monopolized by a red-faced captain, who had once been a visitor in Black Hawk's camp, and who loudly asserted that the gathering volunteers would prove utterly useless in such a campaign, which must eventually be won by the superiority of regular troops. A hot-headed civilian opposite him at the table argued otherwise, claiming that the militia was largely composed of old Indian fighters, who would give a good account of themselves. The discussion became noisy, and apparently endless, interesting me not at all. Once I detected Kirby's voice chime in mockingly, but altogether the talk brought me no information, and possessed little point.

I had moved away, and was engaged busily scraping at the dingy paint of the pilot house, when a negro, evidently a cook from his dress, came up from the lower deck, bearing a tray well-laden with food in one hand, and disappeared aft. He did not even notice my presence, or glance about, but I instantly shrank back out Of sight, for I became immediately conscious that someone was closely following him. This second man proved to be one of the fellows in civilian clothing I had previously noticed at the table below, a tall, sallow individual, attired in a suit of brown jeans, his lean, cracker face ornamented by a grizzled bunch of chin-whiskers.

"Yer wait a minute thar, Jim," he called out, "'til I unlock that thar dore. I ain't ther kind thet takes chances with no nigger."

I recognized the peculiar voice instantly, for I had listened to that lazy drawl before while hidden in the darkness beneath the Beaucaire veranda—the fellow was Tim, the deputy sheriff from St. Louis. The negro rested his tray on the rail, while the white man fumbled through his pockets for a key, finally locating it, and inserting the instrument into the lock of the second cabin from the stern. It turned hard, causing some delay, and a muttered curse, but finally yielded, and the door was pushed partly ajar. I heard no words exchanged with anyone within, but the negro pushed the tray forward without entering, sliding it along the deck, while Tim, evidently satisfied that his charges were quite safe, promptly reclosed and locked the door, returning the key to the security of his pocket. After staring a moment over the rail at the shore past which we were gliding, he disappeared after the negro down the ladder. I was again alone on the upper deck, except for the wheelsman in the pilot house, yet in that broad daylight I hesitated to act on my first impulse. Eager as I certainly was too make the poor girl aware of my presence on board, the chance of being seen, and my purpose suspected by others, restrained me. Besides, as yet, I had no plan of rescue; nothing to suggest.

Even as I hesitated, industriously scrubbing away at the paint, Kirby and the captain appeared suddenly, pausing a moment at the head of the ladder in friendly conversation. Parting at last, with a hearty laugh over some joke exchanged between them, the latter ascended the steps to the pilot house, while the gambler turned aft, still smiling, a cigar between his lips. I managed to observe that he paused in front of the second cabin, as though listening for some sound within, but made no attempt to enter, passing on to the door beyond, which was unlocked. He must have come to the upper deck on some special mission, for he was out of my sight scarcely a moment, returning immediately to the deck below. This occurrence merely served to make clearer in my mind the probable situation—the after-cabin was undoubtedly occupied by Kirby, perhaps in company with the deputy; while next to them, securely locked away, and helpless to escape, were confined the two slave women. In order to reach them I must operate under the cover of darkness, and my only hope of being free to work, even then, lay in the faith that the gambler might become so involved in a card game below as to forget his caution. So far as Tim was concerned I felt perfectly capable of outwitting him; but Kirby was dangerous.

CHAPTER XX

THE STORY OF ELSIE CLARK

The next two hours dragged dreadfully slow, in spite of my pretense at steady work, and the fact that my thoughts were continuously occupied. The shores past which we glided were low and monotonous, while the river was but a tawny sweep of unoccupied water. We were already well above the region of white settlements, in a land beautiful, but uncultivated. The upper deck remained practically deserted, and I was encouraged to observe, by glancing through the skylight, that a stubborn game of poker was being indulged in at the cabin table below. The amount of stakes visible, as well as some of the language reaching me, accounted for the absence of passengers outside, even those not playing circling the table in interest. The deputy, however, was not among these, and occasionally he wandered up the ladder, and patrolled the deck, although making no effort to invade the locked stateroom. Apparently he was merely performing a duty assigned him by Kirby, but possessed no fear that his prisoners would escape. The last time he appeared more at ease, and sat down on a stool close to the rail, smoking his pipe, and staring out glumly at the water. His position was within a foot or two of the closed door, and I ventured to work my passage along the front of the cabin, hoping to attract his attention. Perhaps he was lonely, for he finally observed me in my humble capacity, and broke the silence with a question.

"Hav' yer ever bin up this way afore?"

I paused in my work, and straightened up stiffly.

"Onct," making the fault in pronunciation prominent.

"Wal', how fur is it then, ter thet damn Yellow Banks?"

"I dunno 'sackly in miles," I acknowledged doubtfully. "Everything looks just 'bout alike 'long yere," and I took a squint at the bank, as though endeavoring a guess. "I reckon maybe it'll be 'bout twenty-four hours' steamin' yet—morn'n thet, likely, if we got ter tie up much 'long shore. Are yer goin' fer ter jine the army?"

"Whut, me jine the army?" he laughed as though at a good joke. "Hell, no; I'm a sorter sheriff down Saint Louee way, an' all I want fer ter do now is just git back thar as fast as God Almighty'll let me."

"I see, yer a headin' in the wrong direction. I reckon yer mus' be one o' them parties whut we done yanked outer thet keelboat down river las' night, aint yer?"

"I reckon I wus; whut of it?"

"Nuthin' 'tall; 'tain't no manner o' 'count ter me, fur as thet goes," and I got down on my knees again to resume scrubbing. "All I wus goin' fer ter ask yer wus—wan't thar a couple o' womin 'long with ye? Whut's becom' o' them? I ain't seed hide ner hair ov either since they cum aboard."

I did not glance around, yet knew that Tim spat over the rail, and stroked his chin-beard reflectively, after looking hard at me.

"They'se both of 'em niggers," he said, evidently persuaded my question was prompted only by curiosity. "They belong ter Joe Kirby, an' we got 'em locked up."

"That's whut yer way up yere fur, hey? Goin' ter take 'em back down river ter Saint Louee, I reckon?"

"Furst boat thet cums 'long. They skipped out night afore las', but we cotched 'em all right. Yer goin' back on this steamer?"

"Not me; I'm goin' fer ter enlist whin we git ter Yellow Banks. Thar's a heap more fun in thet, then steam-boatin'."

We continued to talk back and forth for some time but to little purpose, although I endeavored to lead the conversation so as to learn more definitely the exact situation of the two prisoners. Whether Tim was naturally cautious, or had been warned against talking with strangers by Kirby, I do not know, but, in spite of all my efforts, he certainly proved extremely close-mouthed, except when we drifted upon other topics in which I felt no interest. He was not suspicious of me, however, and lingered on in his seat beside the rail, expectorating into the running water below, until Mapes suddenly appeared on deck, and compelled me to resume work. The two disappeared together, seeking a friendly drink at the bar, leaving me alone, and industriously employed in brightening up the front of the cabin. I was still engaged at this labor, not sorry to be left alone, when a cautious whisper, sounding almost at my very ear, caused me to glance up quickly, startled at the unexpected sound. I could perceive nothing, although I instantly felt convinced that whispering voice had issued from between the narrow slats defending the small stateroom window. No one was in sight along the deck, and the rag I was wielding hung limp in my hand.

"Who was it that spoke?" I ventured, the words barely audible.

"Ah did; the prisoner in the stateroom. Have both those men gone?"

"Yes; I am here alone. You are a woman? You are Rene Beaucaire?"

"No, Ah am not her; but Ah thought from the way yer questioned thet brute, yer was interested. Ah know whar Rene Beaucaire is."

"You know? Tell me first, who you are?"

"Elsie Clark. Ah am a mulatto, a free negress. Ah bin helpin' Massa Shrunk, an' a cookin' fer him. Yer know whut it wus whut happened down thar?"

"I know part of it, at least—that Shrunk has been killed. I am not a steamboatman. I was at Shrunk's cabin, and found the bodies. Tell me exactly what occurred there."

"Whut's yer name?"

"Steven Knox; I am a soldier. Rene must have told you about me."

"No, sah; she never done tol' me nuthin'. Ah didn't much mor'n see her enyhow, fur as thet goes."

"Not see her! Then she is not confined there with you?"

"Wiv me? Dar ain't nobody confined yer wiv me. Ah just ain't set eyes on nobody since Ah done got on board, 'cept de cook. Ah reckon dem white men aim fer ter tote me soufe, an' sell me fer a slave; dat's why Ah's locked up yere dis way. But Ah sure does know whar dis yer Rene Beaucaire wus."

"Where?"

"Wal', sah, it wus 'bout like dis. Long 'bout three o'clock in de manning, ol' Bill Sikes cum up frum de lower pint, a drivin' his kivered wagon, an' made Massa Shrunk git up out er bed fer ter git him anodder team o' hosses. Den dey done routed me up fer ter hustle up sum grub."

"Sikes; who is Sikes?"

"He lives down by de lower pike, Sah; he's an abolitionist, sah."

"Oh, I see; he and Shrunk worked together. He helped with the runaway slaves."

"Yas, sah. Ah's bin called up thet way afore. So Ah just nat'larly went ter work cookin', an' purty soon dey all ov 'em cum stragglin' in ter de cabin fer ter eat. Dar was four ov 'em, sah," her voice a husky whisper. "Bill Sikes, totin' a gun in his han', a free nigger whut dey called Pete, an' two wimin. Furst like, bein' Ah wus right busy, Ah didn't take no heed ov dere faces, fer dey wus all muffled 'round like; but dey hed fer ter unwrap dem veils fore dey cud eat—tho' de Lord knows dey didn't no one ov 'em eat much. De bigger one was a quadroon, maybe 'bout forty years ol', an' de odder she wan't much more'n a gal; an' dar wan't nuthin' ov de nigger 'bout her, 'cept it mought be de hair, an' de eyes—dem was sure black 'nough. Ah just nat'larly felt mighty sorry fer her, fer she done cried all de time, an' cudn't eat nuthin'."

"You learned who they were? how they came there?"

"Course Ah did. Sikes he 'splained all 'bout 'em ter Massa Shrunk, an' Ah heerd whut he sed. Ah wus a waitin' on 'em. Seems like, dey hed run off frum de Beaucaire plantation, sumwhar down ribber on de Missouri side, 'cause ol' Beaucaire hed died, an' dey wus goin' fer ter be sold down soufe. De free nigger he wus helpin' fer ter git 'em away in his boat. De way I heerd 'em tell, dey got snagged in de dark, an' den drifted ashore at de lower pine. Wanderin' 'round, dey stumbled on Sikes, an', soon as he heard de story, he just hitched up, an' drove over whar we were. Took him 'bout three hours, Ah reckon, an' 'long de road one ov his hosses wint lame."

"And—and what then?" I asked breathlessly, glancing about to assure myself no one had appeared on deck, as she paused. "They got away?"

"'Cept fer de free nigger, de rest ov 'em started cross kintry fer Beardstown, sah. De nigger Pete, he didn't go, fer he'd made up his min' fer ter git bac' hom' ter ol' Missurry de furst chanst he got. We all ov us helped fer ter put 'em in de wagon, hid undeh a lot o' truck, an' den Sikes he done drove 'em out thro' de bluffs. Ah done walked wif de gal, an' she tol' mor' 'bout herself, an' whar she cum frum; an' dat wus her name, sah."

"Her name? What name?"

"Rene Beaucaire; de quadroon woman, she wus her mother."

I could scarcely voice my surprise, the quick throbbing of my heart threatening to choke me.

"She claimed that name? She actually told you she was Rene Beaucaire?"

"She sure did. Why? Wan't thet her name?"

"I do not know," I confessed. "I had supposed I had met such a person, but if what you tell me is true, I was mistaken. Everything has become confused. Perhaps I shall understand better, if you go on. What happened after they left?"

"Why, we just went back ter bed, an' 'long 'bout daylight, I reckon, sum fellars cum ashore off a steamboat, an' done broke inter de house; muster bin a dozen, er mor', white men, a cussin' an' swearin', an' sayin' dey wus a huntin' dem thar Beaucaire niggers. We never done heerd 'em till dey bust in de dore. One ob dem he knocked me down, an' den Ah saw Massa Shrunk kill one, afore dey got him. Ah don't know just whut did cum ob de free nigger; Ah reckon maybe he run away. Dar's a fellar on board yere whut killed Massa Shrunk; an' he's de same one whut made me cum 'long wid him."

"You mean the deputy sheriff? the man with the chin-whiskers?"

"No, sah. Ah don't mean him. He wus thar all right, but Ah never saw him hit nobody. It wus another fellar, a smooth-faced man, sorter tall like, all dressed up, an' who never talks much."

"Kirby—Joe Kirby, a river gambler."

"Dat's de name—Kurby. Wal', he's de one whut wus lookin' fer dis yere gal, Rene Beaucaire. He wanted her pow'ful bad. Dey hunted all 'round fer ter git hol' her, cussin' an' threatenin', an' a haulin' me round; but 'twan't no sorter use.

So finally dey took me 'long ter a boat in de crick—a keel-boat, run by steam. Most de odder men disappeared; Ah never did know whar dey went, but dis yere Kurby, an' de man wif de chin-whiskers, dey done shut me up in de cabin. Ah don't know much whut did happen after dat, till 'bout de time de steamboat done hit us; an' 'bout de next thing Ah wus yanked up yere on deck."

"But there was another woman on the keel-boat when it was sunk—a prisoner also. Surely you must have seen her," I insisted.

"Ah saw her—yas," eagerly. "But Ah don't know who she wus, sah, nor whar she ever cum frum."

"Then she is not there with you?"

"No, sah; Ah's yere all 'lone. Ah reckon, tho', she sure mus' be on board sumwhar. All what Ah does know is, dat de gal called Rene Beaucaire sure ain't on board; fer she, an' her mah, am at Beardstown long fore dis, an' a headin' right smart for Canady; while Ah's headin' fer down soufe. Ah's a free nigger, an' dey's kidnapped me. Ah's just told yer all dis, Mister White Man, 'cause you's a frien' ob de Beaucaires— yer wus, wusn't yer?"

"Yes," I said soberly, "I am; and, if I can find any chance to help you, I am going to do it, Elsie. Be careful now; don't talk any more—the captain is just coming out of the pilot house."

As greatly as this brief, hastily whispered conversation had served to clear up certain puzzling matters in my mind, the total result of the information thus imparted by Elsie Clark only rendered the situation more complex and puzzling. Evidently the other prisoner had not been confined on the upper deck, but had been more securely hidden away below, where her presence on board would better escape detection. For what purpose? A sinister one, beyond all doubt—the expression of a vague fear in Kirby's heart that, through some accident, her identity might be discovered, and his plans disarranged. I was beginning to suspect I might not have rightly gauged those plans. The first suspicion which assailed me was whether or not the man himself had already determined that his prisoner was not merely a helpless slave in his hands, to be dealt with as he pleased under the law, but a free white woman. If so, and he still desired to keep control, he would naturally guard her all the more closely from either speech, or contact with others. His only safety would lie in such action. I had heard him express boastingly his original design relative to both these girls; I comprehended the part he intended Eloise Beaucaire to play in his future, and realized that he cared more to gain possession of her, to get her into his power, than he did to obtain control of the slave. This knowledge helped me to understand the predicament which this revelation put him into, and how desperately he would strive to retain the upper hand. If, in very truth, she was Judge Beaucaire's white daughter, and could gain communication with others of her class, bringing to them proof of her identity, there would be real men enough on board the *Adventurer* to rally to her support. Those army officers alone would be sufficient to overcome any friends Kirby might call upon, and in that case the gambler's house of cards would fall instantly into ruins. We were already sailing through free territory, and even now he held on to his slaves rather through courtesy than law. Once it was whispered that one of these slaves was white, the daughter of a wealthy planter, stolen by force, the game would be up.

But would she ever proclaim her right to freedom? It seemed like a strange question, and yet there remained a reason still for silence. If she was indeed Eloise Beaucaire—and even as to this I was not as yet wholly convinced—she had deliberately assumed to be Rene, doing so for a specific purpose—that object being to afford the other an opportunity for escape. She, conscious of her white blood, her standing of respectability, had felt reasonably safe in this escapade; had decided that no great harm could befall her through such a masquerade for a few days. If worst came to worst she could openly proclaim her name at any moment, assured of protection at the hands of anyone present, and thus defy Kirby. I recalled to memory their conversation, which I had overheard in the library at Beaucaire; and I understood now what had easily led to all this—her belief, from Kirby's own words, that nothing further could be done until the necessary legal papers had been served on her in person. This faith, coupled with the mysterious disappearance of Rene and the quadroon mother, and her being mistaken for the absent girl, all led her inevitably to the conclusion that she must continue to act out the part assumed until those others were safe beyond pursuit. With quick wit she had grasped this chance for service; had encouraged Kirby to believe her the slave, and then, in sudden desperation, had been driven into trusting me in an effort to keep out of his hands.

This theory seemed possible enough; yet what she might decide to do now, under the stress of these new conditions, was no less a problem. She possessed no knowledge regarding the others, such as I did. She had no means of guessing that the two others had already actually escaped, and were even then beyond the power of their pursuers. Her one thought still would be the continuation of deceit, the insistence that she was Rene. To do otherwise would defeat her purpose, make her previous sacrifice useless. She must still fight silently for delay. Why, she had not so much as trusted me. From the very beginning she had encouraged me in the belief that she was a negress, never once arousing the faintest suspicion in my mind. Not by the slip of the tongue, or the glance of an eye, had she permitted either of us to forget the barrier of race between. Nothing then, I was convinced, short of death or disgrace, could ever compel her to confess the truth yet. Kirby might suspect, might fear, but he had surely never learned who she was from her lips—that she was Eloise Beaucaire.

And was she? Was the proof of her identity, as yet produced, the story of Elsie Clark, sufficiently satisfactory to my own mind? It became more so as I thought, as I remembered. Every link in the chain of evidence seemed to fall noiselessly into its place, now that I compared my own experience with the details furnished me by the mulatto girl. No other conclusion appeared possible, or probable; no other solution fully met the facts in the case. The conviction that this young woman was white, educated, refined, the daughter of good blood—no fleeing negress, cursed with the black stain of an alien race, a nameless slave—brought to me a sudden joy in discovery I made no attempt to conceal. "Eloise Beaucaire, Eloise Beaucaire"—the name repeated itself on my lips, as though it were a refrain. I knew instantly what it all meant— that some divine, mysterious hand had led from the very hour of my leaving Fort Armstrong, and would continue to lead until the will of God was done. It was not in the stars of Fate that such villainy should succeed; such sacrifice as hers fail of its reward. I might not know where to turn, or what to do; yet it was with far lighter heart, a heart stimulated by new hope, the gleam of love, that I faced the task before me.

CHAPTER XXI

THE LANDING AT YELLOW BANKS

Nevertheless, in spite of this resolve, and the fresh courage which had been awakened within me by the faith that from now on I battled for the love of Eloise Beaucaire, no immediate opportunity for service came. All that the dark girl knew of her present whereabouts was that she had been lifted on board, and, in all probability, taken below. Certainly the girl had not been cabined on the upper deck; nor was I at present in any position to seek openly the place of her confinement. I could only wait patiently, and observe.

Supper was served me in front of the boilers, in company with the rest of the crew. Later, I was assigned a sleeping space on the lower deck, barely wide enough to lie in, and was permitted to sit among the others, under the uptilt of the swinging gangway, listening to their boisterousness, and rough play, or watching the dusk of evening descend over the deserted waters, as the laboring steamer battled against the current. It was a still, black night, and the *Adventurer* made extremely slow progress, a leadsman at the bow calling off the depth of water, and a huge light, rather ingeniously arranged, casting a finger of radiance along the ghostly shore line. With no marks of guidance on either bank, the wheelsman felt his uncertain passage upward, advancing so cautiously progress was scarcely noticeable, and I could frequently distinguish the voice of the anxious captain from the upper deck, above the hiss of the steam, as he called some hasty warning. In all probability we should have eventually been compelled to tie up against the bank, and await daylight, but for the disappearance of the heavy masses of clouds overhead, and the welcome gleam of myriads of stars, reflected along the smooth surface of the water.

Three times, at intervals, I made an effort to explore the second deck, but each time met with failure to accomplish my object. The narrow space extending between rail and cabin never seemed entirely deserted, and my last attempt brought me face to face with Mapes, who very curtly ordered me below, accompanying his command with a profane request to remain there. To protest, and thus possibly arouse the mate's suspicion as to the purpose of my presence on board, would have resulted in greater damage to our cause than any probable peril of the coming night. So I obeyed without a word, deeming it best to lie down quietly in the space allotted, and endeavor to think out some feasible plan for the morrow, rather than be caught again prowling around blindly in the dark. To assist me in this decision Mapes hung about the lower deck, until satisfied that I had actually turned in.

But I made no effort to sleep, and my mind remained busy. Even in the course of those brief excursions I had acquired some little information of value, and of a nature to leave me more at ease. I was now convinced that Kirby, whatever might be his ultimate purpose regarding the girl, had no present intention of doing her further injury. He contemplated no immediate attempt at forcible possession, and would be well satisfied if he could only continue to hold her in strict seclusion. The thing he was guarding against now, and while they remained on board, was escape from discovery.

I could easily understand the reason for this. He dare not expose her to the view of others, or permit her the slightest opportunity to appeal to them for rescue. Whether the man still believed her to be of negro blood, or not, the girl's unusual appearance would be certain to exercise more weight than his unsupported word—her refined, Caucasian face, the purity of her language, her simple story, would assuredly win an instant response from many of those on board. These waters were too far to the northward to be a safe hiding place for slave-hunters, and Kirby must be fully aware—knowing the characteristics of the river as he did—that his only security lay in keeping this woman in seclusion, carefully hidden away under lock and key, until he held her completely in his power, in a land where slavery was king. Then he could play the brute, but not here. I was convinced the man possessed brains and caution enough to deliberately choose this course—to do otherwise would mark him a fool, and that was not to be thought of. Even his reckless bravado would never drive him into an utterly unnecessary peril. All that he planned to accomplish later, could wait; but now his only purpose was to protect her from observation; to encourage his fellow-travelers to even forget that he had any slaves on board. There was a game of cards going on in the salon, in which he was participating, but Tim, not concerned in it, was wandering back and forth, up and down the ladder, watchful of every movement about the two decks, and making it extremely difficult for anyone to pass his guard. Satisfied as to this, and being intensely weary from my night without rest, and the hard work of the day, before I even realized the possibility, I fell sound asleep.

It was about the middle of the following afternoon when the *Adventurer* poked her blunt nose around a point of land, and came into full view of the squalid hamlet of Yellow Banks. A half-hour later we lay snuggled up against the shore, holding position amid several other boats made fast to stout trees, busily unloading, and their broad gangplanks stretching from forward deck to bank. All about was a scene of confusion and bustle, mud, and frontier desolation. Inspired by the ceaseless profanity of both mates, the roustabouts began unloading cargo at once, a steady stream of men, black and white, burdened with whatever load they could snatch up, moving on an endless run across the stiff plank, and up the low bank to the drier summit. It chanced to be my good fortune to escape this labor, having been detailed by Mapes to drag boxes, bales and barrels forward to where the hurrying bearers could grasp them more readily. This brought me close to the forward stairs, down which the departing passengers trooped, threading their insecure way among the trotting laborers, in an effort to get ashore.

All this deck was sufficiently unobstructed so as to afford me glimpses without, and for some distance along the bank; and it was not difficult for one with military training quickly to sense the situation, especially as I overheard much of the conversation between Mapes and the young lieutenant quartermaster who immediately came aboard. A more desolate, God-forsaken spot than Yellow Banks I never saw. It had been raining hard, and the slushy clay stuck to everything it touched; the men were bathed in it, their boots so clogged they could hardly walk, while what few horses I saw were yellow to their eyes. The passengers going ashore waded ankle deep the moment they stepped off the plank, and rushes and dried grass had been thrown on the ground to protect the cargo. Only three log houses were visible, miserable shacks, one of them a saloon, evidently doing a thriving business. In most cases it was impossible to distinguish the civilian inhabitants from their soldier guests. Reynolds' troops, all militia, and the greater part of them mounted, were an extremely sorry-looking lot—sturdy enough physically, of the pioneer type, but bearing little soldierly appearance, and utterly ignorant of discipline. They had been hastily gathered together at Beardstown, and, without drill, marched across country to this spot. Whatever of organization had been attempted was worked out en route, the men being practically without uniforms, tents, or even blankets, while the arms they bore represented every separate species ever invented. I saw them straggle past with long squirrel rifles, Hessian muskets, and even one fellow proudly bearing a silver-mounted derringer. The men had chosen officers from out their own ranks by popular election, and these exercised their authority very largely through physical prowess.

We had an excellent illustration of this soon after tying up at the landing. A tall, lank, ungainly officer, with a face so distinctively homely as to instantly attract my attention, led his company of men up the river bank, and ordered them to transport the pile of commissary stores from where they had been promiscuously thrown to a drier spot farther back. The officer was a captain, to judge from certain stripes of red cloth, sewed on the shoulders of his brown jean blouse, but his men were far from prompt in obeying his command, evidently having no taste for the job. One among them, apparently their ringleader in incipient mutiny, an upstanding bully with the jaw of a prize-fighter, took it upon himself openly to defy the officer, exclaiming profanely that he'd be damned if he ever enlisted to do nigger work. The others laughed, and joined in the revolt, until the captain unceremoniously flung off his blouse, thus divesting himself of every vestige of rank, and proceeded to enforce his authority. It was a battle royal, the soldiers crowding eagerly about, and yelling encouragement impartially first to one combatant, and then another.

"Kick him in the ribs, Sam!"

"Now, Abe, yer've got him—crack the damn cuss's neck."

"By golly! that's the way we do it in ol' Salem."

"He's got yer now, Jenkins, he's got yer now—good boy, Abe."

Exactly what occurred I could not see, but when the circle of wildly excited men finally broke apart, the big rebel was lying flat on his back in the yellow mud, and the irate officer was indicating every inclination to press him down out of sight.

"Hav' yer hed 'nough, Sam Jenkins?" he questioned, breathlessly. "Then, blame ye, say so."

"All right, Abe—yer've bested me this time."

"Will yer tote them passels?"

The discomfited Jenkins, one of whose eyes was closed, and full of clay, attempted a sickly grin.

"Hell! yes," he admitted, "I'd sure admire ter dew it."

The conqueror released his grip, and stood up, revealing his full height, and reaching out for the discarded blouse, quietly slipped it on. One of the *Adventurer's* passengers, an officer in uniform, going ashore, another tall, spare man, had halted on the gangplank to watch the contest. Now he stepped forward to greet the victor, with smiling eyes and out-stretched hand.

"Not so badly done, Captain," he said cordially. "I am Lieutenant Jefferson Davis, of General Atcheson's staff, and may have a good word to say regarding your efficiency some time."

The other wiped his clay-bespattered fingers on his dingy Jean pants, and gripped the offered hand, appearing homelier than ever because of a smear of blood on one cheek.

"Thank ye, sir," he answered good humoredly. "I'm Abe Lincoln, of Salem, Illinoy, an' I ain't got but just one job right now—that's ter make them boys tote this stuff, an' I reckon they're goin' ter do it."

With the exchange of another word or two they parted, and not until thirty years later did I realize what that chance meeting meant, there in the clay mud of Yellow Banks, at the edge of the Indian wilderness, when Abraham Lincoln, of Illinois, and Jefferson Davis, of Mississippi, stood in comradeship with clasped hands.

I recognized the majority of those disembarking passengers who passed by me within a few feet, but saw nothing of Kirby, the deputy sheriff, or caught any glimpse of their prisoners. The only conclusion was that they still remained on board. I was not at all surprised at this, as their intention undoubtedly was to continue with the steamer, and return south the moment the cargo of commissary and quartermaster's stores had been discharged. Neither had any interest in the war, and there was nothing ashore to attract them which could not be comfortably viewed from the upper deck. It was safer far to keep close guard over their charges, and see that they remained out of sight.

We had unloaded perhaps a quarter of our supplies, when an officer suddenly appeared over the crest of the bank and hailed the captain. There was a tone of authority in his voice which caused us to knock off work and listen.

"Is Captain Corcoran there? Oh, you are Captain Corcoran. Well, I bring orders from headquarters. You are to discontinue unloading, Captain, retain the remainder of the provisions on board, and prepare at once to take on men. What's your capacity?"

"Take on men? Soldiers, you mean?"

"Exactly; we've got to find quarters for about seven hundred. Two of those boats up yonder will take horses. The troops will be along within an hour."

"We are not to return south, then?"

"No; you're going in the other direction—up the Rock. You better get busy."

He wheeled his horse and disappeared, leaving the angry captain venting his displeasure on the vacant air. Kirby, evidently from some position across the deck, broke in with a sharp question.

"What was that, Corcoran? Did the fellow say you were not going back to St. Louis?"

"That's just what he said. Damn this being under military orders. We've got to nose our way up Rock River, with a lot of those measly soldiers aboard. It's simply hell. Here you, Mapes, stop that unloading, and get steam up—we've got to put in a night of it."

"But," insisted Kirby in disgust, "I'm not going up there; aren't there any boats going down?"

"How the hell should I know? Go ashore and find out—you haven't anything else to do. According to what he said, this boat casts off in half an hour and heads north."

The men below knocked off work willingly enough, and, taking advantage of the confusion on board, I endeavored to creep up the stairs and gain a view of the upper deck. But both Mapes and the second mate made this attempt impossible, forcing me into the ranks of the others, and compelling us to restow the cargo. The methods they adopted to induce sluggards to take hold were not gentle ones, and we were soon jumping at the snarl of their voices, as though each utterance was the crack of a whip. By a little diplomacy, I managed, however, to remain within general view of the gangway and the stairs descending from the deck above, confident that no one could pass me unseen. This watch brought no results, except to convince me that Kirby and his party still remained aboard. So far as I could perceive, no attempt to depart was made by anyone, excepting a big fellow with a red moustache, who swore profanely as he struggled through the mud, dragging a huge valise.

The situation puzzled and confused me. What choice would Kirby and the deputy make? If once up Rock River the *Adventurer* might very likely not return for weeks, and it did not seem to me possible that the impatient gambler would consent to such a delay. Every advance northward brought with it a new danger of exposure. These were Illinois troops to be transported—not regulars, but militia, gathered from a hundred hamlets—and many among them would be open enemies of slavery. Let such men as these, rough with the pioneer sense of justice, once suspect the situation of those two women, especially if the rumor got abroad among them that Eloise was white, and the slave-hunter would have a hard row to hoe. And I made up my mind such a rumor should be sown broadcast; aye, more, that, if the necessity arose, I would throw off my own disguise and front him openly with the charge. Seemingly there remained nothing else to do, and I outlined this course of action, growing more confident as the minutes sped, that the two men had determined to take their chances and remain aboard with the prisoners. No doubt they hesitated to leap from the frying pan into the fire, for perilous as it might prove to continue as passengers of the *Adventurer*, an even greater danger might confront them ashore, in that undisciplined camp. Aboard the steamer they could keep their victims safely locked in the cabins, unseen, their presence unknown; while probably Captain Corcoran and his two mates, all southern men, would protect their secret. It seemed to me that this, most likely, had been the final decision reached, and I determined to stick also, prepared to act at the earliest opportunity. I could do no more.

It was only an accident which gave me a clue to the real program. Mapes sent me back into the vacant space just forward of the paddle-wheel, seeking a lost cant-hook, and, as I turned about to return the missing tool in my hand, I paused a moment to glance curiously out through a slit in the boat's planking, attracted by the sound of a loud voice uttering a command. I was facing the shore, and a body of men, ununiformed, slouching along with small regard to order, but each bearing a rifle across his shoulder, were just tipping the ridge and plowing their way down through the slippery clay in the direction of the forward gangway. They were noisy, garrulous, profane, their mingled voices drowning the shouts of their officers, yet advanced steadily—the troops destined for Rock River were filing aboard. I saw the column clearly enough, all the soldier in me revolting to such criminal lack of discipline, and the thought of hurling such untrained men as these into Indian battle. Yet, although I saw, not for an instant did my gaze linger on their disordered ranks. The sight which held me motionless was rather that of a long, broad plank, protected on either side by a rope rail, stretching from the slope of the second deck across the narrow gulf of water, until it rested its other end firmly against the bank.

The meaning of this was sufficiently apparent. For some reason of his own, Kirby had evidently chosen this means of attaining the shore, and through personal friendship, Corcoran had consented to aid his purpose. The reason, plainly enough, was that by use of this stern gangway the landing party would be enabled to attain the bank without the necessity of pushing their way through the crowd of idle loungers forward. And the passage had just been accomplished, for, as my eyes focussed the scene, they recognized the spare figure of the deputy disappearing over the crest—a vague glimpse, but sufficient. At the same instant hands above began to draw in the plank.

There was but one thing for me to do, one action to take—follow them. Dropping the cant-hook, I turned aft and crept forth through a small opening onto the wooden frame which supported the motionless paddlewheel, choosing for the scene of operations the river side, where the boat effectively concealed my movements from any prying eyes ashore. Everyone aboard would be clustered forward, curiously watchful of that line of soldiers filing across the gangplank and seeking quarters upon deck. The only danger of observation lay in some straggler along the near-by bank. I lowered myself the full length of my arms, dangling there an instant by clinging to the framework; then loosened my grip and dropped silently into the rushing waters beneath.

CHAPTER XXII

MY FRIEND, THE DEPUTY SHERIFF

Well below the surface, yet impelled swiftly downward by the sturdy rush of the current, sweeping about the steamer's stern, I struck out with all the strength of my arms, anxious to attain in that first effort the greatest possible distance. I came panting up to breathe, my face lifted barely above the surface, dashing the water from my eyes, and casting one swift glance backward toward the landing. The high stern of the *Adventurer* was already some considerable distance away, exhibiting no sign of movement along her after-decks, but with that snake-like line of men still pouring over the crest of the bank, and disappearing forward. Great volumes of black smoke swept forth from the funnels, and my ears could distinguish the ceaseless hiss of steam. Again I permitted my body to sink into the depths, swimming onward with easier stroke, satisfied I had not been seen.

When I came up the second time I was quite far enough to be safe, and the stragglers had largely disappeared on board. Content to tread water, yet constantly drifting farther away in the trend of the current, I was able to observe all that took place. The sun had disappeared, and the western shore rested obscured by a purple haze, the wide stretch of water between slowly darkening. Light lingered still, however, along the clay hills of Yellow Banks, crowded with those soldiers left behind, who had gathered to speed the departure of their more fortunate comrades. The decks of the *Adventurer* were black with men, their cheers and shouts echoing to me along the surface of the river. Slowly the steamer parted from the shore, as the paddle-wheel began to revolve, flinging upward a cataract of spray, the space of open water widening, as the advancing bow sought the deeper channel, and headed northward. A great resounding cheer from both ship and shore mingled, rolling out over the darkening waters of the river, and echoed back by the forests along the bank. Farther up two other boats—mere phantoms in their white paint— cast off also, and followed, their smoke wreaths trailing behind as they likewise turned their prows up stream. Ten minutes later the three were almost in line, mere blobs of color, barely distinguishable through the descending dusk.

I swam slowly ashore, creeping up the low bank into the seclusion of a shallow, sandy gully, scooped out by the late rains. The air was mild, and I experienced no chill from my wet clothes, the warmth of the sand helping to dry them on my body. The river and sky were darkening fast, the more brilliant stars already visible. The western shore had entirely vanished, while nothing remained in evidence of those department boats except the dense black smoke smudge still outlined against the lighter arch of sky overhead. To my left the camp fires of the soldiers still remaining at Yellow Banks began to show red with flame through the shadows of intervening trees, and I could hear the noise of hammering, together with an occasional strident voice. Immediately about me all was silent, the steadily deepening gloom rendering my surroundings vaguely indistinct.

Thus far I possessed no plan—except to seek her. How this was to be accomplished appeared in no way clear. I lay there, my mind busy with the perplexing problem. Where could

Kirby go, now that he was ashore? How could he hope to find concealment in the midst of that rough camp? that little, squalid frontier settlement of a few log huts? Could it be possible that he had friends there—old cronies to whom he might venture to appeal for shelter, and protection? men of his own kidney to whom he could confide his secret? As the thought occurred to me it seemed quite possible; indeed it scarcely appeared probable that he would, under any other circumstances, have made the choice he did.

Surely such a man could never have risked going ashore unless some definite plan of action had already formulated itself in his mind. And why should the fellow not possess friends at Yellow Banks? He knew the river intimately and all the river towns; possibly he had even landed here before. He was a man feared, hated, but obeyed the full length of the great stream; his name stood for reckless daring, unscrupulous courage everywhere; he could command the admiration and loyalty of every vicious character in the steamboat service between Fort Crawford and New Orleans. It was hardly likely that none of these men, floaters at best, were in this miscellaneous outpouring of militia; indeed it was almost certain there would be some officers among them, as well as enlisted men.

As my thought grasped these facts, they led to the only possible decision. I would venture forward, rather blindly trusting that good fortune might direct my steps aright. I would have to discover first of all, where Kirby had taken Eloise—into whose hands he had deposited the girl for safe keeping. This task ought not to be difficult. The settlement was small, and the camp itself not a large one; no such party could hope to enter its confines without attracting attention, and causing comment. There was but slight discipline, and the majority of the soldiery were simple-hearted, honest fellows who could be easily induced to talk. Once I had thus succeeded in locating her, the rest ought to prove comparatively easy—a mere matter of action. For I had determined to play the spy no longer; to cease being a mere shadow. To my mind the excuse for masquerade no longer existed. The two fugitives were already safely on their way toward Canada, beyond any possibility of pursuit; and, from now on, I could better play my game in the open, confident that I held the winning hand in my knowledge of the girl's identity.

So I proposed finding Eloise, and telling her the whole truth; following that, and assured of her support, I would defy Kirby, denounce him if necessary to the military authorities, identifying myself by means of my army commission, and insist on the immediate release of the girl. The man had broken no law—unless the wanton killing of Shrunk could be proven against him—and I might not be able to compel his arrest. Whatever he suspected now relative to his prisoner, he had originally supposed her to be his slave, his property, and hence possessed a right under the law to restrain her liberty. But even if I was debarred from bringing the man to punishment, I could break his power, and overturn his plans. Beyond that it would be a personal matter between us; and the thought gave me joy. Certainly this method of procedure looked feasible to me; I saw in it no probability of failure, for, no matter how many friends the gambler might have in camp, or the influence they could exert in his behalf, they could never overcome the united testimony I was now able to produce. The mere statement of the girl that she was Eloise Beaucaire would be sufficient to free her.

I attained my feet, confident and at ease, and advanced up the gully, moving cautiously, so as not to run blindly upon some sentry post in the darkness. There would be nervous soldiers on duty, liable to fire at any sound, or suspicious movement, and it was a part of my plan to penetrate the lines unseen, and without inviting arrest. Once safely within the confines of the camp, the lack in uniforms and discipline, would afford ample freedom, but to be held as a prisoner, even for a short time, might prove a very serious matter. Within a short distance the gully became too shallow for further concealment. I could perceive the red glow of the fires gleaming out between the trees, and the numerous dark figures of men, engaged in various tasks, or lying idly about, waiting a call from the cooks to supper. My judgment told me that I must already be safely within the picket lines, able to walk forward unmolested, and mingle with these groups fearlessly. I was yet standing there, uncertain as to which group I should choose to companion with, when the dim figure of a man, unquestionably drunk, came weaving his uncertain way along a footpath which ran within a yard of my position. Even in that darkness, not yet dense with night, the lank figure possessed an outline of familiarity, and the sudden blazing up of a fire revealed the unmistakable features of the deputy.

"Hullo," I said, happily, stepping directly before him. "When did you come ashore?"

He stopped as though shot, bracing himself with difficulty, and endeavoring to gain a glimpse of my face.

"Hello, yerself," he managed to ejaculate thickly. "Who are yer? frien' o' mine?"

"Why, don't yer remember me, ol' man? I'm the feller who wus scrubbin' the paint on the *Adventurer*. We wus talkin' tergether comin' up. I wus goin' fer ter enlist."

"Hell! yes; glad ter see yer. Sum hot whisky et this camp— tried eny?"

"No," I answered, grasping at the opportunity to arouse his generosity. "I ain't got no coin to buy. They wudn't let me leave ther boat, ner pay me a picayune, so I just skipped out. I'm flat broke; maybe yer cud stake me fer a bite ter eat?"

"Eat!" he flung one arm lovingly about my shoulders, and burst into laughter. "Yer bet yer life, we're a goin' ter eat, an' drink too. I don't go back on none o' ther boys. Yer never heerd nuthin' like thet 'bout Tim Kennedy, I reckon. Eat, sure—yer know Jack Rale?"

"Never heerd the name."

"What, hell! never heerd o' Jack Rale! Ol' river man, half hoss, half alligator; uster tend bar in Saint Louee. He's up yere now, a sellin' forty-rod ter sojers. Cum up 'long with him frum Beardstown. Got a shack back yere, an' is a gittin' rich—frien' o' mine. Yer just cum 'long with me—thas all."

I permitted him to lead me, his voice never ceasing as we followed the dim trail. I made out little of what he said, nor did I question him. Drunk as the man was, I still thought it best to wait until more thoroughly assured that we were alone. Besides I could take no chance now with his garrulous tongue. The trail ended before a two-room log cabin, so deeply hidden in the woods as to be revealed merely by a glimmer of light shining out from within through chinks in the walls. Tim fumbled for the latch and finally opened the door, lurching across the threshold, dragging me along after him. The room was evidently kitchen and bar combined, the latter an unplaned board, resting on two upturned kegs, with a shelf behind containing an array of bottles. There were two men at a sloppy table, a disreputable looking white woman stirring the contents of a pot hung over the open fire, and a fellow behind the bar, attired in a dingy white apron. It was all sordid enough, and dirty—a typical frontier grogshop; but the thing of most interest to me was the proprietor. The fellow was the same red-moustached individual whom I had watched disembark from the steamer that same afternoon, slipping in the yellow mud as he surmounted the bank, dragging his valise along after him. So it was this fellow passenger who had given these fugitives refuge; it was his presence in these parts which had decided Kirby to make the venture ashore. He glanced up at our entrance, the glare of light overhead revealing a deep, ugly scar across his chin, and a pair of deep-set, scowling eyes.

"Back in time fer supper, hey, Kennedy," he growled, none too cordially. "Who's yer frien'?"

"A feller whut's goin' ter enlist. He's all right, Jack," the deputy hiccoughed thickly. "Les' liquor, an' then we'll eat. I'm payin' the bill—so whut the hell is it ter yer?"

"Nuthin' 'tall; eny frien' o' yers gits ther best I hav'. Corn liquor, I reckon?"

He set out a squat bottle on the bar, and thinking it best to humor the both of them I poured out a stiff drink, fully aware that Rale was observing my features closely.

"Seen yer afore sumwhar, ain't I?"

"I reckon," I replied indifferently, watching Tim fill his glass. "I worked my way up on the boat; saw yer on board."

"Sure; that's it; 'tain't in my line fer ter forgit a face. Yer ain't enlisted yit?"

"No; reckon I'll wait till maunin', an' clean up a bit furst. How 'bout sum soap an' water fore I eat? an' yer cudn't loan me a razor, cud ye?"

He rubbed his chin reflectively with stubby fingers.

"Wal' I got plenty o' water, an' maybe cud scare up sum soap. Tim yere he's got a razor, an', if he's a frien' o' yers, I reckon he mought lend it ter yer—thet's sure sum hell ov a beard yer've got."

The deputy gulped down his drink, and smacked his lips, clinging with one hand to the bar, regarding me lovingly.

"Sure; he's friend' o' mine. Shave him myself soon's I git sober. Stand most whisky all righ', but damn if I kin this kind—only hed three drinks, tha's all—whut's thet? Yer can't wait? Oh, all righ' then, take it yerself. Mighty fin' razor, ol' man."

Rale found me a tin basin, water, a bit of rag for a towel, and a small, cracked mirror, in which my reflection was scarcely recognizable. He was a man of few words, contenting himself with uttering merely a dry comment on Kennedy, who had dropped back into a convenient chair, and buried his face on the table.

"Tim's a damn good fellow, an' I never saw him so blame drunk afore," he said, regretfully. "Know'd him et Saint Louee; used ter drop in ter my place. He an' Kirby hed a row, an' I reckon thet's whut started him drinkin'."

"A row; a quarrel, you mean?" forgetting myself in surprise. "Who's Kirby?"

"Joe Kirby; yer sure must know him, if yer a river man. Slim sorter feller, with a smooth face; slickest gambler ever wus, I reckon."

"Why, of course," getting control of myself once more. "We

Randall Parrish

picked him up, 'long with Tim, down river. Hed two women with 'em, didn't they? runaway niggers?"

Rale winked facetiously, evidently rather proud of the exploit as it had been related to him.

"Wal', ther way I understan', they wa'n't both of 'em niggers; however, that was the story told on board. This yere Joe Kirby is pretty damn slick, let me tell you. One of 'em's a white gurl, who just pretended she wus a nigger. I reckon thet even Kirby didn't catch on ter her game et furst; an' when he did he wus too blame smart ter ever let her know. She don't think he knows yet, but she's liable fer ter find out mighty soon."

"But he cannot hold a white woman," I protested stoutly.

"Can't, hey! Wal', I reckon there are ways o' even doin' thet, an' if thar be, Kirby'll find it. They say thar's mor'n one way ter skin a cat, an' Joe never cut his eye teeth yisterday, let me tell yer. Thet gurl's not only white—she's got money, scads ov it, and is a good looker. I saw her, an' she's some beaut; Joe ain't passin' up nuthin' like that. I reckon she won't find no chance ter raise a holler fore he's got her tied good an' strong."

I stared blankly at the fellow, a thousand questions in my mind, and a dim perception of what he meant permeating my brain.

"Do you mean," I asked, horrified, "that he will compel her to marry him?"

"Sum smart little guesser, ain't yer? I reckon she's in a right smart way ter do it, et thet."

"And wus this the cause of the quarrel between Kirby and Kennedy?"

"Wal', I reckon it wus; leastwise Tim wudn't be mixed up in the affair none. They hed it prutty blame hot, an' I reckon thar'd bin a dead deputy if hedn't bin fer me. Tim thought I wus a prutty gud frien' an' cum over yere ter liquor, an' eat. Ther joke ov it is, he never know'd thet Joe hed told me all 'bout the fix he wus in, afore we cum ashore. Hell, it wus all fixed up whut wus ter be done—only we didn't expect the steamer wus goin' on north. Thar's sum boys wantin' a drink; see yer agin."

I finished shaving, making no attempt to hurry, busily thinking over this new situation. In the first place why had Rale told me all this? Quite probably the indiscretion never occurred to him, or a thought that the matter would prove of any personal interest to me. He had been drinking, and was in a reckless mood; he believed me a common river roustabout, with few scruples of conscience, and possibly had even picked me out as an assistant in the affair. I felt convinced the man had some purpose in his conversation, and that he had not finished all he intended to say, when the entrance of customers compelled his return to the bar. His parting words implied that. Perhaps the revolt of the deputy made it necessary for the conspirators to select another helper to properly carry out their nefarious scheme, and Rale had decided that I might answer. I hoped this might prove the explanation, and determined to seek the earliest opportunity to impress upon that individual the fact that I was desperately in need of money, and decidedly indifferent as to how it was obtained. If I could only have a moment alone with Kennedy, in which to learn exactly what he knew. But it was plainly useless to hope for this privilege; the fellow slept soundly, his face hidden in his arms, the sleep of complete drunkenness.

The two soldiers, whose entrance had interrupted our talk, remained at the bar drinking, until after I had completed my toilet; and were still there listening to a story Rale was telling, when the slatternly white woman announced that supper was ready to serve. Seemingly I was the only one prepared to eat, and I sat down alone at a small table, constructed out of a box, and attempted to do the best I could with the food provided. I have never eaten a worse meal, or a poorer cooked one; nor ever felt less inclination to force myself to partake. Finally the soldiers indulged in a last drink, and disappeared through the door into the night without. Tim slept soundly, while the other men remained engrossed in their game of cards. Rale wiped off the bar, glanced about at these, as though to reassure himself that they were intent on their play; then, removing his apron, he crossed the room, and drew up a chair opposite me.

"All right, Sal," he grunted shortly. "Bring on whut yer got."

CHAPTER XXIII

A NEW JOB

He remained silent, staring moodily at the fire, until after the woman had spread out the dishes on the table before him. Then his eyes fell upon the fare.

"Nice looking mess that," he growled, surveying the repast with undisguised disgust. "No wonder we don't do no business with thet kind ov a cook. I reckon I'd a done better to hav' toted a nigger back with me. No, yer needn't stay—go an' make up them beds in the other room. I'll watch things yere."

He munched away almost savagely, his eyes occasionally lifting to observe me from beneath their shaggy brows, his muscular jaws fairly crunching the food. I judged the fellow had come over intending to resume our interrupted conversation, but hardly knew what he had best venture. I decided to give him a lead.

"I ain't got no money, myself," I began to explain, apologetically, "but Tim thar sed he'd pay my bill."

"Sure, that's all right; I ain't a worryin' none. Maybe I might put yer in an easy way o' gittin' hold o' a little coin—thet is if

Randall Parrish

ye ain't too blame perticular."

"Me!" I laughed. "Well, I reckon I don't aim fer ter be thet. I've bin ten years knockin' 'bout between New Orleans an' Saint Louee, steamboatin' mostly. Thet sort o' thing don't make no saint out'r eny kin'd man, I reckon. What sort'r job is it?"

He eyed me cautiously, as though not altogether devoid of suspicion.

"Yer don't somehow look just the same sort o' chap, with them ther' whiskers shaved off," he acknowledged soberly. "Yer a hell sight better lookin' then I thought yer wus, an' a damn sight younger. Whar wus it yer cum frum?"

"Frum Saint Louee, on the boat, if thet's what yer drivin' at."

"Tain't what I'm drivin' at. Whar else did yer cum frum afore then? Yer ain't got no bum's face."

"Oh, I see; well, I can't help that, kin I? I wus raised down in Mississip', an' run away when I wus fourteen. I've been a driftin' 'long ever since. I reckon my face ain't goin' ter hurt none so long as the pay is right."

"No, I reckon maybe it won't. I've seed sum baby faces in my time thet sure hed the devil behind 'em. Whut's yer name?"

"Moffett—Dan Moffett."

He fell silent, and I was unpleasantly aware of his continued scrutiny, my heart beating fiercely, as I endeavored to force down more of the food as an excuse to remain at the table. What would he decide? I dared not glance up, and for the moment every hope seemed to die within me; shaving had evidently been a most serious mistake. Finally he spoke once more, but gruffly enough, leaning forward, and lowering his voice to a hoarse whisper.

"Wal' now see yere, Moffett, I'm goin' fer ter be damn plain with yer. I'm a plain man myself, an' don't never beat about no bush. I reckon yer whut yer say ye are, fer thar ain't no reason, fer as I kin see, why we should lie 'bout it. Yer flat broke, an' need coin, an' I'm takin' at yer own word—thet ye don't care overly much how ye git it. Thet true?"

"Just 'bout—so it ain't no hangin' job."

"Hell, thar ain't really no manner o' risk at all. Yer don't even hav' ter break the law fer as I know. It's just got fer ter be done on the dead quiet, an' no question asked. Now look yere," and he glared at me fiercely, a table knife gripped in one hand. "I'm sum wildcat whin I onct git riled, an' if yer play any dirt I'll sure take it out'r yer hide if I'm ten years a findin' yer. Yer don't want'r try playin' no tricks on Jack Rale."

"Who's a playin' any tricks?" I protested, indignantly. "Whatever I says I'll do, an' thar won't be no talkin' 'bout it nether. So whut's the job? This yere Kirby matter?"

He nodded sullenly, a bit regretful that he had gone so far I imagined, and with another cautious glance about the room.

"I'll tell yer all ye need ter know," he began. "'Tain't such a long story. This yere Joe Kirby he's a frien' o' mine; I've know'd him a long time, an' he's in a hell of a fix. He told me 'bout it comin' up on the boat, an', betwixt us, we sort'r fixed up a way ter stack ther cards. Here's how it all happened: Thar wus an ol' planter livin' down in Missoury at a place called Beaucaire's Landin'. His name wus Beaucaire, an' he hed a son named Bert, a damn good-fer-nuthing cuss, I reckon. Wal' this Bert runned away a long while ago, an' never cum back; but he left a baby behind him—a gurl baby—which a quadroon slave give birth too. The quadroon's name wus Delia, an' the kid wus called Rene. Git them names in yer head. Ol' Beaucaire he knew the gurl wus his son's baby, so he brought her up 'long with his own daughter, who wus named Eloise. They wus both 'bout ther same age, an' nobody seemed ter know thet Rene wus a nigger. Fer sum reason ol' Beaucaire never set her free, ner the quadroon nether. Wal' Kirby he heard tell o' all this sumwhar down the river. Yer see he an' Bert Beaucaire run tergether fer a while, till Bert got killed in a row in New Orleans. I reckon he tol' him part o' the story, an' the rest he picked up in Saint Louee. Enyhow it looked like a damn good thing ter Kirby, who ain't passin' up many bets. Ol' Beaucaire wus rich, an' considerable ov a sport; people who hed seed the gurls sed they wus both ov 'em beauties an' Eloise—the white one—hed an independent fortune left her through her mother. So Kirby, he an' a feller named Carver—a tin-horn—planned it out betwixt 'em ter copper ol' Beaucaire's coin, an' pick up them gurls along with it."

"But how cud they do thet?"

"Luck mostly, I reckon, an' Kirby's brains. The plan wus ter git Beaucaire inter a poker game, ease him 'long a bit, an' then break him, land, niggers, an' all. They didn't figure this wud be hard, fer he wus a dead game gambler, an' played fer big stakes. It wus luck though what giv' 'em their chance. Beaucaire hed sum minin' claims up on the Fevre, an' hed ter go up thar. It's a long, lonesom' trip, I reckon, an' so the other two they went 'long. They got the ol' chap goin' an comin', an' finally coddled him 'long till he put up his big bet on a sure hand. When he found out whut hed happened the of gent got so excited he flung a fit, an' died."

"Leavin' Kirby ownin' all the property?"

"Every picayune, niggers an' all. It wus sum sweep, an' he hed signed bills o' sale. Wa'n't nobody cud git it away frum him. Wal', Joe he didn't want fer ter make no fuss, ner scare the gurl none, so he went down ter' Saint Louee an' made proof o' ownership afore a jedge he know'd. Then, with the papers all straight, he, an' the sheriff, with Tim yere, the deputy, run up the river at night ter serve 'em quietly on the daughter—the white one, Eloise. Kirby he didn't aim ter be seen at all, but just went 'long so thar wudn't be no mistake. Yer see, them papers hed ter be served afore they cud take away the niggers. Kirby wus goin' ter sell them down river, an' not bother 'bout the land fer awhile, till after he'd hed a chance ter shine up ter this yere gurl Eloise. He'd never seen her—but, enyhow, he got thet notion in his hed."

"She wus the daughter; the white one?"

"Sure; he hed the other by law. Wal', when they all got thar, nobody wus home, 'cept one o' the gurls, who claimed fer ter be Rene—the one whut wus a nigger, thet Kirby owned. Nobody know'd which wus which, an' so they hed ter take her word for it. They cudn't do nuthin' legal till they found the other one, an' they wus sittin' round waitin' fer her ter turn up, when the nigger gurl they wus watchin' got away."

"How'd she do thet?"

"Don't noboddy seem ter know. Damn funny story. Way they tell it, sumbody must'r knocked Kirby down an' run oft with her. Whoever did it, stole the boat in which Kirby an' the sheriff cum up the river, an' just naturally skipped out—the sheriff's nigger an' all. It wus a slick job."

"Of course, they chased them?'

"Best they cud, not knowin' which way they'd gone. They reckoned the whol' bunch must'r got away tergether, so the sheriff he started fer Saint Louee, an' the others got onto a troop boat what happened ter cum 'long, and started north. Long 'bout the mouth ov the Illinoy they caught up with a nigger-stealer named Shrunk. They hed a fight in an' about his cabin, an' sum killin'. Two ov the womin got away, but Kirby an' Tim got hold o' this gurl what hed claimed ter be Rene, an' a mulatto cook who wus a workin' fer Shrunk. I reckon maybe yer know the rest."

"I know they wus run down by the *Adventurer*, an' hauled aboard. But how did Kirby learn his prisoner wus white? Did she tell him?"

"I should say not. It wus the mulatto cook who told him, although, I reckon, he hed his doubts afore thet I knew she wusn't no nigger the furst minute I got eyes on her—they can't fool me none on niggers; I wus raised 'mong 'em. But so fur's the gurl's concerned, she don't know yet thet Kirby's found out." He emitted a weak laugh. "It sorter skeered Joe ter be caught way up yere in this kintry, kidnapin' a white gurl. He didn't know whut the hell ter do, till I give him a p'inter."

"You were the one who suggested marriage?"

"Wal', I sed she cudn't do nuthin' 'gainst him onct he wus married to her. I thought o' thet right away. Yer see this wus how it happened: Kirby sed he'd like fer ter marry her, an' I sez, 'why not then? Thar's an ol' bum ov a preacher yere at Yellow Banks, a sorter hanger-on ter one o' them militia companies, what'll do eny damn thing I tell him too. I got the goods on him, an' he knows it.'"

"'But she wouldn't marry me,' he says, 'yer don't know

thet gurl.'"

"'Don't I,' I asked sarcastic. 'Wal', thar ain't no gurl ever I see yet thet won't marry a man if the right means are used. How kin she help herself? Yer leave it ter me.'"

"And he consented?"

"He wus damn glad to, after I told him how it cud be done. But Tim he wudn't go in with us, an' thet's why we got ter hav' anuther man. Come on over ter the bar an' hav' a drink, Moffett; them other fellers are goin' ter eat now."

The diversion gave me opportunity for a moment's thought. The plan was a diabolical one, cold-blooded and desperate, yet I saw no certain way of serving her, except by accepting Rale's offer. I had no satisfactory proof to present against these villains, and, even if I had, by the time I succeeded in locating headquarters and establishing my own identity, the foul trick might be executed without my aid, and the injured girl spirited away beyond reach. I did not even know where she was concealed, or how I could lay hands on Kirby. The genial Rale pushed out a black bottle and we drank together.

"Wal'," he said, picking up the conversation where it had ended, quite satisfied with his diplomacy, and wiping his lips on his sleeve. "What ye say, Moffett? Thar's a hundred dollars in this job."

"Whar is the gurl?"

"Oh, I reckon she ain't fur away; we kin find her all right. I got ter know 'bout yer furst. Are yer game?"

"I'm game 'nough, Jack," assuming a familiarity I thought he would appreciate. "Only I don't want'r jump inter this yere thing without knowin' nuthin' 'bout it. What is it yer got lined up fer me ter do?"

He helped himself to yet another liberal drink, and I was glad to note that the fiery liquor was already beginning to have its effect, increasing his recklessness of speech.

"All right, Dan; have another one on me—no? Wal', hell; I 'spose I might as wal' tell ye furst as last. Thar ain't nuthin' fer eny o' us ter git skeered about. We got it all planned. I sorter picked yer out 'cause thar ain't noboddy knows yer in camp here—see? If yer disappear thar won't noboddy give a damn. An' thar ain't scarcely noboddy what knows the gurl is yere nether—only maybe a few soldiers, who thinks she's a nigger. We don't want this affair talked about none, do we? I reckon not. So we planned it out this way: Thar's a frien' o' mine got a shack down on Bear Crick, 'bout twenty mile below yere. He sells red-eye ter barge an' keel-boatmen, what tie up thar nights. Wal', he's all right—a hell o' a good feller. What we aim ter do is run the gurl down thar ternight, unbekno'nst ter enybody. I reckon yer kin ride a hoss?"

"Yes; so thet's my job?"

"Thet's the whole o' it. Yer Just got ter stay thar with her till Kirby kin git away, without noboddy thinkin' enything 'bout it. It's damn easy money ter my notion."

I thought swiftly. There were several questions I wanted to ask, but dare not. It was better to trust to luck, for I must lull, not arouse suspicion. Thus far the affair had played wonderfully into my hands; if I could maintain my part to the end, there ought to be no reason why the girl should not be saved uninjured. The one thing which I had feared no longer threatened—I was not to be brought face to face with Kirby. If we encountered each other at all, it would be in darkness, where there was only slight probability of recognition. The impatience in Kale's face drove me to declare myself.

"Why, if thet's all I got ter do fer a hundred dollars," I said gaily, "I'm yer man, Jack. An' how soon will Kirby be comin' down ter this yer place on Bear Crick?"

"In a day er two, I reckon. Soon's thar's sum boat headin' down river. Yer see, this yer's all camp; thar ain't no fit place whar we kin hide the gurl, an' make her keep her mouth shet. Them blamed soldiers are a moosin' 'bout every whar, an' if she onct got talkin', our goose wud be cooked. Furst thing we got ter do is git her outer this camp."

"Ternight, yer sed?"

"'Bout midnight; yer'll go'—hey?"

"I reckon; yer got the money?"

With his eyes fastened on the two men eating, he counted out some gold pieces on the bar and shoved them over to me, keeping them under cover of his hand.

"Thar's half o' it, an' the rest is yers when ye bring back the hosses."

"How many hosses? Who's a goin'?"

"Three o' yer. Kirby's fer sendin' the mulatter gurl 'long. She's a free nigger an' might let her tongue wag. Now listen, Moffett, I'm a goin' out putty soon ter git things ready, an' I'll leave Sal yere ter tend bar. Now git this; thar's a right smart trail back o' the cabin, leadin' straight down ter the crick, with a spring 'bout half way. Thar ain't no guard down thar, an' ye can't miss it, even en the dark. The hosses will be thar et midnight waitin' fer yer. All ye got ter do is just put them two gurls on an' ride away. Yer don't never need ter speak ter 'em. Yer understand? All right, then; hav' anuther drink."

I shook my head.

"But how'm I goin' ter git ter this place—whatever it's called?"

"Thar ain't no trouble 'bout thet; all yer got ter do is ride straight south till yer cum ter the crick, an' yer thar. It's Jenkins' Crossing yer after."

"I reckon thar ain't eny Injuns, er nuthin'?"

"Hell, no; they're all t'other direction; nuthin' worse'n wolves. Say, though, yer might have trouble with them gurls—got a gun?"

"No."

He reached back into a small drawer under the shelf, and brought out an ugly-looking weapon, tried the hammer movement with his thumb, and handed it over to me with a grin.

"Some cannon, an' I want it back. Don't fail at midnight."

"An' thar ain't nuthin' fer me ter do till then?"

"Not a thing; take a nap, if ye want'r. Sal kin wake ye up. I reckon I won't be back till after yer off."

I sat down in a chair and leaned back against the wall, tilting my hat down over my eyes and pretending to fall asleep. Through half-closed lids I managed to see all that transpired in the room, and my mind was busy with the approaching crisis. Had Rale revealed all the details of their plan to me, I wondered. It seemed comprehensive enough, and yet it hardly appeared possible that they would thoughtlessly place in the hands of any stranger such an advantage. It would only be natural for them to withhold something—merely trusting me with what I actually had to know. Yet crime was forever making just such mistakes; these men had to place confidence in someone, and, after all, it was not so strange that the saloon keeper had selected me. I had come to him a penniless river bum, representing a class he had dealt with all his life. I had played the part well, and he had found no reason to suspect me. Moreover the course they were pursuing appeared perfectly natural—the only means of carrying out their scheme, with the least possible chance for discovery.

Rale busied himself for some minutes before putting on his hat, counting over some money, and filling his bottles from a reserve stock underneath the shelf. The two men completed their meal and resumed their card game, while Sal hastily washed up the few dishes and tucked them away in a rude cupboard beside the fireplace. Tim slept peacefully on, but had slightly changed his posture, so that his face was now upturned to the light. The sight of his familiar features gave me an inspiration. He was, undoubtedly, an honest fellow, and had quarreled with Kirby over this very matter, refusing to have any hand in it. He had supposed up to that time that he was doing no more than his duty under the law. If I could arouse him from drunken stupor, he might even be willing to work with me in the attempt to rescue Eloise. Rale disappeared through the rear door, after exchanging a few words with the woman, and did not return. I waited motionless for some time, fearful lest he might come back. Suddenly the front door opened noiselessly, and Kirby entered, advancing straight toward the bar. Sal served him, answering his questions, which were spoken so low I could not catch the words. His eyes swept the room, but the hat concealed my face, and he only recognized Tim. He paused long enough to bend above the upturned features of the unconscious deputy, not unpleased, evidently, to discover him in that condition.

"The damned old fool," he muttered, perhaps not aware that he spoke aloud. "Rale has got him fixed, all right."

CHAPTER XXIV

KIRBY AND I MEET

Sal remained seated behind the bar, nodding, and, so soon as I felt reasonably assured that she was without interest in my movements, I leaned forward and endeavored to arouse Kennedy. This was by no means easy of accomplishment, and I was compelled to pinch the fellow rather severely before he sat up angrily, blurting out the first words which came to his lips:

"What the devil—"

His half-opened eyes caught my gesture for silence, and he stopped instantly, his lips widely parted.

"Meet me outside," I whispered, warningly. "But be careful about it."

The slight noise had failed to disturb the woman, and I succeeded in slipping through the unlatched door without noting any change in her posture. Tim, now thoroughly awake, and aware of something serious in the air, was not long in joining me without, and I drew him aside into a spot of deeper blackness under the trees. He was still indignant over the pinching, and remained drunk enough to be

Randall Parrish

quarrelsome. I cut his muffled profanity short.

"That's quite enough of that, Tim," I said sharply, and was aware that he stared back at me, plainly perplexed by the change in my tone and manner. "You are an officer of the law; so am I, and it is about time we were working together."

He managed to release a gruff laugh.

"You—you damn bum; hell, that's a good joke—what'r yer givin' me now?"

"The exact truth; and it will be worth your while, my man, to brace up and listen. I am going to give you a chance to redeem yourself—a last chance. It will be a nice story to tell back in St. Louis that you helped to kidnap a wealthy young white woman, using your office as a cloak for the crime, and, besides that, killing two men to serve a river gambler. Suppose I was to tell that sort of tale to Governor Clark, and give him the proofs—where would you land?"

He breathed hard, scarcely able to articulate, but decidedly sober.

"What—what's that? Ain't you the fellar thet wus on the boat? Who—who the devil are yer?"

"I am an officer in the army," I said gravely, determined to impress him first of all, "and I worked on that steamer merely to learn the facts in this case. I know the whole truth now, even to your late quarrel with Kirby. I do not believe you realized before what you were doing—but you do now. You are guilty of assisting that contemptible gambler to abduct Eloise Beaucaire, and are shielding him now in his cowardly scheme to compel her to marry him by threat and force."

"The damn, low-lived pup—I told him whut he wus."

"Yes, but that doesn't prevent the crime. He's all you said, and more. But calling the man names isn't going to frighten him, nor get that girl out of his clutches. What I want to know is, are you ready to help me fight the fellow? block his game?"

"How? What do ye want done?"

"Give me a pledge first, and I'll tell you."

He took a long moment to decide, not yet wholly satisfied as to my identity.

"Did ye say ye wus an army offercer?"

"Yes, a lieutenant; my name is Knox."

"I never know'd yer."

"Probably not, but Joe Kirby does. I was on the steamer *Warrior* coming down when he robbed old Judge Beaucaire. That was what got me mixed up in this affair. Later I was in that skiff you fellows rammed and sunk on the Illinois. I know the whole dirty story, Kennedy, from the very beginning. And now it is up to you whether or not I tell it to Governor Clark."

"I reckon yer must be right," he admitted helplessly. "Only I quit cold the minute I caught on ter whut wus up. I never know'd she wa'n't no nigger till after we got yere. Sure's yer live that's true. Only then I didn't know whut else ter do, so I got bilin' drunk."

"You are willing to work with me, then?"

"Yer kin bet I am; I ain't no gurl-stealer."

"Then listen, Kennedy. Jack Rale told me exactly what their plans were, because he needed me to help him. When you jumped the reservation, he had to find someone else, and picked me. The first thing he did, however, was to get you drunk, so you wouldn't interfere. That was part of their game, and Kirby came into the saloon a few minutes ago to see how it worked. He stood there and laughed at you, lying asleep. They mean to pull off the affair tonight. Here's the story."

I told it to him, exactly in the form it had come to me, interrupted only in the recital by an occasional profane ejaculation, or some interjected question. The deputy appeared sober enough before I had finished, and fully grasped the seriousness of the situation.

"Now that is the way it stacks up," I ended, "The girl is to be taken to this fellow's shack and compelled to marry Kirby, whether she wants to or not. They will have her where she cannot help herself—away from anyone to whom she could appeal. Rale wouldn't explain what means were to be used to make her consent, and I didn't dare press him for fear he might suspect me. They either intend threatening her, or else to actually resort to force—likely both. No doubt they can rely on this renegade preacher in either case."

"Jack didn't name no name?"

"No—why?"

"Only thar uster be a bum hangin' round the river front in Saint Louee who hed preacher's papers, en wore a long-tailed coat. Thar wan't no low-down game he wudn't take a hand in fer a drink. His name wus Gaskins; I hed him up fer mayhem onct. I'll bet he's the duck, for he hung round Jack's place most o' the time. Whatcha want me ter do?"

"It has seemed to me, Tim," I said, thoughtfully, "that the best action for us to take will be to let them place the girl in my hands, just as they have planned to do. That will throw them entirely off their guard. As things stand, I have no knowledge where she is concealed, or where to hunt for her; but it is evident she is in no immediate danger. They don't dare to force action here, in this camp. Once we succeed in getting her safely away, and remain unknown ourselves, there ought to be very little trouble in straightening out the whole matter. My plan would be to either ride around the camp in the night, and then report the whole affair at headquarters, or else to strike out direct for Fort Armstrong across country. The Indians will all be cleaned out north of here, and they know me at Armstrong. Do you know any place you can pick up a horse?"

"Thar's a slew ov 'em round yere," he admitted. "These fellers are most all hoss-soldiers. I reckon I cud cinch sum sort o' critter. Yer want me along?"

"Perhaps not, Tim. Your disappearance might cause suspicion, and send them after us. My plan is to get away as quietly as possible, and let them believe everything is all right. I want a day or two in which to work, before Rale or Kirby discover we have not gone to Bear Creek. I'll meet them alone at the spring down the trail, but shall want you somewhere near by. You see this is bound to mean a fight if I am recognized—likely three against one; and those men wouldn't hesitate at murder."

"I reckon not, an' it wudn't be their furst one nuther, Looks ter me like yer wus takin' a big chance. I'll be thar, though; yer kin bet on thet, an' ready fer a fight, er a foot race. This is how I size it up—if thar ain't no row, I'm just ter keep still, an' lie low; an' if a fracas starts I'm ter jump in fer all I'm worth. Is thet the program?"

"Exactly—that's my idea."

"Wal' then, I'm a prayin' it starts; I want just one crack et thet Kirby, the ornary cuss."

We talked the whole matter over in detail, having nothing better to do, and endeavoring to arrange for every proba- bility, yet did not remain together for long. With my eyes to a chink between the logs I got a view of the interior of the cabin. The two card players had disappeared, and I imagined they were rolled up in blankets in one corner of the room. Sal was alone, seated on a stool, her head hanging forward, sound asleep. Evidently she had received no orders from Rale to keep watch over the movements of either of us, and was not worried on account of our absence. In all probability the saloon keeper believed the deputy was drunk enough to remain in stupor all night, and he considered my services as bought and paid for. He had traded with derelicts of my apparent kind before.

I felt nervous, anxious, eager for action. The time dragged horribly. If I could only be accomplishing something; or if I knew what was occurring elsewhere. What if something unforeseen should occur to change Rale's plan? Suppose, for instance, those fellows should decide to force the marriage tonight, instead of waiting until after arrival at Jenkins' Crossing? Suppose she resisted them, and was injured? A suspicion came to me that I might have misunderstood all this. My God! if I only knew where it was they had concealed the girl.

The two of us explored about the silent cabin, but discovered nothing. There was no light visible in the rear room, nor any sound of movement within. The two windows were closed, and the door locked. We found a convenient stump in the woods, and sat down to wait, where we could see all that occurred about the cabin. The distant camp fires had died down, and only occasionally did any sound, generally far away, disturb the silence. The night was fairly dark, the stars shining brightly enough, but dense beneath the trees; yet we managed to locate the nearer sentries by their voices when they reported posts. None were stationed close by. Everything indicated that we were safely outside the lines of camp. We conversed in whispers, until Tim, still influenced by his excessive drinking, became sleepy, and slid off the stump onto the ground, where he curled up on a pile of leaves. I let him lie undisturbed, and continued my vigil alone, feeling no inclination to sleep, every nerve throbbing almost painfully. Three or four men straggled into the saloon while I sat there, coming from the direction of the camp, and were doubtless waited upon by Sal. None remained long within, and all I saw of them were indistinct figures revealed for a moment, as the light streamed out through the opened door. One seemed to be an officer, wrapped in a cavalry cloak— hunting after men out of bounds, possibly—but, later than eleven o'clock, there were no more callers. Soon after that hour the light within was turned low.

All the while I remained there, motionless, intently watchful for every movement about me, with Tim peacefully asleep on the leaves, my thought was with Eloise Beaucaire, and my mind torn with doubt as to the wisdom of my choice. Had I determined on the right course? Was there nothing else I could do? Was it best for me to thus rely on my own efforts? or should I have sought the assistance of others? Yet where could I turn? How could I gain in time such assistance? I realized in those moments that selfishness, love, personal desire, had very largely influenced me in my decision; I was eager to rescue her alone, by my own efforts, unaided. I had to confess this to be my secret purpose. I could dream of nothing else, and was actually unwilling to share this privilege with any other. I felt she belonged to me; determined she should belong to me. From that instant when I became convinced that she was of white blood—that no hideous barrier of race, no stain of dishonor, held us apart— she had become my one ambition. I not only knew that I loved her; but I believed almost as strongly that she loved me. Every glance of her eyes, each word she had spoken, remained indelibly in my memory. And beyond doubt she thought me dead. Kirby would have told her that both men in the wrecked boat went down. It would be to his advantage to impress this on her mind, so as thus to emphasize her helplessness, and cause her to realize that no one knew of her predicament. What an awakening it would be when she again recognized me as actually alive, and beside, her. Surely in that moment I should read the whole truth in those wonderful eyes, and reap my reward in her first impulse of gratitude. It was not in nature to share such a moment with another; I wanted it for myself, alone.

It was nearly twelve before even the slightest sound near at hand indicated the approach of others. I was already in an agony of suspense, imagining something might have gone wrong, when the dull scuffling of horses' hoofs being led cautiously up the trail to my right, broke the intense silence. I listened to assure myself, then shook Tim into wakefulness, leaving him still blinking in the shadow of the stump, while I advanced in the direction of the spring. Suddenly the darker shape of the slowly moving animals loomed up through the gloom, and came to a halt directly in front of me. I saw nothing of Rale until he spoke.

"That yer, Moffett?"

"Yes; whar's yer party?"

I caught view of his dim outlines, as he stepped slightly forward, reassured by my voice.

"They'll be yere; thar's a bit o' time ter spare yit. I aimed not ter keep 'em waitin'. Here, this is yer hoss, an' yere's the leadin' strap fer the others. Better tie it ter yer pommel, I reckon, so's ter leave both yer hands free—yer might hav' need fer 'em. We'll tend ter mountin' the gurls, an' then all ye'll hav' ter do will be ter lead off. Thar won't be no talkin' done yere. Better walk the hosses till yer git crost the crick, so the sojers won't hear yer. Got that?"

"I reckon I hav', an' sense 'nough ter know it without bein' told. Did yer think I wanted ter be catched on this job?"

"All right, but thar's no harm a tellin' yer. Don't be so damn touchy. Eneyboddy in the shack?"

"No; only the woman, asleep on a stool."

"Whar's Tim gone to?"

"I reckon he don't even know hisself; he's sure sum drunk."

Rale chuckled, patting the side of the horse next him. "Whole caboodle workin' like a charm," he said, good humoredly. "Thought onct the deputy might show up ugly, but a quart o' red-eye sure fixed him—thar's our party a comin' now. Ye're ter stay right whar ye are."

They were advancing toward us up the bank which sloped down toward the creek. It occurred to me they must be following some well-worn path, from the silence of their approach—the only sound being a faint rustling of dead leaves. Rale moved forward to meet them across the little open space, and a moment later, from my hiding place among the motionless horses, I became able to distinguish the slowly approaching figures. There were four in the party, apparently from their garb two men and two women. The second man might be the preacher, but if so, why should he be there? Why should his presence at this time be necessary? Unless the two main conspirators had special need for his services, I could conceive no reason for his having any part in the action that night. Had I been deceived in their plans? The horror of the dawning conception that possibly I had waited too long, and that the deed I sought to prevent had already been consummated, left me trembling like an aspen. Even as this fear overwhelmed me with consternation, I was compelled to notice how helplessly the first of the two women walked—as though her limbs refused to support her body, even though apparently upheld by the grip of the man beside her. Rale, joining them, immediately grasped her other arm, and, between the two, she was impelled forward. The saloon keeper seemed unable to restrain his voice.

"Yer must'r give her one hell o' a dose," he growled, angrily. "Half o' thet wud a bin 'nough. Why, damn it, she kin hardly walk."

"Well, what's the odds?" it was Kirby who replied sarcastically. "She got more because she wouldn't drink. We had to make her take it, and it wasn't no easy job. Gaskins will tell you that. Have you got your man here?"

"O' course; he's waitin' thar with the hosses. But I'm damned if I like this. She don't know nuthin', does she?"

"Maybe not now; but she'll come around all right, and she signed her name. So there ain't no hitch. She seemed to get worse after that. Come on, we can't stand talking here; let's get them off, Jack, there isn't any time to waste. I suppose we'll have to strap her into the saddle."

I held back, and permitted them to work, merely leading my own horse slightly to one side, and keeping in his shadow. I doubt if Kirby even glanced toward me, although if he did he saw only an ill-defined figure, with no glimpse of my face. But the chances were that I was nothing to him at that moment—a mere floating bum whom Rale had picked up to do this job; and just then his whole attention was concentrated upon the half-conscious girl, and his desire to get her safely out of that neighborhood. My presence meant nothing of special interest. Gaskins brutally jerked the shrinking mulatto forward, and forced her to mount one of the horses. She made some faint protest, the nature of which I failed to catch clearly, but the fellow only laughed in reply, and ordered her to keep quiet. Eloise uttered no word, emitted no sound, made no struggle, as the two other men lifted her bodily into the saddle, where Kirby held her, swaying helplessly against him, while Rale strapped her securely into place.

The entire proceedings were so brutally cruel that it required all my strength of will to restrain myself from action. My fingers closed upon the pistol in my pocket, and every impulse urged me to hurl myself on the fellows, trusting everything to swift, bitter fight. I fairly trembled in eagerness to grapple with Kirby, hand to hand, and crush him helpless to the earth. I heard his voice, hateful and snarling, as he cursed Rale for his slowness, and the hot blood boiled in my veins, when he jerked the girl upright in the saddle.

"Thar," said the saloon keeper, at last, testing his strap. "I reckon she can't fall off nohow, even if she don't sit up worth a damn. Go ahead now, Moffett."

Both the men stepped aside, and I led my horse forward. The movement brought me more into the open, and face to face with Kirby. By some trick of fate, at that very instant a star-gleam, piercing through the screen of leaves overhead, struck full into my eyes. With an oath he thrust my hat back and stared straight at me.

CHAPTER XXV

THE FUGITIVES

I could not see the mingled hate and horror glaring in the man's eyes, but there could be no doubt of his recognition. The acknowledgment found expression in a startled exclamation.

"By God!—you, here!"

That was all the time I gave him. With every pound of strength, with every ounce of dislike, I drove a clenched fist into that surprised face, and the fellow went down as though smitten by an axe. Even as he reeled, Rale leaped on me, cursing, failing to understand the cause, yet instinctively realizing the presence of an enemy. He caught me from behind, the very weight of his heavy body throwing me from balance, although I caught one of his arms, as he attempted to strike, and locked with him in desperate struggle. He was a much heavier and stronger man than I, accustomed to barroom fighting, reckless of method, caring for nothing except to get his man. His grip was at my throat, and, even as his fingers closed savagely, he struck me with one knee in the stomach, and drove an elbow straight into my face. The next instant we were locked together so closely any blow became impossible, youth and agility waging fierce battle against brutal strength. I think I was his match, yet this I never knew—for all my thought centered in an effort to keep his hands from reaching any weapon. Whatever happened to me, there must be no alarm, no noise sufficiently loud so as to attract the attention of sentries on guard. This affair must be fought out with bare knuckles and straining sinews— fought in silence to the end. I held him to me in a bear grip, but his overmastering strength bore me backward, my body bending beneath the strain until every muscle ached.

"Damn you—you sneakin' spy!" he hissed savagely, and his jaws snapped at me like a mad beast. "Let go! damn you—let go!"

Crazed by the pain, I swerved to one side, and half fell, my grip torn loose from about his arms, but as instantly closing again around his lower body. He strained, but failed to break my grasp, and I should have hurled him over the hip, but at that second Gaskins struck me, and I went tumbling down, with the saloon keeper falling flat on top of me, his pudgy fingers still clawing fiercely at my throat. It seemed as though consciousness left my brain, crushed into death by those gripping hands, and yet the spark of life remained, for I heard the ex-preacher utter a yelp, which ended in a moan, as a blow struck him; then Rale was jerked off me, and I sobbingly caught my breath, my throat free. Into my dazed mind there echoed the sound of a voice.

"Is thet 'nough, Jack?—then holler. Damn yer, yer try thet agin, an' I'll spill whut brains ye got all over this kintry. Yes, it's Tim Kennedy talkin', an' he's talkin' ter ye. Now yer lie whar yer are. Yer ain't killed, be ye, Knox?"

I managed to lift myself out of the dirt, still clutching for breath but with my mind clearing.

"No; I guess I'm all right, Tim," I said, panting out the words with an effort. "What's become of Kirby? Don't let him get away."

"I ain't likely to. He's a lyin' right whar yer dropped him. Holy Smoke! it sounded ter me like ye hit him with a pole-axe. I got his gun, an' thet's whut's makin' this skunk hold so blame still—oh, yes, I will, Jack Rale; I'm just a achin' fer ter let ye hav' it."

"And the other fellow? He hit me."

"My ol' frien', Gaskins; thet's him, all right." The deputy gave vent to a short, mirthless laugh. "Oh, I rapped him with the butt; had ter do it. He'd got hold ov a club somwhar, an' wus goin' ter give yer another. It will be a while, I reckon, 'fore he takes much interest. What'll I do with this red-headed gink?"

I succeeded in reaching my feet, and stood there a moment, gaining what view I could through the darkness. The short struggle, desperate as it had been, was not a noisy one, and I could hear nothing about us to indicate any alarm. No hurrying footsteps, no cries told of disturbance in any direction. Kirby rested exactly as he had fallen, and I stared down at the dim outlines of his distended body, unable to comprehend how my swift blow could have wrought such damage. I bent over him wonderingly, half believing he feigned unconsciousness. The fellow was alive, but his head lay upon a bit of jagged rock—this was what had caused serious injury, not the impact of my fist. Kennedy had one hard knee pressed into Rale's abdomen and the star-rays reflected back the steel glimmer of the pistol held threateningly before the man's eyes. The horses beyond stood motionless, and the two women in the saddles appeared like silent shadows. I stood up once more, peering through the darkness and listening. Whatever was to be done, I must decide, and quickly.

"Have Rale stand up, but keep him covered. Don't give him any chance to break away; now wait—there is a lariat rope hanging to this saddle; I'll get it."

It was a strong cord and of good length, and we proceeded to bind the fellow securely in spite of his objections, I taking charge of the pistol, while Tim, who was more expert, did the job in a workmanlike manner. Rale ventured no resistance, although he made no effort to restrain his tongue.

"Thar ain't no use pullin' thet rope so tight, yer ol' fule. By God, but yer goin' ter pay fer all this. Maybe ye think ye kin git away in this kintry, but I'll show ye. Damn nice trick yer two played, wa'n't it? The lafe will be on 'tother side afore termorrer night. No, I won't shet up, an' ye can't make me— ye ain't done with this job yet. Curse ye, Tim Kennedy, let up on thet."

"Now gag him, Tim," I said quietly. "Yes, use the neckerchief. He can do more damage with his mouth than any other way. Good enough; you are an artist in your line; now help me drag him over here into the woods. He is a heavy one. That will do; all we can hope for is a few hours start."

"Is Kirby dead?"

"I'm afraid not, but he has got an ugly bump, and lost some blood, his head struck a rock when he fell. It will be a while, I imagine, before he wakes up. How about your man?"

He crossed over and bent down above the fellow, feeling with his hands in the darkness.

"I reckon he's a goner, Cap," he admitted, as though surprised. "Gosh, I must'r hit the cuss harder than I thought—fair caved in his hed, the pore devil. I reckon it's no great loss ter noboddy."

"But are you sure he is dead? That will put a different aspect on all this, Kennedy!" I exclaimed gravely, facing him as he arose to his feet. "That and the belief I now have that Kirby has already consummated his plan of marriage with Miss Beaucaire."

"You mean he has—"

"Yes, that he has forced the girl to assent to some form of ceremony, probably legal in this country. I overheard enough between him and Rale to suspect it, at least, and she is even now under the influence of some drug. She hasn't spoken, nor does she seem to know what is going on about her. They strapped her into the saddle."

"The hell they did."

"It has been a hellish affair all the way through, and the only way in which I can serve her, if this is so, is by getting her away—as far away as possible, and where this devil can never find her again. She's got to be saved not only from him, but also from the scandal of it."

He stood silent, little more than a shadow before me, his head bent, as though struggling with a new thought, a fresh understanding.

"I reckon I kin see thet, sir, now." His voice somehow contained a new note of respect, as though the truth had suddenly dawned upon him, "I didn't just get hold o' things rightly afore; why an army offercer like yer should be mixed up in this sorter job. But I reckon I do now—yer in love with her yerself; ain't thet it, sir?"

"Yes, Tim," I confessed frankly, and not at all sorry to make the avowal. "That is the truth. Now what would you do if you were in my place?"

"Just exactly whut yer doin', I reckon," he returned heartily. "Only maybe I'd kill thet dirty skunk afore I went away; damned if I wudn't."

I shook my head.

"No, not in cold-blood. I wouldn't have been sorry if he had died fighting, but murder is not my line. He deserves death, no doubt, but it is not possible for me to kill him lying there helpless. What bothers me most right now is your case."

"Mine? Lord, what's the matter with me?"

"Considerable, I should say. You cannot be left here alone to face the result of this night's work. If Gaskins is dead from the blow you struck him, these two fellows will swear your life away just for revenge. Even if you told the whole story, what chance would you have? That would only expose us, and still fail to clear you. It would merely be your word against theirs—you would have no witnesses, unless we were caught."

"I reckon thet's true; I wasn't thinkin' 'bout it."

"Then there is only the one road to take, Tim," I insisted. "We've got to strike the trail together."

"Whar?"

"I cannot answer that now; I haven't thought it out yet. We can talk that matter over as we ride. I have a map with me, which will help us decide the best course to choose. The first thing is to get out of this neighborhood beyond pursuit. If you only had a horse."

"Thar's two critters down in the crick bottom. I reckon thet Kirby an' Gaskins must'r tied 'em thar."

"Good; then you will go; you agree with me?"

"Thar ain't nuthin' else fer me ter do—hangin' ain't never bin no hobby o' mine. As I understand it, this Gaskins wus one o' these yere militia men. I reckon thet if these yere two bug's wus ter swear thet I killed him—as most likely they will— them boys wud string me up furst, an' find out fer sure afterwards. Thar ain't so damn much law up yere, an' thet's 'bout whut wud happen. So the sooner I leave these yere parts, the more likely I am ter live a while yet."

"Then let's start," decisively. "Pick up one of those horses down on the bottom, and turn the other one loose. I'll lead on down the trail and you can meet us at the ford—once across the creek we can decide which way to travel; there must be four hours of darkness yet."

I picked up the trailing rein of my horse and slipped my arm through it. Tim faded away in the gloom like a vanishing shadow. The young woman next me, strapped securely to her saddle, made no movement, exhibited no sign of interest; her head and body drooped, yet her hands grasped the pommel as though she still retained some dim conception of her situation. The face under her hood was bent forward and shaded and her eyes, although they seemed open, gave no heed to my presence. I touched her hands—thank God, they were moist and warm, but when I spoke her name it brought no response. The other horse, ridden by the mulatto girl, was forced in between us.

"Who are ye?" she questioned, wonderingly. "Ye just called her by name, an' ye must know her. Whut ye goin' fer ter do with us, sah?"

I looked up toward her face, without distinguishing its outlines. I felt this was no time to explain; that every moment lost was of value.

"Never mind now; I know who she is and that you are Elsie Clark. We are your friends."

"No he ain't—not thet other man; he ain't no friend o' mine. Ah tell ye. He's de one whut locked me up on de boat. Ah sure know'd his voice; he done locked me up, an' Ah's a free nigger."

"Forget that, Elsie; he's helping you now to get away. You do just what I tell you to and above all keep still. Miss Beaucaire was drugged, wasn't she?"

"Ah don't know, sah. She sure does act mighty queer, but Ah nebber see her take nuthin'. Ah nebber see nuthin' 'tall till dey took me outer de shack an' galivanted me up yere. Whar I heerd yer voice afore?"

"I haven't time to explain that; we are going now."

I started forward on foot, leading my horse, the others trailing after through the darkness. Knowing nothing of the way, I was thus better able to pick the path, yet I found this not difficult, as it was rather plainly outlined by the forest growth on either side. It led downward at a gentle slope, although the grade was sufficiently steep so as to force

Eloise's body forward and compel me to support her as best I could with one arm. She still appeared to be staring directly ahead, with unseeing eyes, although her hands clung as tightly as ever to the saddle pommel. I clinched my teeth, half crazed at the sight of her condition, yet feeling utterly helpless to do more. I spoke to her again, but received no answer, not the slightest evidence that she even heard my voice or recognized her name.

The trail was clay with a few small stones embedded in it, and the horses made little noise in their descent, except once when Elsie's animal slipped and sent a loosened bit of rock rolling down to splash in some pool below. We came to the bank of the creek at last, a narrow stream, easily fordable, but with a rather steep shore line beyond, and waited there a moment until Tim emerged from out the black woods at our right and joined us. He was mounted, and, believing the time had arrived for more rapid movement, I also swung up into saddle and ranged the girl's horse beside mine.

"It looks to be open country beyond there," I said, pointing across, "what little I can see of it. You better ride the other side of Miss Beaucaire, Tim, and help me hold her up—the colored girl can trail behind. We'll jog the horses a bit."

They were not stock to be proud of, yet they did fairly well, Tim's mount evidently the best of the four. The going was decidedly better once we had topped the bank. The stars were bright enough overhead to render the well-marked trail easily visible, and this led directly southward, across a rolling plain. We may have ridden for two miles without a word, for, although I had no intention of proceeding far in this direction, I could discover no opportunity for changing our course, so as to baffle pursuit. That Kirby and Rale would endeavor to follow us at the earliest opportunity was most probable. They were neither of them the sort to accept defeat without a struggle, and, after the treatment they had received, the desire for revenge would be uppermost. Nor thus far would there be any difficulty in their picking up our trail, at least as far as the creek crossing, and this would assure them the direction we had chosen. Beyond the ford tracing our movements might prove more troublesome, as the short, wiry grass under foot, retained but slight imprint of unshod hoofs, the soil beneath being of a hard clay. Yet to strike directly out across the prairie would be a dangerous experiment.

Then suddenly, out of the mysterious darkness which closed us in, another grove loomed up immediately in our front, and the trail plunged sharply downward into the depths of a rugged ravine. I was obliged to dismount and feel my way cautiously to the bottom, delighted to discover there a smoothly flowing, narrow stream, running from the eastward between high banks, overhung by trees. It was a dismal, gloomy spot, a veritable cave of darkness, yet apparently the very place I had been seeking for our purpose. I could not even perceive the others, but the restless movement of their horses told me of their presence.

"Kennedy."

"Right yere, sir. Lord, but it's dark—found enything?"

"There is a creek here. I don't know where it flows from, but it seems to come out of the east. One thing is certain, we have got to get off this trail. If we can lead the horses up stream a way and then circle back it would keep those fellows guessing for a while. Come here and see what you think of the chance."

He was not to exceed two yards away from me, but came shuffling uncertainly forward, feeling gingerly for footing in the blackness along the rock-strewn bank. His outstretched hand touched me, startling us both, before we were aware of our close proximity.

"Hell, but I'm as blind as a bat," he laughed. "Is this the crick? How wide is it?"

"I just waded across; about five yards and not more than two feet deep."

"Maybe it's blocked up above."

"Of course, it might be, but it seems like a chance worth taking. We are sure to be caught if we hang to this trail."

"I reckon thet's so. Ye let me go ahead with the nigger gurl, an' then follow after us, leadin' Miss Beaucaire's boss. By jeminy crickets, 'tain't deep 'nough fer ter drown us enyway, an' I ain't much afeerd o' the dark. Thar's likely ter be sum place whar we kin get out up thar. Whar the hell are them hosses?"

We succeeded in locating the animals by feeling and I waited on the edge of the bank, the two reins wrapped about my arm, until I heard the others go splashing down into the water. Then I also groped my own way cautiously forward, the two horses trailing behind me, down the sharply shelving bank into the stream. Tim chose his course near to the opposite shore, and I followed his lead closely, guided largely by the splashing of Elsie's animal through the shallow water. Our movement was a very slow and cautious one, Kennedy halting frequently to assure himself that the passage ahead was safe. Fortunately the bottom was firm and the current not particularly strong, our greatest obstacle being the low-hanging branches which swept against us. Much of my time was expended in holding these back from contact with Eloise's face, our horses sedately plodding along behind their leaders.

I think we must have waded thus to exceed a mile when we came to a fork in the stream and plumped into a tangle of uprooted trees, which ended our further progress. Between the two branches, after a little search, we discovered a gravelly beach, on which the horses' hoofs would leave few permanent marks. Beyond this gravel we plunged into an open wood through whose intricacies we were compelled to grope blindly, Tim and I both afoot, and constantly calling to each other, so as not to become separated. I had lost all sense of direction, when this forest finally ended, and we again emerged upon open prairie, with a myriad of stars shining overhead.

CHAPTER XXVI

THE ISLAND IN THE SWAMP

The relief of thus being able to perceive each other and gain some view of our immediate surroundings, after that struggle through darkness, cannot be expressed in words. My first thought was for the girl, whose horse I had been leading, but her eyes were no longer open and staring vacantly forward; they were now tightly closed, and, to all appearances, she slept soundly in the saddle. In the first shock of so discovering her, I touched her flesh to assure myself that she was not dead, but the blood was flowing warm and life-like through her veins. She breathed so naturally I felt this slumber must be a symptom of recovery.

We were upon a rather narrow tongue of land, the two diverging forks of the stream closing us in. So, after a short conversation, we continued to ride straight forward, keeping rather close to the edge of the woods, so as to better conceal our passage. Our advance, while not rapid, was steady, and we must have covered several miles before the east began to show gray, the ghastly light of the new dawn revealing our tired faces. Ahead of us stretched an extensive swamp, with pools of stagnant water shimmering through lush grass and brown fringes of cat-tails bordering their edges. Seemingly our further advance was stopped, nor could we determine the end of the morass confronting us. Some distance out in this desolation, and only half revealed through the dim light, a somewhat higher bit of land, rocky on its exposed side, its crest crowned with trees, arose like an island. Tim stared across at it, shading his eyes with one hand.

"If we wus goin' ter stop enywhar, Cap," he said finally, "I reckon thar ain't no better place then thet, pervidin' we kin git thar."

I followed his gaze, and noticed that the mulatto girl also lifted her head to look.

"We certainly must rest," I confessed. "Miss Beaucaire seems to be sleeping, but I am sure is thoroughly exhausted. Do you see any way of getting across the swamp?"

He did not answer, but Elsie instantly pointed toward the left, crying out eagerly:

"Sure, Ah do. The lan' is higher 'long thar, sah—yer kin see shale rock."

"So you can; it almost looks like a dyke. Let's try it, Tim."

It was not exactly a pleasant passage, or a safe one, but the continual increase in light aided us in picking our way above the black water on either hand. I let my horse follow those in front as he pleased and held tightly to the bit of the one bearing Eloise. It had to be made in single file, and we encountered two serious breaches in the formation where the animals nearly lost their footing, the hind limbs of one, indeed, sliding into the muck, but finally reached the island end, clambering up through a fissure in the rock and emerging upon the higher, dry ground. The island thus attained proved a small one, not exceeding a hundred yards wide, rather sparsely covered with forest trees, the space between these, thick with undergrowth. What first attracted my gaze after penetrating the tree fringe was the glimpse of a small shack, built of poles, and thatched with coarse grass, which stood nearly in the center of the island. It was a rudely constructed, primitive affair, and to all appearances deserted. My first thought was that we had stumbled upon some Indian hut, but I felt it safer to explore its interior before permitting the others to venture closer.

"Hold the horses here, Tim; let me see what we have ahead first."

I approached the place from the rear, peering in through the narrow openings between the upright poles. The light was so poor I was not able to perceive much, but did succeed in fully convincing myself that the dismal shack was unoccupied. The door stood unlatched and I pushed it open. A single glance served to reveal everything the place contained. Without doubt it had been the late abode of Indians, who, in all probability had fled hastily to join Black Hawk in his foray up Rock River. There was no pretense at furniture of any description—nothing, indeed, but bare walls and trampled dirt floor, but what interested me most was a small bit of jerked deer meat which still hung against an upright and the rude stone fireplace in the center of the hut, with an opening above to carry away the smoke. I had found during the night a fair supply of hard bread in my saddle-bag, and now, with this additional gift of Providence, felt assured, at least, of one sufficient meal. I stood there for perhaps a minute, staring wonderingly about that gloomy interior, but making no further discoveries, then I returned without and called to the others.

"It is all right, Tim, there is no one here. An old Indian camp, with nothing but a junk of jerked deer meat left behind.

Elsie, gather up some of that old wood yonder and build a fire. Kennedy and I will look after Miss Beaucaire."

It was bright day by this time, the red of the rising sun in the sky, and I could trace the radius of swamp land stretching about us on every hand, a grim, desolate scene even in the beauty of that clear dawn. We had been fortunate enough to approach the spot along the only available pathway which led to this little oasis, and a more secure hiding place it would be difficult to find. The tree growth and heavy underbrush completely concealed the miserable shack from view in every direction, and what faint trail we had left behind us since we took to the water of the creek would be extremely hard to follow. I felt almost at ease for the present and satisfied to rest here for several hours.

Tim assisted me in unstrapping Eloise, and lifting her from the saddle, and, as she made no effort to help herself, the two of us carried her to a warm, sunny spot beside the wall of the hut. Her cramped limbs refused to support her body, and her eyes, then open, yet retained that vacant look so noticeable from the first. The only change was in the puzzled way with which she stared into our faces, as though memory might be struggling back, and she was vaguely endeavoring to understand. Except for this pathetic look, she had never appeared more attractive to my eyes, with color in cheeks and lips. Her hood had fallen backward, revealing her glossy hair still smoothly brushed, while the brilliancy of the sunlight only made more manifest the delicate beauty of her features. Tim led the horses away and staked them out where they could crop the rich, dewy grass. After removing the saddles, he followed the mulatto girl into the hut, and I could hear the murmur of their voices. I endeavored to address Eloise, seeking thus to awaken her to some sense of my presence, but she merely smiled meaninglessly, leaned her head wearily back against the poles and closed her eyes.

It was a poor meal enough, although it sufficed to dull hunger, and yield us some strength. Eloise succeeded in choking down a few morsels, but drank thirstily. It was pitiful to watch her, and to mark the constant effort she was making to force the return of memory. Her eyes, dull, uncomprehending, wandered continually from face to face in our little group, but no flash of intelligence lighted up their depths. I had Elsie bathe her face with water and while, no doubt, this refreshed her somewhat, she only rested her head back on my coat, which I had folded for a pillow, and again closed her heavy eyes. The negress appeared so tired I bade her lie down and sleep, and soon after Tim also disappeared. I remained there alone, guarding the woman I loved.

I myself had reason enough to be weary, yet was not conscious of the slightest desire to rest. My mind did not crave sleep. That Eloise had been drugged for a purpose was now beyond controversy, but what the nature of that drug might be, and how it could be combated, were beyond my power to determine. Even if I knew, the only remedies at hand were water and fresh air. And how were we to escape, burdened by this helpless girl, from pursuit, which, perhaps, had already started from Yellow Banks? At all hazards I must now prevent this dazed, stupified woman from ever again falling into the power of Joe Kirby. That was the one fact I knew. I would rather kill her with my own hand, for I was convinced the fellow actually possessed a legal right, which I could not hope to overthrow. However it had been accomplished, through what villainy, made no odds—she was his wife, and could only be released through process of law. He could claim her, hold her in spite of me, in spite of herself. No influence I might bring to bear would save her now from this contamination. It would all be useless, a thing for laughter. Her signature—of which Kirby had boasted—and the certificate signed by the dead Gaskins, would offset any possible efforts I might put forth. There remained no hope except through flight; outdistancing our pursuers; finding a route to safety through the wilderness which they would never suspect.

Where could such a route be found? In which direction was it safest for us to turn? Surely not southward down the river seeking refuge at Fort Madison, nor in the opposite direction toward Fort Armstrong. I thought of both of these, but only to dismiss them from consideration. Had it not been for this marriage, either might have answered, but now they would prove no protection. Those men whom we were seeking to escape would remember these points at once, and suspect our fleeing to either one or the other. There was no power there able to protect her from the lawful authority of a husband; nor could she deny that authority, if he held in his hands the proof. No, I must find an unknown path, an untraveled trail. Our only hope lay in baffling pursuit, in getting far beyond Kirby's grip. For the moment I felt reasonably safe where we were—but only for the moment. We could rest on this isolated island, barely lifting itself above the swamp, and plan our future, but within the limits of another day, probably, those fellows would discover signs of our passage, faint as they were, and follow us. I dragged the map out from its silk wrapping and spread it forth on the ground between my knees. It was the latest government survey, given me when I first departed for the North, and I already knew every line and stream by heart. I bent over it in uncertainty, studying each feature, gradually determining the better course, weighing this consideration and that.

I became so interested in the problem as to entirely forget her presence, but, when I finally lifted my head, our eyes met, and I instantly read in the depths of hers the dawning of recognition. They were no longer dull, dead, emotionless, but aglow with returning life—puzzled, unassured, yet clearly conscious.

"Who are you?" she breathed incredulously, lifting herself upon one hand. "Oh, surely I know—Lieutenant Knox! Why, where am I? What has happened? Oh, God! you do not need to tell me that! But you; I cannot understand about you. They—they said you died."

"They must have said much to deceive you," and I bent forward to touch her hand. "See, I am very much alive. Let me tell you—that will be the quickest way to understand. In the first place I did not drown when the boat was smashed, but was rendered helpless and borne away on the water. I drifted through the darkness out into the Mississippi, and later became caught on a snag in the middle of that stream. The *Adventurer* rescued me about daylight the next morning, and I was no sooner on board than I was told how the keel-boat had been run down below on the river during the night and that your party had all been saved—two white men and two negress slaves. Of course, I knew you must be one of them."

"Then—then we were actually together, on the same boat, all the way up here?"

"Yes; I tried hard to find where you were concealed on board, but failed. I might not have helped you, but I thought you would be glad to know I was alive. Kirby guarded you with great care from all observation. Do you know why?"

Her wide-opened eyes gazed into mine frankly, but her lips trembled.

"Yes," she answered, as though forcing herself to speak. "I do know now. I thought I knew then, but was mistaken. I supposed it might be because I looked so little like a negress, but now I realize it was his own conscience. He knew I was a white woman; he had become convinced that I was Eloise

Beaucaire. Did you know that, also?"

"I learned the truth on the boat, from the same source where Kirby obtained his information. Elsie Clark told me."

"Elsie Clark! Who is she? How did she know?"

"A free negress, who had been employed by Amos Shrunk. She was the other prisoner on the keel-boat when you were captured, kept locked below in the cabin. Surely you knew there was another woman taken aboard the *Adventurer*?"

"Yes, but we never spoke; she was below, and they kept me on deck. How could she know who I was?"

"She did not. Only she was positive that you could not be Rene Beaucaire, because she knew that Rene, in company with her mother, had departed from Shrunk's cabin before those raiders came. The two had already started for Beardstown."

She sat upright, all lassitude gone from her body, leaning eagerly toward me, her eyes alight with interest.

"Gone! Rene escaped them!" she exclaimed, her voice choking, "Oh, tell me that again. Was the girl sure?"

"Quite sure; she had cooked them breakfast and talked with Rene afterwards. She saw and spoke with both the women before they left in a wagon. They were on the Underground, bound for Canada, and safety."

"Thank God! Oh, I thank God!" Her face sank until it was concealed within her hands. When it lifted again the eyes were brimming with tears.

"I am so glad—so glad," she said simply. "Now I am strong enough to hear the rest, Lieutenant Knox. You must tell me."

"There is not so much to tell, that I am cock-sure about." I began slowly. "Kirby had you securely hidden away somewhere on the second deck, while this Clark girl had been locked into a stateroom above. I possessed such a growth of beard and was altogether so disreputable looking as to be mistaken for a roustabout by the boat's officers, who set me at work to earn my passage. In this way I managed to talk with Elsie, but failed to locate your quarters. The only glimpse I gained of you was when you were being taken ashore. Then I followed, and a little later succeeded in getting you out of Kirby's hands. That is about all."

"Oh, no, it is not—you—you came too late."

"Too late! Perhaps I may know what you mean."

"Do you? Surely not to blame me! I—I wish to tell you, Lieutenant Knox, but—but I scarcely know how. It is all so dim, indistinct in my own mind—and yet I remember. I am trying so hard to recall how it all happened, but nothing remains clear in my mind. Have I been drugged?"

"Without question. We have been riding all night and you were strapped to your horse. Probably you have no recollection of this?"

She shook her head in bewilderment, gazing about as though noting the strange surroundings for the first time.

"No; the last I remember I was with Kirby and another man. He—he was dressed like a minister, but—but he was half drunk, and once he swore at me. The place where we were was a little shack in the side of a hill, with stone walls. Kirby took me there from the steamer, together with a man he called Rale—Jack Rale. They locked me in and left me alone until after dark. Then this other man, who dressed like a minister, came back with Kirby. They had food and something to drink with them, and lit a lamp, so that we could see. It was awfully dismal and dark in there." She pressed her hands to her head despairingly. "I can remember all this, but later it is not so clear; it fades out, like a dream."

"Try to tell me all you can," I urged. "They fed you?"

"Yes, I managed to eat a little, but I would not drink. They both became angry then and frightened me, but they did compel me to swallow some of the stuff. Then I became dazed and partially helpless. Oh, I cannot tell you; I do not really know myself—it seemed as though I had to do just what they told me; I had no will of my own, no power of resistance."

"You were married to Kirby."

"Oh, God!—was I? I wondered; I did not really know; truly I did not know. I seem to remember that I stood up, and then signed some paper, but nothing had any meaning to me. Is that true? Do you know that it is true?"

I grasped her hand and held it closely within my own.

"I am afraid it is true," I answered. "I know very little law, and it may be that such a ceremony is not legal. Yet I imagine those men were certain as to what they could do. Kirby had planned to marry you from the very first, as I explained to you before. He told me that on the *Warrior* the night your father died."

"Yes, you said so; but I did not quite understand—he

planned then—why?"

"Because he had heard of your beauty and that you were rich. Were these not reasons enough? But, after he had mistaken you for Rene, the only possible way in which he could hope to gain you was by force. Jack Rale suggested that to him and how it could be done. The other man was a friend of Rale's, a renegade preacher named Gaskins; he is dead."

"Dead! Killed?"

"Yes; we brought you away after a fight with those fellows. We left Rale bound and Kirby unconscious."

"Unconscious, hurt—but not dead?"

"He had a bad gash in his skull, but was alive."

Kennedy, puffing happily upon a pipe, came loitering about the corner of the hut and approached us. Eloise staggered to her feet, shrinking back against the wall of the shack, her eyes on his face.

"That man here!" she cried in terror. "That man? Why, he was at Beaucaire! He is the one to whom I claimed to be Rene."

CHAPTER XXVII

WE CHOOSE OUR COURSE

Tim grinned at me, but did not appear particularly flattered at his reception.

"Not quite so fast, yung lady," he said, stuttering a bit and holding the pipe in his hand. "I reckon I wus thar all right, just as ye say, an' thet I did yer a mighty mean turn, but I ain't such a dern ornary cuss as ye think—am I, Cap?"

"No, you are not," I hastened to explain. "Miss Beaucaire does not understand, that is all. We have been talking together for some time, but I had forgotten to tell her that you were one of her rescuers. Kennedy here, merely supposed he was doing his duty, until he learned what Kirby contemplated. Then he refused to have any hand in it and the two quarreled. Shall I relate that part of the story?"

Her eyes softened, her lips almost smiling.

"Yes," she said. "I am glad to know; tell me all."

I described Tim's part in the whole tragedy swiftly, while he shifted awkwardly from one foot to the other and occasionally interjected some comment or correction. He was not wholly at ease in the role of hero, nor under the steadfast gaze of her eyes. As I stopped speaking she held out her hand frankly.

"Then I shall count you my friend now," she said simply. "And I am so delighted to understand everything. There are four of us here, counting the mulatto girl, and we are in hiding not far from Yellow Banks. You both think that Kirby and Rale must be hunting us already?"

"Probably; they are very certain not to be very far away. I was planning our course when I glanced up and caught your eyes watching me—"

"And I—I thought I saw a ghost," she interrupted. "And then, when, you actually spoke, I—I was so glad."

Tim's eyes fell upon the map, lying outspread on the ground.

"An' whut did ye think wus best, Cap?" he inquired gravely. "'Tain't likely we got all summer ter sit 'round yere an' talk in. I reckon we done rested 'bout long 'nough. 'Tain't such a bad place, but my notion is, we ought ter be joggin' 'long."

"Mine also. Come over here, both of you, and I'll give you my idea. I figured our chances in this way."

In a few words I explained my choice of route, pointing it out on the map and telling them briefly why I was afraid to seek refuge either at Fort Madison or Fort Armstrong, or, indeed, at any of the nearer settlements. Eloise said nothing, her gaze rising from the map to our faces as we debated the question, for Tim spoke his mind freely, his stubby forefinger tracing the course I had indicated.

"Thar's a trail south o' yere thet leads ter a town called

Ottaway, an' thar's another trail north o' yere—Injun, I reckon—whut runs straight east. Whar we are is plum in atween the two ov 'em, but it looks like it might be gud travelin'. Enyhow, thar ain't no rivers er nuthin' so fer as I see. What's this Ottaway, enyhow?"

"There is a small settlement there and a blockhouse. Possibly there are other settlements between here and there, not on the map."

"How fer do yer make it—frum this place ter thar?"

"Well, here is probably the stream we waded up last night— see. I should say we must be about where I make this mark. To Ottawa? I will make a guess that it is a bit over a hundred miles, and from there to Chicago sixty or seventy more. Those last would be over a good trail."

"An' whar do yer reckon are them Injuns—the hostile ones; this yere bunch o' Black Hawk's?"

"Somewhere up Rock River, or along the Green Valley. I'll point it out to you—see; there is where Black Hawk had his village and his hunters ranged all over this country, down as far as the Illinois. Of course, I cannot tell where they are now, for that depends on how far the soldiers have driven them, but it would be my guess they will be somewhere in here—between Prophetstown and the Winnebago Swamp."

"Let's see; thet ain't so dern fer away either. I reckon this yere course ye've just picked out wudn't take us mor'n twenty mile er so away. 'Spose we'd run inter a raidin' party o' them red bucks. I ain't got much hair, but I kin use whut I hav' got."

"I am not sure, Tim, but I would even prefer that to being

overtaken by Joe Kirby and the gang he'll probably have with him," I retorted, my gaze on the questioning face of the girl. "However, there is little chance of our encountering such a party. The soldiers are all coming up from the south and are bound to force Black Hawk's warriors to the other bank of the Rock. There will be nothing but barren country east of here. What do you say, Miss Eloise?"

Her eyes met mine bravely, without a shadow of doubt in them.

"I shall go wherever you say," she replied firmly, "I believe you will know best."

"Then I decide on this route. Once we get beyond the swamp, those fellows are going to have a hard task following us, unless they have an Indian trailer along with them. We have been here several hours; the horses must be rested. Let's eat what we can again and then start. We must find a way out of this labyrinth while we have daylight."

Kennedy stood up and stared about us at the desolate scene, the expression of his face proving his dissatisfaction with the prospect.

"O' course, I'm a goin' 'long with yer, Cap," he acknowledged, dryly. "I never wus no quitter, but this yere trip don't look so damned easy ter me, fer all thet. Howsumever I reckon we'll pull through som'how, on fut, er hossback. I'll wake up thet dark gurl an' then saddle the hosses."

I watched him round the corner of the cabin, not wholly at ease in my own mind, then gathered up the map and replaced it in my pocket, aware that Eloise had not moved from her position on the grass.

"Is he right?" she questioned, looking up at me. "Is there any real danger of Indians?"

"Some, perhaps; it is all Indian country, north and east of here—or has been. I am not denying that, but this danger does not compare, in my mind, with the peril which confronts us in every other direction. I am trying to choose the least. Our greatest difficulty will be the lack of food—we possess no guns with which to kill game, only pistols, and an exceedingly small stock of ammunition. That is what troubles Tim; that, and his eagerness to get back down the river. He fails to realize what it would mean to you to fall again into Kirby's hands."

"Do you realize?"

"Do I? It is the one memory which controls me. Tell me, am I not right? No, not about the route, but about the man. You despise the fellow; you are willing to face any hardship so as to escape him?"

"I would rather die than have him touch me. I never knew the meaning of hate before. Surely you cannot deem it possible that I could ever forgive?"

"No; that would be hard to conceive; and yet, I wished to hear the words from your own lips. Will you answer me one thing more—why did you first assume the character of Rene, and why did you repose such instant trust in me?"

She smiled rather wistfully, her long lashes concealing her eyes.

"I think I myself hardly knew," she admitted timidly. "It all happened, was born of impulse, rather than through any plan. Perhaps it was just the woman in me. After my father died,

Delia thought it best to tell us the story of Rene's birth. This—this was such a terrible tale, and later we sought all through his private papers, hoping he had taken some action to set those two free. There was no proof that he had, no mention, indeed, except a memorandum of intention to refer the matter to Lawyer Haines at the Landing. This merely served to confirm what Delia had told us, and, as Haines had gone to St. Louis, we were unable to see him. We were all of us nearly crazed; I was even afraid Rene would throw herself into the river. So I suggested that we run away and drew money out of my private account for that purpose. My only thought was to take a steamer up the Ohio, to some place where we were not known, and begin life over again. Rene had been a sister to me always; we were playmates from childhood, and I had grown up loving and trusting Delia ever since I was a baby. No sacrifice was too great to prevent their being sold into slavery. Oh, you cannot understand—I had no mind left; only a blind impulse to save them."

I caught her hand in mine and held it firmly.

"Perhaps I do understand. It was my knowledge of this very condition which first brought me to you."

"You heard about us on the boat—the *Warrior*? Did father tell you?"

"No; it was Kirby. He was actually proud of what he had done—boasted to me of his success. I have never known a man so heartlessly conceited. Eloise, listen. You may have thought this was largely an accident. It was not; it was a deliberately planned, cold-blooded plot. I tell you that Joe Kirby is of the devil's own breed; he is not human. Rene's father told him first of the peculiar conditions at Beaucaire."

"Rene's father! Does—does he still live?"

"No; but he did live for years after he disappeared, supporting himself by gambling on the lower river. At one time he and Kirby were together. After he died Kirby investigated his story in St. Louis and found that it was true. Then he laid this plot to gain control of everything, including both of you girls—a plot surely hatched in hell."

"You know this to be true? How?"

"Partly, as I have said, from Kirby's own lips. In addition Jack Rale added what he knew—they are birds of a feather."

"But it seems so impossible, so like fiction. How could the man hope to succeed; to consummate such a crime? Besides, why should he desire us—Rene and I—whom he had never seen?"

"It can only be explained when you know the man. He had heard you described as a beautiful woman—that was enough for his type. He had convinced himself that Rene was a slave—his slave, once he had successfully played his trick. He knew you to be an heiress with a sum of money in your own right, which he could only hope to touch through marriage. The man dreamed of owning Beaucaire, of possessing all it contained. He was willing to risk everything to carry out his hell-born scheme, and to ruin everyone who interfered with him. I am telling you all this, Eloise, because it is now time you should know. Will you not tell me just how it all came to you?"

Her hands clung to me, as though she dare not let go; her eyes were filled with a mingling of wonderment and pain.

"Why, of course. We thought it best not to go until after we could see the lawyer. I could not believe my father had neglected to set those two free—he—he loved them both.

Delia and Rene had gone down to the Landing that night to see if he had returned. We were both of us afraid to leave Rene alone—she was so despondent, so unstrung. It was dark and I was all alone in the house. Then these men came. They did not know me and I did not know them, but I was sure what they came for. I was terribly frightened, without an idea what to do—only I refused to talk. All I could do was to pray that the others might be warned and not return. They searched the house and then left this man Tim to guard me. He told me he was a deputy sheriff from St. Louis, and—and I encouraged him to explain all he knew about the case. Then I made up my mind what to do—I would pretend to be Rene, and let them carry me off instead of her."

"But did you not realize the danger to yourself?"

"No, I suppose I didn't; or rather I did not care. All I thought about was how to save her. These were law officers; they would take me to St. Louis before a court. Then I could make myself known and would be set free. They couldn't do anything else, could they? There was no law by which I could be held, but—but, don't you see? The delay might give Rene time to escape. That was not wrong, was it?"

"Wrong! It was one of the bravest things I ever heard of. And I know the rest—your encounter with Kirby in the library. I overheard all of that through the open window, and how you learned from him that certain legal papers would have to be served on Eloise Beaucaire before any of the slaves could be touched, or removed from the estate. That knowledge only brought you new courage to play out your part. But why did you trust me enough to go with me? And, after trusting me so fully, why did you refuse to tell me who you really were?"

Her eyes fell before mine, and her cheeks were flushed.

"I—I do not believe I can tell you that, Lieutenant. You— you see I am not even sure I know. At first, there in the library, I was compelled to choose instantly between you, and—and something infinitely worse. I—I supposed that man Kirby was dead; that—that you had killed him to save me. I—I looked into your face, and—and it was a man's face; you said you were an army officer. I—I had to believe and trust you. There was no other way. Please do not ask me to explain any more."

"I shall not—only just this. If you actually believed in me, trusted me, as you say, why should you still claim to be Rene; and continually remind me there was negro blood in your veins; that you were a negress and a slave?"

"You think that strange? I did trust you, Lieutenant Knox, and I trusted you more completely the longer we were together. But—but I did not wholly understand. You were endeavoring to rescue Rene from slavery. I could not conceive what interest you might feel if I should confess myself Eloise. You were strange to me; we were there alone with the negro, and—and somehow it seemed a protection to me to claim a drop of black blood. Twice I thought to tell you—the words were on my lips—but something stopped them. Possibly, just a little, I was afraid of you."

"Then—but not now?"

"No, not now—not even a little; you have proven yourself all I ever hoped you would be. I am glad—so glad—to say to you now, I am Eloise Beau—"

She stopped suddenly, the word half uttered, the smile fading from her lips. She withdrew her hands from my clasp and pressed them over her eyes.

"My God!" she burst forth. "But I am not! I am not! Why, I never felt the horror of it all before—I am not Eloise Beaucaire!"

A moment I stood motionless, seeming to hold my breath, my eyes open, struck silent by the intense bitterness of that cry. Then the reaction came, the knowledge that I must turn her thought elsewhere.

"Do not say that, or even think it," I urged, scarcely able to restrain myself from grasping her in my arms. "Even if it shall prove true—legally true—some way of escape will be found. The others are safe, and you are going to need all your courage. Pledge me to forget, to ignore this thing. I need you."

Her hands fell nerveless and her questioning eyes sought my face. They were tearless, unabashed.

"You are right, Lieutenant Knox," she said frankly. "I owe my loyalty now to you. I shall not yield again to despair; you may trust me—my friend."

The day was not yet ended when we finally retraced our way across the narrow dyke to the mainland, prepared to resume our journey. The passage was slow and dangerous, and we made it on foot, leading the horses. The woods were already beginning to darken as we forded the north branch of the creek, and came forth through a fringe of forest trees into a country of rolling hills and narrow valleys. The two girls were already mounted, and Tim and I were busily tightening the straps for a night's ride, when, from behind us, back in the direction of the peninsula we had just quitted, there sounded the sharp report of a rifle. We straightened up, startled, and our eyes met. There could be but one conclusion—our pursuers had found the trail.

CHAPTER XXVIII

A FIELD OF MASSACRE

To my mind, seated on that island in the morass, a map spread before me, a hundred miles of travel had not appeared a very serious matter, but I was destined to learn my mistake. The close proximity of the men seeking to overtake us—as evidenced by that rifle shot—awoke within us a sense of imminent danger and drove us forward through the fast gathering darkness at a perilous pace, especially as our mounts were not of the best. The fringe of trees along the bank of the stream was sufficiently thick to securely screen our movements until we had safely merged into the darkness beyond, nor could our trail be followed before daylight. Yet the desire was in all of our hearts to cover as much ground as possible. The available course lay across rough country, along steep sidehills, and into stagnant sloughs. Twice we mired through carelessness, and several times were obliged to skirt the edge of marshes for considerable distances, before discovering a safe passage beyond. The night shut about us black, and discouraging, with scarcely a star visible in the sky, by which we could determine our direction. I was quickly lost in this blind groping, unable to even guess the points of the compass, but Tim apparently possessed the mysterious instinct of the pathfinder, although what dim signs guided him I could not decipher. To me it was all chance; while he kept steadily moving, occasionally relieving his feelings by an oath, but never hesitating for longer than a moment.

We became mere shadows, groping through the void, barely perceptible to our own strained eyes. Now and then we drifted apart, and were obliged to call out so as to locate the others. We seemed to be traveling across a deserted, noiseless land, the only sound the stumbling hoofs of the horses, or the occasional tinkle of some near-by stream, invisible in the darkness. Kennedy led the way, after I had confessed my inability to do so, and, I think, must have remained afoot most of the time, judging from the sound of his voice; advising us of the pitfalls ahead. It was some hours before we finally emerged from this broken land, and came forth onto a dry, rolling prairie, across which we advanced at a somewhat swifter gait. In all this time I had never relaxed my grip on the bridle-rein of Eloise's horse, drawing her up close beside me, whenever the way permitted, conscious that she must feel, even as I did, the terrible loneliness of our surroundings, and the strain of this slow groping through the unknown. We conversed but little, and then in whispers, and of inconsequential things—of hope and fear, even of literature and music, of anything which would take our minds off our present situation. I smiled afterwards to remember the strange topics which came up between us in the midst of that gloom. And yet, in some vague way, I comprehended that amid the silence, the effort to converse, a bond was strengthening between us both—a bond needing no words. It seemed to me that I could feel the beating of her heart in response to my own; and that while to my eyes she was but a mere outline, her features invisible, in imagination I looked into that face again, and dreamed dreams the lips dared not express.

Surely we both understood. Even as I knew my own heart, I

believed that I knew hers. I do not think she cared then to conceal, or deny; but, nevertheless, there existed continually between us a sinister face, a leering, sarcastic face, with thin lips and sneering eyes forever mocking—the hateful face of Joe Kirby. It was there before me through all those hours, and I doubt not it mocked her with equal persistency. Whenever I would speak, that memory locked my lips, so that all I ventured upon was to quietly reach out my hand through the darkness, and touch hers. Yet that was enough, for I felt her fingers close on mine in silent welcome.

Yet, perhaps, I ought not to say that it was any memory of the gambler which held me dumb. For it was not thought of the man, but rather of the woman, whose honor I felt bound to guard by closed lips. Some instinct of my own higher nature, or some voiceless message from her personality, told me the line of safety—told me that she would secretly resent any familiarity she was not free to welcome. She might ride through the black night beside me, our hands clasped in friendship, our hearts thrilling with hope. We could understand, could dream the dream of ages together—and yet, this was not now to be expressed in words; and there must still remain between us a barrier blacker than the night. She needed not to tell me this truth—I felt it; felt it in the purity of her soul, her silence, her perfect trust in me. For this I knew, then and forever—only by respect could I win the love of her. This knowledge was restraint enough.

We rested for an hour at midnight, on the banks of a small stream. The sky had lightened somewhat, and we could perceive the way fairly well when we again advanced, now traveling through a more open country, a prairie, interspersed with groves of trees. Daylight overtook us at the edge of a slough, which bordered a little lake, where in the gray dawn, Tim, by a lucky shot, managed to kill a crippled duck, which later furnished us with a meager breakfast. In the security of a near-by cluster of trees, we ventured to build a fire, and, sitting about it, discussed whether to remain there, or press on. It was an ideal spot for a camp, elevated enough to afford a wide view in every direction. No one could approach unseen, and thus far we had no evidence that our pursuers were even on our trail. Only the crack of that single rifle shot the evening before had suggested that we were being followed—yet, even if this were true, the black hours since would have prevented any discovery of the direction of our night. Not even an Indian tracker could have picked up our trail amid that darkness. So it was decided to remain where we were, and rest.

I need not dwell on the details of our flight. They remain in my memory in all clearness, each scene distinct, each incident a picture engraved on the mind. I came to believe in, implicitly rely on, all my comrades—on the black-eyed, dusky Elsie, emotional and efficient, whose care-free laugh was contagious, and whose marvelous skill in cooking only increased our hunger, who knew every wild plant that grew, and unearthed many a treasure to help out our slim larder from the forest and prairie soil; on the solemn-faced Kennedy, whose profanity could not be restrained, and whose sole happiness was found in an ample supply of tobacco; who persistently saw only the dark side of things, yet who was ever competent, tireless, and full of resource; but most of all on Eloise, her patient, trustful eyes following my every movement, uncomplaining, cheerful, with a smile for every hardship, a bright word of hope for every obstacle. In the darkness of night travel, when no eye could see her, she might droop from weariness, clinging to her pommel to keep in the saddle, yet it was always her voice which revived courage, and inspired new endeavor.

The way was generally rough and puzzling, bringing before us no familiar landmarks by which to guide our course. My map proved utterly useless, confusing me by its wrong location of streams, and its inaccuracy in the estimation of distances. We must have wandered far to the north from our direct course, led astray in the dark, and by our desire to advance swiftly. For there soon came to us warning signs that we were indeed being pursued; and some evidence also that we were even within Indian territory. Once we beheld from an eminence the wisp of a camp fire far in our rear, a mere misty curl of smoke showing against the distant blue of the sky. And once, from out the shadow of a grove, we stared perplexed across a wide valley, to where appeared a dim outline of bluffs, and watched a party of five horsemen creep slowly along their summit, too far away to be recognized— mere black dots, we could not identify as either white men, or red.

But the savages had left their unmistakable mark for our finding. It was in the early twilight of the second day, the western sky already purple with the last fading colors, the prairie before us showing in patches of green and brown. To our left was a thick wood, even then grown gloomy and dark in shadows, and slightly in advance of us Kennedy rode alone, hopeful of thus dislodging some wild animal. I could see the gleam of the pistol in his hand, held in instant readiness, cocked and primed. Suddenly he drew rein, and then, turning his horse's head sharply, advanced cautiously toward the miniature forest, leaning forward to gaze intently at something unseen from where we were. I halted the others in a thrill of expectancy, anticipating the report of his weapon, and hopeful of a successful shot. He halted his horse, which pawed restlessly, and sat motionless, staring down into a little hollow immediately in front of him; then he turned in the saddle, and beckoned me.

"Cum over yere, Cap," he called, his voice sounding strange. "No, not the gurls; you cum alone."

I rode forward and joined him, only to stare also, the heart within me almost ceasing to beat, as I beheld the gruesome sight so suddenly revealed. There, within the confines of that little hollow, almost at the edge of the wood, lay the dead and mutilated bodies of eleven men, in every distorted posture imaginable, some stripped naked, and showing ghastly wounds; others fully clothed; but with the cloth hacked into rags. It had once been a camp, the black coals of a fire still visible, with one man lying across them, his face burnt and unrecognizable. With the exception of one only—a mere boy, who lay at few rods away, as though brought down in flight—the entire group were together, almost touching each other in death. Beyond question they had been soldiers—militia volunteers—for while there was only one uniform among them, they all wore army belts, and a service insignia appeared on their hats. Tim vented his feelings in a smothered oath.

"Militia, by God!" he muttered gruffly. "No guard set; the bloody Injuns jumped 'em frum out them woods. Those poor devils never hed no chanct. Ain't thet it, Cap?"

"No doubt of it; the whole story is there. None of them alive?"

"I reckon not—cudn't be hacked up like thet, an' most o' 'em skelped. Them reds never left a damn gun behind neither. Why say, this affair must a took place this yere very maunin', 'bout breakfast time."

He stood up in his stirrups, and swept his eyes anxiously about in every direction.

"Good Lord! maybe we better be gittin' 'long out o' yere right smart. Thar ain't nuthin' ter stay fer; we can't help them ded men none, an' only the devil himself knows whar them

Injuns hav' gone. Yer git the gurls away afore they see whut's yere—down yonder, inter the valley."

I took one more glance at the sight, fascinated by its very horror, then wheeled my terrified horse, and rode back. Heartless as his words sounded, they were nevertheless true. We could be of no aid to the dead, while upon us yet rested the duty of guarding the living. The young negress lifted her head, and gazed at me dully, so thoroughly tired as to be indifferent as to what had occurred; but Eloise read instantly the message of my face.

"You have looked upon something terrible," she cried. "What was it? a dead body?"

"Eleven dead bodies," I answered gravely, my lips trembling. "A squad of militiamen were surprised by Indians over there, and slaughtered to a man, apparently with no chance to even defend themselves. I have never seen a more terrible sight."

"Indians, you say! Here?" her eyes widening in horror. "When do you suppose this happened? how long ago?"

"Within twelve hours certainly; probably soon after dawn. The attack must have been made while the soldiers were at breakfast."

"Then—then those Indians cannot be far away?"

"We have no means of knowing; but it will be assuredly safer for us to get under cover. Come, both of you."

"They were all killed—all of them? You are sure?"

"Yes; it would be impossible for any among them to be alive—the bodies were scalped, and mutilated."

I caught the rein of her horse, and Elsie, who was now wide awake, and trembling with fear, pressed forward, close to my other side, moaning and casting her frightened glances backward. Kennedy was already started in advance of us on foot, leading his animal, and seeking to discover the quickest passage to shelter. The valley below was a deep and pleasant one, with sides forest clad, and so thickly timbered we were almost immediately concealed the moment we began the descent. On a narrow terrace the deputy halted us.

"I reckon maybe this yere is as gud as eny place fer ter stop," he said rather doubtfully. "Thar ain't noboddy kin see us, nohow, an' thar's a gud spring over yonder. It'll be mighty dark in an hour, an' then we kin go on; only my hoss is about did up. Whut ye say, Cap?"

"We are probably as safe here as anywhere in the neighborhood. Let me help you down, Eloise. Is that all you have to report, Tim?"

He lifted his hat, and scratched gently his thin hair.

"Only thet them Injuns went south. I done run onto their trail after yer left—it wus plain as the nose on yer face. Thar must'r bin a slew o' 'em, an' sum a hoss-back; they wus a strikin' straight across yonder, an' I reckon they fetched a prisoner 'long, sumbody wearin' boots enyhow, fer I saw the tracks in the mud."

"Poor fellow. We'll not remain here, Kennedy, only to rest for an hour, or two. We'll not risk a fire."

"Sure not—ain't got nuthin' ter cook, enyhow." He hesitated, as though something was on his mind, glancing toward the girls, and lowering his voice. "I ain't so very dern tired, an' reckon I'll scout 'round a bit. Them red devils might'r overlooked a rifle er two back thar in the timber, an' I'd sure like ter git my fingers on one."

I nodded indifferently, too completely exhausted myself to care what he did, and then dull-eyed watched him disappear through the trees. No one spoke, even Eloise failing to question me, as I approached where she and Elsie had flung themselves on the short grass, although her heavy eyes followed my movement, and she made an effort to smile.

"One can easily see by your face how tired you are," I said, compassionately, looking kindly down at her. "I am going to sleep for an hour or two, and you had both better do the same. Tim is going to keep guard."

She smiled wearily at me, her head sinking back. I did not move, or speak again; indeed I had lost consciousness almost before I touched the ground.

I could not have slept long, for there was a glow of light still visible in the western sky, when a strong grip on my arm aroused me, causing me instantly to sit up. Tim stood there, a battered, old, long rifle in his hand, and beside him a boy of eighteen, without a hat, tousled headed, with an ugly red wound showing on one cheek.

"Mighty sorry fer ter wake ye, Cap," the deputy grinned. "This yere young chap is one o' them sojers; an' it strikes me, he's got a damn queer tale ter tell."

CHAPTER XXIX

THE VALLEY OF THE BUREAU

I glanced backward across my shoulder toward the others. Both girls were sleeping soundly, while beyond them, down the slope, the three horses were quietly cropping away at the herbage. I managed to rise.

"Let's move back to the spring, where we will not wake them up," I suggested. "Now we can talk."

My eyes sought the face of the lad questioningly. He was a loose-lipped, awkward lout, trembling still from a fright he could not conceal.

"You belonged to that squad killed out yonder?"

"Yes, seh; I reckon I'se the only one whut ain't ded," he stammered, so tongue-tied I could scarcely make out his words. "I wus gone after wahter, an' when them Injuns begun fer ter yell, I never dun nuthin' but just run, an' hid in the bush."

"But you are wounded?"

He put a red hand to his face, touching it gingerly.

"I dun got racked with a branch; I wus thet skeered I just cudn't see nuthin', seh."

"I understand. What is your name?"

"Asa Hall."

"Well, Asa, I suppose those were militiamen; you belonged to the company?"

He nodded, his eyes dull, his lips moving, as though it was an effort to talk. Quite evidently whatever little intellect he had ever possessed, now refused to respond. Kennedy broke in impatiently.

"It takes thet boy 'bout an hour fer ter tell enything, Cap," he explained gruffly. "I reckon he's skeered half ter death in the furst place, an' then thar's sumthin' wrong with him enyhow. Maybe I kin give ye the main pints. Them thar fellers belonged ter Cap. Hough's company frum down Edwardsville way—greener then grass, most ov 'em. They'd cum up frum sumwhar on the Illinoy, an' wus a headin' fer Dixon. Never onct thought thar might be Injuns down yere, an' never kept no guard. Them Injuns jumped 'em at daybreak, an' not a soul knew they wus thar, till they yelled. 'Twan't no fight, just a massacre. This feller he got away, just as he sed he did, by a hidin' in the bush. I reckon he wan't even seed at all, but he wus so blame close thet he heerd 'bout all thet went on, an' even seed a bit ov it. Lord! I hed ter poke him out; he wus thet skeered he cudn't stand."

"Wal, I reckon yer'd a bin too," the boy stuttered angrily. "I ain't never seed no Injuns afore."

"An' don't wanter ever see no more, I reckon. Hell! I don't hanker after eny myself. Howsumever, it's whut he seed an' heerd, Cap, thet sounds mighty queer ter me. He sez thar wus mor'n fifty bucks in thet party, an' that ol' Black Hawk wus thar hisself, a leadin' 'em'—he done saw him."

I turned, surprised at this statement, to stare into the boy's face. He half grinned back at me, vacantly.

"Black Hawk! He could scarcely be down here; what did he look like?"

"'Bout six feet high, I reckon, with a big hooked nose, an' the blackest pair o' mean eyes ever yer saw. I reckon he didn't hav' no eyebrows, an' he wore a bunch o' eagle feathers, an' a red blanket. Gosh' Mister, but the Devil cudn't look no worse'n he did."

"Wus thet him, Cap?" burst in Tim, anxiously.

"It's not a bad description," I admitted, yet not convinced. "I can't believe he would be here with a raiding party. If he was, there must be some important object in view. Is that all?"

"No, 'tain't; the boy swears thar was a white man 'long with 'em, a feller with a short moustache, an' dressed in store clothes. He wan't no prisoner nuther, but hed a gun, an' talked ter Black Hawk, most like he wus a chief hisself. After the killin' wus all over, he wus the one whut got 'em ter go off thar to the south, the whole kit an' kaboodle. Onct he spoke in English, just a word, er two. Asa cudn't make out whut he sed, but 'twas English, all right."

"I don't doubt that. There have always been white renegades among the Sacs and plenty of half-breeds. Those fellows are more dangerous than the Indians themselves—more savage, and revengeful. If Black Hawk, and this other fellow are leading this band, they are after big game somewhere, and we had better keep out of their way. I favor saddling up immediately, and traveling all night."

"So do I," and Tim flung a half-filled bag from his shoulder to the ground. "But I vote we eat furst. 'Tain't much, only a few scraps I found out thar; but it's a way better then nuthin'. Here you, Hall, give me a hand, an' then we'll go out, an' round up them hosses."

If the party of raiding Indians, whose foul deed we had discovered, had departed in a southerly direction, as their trail would plainly seem to indicate, then our safest course would seemingly be directed eastward up the valley. This would give us the protection of the bluffs, and take us more and more out of the territory they would be likely to cover. All this I explained to Eloise as we struggled with the hard bread, and a few strips of smoked bacon. Most of the bag had held corn meal, but no one suggested a fire, as we were glad enough to possess anything which would still the pangs of hunger. Eloise, filled with sympathy, attempted to converse with Hall, who ate as though half-starved, using hands and teeth like a young animal, but the boy was so embarrassed, and stuttered so terribly, as to make the effort useless. Within twenty minutes we were in saddle, descending the steep hillside through the darkness, Tim walking ahead with the lad, his horse trailing behind, and the long rifle across his shoulder.

It was a hard night journey. Occasionally as we toiled onward I could hear Elsie moan and sob, but Eloise gave utterance to no sound, except to reply cheerfully whenever I addressed her. The exceeding roughness of the passage made our progress slow, and quite frequently we were all obliged to dismount, generally glad enough of the change, and plod forward for some distance on foot. I possessed no knowledge then as to where we were, the map having deceived me so often I had long since lost all confidence in it as a guide, but now, in this later day, I can trace our progress with some degree of accuracy, and know that we passed that night in the valley of Bureau Creek, blindly groping our way forward toward a fate of which we little dreamed.

Nor did those weary hours of darkness bring to us the slightest warning, I do not recall feeling any special fear. In the first place I was convinced that we must already be at the extreme limit of Black Hawk's radius, and that, traveling as we were eastward, must before morning be well beyond any possible danger of falling into the hands of his warriors. The other pursuers I had practically dismissed from thought. Not for twenty-four hours had we perceived the slightest signs of Kirby's presence in our rear, and my faith was strong that his party had either lost our trail, or been turned aside by fear of encountering Indians. In this respect Kennedy remained more pessimistic than I, yet even in his mind confidence began to dawn that we had outstripped our enemies, both white and red, and that a few miles more must bring us in safety to some pioneer settlement. The poor condition of our horses compelled us to rest frequently, and our own utter exhaustion led to our dropping asleep almost the moment we halted. We were without food, and in no mood to converse. Shortly after midnight my horse strained a tendon, and could no longer uphold my weight. On foot, with the poor beast limping painfully behind me, I pressed on beside Eloise, both of us silent, too utterly wearied with the strain for any attempt at speech.

The early dawn found us plodding along close beside the creek, a fair sized stream, which meandered quietly through a beautiful valley protected on either side by high bluffs, rising to the plateau of prairie beyond. The bluffs themselves were wooded, but the lower expanse was open, covered with luxuriant grass, and containing only an occasional tree, like some lone sentinel, diversifying the landscape with the darker coloring of its leaves. It was a delightful scene, a bit of wilderness beauty undefiled, appearing so peaceful and perfect in its outer aspect as to cause even our tired, jaded eyes to open in eager appreciation. I noticed Eloise straighten up in the saddle, her face brightening in the early light as she gazed enraptured at the varied shades of green decorating the near-by bluff, fading gradually into the delicate blue of the arching sky overhead. The clear water of the creek sparkled and rippled musically over a bed of yellow gravel, while the soft lush grass clothing each bank waved gracefully in the light wind, rising and falling like the waves of the sea. It was all primitive nature untouched, nor was there evidence anywhere within our vision, that this isolated valley in the midst of the prairie, had ever before been visited by man. No dim trail crossed our path; no appearance of life, human or animal, met our eyes; we forced our own passage onward, with nothing to guide us, feeling more and more deeply the dread loneliness and silence of this strangely desolate paradise.

The rising sun topped the summit of the bluff, its red rays seeming to bridge with spans of gossamer the little valley up which we toiled. I had lost my interest, and was walking doggedly on, with eyes bent upon the ground, when the girl beside me cried out suddenly, a new excitement in her voice.

"Oh, there is a cabin! see! Over yonder; just beyond that big oak, where the bluff turns."

Her eager face was aglow, her outstretched hand pointing eagerly.

The logs of which the little building had been constructed, still in their native bark, blended so perfectly with the drab hillside beyond, that for the moment none of us caught the distant outlines. Tim possessed the keenest sight, and his voice was first to speak.

"Sure, Miss, thet's a cabin, all right," he said grimly. "One room, an' new built; likely 'nough sum settler just com' in yere. I don't see no movement, ner smoke."

"Fled to the nearest fort probably," I replied, able myself by this time to decipher the spot. "Be too risky to stay out here alone. We'll look it over; there might be food left behind, even if the people have gone."

We must have been half an hour in covering the distance. There were a number of shallow gullies to cross, and a long, gently sloping hill to climb. The cabin stood well up above the stream, within the shade of the great oak, and we were confirmed, long before we reached it, of our former judgment that it was uninhabited. The door stood ajar, and the wooden shutter of the single window hung dejectedly by one hinge. No sign of life was visible about the place; it had the appearance of desertion, no smoke even curling from out the chimney. A faint trail, evidently little used, led down toward the creek, and we followed this as it wound around the base of the big tree. Then it was that the truth dawned suddenly upon us—there to our right lay a dead mule, harnessed for work, but with throat cut; while directly in front of the cabin door was a dog, an ugly, massive brute, his mouth open, prone on his back, with stiffened legs pointing to the sky. I dropped my rein, and strode forward.

"Wait where you are," I called back. "There have been savages here; let me see first what has happened inside."

The dog had been shot, stricken by two bullets, and I was obliged to drag his huge body to one side before I could press my way in through the door. The open doorway and window afforded ample light, and a single glance was sufficient to reveal most of the story. It was a well-built cabin, recently erected, with hip roof and puncheon floor, the inside of the logs peeled, and white-washed. It had a homelike look, the few scattered articles of furniture rudely but skillfully made. A bit of chintz fluttered at the window, and a flower in a can bloomed on the sill. The table had been smashed as by the blow of an axe, and pewter dishes were everywhere. The bed in one corner had been stripped of its coverlets, many of them slashed by a knife, and the straw tick had been ripped open in a dozen places. Coals from the fireplace lay widespread, some of them having eaten deeply into the hard wood before they ceased smouldering.

I saw all this, yet my eyes rested upon something else. A man lay, bent double across an overturned bench, in a posture which hid his face from view. His body was there alone, although a child's shoe lay on the floor, and a woman's linsey dress dangled from a hook against the wall. I crept forward, my heart pounding madly, until I could gain sight of his face. He was a big fellow, not more than thirty, with sandy hair and beard, and a pugnacious jaw, his coarse hickory shirt slashed into ribbons, a bullet wound in the center of his forehead, and one arm broken by a vicious blow. His calloused hands yet gripped the haft of an axe, just as he had died—fighting.

The sight of the man lying in that posture of horror was so terrible that I instantly grasped the body, dragging it from off the overturned bench, and seeking to give it a resting place on the floor. But it was already stiffened in death, and I could only throw over it a blanket to hide the sight. Tim's voice spoke from the doorway.

"Injuns, I reckon?"

"Yes, they have been here; the man is dead. But there must have been others, a woman and child also—see that shoe on the floor, and the dress hanging over there. The poor devil fought hard."

Kennedy stepped inside, staring about him.

"I reckon likely he wus yere alone," he commented slowly, evidently thinking it out. "I figure like this—thet he'd heerd rumors o' Injuns bein' raidin' this way, an' hed sent his fam'ly back ter sum fort 'round yere, but decided fer ter take his own chances. Thar ain't no waggon round yere, an' no hosses, 'cept thet muel. He'd sure hav' sum sorter contivance fer ter ride in. Then agin he sorter looks like thet kind ov a feller ter me—he wudn't do no runnin' hisself, but I reckon he'd take keer o' his folks. Whut's this yere under the bench?—hell, a letter." He held it up to the light, in an effort to decipher the description. "'Herman Slosser, Otterway, Illinoy—ter be held till called fer.' Thet's it, Cap; thet's his name, I'll bet ye; an' so we can't be so blamed fur frum this yere Otterway fort. Good Lord! won't I be glad fer ter see it."

"Do you think it best to stop here?"

"Why not? 'Tain't likely them devils will be back agin. Thar sure must be somethin' fer us ter eat in the place, an' the Lord kno's we can't go on as we are. Them gurls be mighty nigh ready ter drop, an' two o' the hosses has plum giv' out. I'm fer liftin' this body out'r yere, an' settlin' down fer a few hours enyhow—say till it gits middling dark."

Undoubtedly this was the sensible view. We would be in far less danger remaining there under cover than in any attempt to continue our journey by daylight. Together we carried Slosser's body out, and deposited it in a thicket behind the cabin, awaiting burial; and then dragged the dead dog also out of sight. The disorder within was easily remedied, and, after this had been attended to, the girls were permitted to enter. Little was said to them, for they had seen enough with their own eyes to render the situation sufficiently clear, although in truth both were so wearied with the night ride, and the strain of those hours of night, as to be practically incapable of feeling any occurrence deeply. Horror after horror had followed us, until all sense of such things had become seared and deadened. The mind had reached the limit of endurance, and refused longer to respond. Even as I repeated briefly what it was we had discovered, and the conclusions drawn, their faces expressed only a dull compre- hension, and they seemed rather to be struggling to even keep an appearance of interest. Eloise sank back on the bench, her head supported against the wall, the lashes of her half-closed eyes showing dark against the whiteness of her cheeks. She looked so pitifully tired, the very heart choked in my throat.

The rest of us found a small stock of provisions, and Elsie, with Tim to aid her, built a fire and prepared breakfast. A half-filled bottle of whisky discovered in the cupboard, helped to revive all of us slightly, and gave Asa sufficient courage to seek outside for a spring. Tim, comparatively unwearied himself, and restless, located a trapdoor in the floor, rather ingeniously concealed, which disclosed the existence of a small cellar below. Candle in hand he explored this, returning with two guns, together with a quantity of powder and ball, and information that there remained a half-keg of the explosive hidden below.

"Must a bin aiming ter blow up stumps, I reckon," he commented, exhibiting a sample. "Coarsest I ever saw; cudn't hardly use thet in no gun, but it's powder all right," and he crumbled the particles between his fingers, flinging the stuff into the fire.

To remove the debris out of our way, I was gathering up the straw tick and slit blankets, and piled them all together back on the bed. Clinging to one of the blankets, caught and held by its pin, was a peculiar emblem, and I stood for a moment with it in my hand, curiously examining the odd design. Eloise unclosed her eyes, and started to her feet.

"What is that you have?" she asked,

"A pin of some kind—a rather strange design; I just found it here, entangled in this blanket."

She took it from my hand, her eyes opening wide as she, stared at the trinket.

"Why," she exclaimed in surprise, "I have seen one exactly like it before—Kirby wore it in his tie."

CHAPTER XXX

WE ACCEPT A REFUGEE

I looked again at the thing with a fresh curiosity, yet with no direct thought of any connection. The undisguised terror manifest in her face, however, caused me to realize the sudden suspicion which this discovery had aroused.

"That means nothing," I insisted, taking the pin back into my own possession. "It is probably the emblem of some secret order, and there may be thousands of them scattered about. Anyhow this one never belonged to Joe Kirby. He could never have been here. My guess is the fellow is back at Yellow Banks before now. Forget it, Eloise, while we eat. Then a few hours' sleep will restore your nerves; you are all worn out."

We had nearly completed the meal, seated around what remained of the shattered table. I do not recall what we conversed about, if indeed we conversed at all. My own thoughts, rambling as they were, centered on Eloise, and my desire to bring her safely to the Ottawa fort. How white and drawn the poor girl's face looked in the bright daylight; and how little of the food on her plate she was able to force down. What intense weariness found expression in those eyes which met mine. And she continued to try so hard to appear cheerful, to speak lightly. It was pitiful. Yet in spite of all this never to my sight had she seemed more attractive, more sweet of face. I could not remove my eyes from her, nor do I think she was unobservant, for a tinge of red crept slowly into the white cheeks, and a new light flashed across at me from beneath the shadowing lashes.

The boy Asa sat at the very end of the table, facing the open door, eating as though he had not tasted food for a week. He was a homely, uninteresting lout, but Tim had compelled him to wash, and in consequence his freckled face shone, and the wet shock of hair appeared more tousled than ever. From the time of sitting down he had scarcely raised his eyes from off the pewter plate before him; but at last this was emptied, and he lifted his head, to stare out through the open door. Into his face came a look of dumb, inarticulate fright, as his lips gave utterance to one cry of warning.

"Look! Look!"

With swift turn of the head I saw what he meant—a man on horseback, riding at a savage gait up the trail, directly for the cabin, bent so low in the saddle his features could not be discerned, but, from his clothing, unquestionably white. I was without the door, Tim beside me rifle in hand, when the fellow swept around the base of the oak, still staring behind him, as though in fright of pursuers, and flogging his straining horse with the end of a rein. He appeared fairly crazed with fear, unaware in his blind terror of the close proximity of the cabin.

"Hold on!" I yelled, springing forward, my arms thrown up, directly in the animal's course. "Stop, you fool!"

I know not whether the frantic horse checked itself, or if the rider drew rein, but the beast stopped, half rearing, and I gazed with amazement into the revealed face of the man—he was Joe Kirby. Before I could speak, or move, he burst into words.

"You! Knox! My God, man, whoever you are, don't refuse me shelter!"

"Shelter? from what?" my hand closing on a pistol butt.

"Indians! Be merciful, for God's sake. They are there in the valley, they are after me. I just escaped them—they were going to burn me at the stake!"

I glanced aside at Tim; his rifle was flung forward. Then I looked quickly back at the man, who had already dropped from his horse, and seemed scarcely able to stand. Was this true, had he ridden here unknowing whom he would meet, with no other thought but to save his life? Heaven knows he looked the part—his swarthy face dirtied, with a stain of blood on one cheek, his shirt ripped into rags, bare-headed, and with a look of terror in his eyes not to be mistaken. Villain and savage as I knew him to be, I still felt a strange wave of pity sweep me—pity and tenderness, mingled with hatred and distrust.

"Kirby," I said, and strode in between him and Tim's levelled weapon. "There is no friendship between us—now, or at any time. I believe you to be a miserable, snarling dog; but I would save even a cur from Indian torture. Did you know we were here?"

"No, so help me God. I saw the cabin, and hoped to find help."

"The savages are following you?"

"Yes—yes; see! Look down there—there are half a hundred of the devils, and—and Black Hawk."

"By the Holy Smoke, Cap, he's right—there they are!" sung out Kennedy, pointing excitedly. "The cuss ain't a lyin'. What'll we do?"

I saw them also by this time, my mind in a whirl of indecision. What should we do? What ought we to do? We should have to fight to the death—there was no doubt of that. An attempt to get away was manifestly impossible. But what about this renegade? this infernal scoundrel? this hell-hound who had been trailing us to kill and destroy? Should we turn him back now to his deserved fate? or should we offer him the same chance for life we had? He might fight; he might add one rifle to our defense; he might help us to hold out until rescuers came. And then—then—after that—we could settle our score. Tim's voice broke the silence.

"I reckon we ain't got much time," he said grimly. "It's one thing, 'er the other. I'm fer givin' the damn begger a chanst. I can't turn no white man over ter Injuns—not me. Kirby's got a gun, an' I reckon we're goin' fer ter need 'em all afore this blame fracas is over with."

"And I agree with you, Mr. Kennedy," said Eloise, clearly, speaking from the open door. "Lieutenant Knox, no one here has more to forgive than I. We must give the man refuge—it would be inhuman not to."

My questioning eyes sought her face, and I read there a plea for mercy not to be resisted. She meant her words, and the hate and distrust in my own heart seemed mean and vile. I stepped forward and struck the horse sharply, sending him scurrying around the end of the cabin.

"Go in!" I said, grimly, to Kirby, looking him squarely in the eyes. "And then play the man, if you care to live."

I lingered there upon the outside for a moment, but for a moment only. The advancing cloud of savages were already coming up the slope, gradually spreading out into the form of a fan. The majority were mounted, although several struggled forward on foot. Near their center appeared the ominous gleam of a red blanket, waved back and forth as though in signal, but the distance was too great for my eyes to distinguish the one manipulating it. We were trapped, with our backs to the wall.

There were but few preparations to be made, and I gave small attention to Kirby until these had been hastily completed. The door and window were barred, the powder and slugs brought up from below, the rifles loaded and primed, the few loopholes between the logs opened, and a pail of water placed within easy reach. This was all that could be done. Kennedy made use of the fellow, ordering him about almost brutally, and Kirby obeyed the commands without an answering protest. To all appearances he was as eager as we in the preparations for defense. But I could not command him; to even address the fellow would have been torture, for even then I was without faith, without confidence. The very sneaking, cowardly way in which he acted, did not appeal to me as natural. I could not deny his story—those approaching Indians alone were proof that he fled from a real danger; and yet—and yet, to my mind he could not represent anything but treachery. I possessed but one desire—to kick the cringing cur.

I stood at a loophole watching the approaching savages. They had halted just below the big tree, and four or five, half hidden by the huge trunk, were in consultation, well beyond rifle shot. Assured by their attitude that the attack would not be made immediately, I ventured to turn my face slightly, and take final survey of the room behind. Tim had stationed himself at the other side of the door, his eyes glued to a narrow opening, both hands gripped on his gun. Eloise and the colored girl, the one dry-eyed and alert, the other prone on the floor crying, were where I had told them to go, into the darkest corner. The boy I did not see, nor even remember; but Kirby stood on the bench, which enabled him to peer out through the loop-hole in the window shutter. What I noticed, however, was, that instead of keeping watch without, his eyes were furtively wandering about the room, and, when they suddenly encountered mine, were as instantly averted.

"Where was it you met those Indians, Kirby?" I questioned sternly.

"Down the valley."

"Last night?"

"This morning; they surprised us in camp."

"In camp! there were others with you, then. Who were they? the party you had trailing us?"

"Yes," a decidedly sullen tone creeping into his voice. "Five of them; one was a Winnebago."

"And Rale was along, I presume. What became of the others?"

He shook his head, but with no show of feeling.

"That's more than I know. Things were hot enough for me without bothering about the rest. I never saw any of them again, except Rale. He was killed in the fight. About an hour after that I shot the buck who was guarding me, and got away on his horse."

"What Indians were they?"

"Sacs mostly; some Foxes, and maybe a Winnebago or two."

"Was Black Hawk with them?"

"I don't know—I never saw Black Hawk."

I felt firmly convinced that he was deliberately lying, and yet there was nothing in his story which might not be true. No doubt it was prejudice, personal hatred, and distrust which led me to come to this conclusion. Well, true or not, I meant to see that he fought now.

"All right, but I advise you to keep your eyes outside," I said sternly. "Don't be staring about the cabin any more."

"I was looking for something to eat."

"Is that so? Well, you better stand it for awhile without eating. What is it, Eloise?"

"Please let me hand him some food."

I hesitated, conscious that I disliked even the thought of her serving the fellow in any way, yet unable to resist the eager plea in her eyes.

"Very well, if you wish to; only keep down out of range; those Indians may try for the loopholes. It is more than you deserve, Kirby."

He made no response, and I watched him closely as he endeavored to eat what she proffered him, and felt convinced that it was hard work. The man had lied about being hungry; he was not in need of food, and my deep-rooted suspicion of him only flamed up anew. A hand gripped at my sleeve timidly, and I turned quickly to encounter the eyes of Asa Hall. Never did I read such depth of fear in the expression of any face—it was the wild, unreasoning terror of an animal.

"What is it, my boy?"

"It's him, seh," he whispered, his lips trembling so I could scarce catch the words. "Thet feller thar. He's—he's the one I saw las' night with Black Hawk."

"Are you sure?"

"Yes, seh; I know him. I saw him plain as I do now."

I do not know why, but every bit of evidence against the man came instantly thronging back to my mind—the chance remark of Thockmorton on the *Warrior* about his suspicion of Indian blood; the high cheek bones and thin lips; the boy's earlier description; the manner in which our trail had been so relentlessly followed; the strange emblem found pinned to the blanket. I seemed to grasp the entire truth—the wily, cowardly scheme of treachery he was endeavoring to perpetrate. My blood boiled in my veins, and yet I felt cold as ice, as I swung about, and faced the fellow, my rifle flung forward.

"Kirby, stand up! Drop that rifle—take it, Eloise. Now raise your hands. Tim."

"Whut's up?"

"Is there anything serious going on outside?"

"No; nuthin' much—just pow-wowin'. Yer want me?"

"Search that scoundrel for weapons. Don't ask questions; do what I say."

He made short work of it, using no gentle methods.

"Wal' the gent wasn't exactly harmless," he reported, grinning cheerfully, "considerin' this yere knife an cannon. Now, maybe ye'll tell me whut the hell's up?"

Kirby stood erect, his dark eyes searching our faces, his lips scornful.

"And perhaps, Mr. Lieutenant Knox," he added sarcastically. "You might condescend to explain to me also the purpose of this outrage."

"With pleasure," but without lowering my rifle. "This boy here belonged to the company of soldiers massacred yesterday morning. You know where I mean. He was the only one to escape alive, and he saw you there among the savages—free, and one of them."

"He tells you that? And you accept the word of that half-wit?"

"He described your appearance to us exactly twenty-four hours ago. I never thought of you at the time, although the description was accurate enough, because it seemed so impossible for you to have been there. But that isn't all, Kirby. What has become of the emblem pin you wore in your tie? It is gone, I see."

His hand went up involuntarily. It is possible he had never missed it before, for a look of indecision came into the man's face—the first symptom of weakness I had ever detected there.

"It must have been lost—mislaid—"

"It was; and I chance to be able to tell you where—in this very room. Here is your pin, you incarnate devil. I found it caught in those blankets yonder. This is not your first visit to this cabin; you were here with Indian murderers."

"It's a damned lie—"

But Kennedy had him, locked in a vise-like grip. It was well he had, for the fellow had burst into a frantic rage, yet was bound so utterly helpless as to appear almost pitiful. The knowledge of what he had planned, of his despicable treachery, left us merciless. In spite of his struggles we bore him to the floor, and pinned him there, cursing and snapping like a wild beast.

"Tear up one of those blankets," I called back over my shoulder to Hall. "Yes, into strips, of course; now bring them here. Tim, you tie the fellow—yes, do a good job; I'll hold him. Lie still, Kirby, or I shall have to give you the butt of this gun in the face."

He made one last effort to break free, and, as my hand attempted to close on his throat, the clutching fingers caught the band of his shirt, and ripped it wide open. There, directly before me, a scar across his hairy, exposed chest, was a broad, black mark, a tribal totem. I stared down at it, recognizing its significance.

"By Heaven, Tim, look at this!" I cried. "He is an Indian himself—a black Sac!"

CHAPTER XXXI

THE VALLEY OF THE SHADOW

I do not know what delayed the attack of the savages, unless they were waiting for some signal which never came. I passed from loophole to loophole, thus assuring myself not only that they still remained, but that the cabin was completely surrounded, although the manner in which the warriors had been distributed left the great mass of them opposite the front. The others evidently composed a mere guard to prevent escape. No movement I could observe indicated an immediate assault; they rather appeared to be awaiting something.

Those I saw were all dismounted, and had advanced toward the cabin as closely as possible without coming within the range of guns. They had also sheltered themselves as far as possible behind clumps of brush, or ridges of rock, so that I found it difficult to estimate their number. Only occasionally would a venturesome warrior appear for a moment in the open, as he glided stealthily from the protection of one covert to another. No doubt some were brought within range of our rifles, as these efforts were usually made to more advanced positions, but I forbade firing, in the vague hope that, not hearing from Kirby, the chiefs might become discouraged and draw off without risking an open attack.

Randall Parrish

This was more a desperate hope, rather than any real faith I possessed. Beyond doubt the Indian chief knew, or thought he knew, our exact strength before he consented to use his warriors in this assault. If the band had trailed us to this spot, it had been done through the influence of Kirby, and he had, beyond question, informed them as to whom we were, and the conditions under which we had fled from Yellow Banks. The only addition to our party since then was the rescued boy. They would have little fear of serious loss in an attack upon two men, and two women, unarmed, except possibly with a pistol or two, even though barricaded behind the log walls of a cabin. And, with one of their number within, any attempt at defense would be but a farce. This same gang had already sacked the cabin, taking with them, as they believed, every weapon it contained. In their haste they had over-looked the cellar below. They had no thought of its existence, nor that we awaited them rifles in hand and with an amply supply of powder and lead. Whatever might be the final result, a surprise of no pleasant nature was awaiting their advance.

Convinced, as I had become, that Black Hawk was actually with the party, although I was unable to obtain any glimpse of him, I felt there was small chance of his departure, without making at least one effort to capture the cabin. That was his nature, his reputation—that of a bulldog to hang on, a tiger to strike. More even, this band of raiders must be far south of the main body of the Hawk's followers, and hence in danger themselves. They would never remain here long, facing the possibility of discovery, of having their retreat cut off. If they attacked, the attempt would not be long delayed.

Still there was nothing left to do but wait. We were already as completely prepared as possible with our resources. The main assault would undoubtedly be delivered from the front, directed against the door, the only point where they could hope to break in. Here Tim and myself held our positions, as ready as we could be for any emergency, and watchful of the slightest movement without. Tim had even brought up the half-keg of coarse powder from the cellar, and rolled it into one corner out of the way. His only explanation was, a grim reply to my question, that "it mought be mighty handy ter hav' round afore the fracus wus done." We had stationed Asa on the bench, as a protection to any attack from the rear, although our only real fear of danger from that direction lay in an attempt to fire the cabin during the engagement in front. I had instructed the boy to stay there whatever happened, as he could be of no help anywhere else, and to shoot, and keep shooting at anything he saw. Not overly-bright, and half-dead with fear as he was, I had no doubt but what he would prove dangerous enough once the action started; and, if he should fail, Eloise, crouching just behind him in the corner, could be trusted to hold him to his duty. There was no fear in her, no shrinking, no evidence of cowardice. Not once did I feel the need of giving her word of encouragement—even as I glanced toward her it was to perceive the gleam of a pistol gripped in her hand. She was of the old French fighting stock, which never fails.

My eyes softened as I gazed at her, her head held proudly erect, every nerve alert, her eyes steadfast and clear. Against the log wall a few yards away, Kirby strained at his blanket bonds, and had at last succeeded in lifting himself up far enough so as to stare about the room. There was none of the ordinary calm of the gambler about the fellow now—all the pitiless hate, and love of revenge which belonged to his wild Indian blood blazed in his eyes. He glared at me in sudden, impotent rage.

"You think you've got me, do you?" he cried, scowling across; then an ugly grin distorted his thin lips. "Not yet you haven't, you soldier dog. I've got some cards left to play in this game, you young fool. What did you butt in for anyway? This was none of your affair. Damn you, Knox, do you know who she is? I mean that white-faced chit over there—do you know who she is? You think you are going to get her away from me? Well, you are not—she's my wife; do you hear?— my wife! I've got the papers, damn you! She's mine!—mine; and I am going to have her long after you're dead—yes, and the whole damn Beaucaire property with her. By God! you talk about fighting—why there are fifty Indians out there. Wait till they find out what has happened to me. Oh, I'll watch you die at the stake, you sneaking white cur, and spit in your face!"

"Kirby," I said sternly, but quietly, stepping directly across toward him, "I've heard what you said, and that is enough. You are a prisoner, and helpless, but I am going to tell you now to hold your tongue. Otherwise you will never see me at the stake, because I shall blow your brains out where you lie. One more word, and I am going to rid this world of its lowest specimen of a human being."

"You dare not do—"

"And why not? You promise me death either way; what have I to lose then by sending you first? It will rid the girl of you, and that means something to me—and her. Just try me, and see."

He must have read the grim meaning in my face, for he fell back against the log, muttering incoherently, his dark eyes wells of hate, his face a picture of malignancy, but utterly helpless—the lurking coward in him, unable to face my threat. I left him and stooped above her.

"We shall be busy presently; the delay cannot be much longer. I am afraid that fellow may succeed somehow in doing us harm. He is crazed enough to attempt anything. May I trust you to guard him?"

Her eyes, absolutely fearless and direct, looked straight up into mine.

"Yes, he will make no movement I shall not see. Tell me; do you believe there is hope?"

"God knows. We shall do our best. If the worst comes—what?"

"Do not fear for me; do not let any memory of me turn you aside from your work," she said quietly. "I know what you mean and pledge you I shall never fall into his hands. It—it cannot be wrong, I am sure, and—and I must tell you that. I—I could not, Steven, for—for I love you."

My eager hands were upon hers, my eyes greedily reading the message revealed so frankly in the depths of her own. She only was in my thoughts; we were there alone—alone.

"They're a comin', Cap," yelled Kennedy and his rifle cracked. "By God! they're here!"

With one swift spring I was back at my deserted post and firing. Never before had I been in an Indian battle, but they had told me at Armstrong that the Sacs were fighting men. I knew it now. This was to be no play at war, but a grim, relentless struggle. They came en masse, rushing recklessly forward across the open space, pressing upon each other in headlong desire to be first, yelling like fiends, guns brandished in air, or spitting fire, animated by but one purpose—the battering of a way into that cabin. I know not who led them—all I saw was a mass of half-naked bodies bounding toward me, long hair streaming, copper faces aglow, weapons glittering in the light. Yes, I saw more—the meaning of that fierce rush; the instrument of destruction they brought with them. It was there in the center of the maelstrom of leaping figures, protected by the grouped bodies, half hidden by gesticulating red arms—a huge log, borne irresistibly forward on the shoulders of twenty warriors, gripped by other hands, and hurled toward us as though swept on by a human sea. Again and again I fired blindly into the yelping mob; I heard the crack of Tim's rifle echoing mine, and the chug of lead from without striking the solid logs. Bullets ploughed crashing through the door panels and Elsie's shrill screams of fright rang out above the unearthly din. A slug tore through my loophole, drawing blood from my shoulder in its passage, and imbedded itself in the opposite wall. In front of me savages fell, staggering, screams of anger and agony mingling as the astonished assailants realized the fight before them. An instant we held them, startled, and demoralized. The warriors bearing the log stumbled over a dead body and went down, the great timber crushing out another life as it fell. Again we fired, this time straight into their faces—but there was no stopping them. A red blanket flashed back beyond the big tree; a guttural voice shouted, its hoarse note rising above the hellish uproar, and those demons were on their feet again, filled with new frenzy. It was a minute—no more. With a blow that shook the cabin, propelled by twenty strong arms, the great tree butt struck, splintering the oak wood as though it were so much pine, and driving a jagged hole clear through one panel. Kennedy was there, blazing away directly into the assailants eyes, and I joined him.

Again they struck, and again, the jagged end of their battering ram protruded through the shattered wood. We killed, but they were too many. Once more the great butt came crashing forward, this time caving in the entire door, bursting it back upon its hinges. In through the opening the red mob hurled itself, reckless of death or wounds, mad with the thirst for victory; a jam of naked beasts, crazed by the smell of blood—a wave of slaughter, crested with brandished guns and gleam of tomahawk.

There is nothing to remember—nothing but blows, curses, yells, the crunch of steel on flesh, the horror of cruel eyes glowering into yours, the clutching of fingers at your throat, the spit of fire singeing you, the strain of combat hand to hand—the knowledge that it is all over, except to die. I had no sense of fear; no thought but to kill and be killed. I felt within me strength—desperate, insane strength. The rifle butt splintered in my hands, but the bent and shapeless barrel rose and fell like a flail. I saw it crush against skulls; I jabbed it straight into red faces; I brought it down with all my force on clutching arms. For an instant Tim was beside me. He had lost his gun and was fighting with a knife. It was only a glimpse I had of him through red mist—the next instant he was gone. A huge fellow faced me, a Winnebago I knew, from his shaven head. I struck him once, laying open his cheek to the bone; then he broke through and gripped me.

The rest is what—a dream; a delirium of fever? I know not; it comes to me in flashes of mad memory. I was struck again and again, stabbed, and flung to the floor. Moccasined feet trod on me, and some fiend gripped my hair, bending my head back across a dead body, until I felt the neck crack. Above me were naked legs and arms, a pandemonium of dancing figures, a horrible chorus of maddened yells. I caught a glimpse of Asa Hall flung high into the air, shot dead in mid-flight, the whirling body dropping into the ruck below. I saw the savage, whose fingers were twined in my hair, lift a gleaming tomahawk and circle it about his head; I stared into the hate of his eyes, and as it swept down—there was a glare of red and yellow flame between us, the thunder of an explosion; the roof above seemed to burst asunder and fall in—and darkness, death.

CHAPTER XXXII

THE TRAIL TO OTTAWA

When my eyes again opened it was to darkness and silence as profound as that of my former unconsciousness. My mind was a blank, and seemingly I retained no sense of what had occurred, or of my present surroundings. For the moment I felt no certainty even that I was actually alive, yet slowly, little by little, reality conquered, and I became keenly conscious of physical pain, while memory also began to blindly reassert itself. It was a series of dim pictures projecting themselves on the awakening brain—the Indian attack on the cabin, the horrors of that last struggle, the gleaming tomahawk descending on my head to deal the death blow, the savage eyes of my assailant glaring into mine, and that awful flash of red and yellow flame, swept across my mind one by one with such intense vividness as to cause me to give vent to a moan of agony.

I could see nothing, hear nothing. All about was impenetrable blackness and the silence of the grave. I found myself unable to move my body and when I desperately attempted to do so, even the slightest motion brought pain. I became conscious also of a weight crushing down upon me, and stifling my breath. One of my arms was free; I could move it about within narrow limits, although it ached as from a serious burn. By use of it I endeavored through the black darkness to learn the nature of that heavy object lying across my chest, feeling at it cautiously. My fingers touched cold, dead flesh, from contact with which they shrank in horror, only to encounter a strand of coarse hair. The first terror of this discovery was overwhelming, yet I persevered, satisfying myself that it was the half-naked body of an Indian—a very giant of a fellow—which lay stretched across me, an immovable weight. Something else, perhaps another dead man, held my feet as though in a vise, and when I ventured to extend my one free arm gropingly to one side, the fingers encountered a moccasined foot. Scarcely daring to breathe, I lay staring upward and, far above, looking out through what might be a jagged, overhanging mass of timbers, although scarcely discernible, my eyes caught the silver glimmer of a star.

I was alive—alive! Whatever had occurred in that fateful second to deflect that murderous tomahawk, its keen edge had failed to reach me. And what had occurred? What could account for my escape; for this silence and darkness; for these dead bodies; for the flight of our assailants? Indians always removed their dead, yet seemingly this place was a perfect charnel house, heaped with slain. Surely there could be but one answer—the occurrence of a disaster so complete, so horrifying, that the few who were left alive had thought only of instant flight. Then it was that the probable truth came to me—that flash and roar; that last impression imprinted on my brain before utter darkness descended upon me, must have meant an explosion, an upheaval shattering the cabin, bringing the roof down upon the struggling mob within, the heavy timbers crushing out their lives. And the cause! But one was possible—the half-keg of blasting power Kennedy had placed in the corner as a last resort. Had Tim reached it in a final, mad effort to destroy, or had some accidental flame wrought the terrible destruction? Perhaps no one could ever answer that—but, was I there alone, the sole survivor? Had those others of our little party died amid their Indian enemies, and were they lying now somewhere in this darkness, crushed and mangled in the midst of the debris?

Kennedy, Elsie Clark, the half-witted boy Asa Hall—their faces seemed to stare at me out of the blackness. They must be dead! Why, I had seen Kennedy fall, the heedless feet crunching his face, and Asa Hall tossed into the air and shot at as he fell. Eloise! Eloise! I covered my eyes with the free hand, conscious that I was crying like a child—Eloise. My God, Eloise! I wonder if I fainted; I knew so little after that; so little, except that I suffered helplessly. That awful, pressing weight upon my chest, the impossibility of moving my limbs, the ceaseless horror of the dark silence, the benumbing knowledge that all about me lay those dead bodies, with sightless eyes staring through the black. If I did not faint, then I must have been upon the verge of insanity, for there was a time—God knows how long—when all was blank.

Some slight, scarcely distinguishable noise aroused me. Yes, it was actually a sound, as though someone moved in the room—moved stealthily, as though upon hands and knees, seeking a passage in the darkness. I imagined I could distinguish breathing. Who, what could it be? A man; a prowling wild animal which had scented blood? But for my dry, parched lips I would have cried out—yet even with the vain endeavor, doubt silenced me. Who could be there—who? Some sneaking, cowardly thief; some despoiler of the dead? Some Indian returned through the night to take his toll of scalps, hoping to thus proclaim himself a mighty warrior? More likely enemy than friend. It was better that I lie and suffer than appeal to such fiend for mercy.

The slight sound shifted to the right of where I lay, no longer reminding me of the slow progress of a moving body, but rather as though someone were attempting blindly to scrape together ashes in the fireplace. Yes, that must be what was being done; whoever the strange invader might be, and whatever his ultimate purpose, the effort now being made was to provide a light, a flame sufficient to reveal the horror of the place—to facilitate his ghastly work. I would wait then; lie there as one dead until the coming of light helped me to solve the mystery. Some life must still have lingered amid those ashes, for suddenly I caught, reflected on the log wall, the tiniest spurt of flame. It grew so slowly, fed by a hand I could not see; then on that same wall there appeared the dark shadow of an arm, and the bent, distorted image of a head. I pressed my one free hand beneath my neck, and thus, by an effort, lifted myself so as to see more clearly beyond the shoulder of the dead Indian. The first tiny, flickering spark of fire had caught the dry wood, and was swiftly bursting into flame. In another moment this had illumined that stooping figure, and rested in a blaze of light upon the lowered face, bringing out the features as though they were framed against the black wall beyond—a woman's face, the face of Eloise!

I gave vent to one startled, inarticulate cry, and she sprang to her feet, the mantling flames girdling her as though she were a statue. They lit up the white-washed wall, splashed with blood, and gave a glimpse of the wrecked timbers dangling from above. In that first frightened glance she failed to see me; her whole posture told of fear, of indecision.

"Who was it spoke? Who called? Is someone alive here?"

The trembling words sounded strange, unnatural, I could barely whisper, yet I did my best.

"It is Steven, Eloise—come to me."

"Steven! Steven Knox—alive! Oh, my God; you have answered my prayer!"

She found me, heedless of all the horror in between, as though guided by some instinct, and dropped on her knees beside me. I felt a tear fall on my cheek, and then the warm, eager pressure of her lips to mine, I could not speak; I could only hold her close with my one hand. The flames beyond leaped up, widening their gleam of light, revealing more clearly the dear face and the joy with which she gazed down upon me.

"You are suffering," she cried. "What can I do? Is it this Indian's body?"

"Yes," I breathed, the effort of speaking an agony. "He lies directly across my chest, a dead weight."

It taxed her strength to the utmost, but, oh, the immediate relief! With the drawing of a full breath I felt a return of manhood, a revival of life. Another body pinned my limbs to the floor, but this was more easily disposed of. Then I managed to lift myself, but with the first attempt her arm was about my shoulders.

"No; not alone—let me help you. Do you really think you can stand! Why, you are hurt, dear; this is a knife wound in your side. It looks ugly, but is not deep and bleeds no longer. Are there other injuries?"

"My head rings, and this left arm appears paralyzed, from blows, no doubt, and there are spots on my body which feel like burns. No, I am not in bad shape. Now let me stand alone; that's better. Good God, what a scene!"

The fire, by this time blazing brightly, gave us a full view of the entire dismantled interior. The cabin was a complete wreck, the roof practically all gone and the upper logs of the side walls either fallen within or dangling in threat. Above clung jagged sections, trembling with their own weight; the lower walls were blackened by powder and stained with blood; the floor was strewn with dead bodies, disfigured and distorted, lying exactly as they fell, while littered all about were weapons, dropped by stricken hands. Clearly enough it had been the sudden plunge of heavy timbers and the dislodgment of those upper logs, which accounted for this havoc of death. There were dead there pierced by bullets and brained by rifle stocks, but the many had met their fate under the avalanche of logs, and amid the burning glare of exploding powder.

Only between arched timbers and sections of fallen roof could we move at all, and beneath the network of this entanglement the majority of the bodies lay, crushed and mangled. I saw Kirby, free from his bonds, but dead beneath a heavy beam. His face was toward us and the flicker of flame revealed a dark spot on his forehead—his life had never been crushed out by that plunging timber which pinned him there; it had been ended by a bullet. My eyes sought hers, in swift memory of my last order, and she must have read my thought.

"No," she said, "not that, Steven. It was the boy who shot him. Oh, please, can we not go? There is light already in the sky overhead—see. Take me away from here—anywhere, outside."

"In a moment; all these surely are dead, beyond our aid, and yet we must not depart foodless. We know not how far it still may be to Ottawa. Wait, while I search for the things we need."

"Not alone; I must be where I can touch you. Try to understand. Oh, you do not know those hours I have spent in agony—I have died a thousand deaths since that sun went down."

"You were conscious—all night long?"

"Conscious? Yes, and unhurt, yet prisoned helpless beneath those two logs yonder, saved only by that over-turned bench. Elsie, poor thing, never knew how death came, it was so swift, but I lay there, within a foot of her body unscratched. I could think only of you, Steven, but with never a dream that you lived. There were groans at first and cries. Some Indians crept in through the door and dragged out a few who lived. But with the coming of darkness all sounds ceased and such silence was even more dreadful than the calls, for help. Oh, I cannot tell you," and she clung to me, her voice breaking. "I—I dared not move for hours, and then, when I did try, found I could not; that I was held fast. Only for a knife in the hand of a dead savage, which I managed to secure, I could never have freed myself. And oh, the unspeakable horror of creeping in the darkness among those bodies. I knew where the fireplace must be; that there might be live coals there still. I had to have light; I had to know if you were dead."

"Don't think about it any more, dear heart," I urged. "Yes, we can go now—nothing else holds us here."

We crept out through the door, underneath a mass of debris, into the gray of the dawn. How sweet the air, how like a benediction the song of birds. Neither of us looked back, and I held her close against me as we moved onward, past the big tree, and down the long slope. It was a wondrous view of peace and beauty, the broad green valley, with the silver thread of water shining in its center—the valley of the Bureau. We followed the faint trail, which wound in and out among small copses of trees; the sun began to brighten the far east and her hand stole into mine. The light was upon her face, and gave me a glimpse of the sadness of her eyes. Beyond a little grove we found some horses browsing in the deep grass; they were those that had brought us from Yellow Banks, and whinnied a greeting as we drew near. Two of them were fit to ride and the others followed, limping along behind.

A half mile up the valley we came to a beaten trail, running straight across from bluff to bluff, and disappearing into the prairie beyond, heading directly toward the sunrise. We stopped and looked back for the first time. There on the side of the slope, under the shade of the big tree, stood the cabin. Only for the wreck of the roof it spoke no message of the tragedy within. The sun's rays gilded it, and the smoke from its chimney seemed a beckoning welcome. I reached out and took her hand, and our eyes met in understanding. What I whispered need not be told, and when we again rode forward, it was upon the trail to Ottawa.

Choose from Thousands of 1stWorldLibrary Classics By

A. M. Barnard
Ada Leverson
Adolphus William Ward
Aesop
Agatha Christie
Alexander Aaronsohn
Alexander Kielland
Alexandre Dumas
Alfred Gatty
Alfred Ollivant
Alice Duer Miller
Alice Turner Curtis
Alice Dunbar
Allen Chapman
Alleyne Ireland
Ambrose Bierce
Amelia E. Barr
Amory H. Bradford
Andrew Lang
Andrew McFarland Davis
Andy Adams
Angela Brazil
Anna Alice Chapin
Anna Sewell
Annie Besant
Annie Hamilton Donnell
Annie Payson Call
Annie Roe Carr
Annonaymous
Anton Chekhov
Archibald Lee Fletcher
Arnold Bennett
Arthur C. Benson
Arthur Conan Doyle
Arthur M. Winfield
Arthur Ransome
Arthur Schnitzler
Arthur Train
Atticus
B.H. Baden-Powell
B. M. Bower
B. C. Chatterjee
Baroness Emmuska Orczy
Baroness Orczy
Basil King
Bayard Taylor
Ben Macomber
Bertha Muzzy Bower
Bjornstjerne Bjornson

Booth Tarkington
Boyd Cable
Bram Stoker
C. Collodi
C. E. Orr
C. M. Ingleby
Carolyn Wells
Catherine Parr Traill
Charles A. Eastman
Charles Amory Beach
Charles Dickens
Charles Dudley Warner
Charles Farrar Browne
Charles Ives
Charles Kingsley
Charles Klein
Charles Hanson Towne
Charles Lathrop Pack
Charles Romyn Dake
Charles Whibley
Charles Willing Beale
Charlotte M. Braeme
Charlotte M. Yonge
Charlotte Perkins Stetson
Clair W. Hayes
Clarence Day Jr.
Clarence E. Mulford
Clemence Housman
Confucius
Coningsby Dawson
Cornelis DeWitt Wilcox
Cyril Burleigh
D. H. Lawrence
Daniel Defoe
David Garnett
Dinah Craik
Don Carlos Janes
Donald Keyhoe
Dorothy Kilner
Dougan Clark
Douglas Fairbanks
E. Nesbit
E. P. Roe
E. Phillips Oppenheim
E. S. Brooks
Earl Barnes
Edgar Rice Burroughs
Edith Van Dyne
Edith Wharton

Edward Everett Hale
Edward J. O'Biren
Edward S. Ellis
Edwin L. Arnold
Eleanor Atkins
Eleanor Hallowell Abbott
Eliot Gregory
Elizabeth Gaskell
Elizabeth McCracken
Elizabeth Von Arnim
Ellem Key
Emerson Hough
Emilie F. Carlen
Emily Bronte
Emily Dickinson
Enid Bagnold
Enilor Macartney Lane
Erasmus W. Jones
Ernie Howard Pie
Ethel May Dell
Ethel Turner
Ethel Watts Mumford
Eugene Sue
Eugenie Foa
Eugene Wood
Eustace Hale Ball
Evelyn Everett-green
Everard Cotes
F. H. Cheley
F. J. Cross
F. Marion Crawford
Fannie E. Newberry
Federick Austin Ogg
Ferdinand Ossendowski
Fergus Hume
Florence A. Kilpatrick
Fremont B. Deering
Francis Bacon
Francis Darwin
Frances Hodgson Burnett
Frances Parkinson Keyes
Frank Gee Patchin
Frank Harris
Frank Jewett Mather
Frank L. Packard
Frank V. Webster
Frederic Stewart Isham
Frederick Trevor Hill
Frederick Winslow Taylor

Friedrich Kerst
Friedrich Nietzsche
Fyodor Dostoyevsky
G.A. Henty
G.K. Chesterton
Gabrielle E. Jackson
Garrett P. Serviss
Gaston Leroux
George A. Warren
George Ade
Geroge Bernard Shaw
George Cary Eggleston
George Durston
George Ebers
George Eliot
George Gissing
George MacDonald
George Meredith
George Orwell
George Sylvester Viereck
George Tucker
George W. Cable
George Wharton James
Gertrude Atherton
Gordon Casserly
Grace E. King
Grace Gallatin
Grace Greenwood
Grant Allen
Guillermo A. Sherwell
Gulielma Zollinger
Gustav Flaubert
H. A. Cody
H. B. Irving
H.C. Bailey
H. G. Wells
H. H. Munro
H. Irving Hancock
H. R. Naylor
H. Rider Haggard
H. W. C. Davis
Haldeman Julius
Hall Caine
Hamilton Wright Mabie
Hans Christian Andersen
Harold Avery
Harold McGrath
Harriet Beecher Stowe
Harry Castlemon
Harry Coghill
Harry Houidini

Hayden Carruth
Helent Hunt Jackson
Helen Nicolay
Hendrik Conscience
Hendy David Thoreau
Henri Barbusse
Henrik Ibsen
Henry Adams
Henry Ford
Henry Frost
Henry James
Henry Jones Ford
Henry Seton Merriman
Henry W Longfellow
Herbert A. Giles
Herbert Carter
Herbert N. Casson
Herman Hesse
Hildegard G. Frey
Homer
Honore De Balzac
Horace B. Day
Horace Walpole
Horatio Alger Jr.
Howard Pyle
Howard R. Garis
Hugh Lofting
Hugh Walpole
Humphry Ward
Ian Maclaren
Inez Haynes Gillmore
Irving Bacheller
Isabel Cecilia Williams
Isabel Hornibrook
Israel Abrahams
Ivan Turgenev
J.G.Austin
J. Henri Fabre
J. M. Barrie
J. M. Walsh
J. Macdonald Oxley
J. R. Miller
J. S. Fletcher
J. S. Knowles
J. Storer Clouston
J. W. Duffield
Jack London
Jacob Abbott
James Allen
James Andrews
James Baldwin

James Branch Cabell
James DeMille
James Joyce
James Lane Allen
James Lane Allen
James Oliver Curwood
James Oppenheim
James Otis
James R. Driscoll
Jane Abbott
Jane Austen
Jane L. Stewart
Janet Aldridge
Jens Peter Jacobsen
Jerome K. Jerome
Jessie Graham Flower
John Buchan
John Burroughs
John Cournos
John F. Kennedy
John Gay
John Glasworthy
John Habberton
John Joy Bell
John Kendrick Bangs
John Milton
John Philip Sousa
John Taintor Foote
Jonas Lauritz Idemil Lie
Jonathan Swift
Joseph A. Altsheler
Joseph Carey
Joseph Conrad
Joseph E. Badger Jr
Joseph Hergesheimer
Joseph Jacobs
Jules Vernes
Julian Hawthrone
Julie A Lippmann
Justin Huntly McCarthy
Kakuzo Okakura
Karle Wilson Baker
Kate Chopin
Kenneth Grahame
Kenneth McGaffey
Kate Langley Bosher
Kate Langley Bosher
Katherine Cecil Thurston
Katherine Stokes
L. A. Abbot
L. T. Meade

L. Frank Baum
Latta Griswold
Laura Dent Crane
Laura Lee Hope
Laurence Housman
Lawrence Beasley
Leo Tolstoy
Leonid Andreyev
Lewis Carroll
Lewis Sperry Chafer
Lilian Bell
Lloyd Osbourne
Louis Hughes
Louis Joseph Vance
Louis Tracy
Louisa May Alcott
Lucy Fitch Perkins
Lucy Maud Montgomery
Luther Benson
Lydia Miller Middleton
Lyndon Orr
M. Corvus
M. H. Adams
Margaret E. Sangster
Margret Howth
Margaret Vandercook
Margaret W. Hungerford
Margret Penrose
Maria Edgeworth
Maria Thompson Daviess
Mariano Azuela
Marion Polk Angellotti
Mark Overton
Mark Twain
Mary Austin
Mary Catherine Crowley
Mary Cole
Mary Hastings Bradley
Mary Roberts Rinehart
Mary Rowlandson
M. Wollstonecraft Shelley
Maud Lindsay
Max Beerbohm
Myra Kelly
Nathaniel Hawthrone
Nicolo Machiavelli
O. F. Walton
Oscar Wilde

Owen Johnson
P.G. Wodehouse
Paul and Mabel Thorne
Paul G. Tomlinson
Paul Severing
Percy Brebner
Percy Keese Fitzhugh
Peter B. Kyne
Plato
Quincy Allen
R. Derby Holmes
R. L. Stevenson
R. S. Ball
Rabindranath Tagore
Rahul Alvares
Ralph Bonehill
Ralph Henry Barbour
Ralph Victor
Ralph Waldo Emmerson
Rene Descartes
Ray Cummings
Rex Beach
Rex E. Beach
Richard Harding Davis
Richard Jefferies
Richard Le Gallienne
Robert Barr
Robert Frost
Robert Gordon Anderson
Robert L. Drake
Robert Lansing
Robert Lynd
Robert Michael Ballantyne
Robert W. Chambers
Rosa Nouchette Carey
Rudyard Kipling
Saint Augustine
Samuel B. Allison
Samuel Hopkins Adams
Sarah Bernhardt
Sarah C. Hallowell
Selma Lagerlof
Sherwood Anderson
Sigmund Freud
Standish O'Grady
Stanley Weyman
Stella Benson
Stella M. Francis

Stephen Crane
Stewart Edward White
Stijn Streuvels
Swami Abhedananda
Swami Parmananda
T. S. Ackland
T. S. Arthur
The Princess Der Ling
Thomas A. Janvier
Thomas A Kempis
Thomas Anderton
Thomas Bailey Aldrich
Thomas Bulfinch
Thomas De Quincey
Thomas Dixon
Thomas H. Huxley
Thomas Hardy
Thomas More
Thornton W. Burgess
U. S. Grant
Upton Sinclair
Valentine Williams
Various Authors
Vaughan Kester
Victor Appleton
Victor G. Durham
Victoria Cross
Virginia Woolf
Wadsworth Camp
Walter Camp
Walter Scott
Washington Irving
Wilbur Lawton
Wilkie Collins
Willa Cather
Willard F. Baker
William Dean Howells
William le Queux
W. Makepeace Thackeray
William W. Walter
William Shakespeare
Winston Churchill
Yei Theodora Ozaki
Yogi Ramacharaka
Young E. Allison
Zane Grey

www.ingramcontent.com/pod-product-compliance
Lightning Source LLC
Chambersburg PA
CBHW031056260626
47172CB00001B/99